ALSO BY BORIS AKUNIN

*The Winter Queen*

*The Turkish Gambit*

*Murder on the Leviathan*

*The Death of Achilles*

# Sister Pelagia
## and the
## White Bulldog

RANDOM HOUSE TRADE PAPERBACKS

NEW YORK

# Sister Pelagia and the White Bulldog

A NOVEL

# BORIS AKUNIN

Translated by Andrew Bromfield

A Random House Trade Paperback Original

Published in the United States by Random House Trade Paperbacks, an imprint of The Random House Publishing Group, a division of Random House, Inc., New York.

RANDOM HOUSE TRADE PAPERBACKS, MORTALIS, and colophons are trademarks of Random House, Inc.

Originally published in Russian as *Pelagia i Belyi Buldog* by AST Publishers, Moscow, in 2000, copyright © 2000 by Boris Akunin. This English translation was originally published by Weidenfeld & Nicolson, London, in 2006.

Grateful acknowledgment is made to Il Messaggero SpA of Rome for permission to print an English translation of "Akunin: La mia Russia a un bivio" by Francesco Fantasia, originally published in *Il Messaggero,* May 30, 2003. Used by the kind permission of Il Messaggero SpA of Rome.

ISBN 978-0-8129-7513-0

Library of Congress Cataloging-in-Publication Data
Akunin, B. (Boris)
   [Pelagiia i belyi bul'dog. English]
   Sister Pelagia and the white bulldog : a mystery / Boris Akunin ; translated by Andrew Bromfield.
      p.   cm.
   A trilogy.
   ISBN-13: 978-0-8129-7513-0
   ISBN-10: 0-8129-7513-8
   I. Bromfield, Andrew.   II. Title.
PG3478.K78P4513 2007
891.73'5—dc22          2006050387

Printed in the United States of America

www.mortalis-books.com

2  4  6  8  9  7  5  3  1

*Book design by Victoria Wong*

# PART ONE

# Beware of Dogs

# The Death of Zagulyai

. . . BUT I SHOULD tell you that, come the apple festival of Transfiguration Day, when the sky begins to change from summer to autumn, it is the usual thing for our town to be overrun by an absolute plague of cicadas, so that by night, much as you might wish to sleep, you never can, what with all that interminable trilling on all sides, and the stars hanging down low over your head, and especially with the moon dangling just above the tops of the bell towers, for all the world like one of our renowned "smetana" apples, the kind that the local merchants supply to the royal court and even take to shows in Europe. If someone should ever happen to glance down at Zavolzhsk from those heavenly spheres out of which the lamps of the night pour forth their bright rays, then the picture presented to that fortunate person's eyes would surely be one of some enchanted kingdom: the River sparkling lazily, the roofs glittering, the gas lamps flickering in the streets, and, hovering over all the shimmer and glimmer of this multifarious radiance, the tremulous silvery chiming of the cicada choir.

But let us return to the reverend Mitrofanii. Our passing reference to nature was made purely and simply to explain why on such a night even the most ordinary of men, far less burdened with cares than the bishop of the province, would find sleep hard to come by. It is hardly surprising that ill-wishers, of whom every man has some, even this worthy pastor being no exception, should claim that it is not our governor, Anton Antonovich von Haggenau, but His Grace who is the true ruler of this extensive region.

Extensive indeed the region may be, but densely populated it is not.

The only genuine town it can really be said to possess is Zavolzhsk, and the others, including the district centers, are more like overgrown villages with a few stone administrative buildings clustered around a single square, a small cathedral, and a hundred or two little log houses with tin roofs of the kind that since time immemorial have for some reason always been painted green in these parts.

And, God knows, even the provincial capital is no Babylon—at the time we are describing, its entire population amounted to twenty-three thousand five hundred eleven individuals of both sexes. Although, of course, during the week following Transfiguration, if no one was to die, the number of inhabitants was expected to increase by two souls, because the wife of the manager of the provincial chancelry, Shtops, and the tradesman's wife, Safulina, were near their time, and the general opinion was that the latter was already overdue.

The custom of maintaining a strict accounting of the population had only been introduced recently, under the current administration, and then only in the towns. How many folk there may be making a living out in the forests and the swamps is something known only to God—go try counting them! The dense, impenetrable thickets extend for hundred of miles from the River all the way to the Ural Mountains, with schismatic monastic communities and salt factories buried among them, and along the banks of the dark, deep rivers that, for the most part, have no names at all, dwells the Zyt tribe, a quiet and submissive people of Ugrian blood.

The only mention of the ancient life of our obscure province is contained in the *Nizhny-Novgorod Miscellany*, a chronicle from the fifteenth century. It speaks of a Novgorodian visitor by the name of Ropsha who was captured by "the wild, bare-bellied pagans" in the green forests and lost his head in a sacrifice to the stone idol Shishiga, and as the chronicler for some reason finds it necessary to explain, "this Ropsha did perish and give up the ghost and was buried without a head."

But that was long ago, in the time of myth. Nowadays a splendid peace reigns supreme in these parts, with no brigandage on the roads, no killing, and even the wolves in the local forests are noticeably fatter and lazier than in other provinces, due to the abundance of wildlife here. God grant everyone a life as good as ours. And as for the murmurings of the bishop's detractors, we shall not undertake to discuss here who is the genuine ruler of the Zavolzhie region—the reverend Mitrofanii, the governor Anton Antonovich, the governor's most learned advisers, or even, perhaps, the governor's wife, Ludmila Platonovna—because it is not for us to judge such things. Let us merely say that His Grace has far more allies and admirers in Zavolzhie than enemies.

Recently, however, certain events had encouraged and emboldened the latter, thereby giving Mitrofanii particular reasons for his insomnia, in addition to those related to the frenzied trilling of the cicadas. This was the reason for the frown that pleated his high forehead into three folds and knitted his thick black brows together.

The Bishop of Zavolzhsk was fair of face, not merely good-looking but strikingly handsome, so that instead of being a pastor, he might easily have been some Old Russian prince or Byzantine *archistrategus*. His hair was long and gray, but his beard, also long and silky, was still half black as yet, and there was not so much as a single silver thread in his mustache. His glance was keen, but generally gentle and clear, which made it all the more frightening when it clouded over with anger and flashed with lightning. At such terrible moments the stern creases over his cheekbones were more pronounced, as was the aquiline curve of his large, noble nose. The reverend bishop's deep, resonant voice with its rumble of thunder was equally well suited for a cordial private conversation, an inspired sermon, or a civic speech on one of the occasions when he attended the Holy Synod.

In his young days, Mitrofanii had been an adherent of asceticism. He used to wear a cassock made of sackcloth, mortify the flesh by constant fasting, and even, so they say, wear chains of cast iron beneath his undershirt, but he had long since abandoned these austerities, having come to regard them as vain, immaterial, and even harmful to a genuine love of God. Having reached the age of maturity and attained wisdom, he became more considerate of his own flesh and that of others, and for his everyday vestments his preference lay in cassocks of fine cloth, blue or black. And on occasion, when the authority of his bishop's title required it, he would robe himself in a mantle of extremely precious purple velvet, order a team of six horses to be harnessed to the bishop's formal carriage, and insist that there must be two stately lay brothers with thick beards standing on the runningboards, wearing green cassocks trimmed with galloons that looked very much like livery.

Of course, there were those who surreptitiously reproached His Grace for his sybaritic habits and devotion to grand style, but even they did not condemn him too harshly, remaining mindful of the exalted origins that had accustomed Mitrofanii to luxury from his childhood, so that he did not regard it as being in any way important—"he did not deign to notice it," as his clerk, Father Serafim Userdov, put it.

His Grace the Bishop of Zavolzhsk was born into a family of courtly nobles and graduated from the Corps of Pages, from where he moved to the Horse Guards (that was back in the reign of Nikolai Pavlovich). He led the life usual for a young man of his circle, and if he was distinguished in any way from his peers, it was perhaps only by a tendency to philosophize, but then that is not such a very rare thing among educated and sensitive youths. In his regiment the "philosopher" was considered a good comrade and an excellent cavalryman, his superiors liked him and they promoted him, so that by the age of thirty he would certainly have risen to the rank of colonel had the Crimean campaign not intervened. God only knows what insights were revealed to the future Bishop of Zavolzhsk during his first taste of active combat, a cavalry skirmish near Balaclava, but after recovering from his saber wound, he had no wish to take a weapon into his hand ever again. He retired from the army, said his farewells to his family, and soon thereafter was serving his novitiate in one of the country's most isolated monasteries. Even now, however, especially when Mitrofanii conducted the service in the cathedral on the occasion of one of the twelve great feasts or took the chair at a meeting of the consistory, it was easy to imagine how he used to command his lancers in his booming voice: "Squadron, sabers at the ready! At a trot, forward!"

An extraordinary man will make his mark in any field of endeavor, and Mitrofanii did not languish in the obscurity of remote monastic life for long. Just as he had previously become the youngest squadron commander in the entire light cavalry, so now it fell to him to become the youngest Orthodox bishop. Initially appointed to be suffragan bishop here in Zavolzhsk, and then as the pastor of the province, he demonstrated so much wisdom and zeal that he was soon summoned to the capital to take up a high position in the church. There were many who predicted that in the none too distant future Mitrofanii would don the black veil of a metropolitan, but he astonished everyone by once again turning off the beaten track and requesting out of the blue to be allowed to return to us in the back of beyond, and, following long attempts to dissuade him, to the joy of us Zavolzhians he was released with a blessing, never again to abandon his modest see, so remote from the capital.

And what does it matter if it is remote? It is a well-known fact that the farther one travels from the capital, the nearer one approaches to God. And our exalted and far-seeing capital will reach out a thousand miles should such an idea ever come into its head.

It was indeed due to precisely such an idea that His Grace was not sleeping on this night, but attending drearily and without pleasure to the endless crescendos of the cicadas. The capital's idea possessed a face and a name, it was called Synodical Inspector Bubentsov, and as he pondered how to deal with this gentleman, the reverend bishop turned for the hundredth time from one side to the other on his soft duck-down mattress, groaning and sighing and occasionally gasping.

The bed in the bishop's bedchamber was special, an old four-poster from Empress Elizabeth's time, with a canopy representing a starry sky. During the period of Mitrofanii's aforementioned enthusiasm for asceticism, he slept quite contentedly on either straw or bare boards until he came to the conclusion that to mortify the flesh was pointless folly and that was not why the Lord had molded it in His own image and likeness, nor was it appropriate for the arch-pastor to make a show of himself to the clergy in his care, compelling them to adopt a self-tormenting severity for which some do not feel any spiritual inclination— nor indeed are they obliged to do so according to the statute of the church. As he reached his years of maturity, His Grace inclined more and more to the opinion that genuine trials are sent down to us not in the realm of the physiological but in the realm of the spiritual, and the scourging of the body by no means always leads to the salvation of the soul. Therefore the bishop's chambers were furnished no worse than the governor's house, the board set in the refectory was incomparably superior, and the orchard of apple trees was the finest in all the town, with arbors, rotundas, and even a fountain. It was peaceful and shady there, inclining one to thought, and so let the detractors whisper among themselves—one can never silence malicious gossip.

So the way to deal with this perfidious inspector Bubentsov is this, the reverend bishop concluded. The first thing is to write to Konstantin Petrovich in St. Petersburg about all the tricks that his trusted nuncio gets up to and the disaster that the church could suffer as a result of them. The chief procurator was a man of intelligence; it was possible that he might heed the warning. But action should not be limited to a letter; Mitrofanii must also summon the governor's wife, Ludmila Platonovna, for a talk, to shame her and stir her conscience. She was a good, honest woman. She must be brought to her senses.

And then everything would be put to rights. The matter could hardly be simpler.

But even now that his heart felt eased, sleep still would not come, and the problem did not lie in the round-faced moon, or even in the cicadas.

Knowing his own character as he did and being in the habit of analyzing the workings of its mechanism in detail, down to the last nut and bolt, Mitrofanii set about trying to identify the worm that was gnawing at him and preventing his reason from shrouding itself in the veil of sleep. What was the cause?

Could it possibly be his recent conversation with a giddy young novice from a noble family who had been denied permission to take the veil? The reverend bishop had not beaten about the bush; he had blurted out his opinion without equivocation: "My daughter, what you need is not the Sweet Bridegroom of Heaven—that is merely your delusion. What you need is a perfectly ordinary bridegroom, a state official or, even better, an officer. With a mustache." He ought not to have put it like that, of course. There had been hysterics, followed by a long, exhausting argument. But never mind that, it was unimportant. What else was there?

He had been obliged to take a disagreeable decision concerning the steward at the Monastery of the Epiphany. For riotous drunken behavior and the lecherous visiting of indecorous women, the offender had been condemned to dismissal from the cloister and returned to his original lay status. Now the scribbling would begin, with letters to His Grace himself and to the synod. But this too was an ordinary matter; the root cause of his alarm did not lie here.

Mitrofanii thought a little more, groping about inside himself, as he used to do in childhood, to see if he was getting "warm" or "cold," and suddenly he realized: It was the letter from his great aunt, the general's widow, Tatishcheva, that was apparently the spot where the worm was gnawing. He was surprised, but his heart immediately confirmed it— he was "hot," he had hit the mark. It seemed like a piece of stupid nonsense, but he could feel the cat's claws scraping at his soul. Perhaps he should get it and read it again?

He sat up in the bed, lit a candle, and put on his pince-nez. Now, where was that letter? Ah, there it was, on the side table.

"My dear Mishenka," the old lady Marya Afanasievna wrote, out of ancient habit still addressing her relative by his long-forgotten secular name, "I hope you are well. Has that cursed gout of yours eased? Are you applying cabbage leaves to it, as I told you to do? The late Apollon Nikolaevich always used to say that—" There then followed a long and verbose description of the wonderworking properties of homegrown cabbage, and His Grace's glance began slipping impatiently along the even lines of old-fashioned handwriting. His eyes stumbled over a disagreeable name. "Vladimir Lvovich Bubentsov has visited me again. What terrible lies they have told about him, saying that he is a scoundrel and very nearly a murderer. He is a fine young man, and I liked him. Direct, with no snobbish pretensions to him, and he knows about dogs, too. Did you know that he is apparently related to me through the Strekhinin line? In her second marriage my grandmother Adelaida Sekandrovna—" No, that was not it, farther on.

Aha, here it was: "But this is all by the way and it has only been written because in the weakness of my heart I have been putting off coming to the point. The moment I gather myself and steel my spirit to it, the tears start flooding down my cheeks again, and my hand shakes, and I get a cold, tight feeling in my chest. I have a special reason for writing to you, Mishenka. I have suffered a great misfortune of such a kind that only you will understand, but I should not wonder if others will poke fun at me and say that the old fool has gone totally cuckoo. I wanted to come to see you myself, but I do not have the strength, although the journey is not really so very long. I lie flat on my back and do nothing but cry. You know how many years, how much effort, and how much money I have invested in order to complete the work to which Apollon Nikolaevich devoted his life." (At this point the reverend bishop shook his head, because he took a skeptical view of the work to which his deceased uncle had devoted his life.) "Learn then, my friend, what villainy has been committed here at my Drozdovka. Some enemy of mine, and it must be someone who is close to me, put poison into Zagulyai's and Zakidai's food. Zakidai is younger; I saved him with emetic stone of antimony and nursed him back to health. But my little Zagulyai passed away. All night long he suffered, tossing and turning, weeping human tears and gazing at me so mournfully, as if to say: Save me, mother, you are my only hope. But I did not save him. In the early morning he gave a pitiful cry, fell over on his side, and gave up the ghost. I fell down in a dead faint and they tell me I spent three hours like that until the doctor arrived from the town. And now I am lying here weak and exhausted, and most of all frightened. It is a conspiracy, Mishenka, a villainous conspiracy. Someone is trying to do away with my little children, and me, an old woman, along with them. In the name of God Almighty I implore you, come. Not to bring me priestly consolation—that is not what I need—but to investigate. Everybody says you have the gift of seeing straight through any villain and unraveling any criminal's cunning trickery. And what villainy could possibly be worse than this? You must come save me. And I shall adore you eternally and leave you a generous bequest for the cathedral, or some monastery, or the poor orphans, if you like." At the very end of her letter his aunt switched from a familial tone to an official and respectful one: "Commending myself to your fatherly attention and pastoral prayers and imploring Your Grace's blessing, I remain your Eminence's most devoted servant, Marya Tatishcheva."

At this point we ought perhaps to offer some explanation concerning the gift about which the general Tatishchev's widow wrote, and which might appear not entirely becoming to a churchman of bishop's rank. Be that as it may, reckoned among the reverend bishop's more sublime merits was the precious talent, one very rarely encountered, for unraveling all sorts of baffling mysteries, especially those of a criminal complexion. One might even say that Mitrofanii had a genuine passion for mental gymnastics of this sort, and on more than one occasion the police authorities, even those from neighboring provinces, had respectfully requested his advice in some confusing investigation. The Bishop of Zavolzhsk secretly took great pride in this reputation of his, but not without certain pangs of conscience—first, because this pride undoubtedly deserved to be categorized as idle vanity, and, second, for another reason known only to himself and a certain other individual, which we will therefore pass over in silence.

The previous evening, on first reading the letter, His Grace had found his aunt's request—to go dashing to her estate and investigate the circumstances of Zagulyai's death—somewhat amusing. And even now, having reread the letter, he thought: Nonsense, it's just an old woman's fancies. She'll spend a day or two in bed and then get up.

He snuffed out the candle and lay down, but his heart still felt uneasy. He tried to pray for his aunt's recovery. It is well known that prayers at night ascend to God's ears more easily. Saint Ioann Zlatoust writes that the Lord's gracious mercy is aroused most powerfully by nocturnal prayers, "when you make the time of rest for many the time of your lament."

But his prayer had no soul, it was no more than an idle parroting of words, and the reverend bishop did not acknowledge prayers of that kind. He had never even imposed penances of prayer on anyone, regarding it as sacrilege. Prayer was not prayer at all if it merely passed through the lips without touching the heart.

Very well, Pelagia can go, Mitrofanii decided. Let her find out what happened to that thrice damned Zagulyai.

Immediately he felt easier, and the cicadas' polyphonic chirping no longer chafed his weary soul but lulled it instead, and the moon no longer stung his eyes but seemed to bathe his face with warm milk. Mitrofanii closed his eyes and the wrinkles on his stern face relaxed. He slept.

. . .

IN THE MORNING they blessed the fruit in the bishop's chapel on the occasion of the Lord's Transfiguration, otherwise known as the Feast of Our Savior of the Apples. Mitrofanii loved this festival, though it was not the greatest of the twelve, for its brilliance and pious frivolity. He did not lead the service himself but stood at the back, on the bishop's dais at the side, which afforded him a better view of the apple-bedecked church, the large congregation, and the priests and deacons in their special "apple" chasubles of blue and gold with a pattern of fruits and leaves embroidered around the top. As they walked in from both sides, the choristers of the famous bishop's choir thundered so loudly that up under the white vault the rainbow-bright pendants on the heavy crystal chandelier began to shake. Father Amfiteatrov began blessing the apples: "Our Lord and God, Who hast vouchsafed the use of Thy creations to those who believe in Thee, we pray Thee, bless these fruits we offer with Thy word . . ."

It was good.

The service at Transfiguration is short and joyful. The cathedral is filled with the smell of fresh fruit, because everybody has brought their baskets along to have their apples sprinkled with holy water. Even the table beside Mitrofanii bore a silver dish with immense red king-pineapple apples from His Grace's orchard—succulent, sweet, and aromatic. When the reverend bishop gave these to someone, it was a mark of special distinction and favor.

Mitrofanii sent the servant who looked after his bishop's crook to the left-hand choir, where the nuns appointed to serve by teaching in the diocesan school for girls were standing placidly in a row. The emissary whispered into the ear of the tall, gaunt directrix, Sister Christina, that the reverend bishop wished to give her an apple, and she glanced around and made a slow grateful bow. Standing on her right, I think (one cannot be certain at first glance from the back), was Sister Emilia, who taught arithmetic, geography, and several other subjects. Then came the lopsided Sister Olympiada, the one who taught Scripture. After her came two equally stooped sisters, Ambrosia and Apollinaria, and there was no way to distinguish one from the other; one taught grammar and history and the other taught the domestic arts. And at the end, by the wall, stood the short, thin Sister Pelagia (literature and gymnastics). Even if one wished, it would be impossible to confuse her with anyone else: Her wimple had slipped over to one side, and protruding from under its edge in a manner quite shameful and impermissible for a nun was a lock of ginger hair, shimmering with a bronze sheen in a ray of sunlight.

Mitrofanii sighed, wondering yet again whether he had not committed an error when he gave his blessing to Pelagia's taking the veil. It had been impossible not to give it—the girl had been through such great grief and terrible suffering that not every soul would have withstood it, but she was really not cut out to be a nun: She was far too lively, fidgety, curious, and undignified in her movements. But you are just the same yourself, you old fool, the reverend bishop rebuked himself, and he sighed again even more ruefully.

When the nuns lined up to receive an apple each from His Grace, he greeted each of them in a distinctive manner—some he allowed to kiss his hand, some he patted gently on the head, at some he simply smiled, but with the last of them, Pelagia, there was a mishap. The clumsy girl stepped on the father subdeacon's foot, started back, apologizing, threw her arms out, and knocked the bowl over with her elbow. A loud rumbling, the ring of silver against the stone floor, red apples tumbling merrily in all directions, and the boys from the seminary, who were not supposed to have any apples because they were mischief-makers and scamps, had already grabbed up the precious king-pineapples and left nothing for the worthy and deserving people waiting their turn behind Pelagia. And so it always was with her—she was not a nun, but a walking disaster with freckles.

Mitrofanii gnawed his lips, but he refrained from rebuking her, because this was the house of God and it was a holiday.

He merely said as he blessed her: "Tuck away that lock of hair; it's shameful. And get along to the library. I have something to say to you."

"A CERTAIN ASS once imagined himself to be a racehorse and began flaring his nostrils and stamping his hoof on the ground." (This was how His Grace began the conversation.) " 'I'll beat you all!' he shouted.

'I'm the swiftest and the fleetest!' And he shouted so convincingly that everyone believed him and began repeating what he said: 'Our ass is no ass at all; he is the purest possible thoroughbred. Now we must run him in the races so that he can win every last prize.' And from that time on the ass knew no peace; whenever there was a race anywhere, they immediately bridled him and dragged him off to it, saying: 'Come on, long-ears, don't let us down.' And so the ass now led a quite wonderful life."

The nun, long since accustomed to the bishop's allegories, listened intently. At first glance she seemed a young girl: the clear, sweet, oval face was winsome and naïve, but this deceptive impression was created by the snub nose and the astonished look of the raised eyebrows, while the round brown eyes gazed out keenly through equally round spectacles with a look that was far from simple, and from the eyes one could tell that this was certainly no young innocent—she had already known suffering, seen something of life, and had time to reflect on her experiences. The air of youthful freshness came from the white skin that often complements ginger hair, and from its speckling of ineradicable orange freckles.

"Tell me then, Pelagia, what is the point of this fable?"

The nun pondered, taking her time before she answered. Her small white hands reached involuntarily for the canvas bag hanging at her belt, and the reverend bishop, knowing that Pelagia found it easier to think with her knitting in her hands, told her, "You may knit."

The pointed steel needles began clacking furiously and Mitrofanii frowned as he recalled what dreadful creations those deceptively deft hands brought into the world. At Eastertide the sister had presented the bishop with a white scarf adorned with the letters CA for "Christ is Arisen," rendered so crookedly that they seemed already to have celebrated the ending of the fast with some gusto.

"Who is this for?" His Grace inquired cautiously.

"Sister Emilia. A belt; I shall run a pattern of skulls and crossbones along it."

"Very good," he said, relieved. "Well, what about the fable?"

"I think," sighed Pelagia, "that it is about me, sinner that I am. With this allegory, father, you were trying to say that I make as good a nun as an ass makes a racehorse. And you have reached this uncharitable judgment about me because I spilled the apples in the cathedral."

"Did you spill them deliberately? To create a commotion in the cathedral? Confess." Mitrofanii glanced into her eyes, but then he felt ashamed, because the response he read in them was meek reproach. "All right, all right, I didn't mean that . . . but that is not the point of my fable; you have guessed wrong. What is it about the way we human beings are constituted that makes us think every event that occurs and every word that is spoken center on ourselves? That is pride, my daughter. And you are too small a bird for me to go concocting fables about you."

Feeling suddenly annoyed, he rose, put his hands behind his back, and paced up and down the library.

The bishop's library, to which it is probably worth our while to pay some attention, was maintained in perfect order under the management of his secretary, Userdov, a most assiduous worker. The bookcase with the works on theology and patrology was located at the center of the longest of the walls (the one that had no windows or doors). It contained doctrinal compositions in Church Slavonic, Latin, Greek, and ancient Hebrew. Extending to its left were the bookcases of hagiography, with lives of the saints, both Orthodox and Roman Catholic; to the right were works on ecclesiastic history, liturgics, and canonics. A separate place was accorded to a broad bookcase with tracts on asceticism, a reminder of His Grace's former enthusiasm. The same bookcase also contained extremely precious bibliographical rarities such as a first edition of Saint Teresa Avila's *The Internal Castle* and Reisbruck the Amazing's *Robes of the Spiritual Marriage.* Lying on a long table running the entire length of the room were bound files of Russian and foreign newspapers and magazines, among which pride of place was given to *The Zavolzhsk Diocesan Gazette,* a provincial newspaper that the bishop himself edited.

Non-religious literature of the most various kinds, from mathematics to numismatics and from botany to mechanics, stood on the stout oak shelves that completely covered the surface of the other three walls of the library. The only kind of reading that the reverend bishop avoided and considered of little value was fiction. He used to say that the Heavenly Creator had contrived more than enough miracles, mysteries, and unique stories in this world, so there was no point in mere mortals inventing their own worlds peopled with puppets; besides, anything contrary to God's own inventions would certainly be wretched and fail to delight. Sister Pelagia argued this point with the bishop, claiming that since the Lord had implanted the desire to create in the soul of man, He was the best judge of whether there was any sense and benefit in the writing of novels. However, this theological dispute was not initiated by Mitrofanii and his spiritual daughter and it will not conclude with them, either.

Halting in front of Pelagia, who was waiting meekly for her spiritual teacher's rather incomprehensible irritation to subside, Mitrofanii suddenly asked: "Why is your nose shiny? Have you been bleaching your freckles with elixir of dandelion again? Is that the right sort of thing for a bride of Christ to concern herself with? You are an intelligent woman, after all. And as the blessed Diadochus teaches us: 'She who adorns her flesh is guilty of love of the body, which is the sign of disbelief.' "

From his jesting tone of voice, Pelagia realized that the cloud had blown over, and she replied spryly: "Your Diadochus, my lord, is a well-known obscurantist. He even forbids us to wash. How does he put it in his *Love of Virtue*? 'It is best, for the sake of abstinence, to avoid the bathhouse, for our body is weakened by its sweet wetness.'"

Mitrofanii knitted his brows.

"I'll have you make a hundred bows to the ground for speaking so disrespectfully of an ancient martyr. And his teaching on the adornment of the flesh is correct."

Embarrassed, Pelagia launched into voluble excuses, claiming that she waged war on her freckles not for the sake of bodily beauty, God forbid, but exclusively out of a sense of decorum—a nun with a freckly nose was a ridiculous sight.

"Oh, indeed?" said the bishop, shaking his head dubiously, still putting off getting down to the important business.

Sister Pelagia's transitions from boldness to meekness and back again always occurred with such lightning speed that it was impossible to keep track of them. And now again she asked in a bold voice, with a glint in her eye: "Your Grace, surely you did not summon me because of my freckles?"

And once more Mitrofanii could not bring himself to speak of his business. He cleared his throat and walked up and down the length of the library yet again. He asked how her pupils were doing in school. Were they diligent, did they want to learn, were the sisters not perhaps teaching them anything superfluous that would not help, but merely hinder them, in their life?

"I am told that you have begun to teach them swimming. Why? They say you have ordered a bathing hut to be set up on the River and you splash about with them there. Is this a good thing?"

"Swimming is essential for girls, in the first place because it is good for their health and develops the flexibility of their limbs, and in the second place because it is good for their figures," the nun replied. "They are from poor families, and most of them have no dowries. When they grow up, they will have to find husbands . . . Your Grace, you did not summon me here because of the school, either. We spoke about it only two days ago, and about the swimming, too."

Pelagia was not one of those people who can be duped for long, and so Mitrofanii finally began talking about the idea he had conceived before he fell asleep the night before.

"The ass that I spoke of is myself. Acceding to your requests, and even more to the promptings of my own wretched vanity, which is absolutely improper for a pastor, I keep it a secret from everyone that it is not I who am the genuine expert in the field of unraveling obscure secrets and piercing through false appearances, but you, the meek and mild nun Pelagia. And now, like the ass who was so fond of fame, I am expected by everyone to produce new miracles and new revelations. Now no one will ever believe that the whole business was entirely your doing, and I did no more than to set you a work of penance."

The needles stopped clacking against each other and bright sparks sprang to the surface of the round brown eyes.

"What has happened, father? It clearly can't be in our province, or I should know about it. Has someone stolen the church treasury again, as they did last year at Shrovetide?" the sister asked with impatient curiosity. "Or, God forbid, killed a clergyman? What work of penance will Your Grace set me to perform this time?"

"No, nobody has been killed," said Mitrofanii, turning away in embarrassment. "This is something different. Not a criminal matter. At least, it is not a matter for the police . . . I'll tell you what it is, and for the time being, you just listen. You can tell me afterward what you think. Yes, do knit. Knit and listen."

He walked across to the window and delivered the following explanation, gazing all the while out into the orchard, from time to time drumming on the window frame with his fingers.

"Not far from here, about eight miles away, is the estate of my great aunt, Marya Afanasievna Tatishcheva. She is extremely old now, but there was a time, long ago, when she was considered one of the greatest beauties in St. Petersburg. I remember her coming to visit us when I was a boy. She was fun-loving then, young, and she used to play checkers with me. . . . She married an officer, a regimental commander, and made the rounds of various remote garrisons with him, then he retired and they settled at Drozdovka. Her husband, Apollon Nikolaevich, who is now deceased, was passionately fond of dogs. He kept the finest kennels in the entire province. He had racing dogs and hunting dogs and gundogs. He once bought a puppy for a thousand rubles, that's the kind of reckless man he was. But he still felt that all this was not enough, and he began to dream of producing some special new breed, something absolutely new. He frittered away all the rest of his life on this project. He called the breed the 'white Russian bulldog.' It is a different color from an ordinary bulldog, as white as milk all over, and has a very distinct flatness of profile (I have forgotten the special term that dog-lovers use for it), and it is quite exceptionally slack-lipped—that is, its lips are droopy. But the most important feature, the real point of all this, is that while it is white all over, its right ear has to be brown. I don't recall what the meaning of that is—something to do with a helmet . . . I think that when Apollon Nikolaevich served in the Horse Guards, it was the custom in his squadron to wear one's helmet cocked slightly to one side. So the ear represents that daredevil attitude. Ah, yes, I forgot, they also have to be extremely slobbery—I don't know what practical purpose that serves. All in all, as ugly a monster as you are likely to find anywhere. Apollon Nikolaevich proceeded as follows. He requested every bulldog-owning noble house in Russia not to drown the degenerate albino pups as they usually do, but send them immediately to Major-General Tatishchev, and he would pay good money for the rejects. White bulldog pups, especially pups with a brown right ear, are very rare. I don't remember how rare, although I heard it many times from my uncle, and from my aunt . . . perhaps one in every hundred litters. Well, anyway, Apollon Nikolaevich collected these little freaks and bred them. The pups mostly came out as usual, reddish-brown, but sometimes there were white ones, too, with brown ears, and now they were more frequent—say, one in every ten litters. Again he selected those and bred them, and took care that they were as slack-lipped and slobbery as possible. A particular difficulty arose, of course, with that thrice-cursed ear. A very large number of pups had to be culled. And so on and on, generation after generation. By the time my uncle passed away, he had made a great deal of progress toward his dream, but even so he was still only halfway there, so to speak. As he was dying, he entrusted the completion of the work that he had begun to his wife. And Marya Afanasievna was an absolute treasure as a wife. She had made the change from high-society charmer to mother and commander's wife and later to lady of the manor in stride. All with absolute sincerity and with a willing heart. Such was the womanly talent granted to her by God. If her husband had not given her any instructions to carry out on his deathbed, she would probably have withered away; she would never have coped with her grief. But as it is she has been a widow for twenty years now and is still strong, active, and cheerful. She talks about dogs all the time and thinks about absolutely nothing else. I have reproached her for her excessive passion and enthusiasm, upbraided her—but she does not listen. One day, as a joke, I teased her: 'Aunty, what if Lucifer himself should suddenly appear and demand your Christian soul in exchange for a pure white breed, would you give it to him?' 'Lord bless you, Misha,' she replied, 'what nonsense is that you're talking?' And then she suddenly fell silent and started thinking about it. I tell you, Pelagia, this is no joking matter. But in any case, she continued her deceased husband's work breeding the Russian white bulldog and was actually rather successful at it, especially along the lines of droopiness, slobberiness, and flatness of profile. But things did not go so well for her with the ear. Until just recently she had only accumulated three absolutely ideal male dogs. An old grandfather by the name of Zagulyai, already over eight years old. Then his son Zakidai, a four-year-old. And two or three months ago the old woman was delighted when Zagulyai's grandson was born. They called him Zakusai. He turned out so exemplary in all points that my aunt ordered all the other dogs who were not perfect enough to be drowned, in order not to spoil the breed, and kept only those three for breeding. Oh, I forgot another important point: They have bandy legs and their noses are pink with black spots. That is also an important feature . . ."

At this point the reverend bishop began feeling completely silly, and he cast an awkward sideways glance at his listener. She was moving her lips silently as she counted her stitches, showing no sign of astonishment.

"Well, anyway, here, read this letter. It came yesterday. If you tell me that the old woman is raving, that she has lost her mind, I'll write something to reassure her, and that will be the end of the matter."

Mitrofanii took the letter out of the sleeve of his cassock and handed it to Pelagia.

The sister pressed her spectacles up against the bridge of her nose with one finger and began reading. Having read the letter, she asked in alarm: "Who could have wanted to poison the dogs? And why?"

Reassured by the serious tone of her question, His Grace immediately stopped feeling embarrassed.

"That is the very point—why? Just consider. Marya Afanasievna is a rich old woman and she has no shortage of heirs. Her children have died, but she has a grandson and granddaughter—the prince and princess Telianov. In addition there are countless distant relatives, some hangers-on, all sorts of friends. She is a kind woman, but foolish. And she has one tyrannical habit—almost every week she summons the attorney from the town and changes her will. If she gets angry with someone, she disinherits them; if she feels pleased with someone, she increases their share. So this is what I was thinking, Pelagia: We need to check who benefited from the last time she changed her will. Or, on the contrary, who she was angry with and threatened to cut off. I cannot see any point to this barbaric poisoning of the dogs unless someone was doing it in order to send the old woman to her grave. You see how ill she has become because of this dog. And if both of them had died, they would have had to bury Marya Afanasievna there and then. What do you make of my suppositions?" the bishop asked his perceptive pupil anxiously. "They do not seem too unlikely?"

"Your suspicion is reasonable and highly probable; no other reason comes to mind," the novice nun said approvingly, adding, however: "But of course, someone really needs to visit the scene. Some other reason might perhaps come to light. Is your aunt's fortune very large?"

"It is. A large estate, maintained in exemplary order. Forests, meadows, mills, flax meadows, fields of top-grade oats. And capital as well, securities in the bank. I should not be surprised if altogether she had a million."

"And do you know her heirs, Your Grace? It requires a very low individual to undertake something of this kind. Killing someone outright would hardly be a more grievous sin."

"You are judging from the standpoint of God, and you are right to do so. But man's laws are very far removed from those of God. Kill someone outright, and the police will attempt to discover who did it and why. Do things that way and you end up serving hard labor. But from the human viewpoint, poisoning dogs is no great sin, and from the legal standpoint it is none at all, even though it is a surer way of killing the old woman than a knife or a bullet."

Pelagia threw her hands up in the air and her knitting went flying to the floor.

"It is a great sin in the human sense, very great! Even if your Marya Afanasievna were the devil incarnate and someone she had offended wished to settle accounts with her, what could these innocent creatures be guilty of? A dog is a trusting creature, affectionate, so generously endowed by God with faithfulness and the gift of love that it would do people no harm to learn from it. I believe, Your Grace, that it is even worse to kill a dog than a man."

"Now, just you stop that pagan talk!" the bishop cried. "I do not wish to hear any more of that. Comparing a living soul with a dumb creature!"

"What does it matter that it is dumb," the stubborn nun persisted. "Have you ever looked into a dog's eyes? Even your own Zhuk, who is chained at your gate? You should try it. Zhuk's eyes have more feeling and life in them than your precious Userdov's dull saucers!"

The bishop was on the point of opening his mouth to vent his righteous anger, but he stopped himself. In recent times he had been waging a struggle against the sin of wrath of the heart, and occasionally he was victorious.

"I have no time to waste looking into the eyes of yard dogs," the bishop said in a stiff, dignified tone of voice. "Leave Userdov alone; he is thorough and conscientious, and as for his soul being buried so deep—that is his character. And I shall not argue with you, especially over the obvious. Tell me one thing: Will you do as I ask?"

"I will, father," the nun said with a bow.

"Then this is your task. Go to Drozdovka this very day. Give Marya Afanasievna my blessing and the letter that I shall give you. Reassure the old woman. And most important of all, find out what is going on there. If you uncover malicious intent—nip it in the bud. But I do not need to tell you; you know what to do. And do not return until you have resolved this business."

"Your Grace," Pelagia began anxiously. "On Saturday I have lessons in the school."

"Well, you can come back for the lessons and then return to Drozdovka. That is all, off you go. But first, approach me and I will give you my blessing."

BEFORE SISTER PELAGIA sets out for the estate of the widow Tatishcheva, we need to offer certain explanations concerning the local geography, without which anyone who has never been to Zavolzhsk will find it a little difficult to believe everything that occurred subsequently, or even to understand how it possibly could have occurred.

The central character in this tale is the River, the greatest and most glorious not only in Russia, but in the whole of Europe. The provincial capital is built on its left bank, atop a steep ravine. Here the flow of the waters is restricted by cliffs on both sides, and therefore the current that is so famous for its stately grandeur temporarily abandons its placid humor, absentmindedly and unhurriedly accelerating to a gallop, its waves foaming into white crests and swirling in dark whirlpools as it maintains its centuries-old siege of the sheer cliff at Zavolzhsk, undercutting the high precipice with its insidious thrusts. About five miles farther downstream the steep slope of the left bank gradually starts to level out until it is eventually replaced by sandy shoals, so that the River, now allowed greater freedom, breathes more easily after its enforced sprint and expands to a width of almost a mile.

But this respite is merely temporary—at the very point where Drozdovka stands, the obstinate bank rears sharply upward once again; the manor house and the garden are elevated high above the watery expanse, and the view presented to the eye from that spot is rightly regarded as the most beautiful in the entire district.

And so Sister Pelagia's route lay in a southerly direction, out through the Kazan Gates and onto the Astrakhan highway, which extends along the River, obediently following all its capricious curves and never departing from it by more than five miles.

Before she left her little room in the episcopal see, referred to in convent fashion as a cell, Pelagia followed her old superstitious habit of opening the Gospels and setting her finger on a line at random. On this occasion the work of penance she had been set was not frightening, one might even call it trivial, but this was the young nun's normal ritual. However, the line of text that she hit on (from Saint Paul's Epistle to the Ephesians) was clearly not fortuitous, for it contained either an admonition or a warning: "Beware of dogs and beware of evildoers."

Apparently it *was* a warning, because as she was leaving the town, after she had already walked past the turnpike, Pelagia was granted a sign that was unambiguously menacing. Glancing around and seeing that no one seemed to be nearby, the novice took a little mirror out from the same waist bag in which she kept her knitting and began examining her nose to see whether the brazen freckles had faded at all after being treated with the dandelion milk. And then there was a sudden rustling in the bushes beside the road as two women emerged, having left the highway for some unknown reason. Sister Pelagia tried to hide her hand behind her back, but was so clumsy that she dropped the mirror. When she picked it up she saw the bad omen: two cracks set in a cross, and everyone knows what that sign means. It bodes nothing good.

In defiance of convent rules, Pelagia took bad omens seriously, not out of ignorance, but because she had been convinced by numerous instances that people had had good reason for identifying and enumerating them over the centuries. She did what is required in such a case—scooped up a handful of earth, threw it over her left shoulder, crossed herself (which she never did idly), recited a prayer to the Holy Trinity, and went on her way.

She did not wish to think of alarming matters (and in any case, she had no reason to do so). She had in prospect a small but nonetheless rather intriguing adventure, and so the nun's mood, briefly clouded by the mirror's demise, was rapidly restored, especially since this was one of those magical summer days when the mature sun turns the air as gold as honey, the sky is high and the earth is wide and everything is filled with bounteous life and sweet languor. But what point is there in description, since after all, everyone knows what a fine August day looks like when the month has only recently passed its midpoint.

For the first mile Pelagia was lucky—a little old peasant gave her a seat in his wagon. The roads in our province are new and even, so riding over them feels as smooth as gliding across ice, and Pelagia rode on soft straw in perfect comfort as far as the turn from the Astrakhan highway toward Drozdovka.

But here, right beside a fork in the road, there was another omen, this time so bad that a worse one could not possibly be imagined. After she got down from the cart and thanked the old man, Pelagia spotted a small group of people off to one side, crowding around a dray and looking at something on it without speaking. Her innate curiosity would not permit the sister simply to walk past an event like this, and she went over to see what this wonder might be. Squeezing her way among the peasant men and wandering pilgrims, she peered short-sightedly through her spectacles: a perfectly ordinary accident on the road—the axle had broken. But for some reason a district police officer was loitering beside the dray, and two police constables were grunting as they mounted a wheel on a freshly cut and roughly trimmed young oak tree. The officer was an acquaintance of hers, Captain Nerushailo from the nearby Chernoyarsk district, and there was something long lying on the dray, covered with a tarpaulin.

"What is it, Pakhom Sergeevich, has someone drowned?" asked Pelagia after she said hello, and to be on the safe side she made the sign of the cross over the tarpaulin.

"No, mother, something more terrible than that," the officer replied with a mysterious air, mopping at his crimson bald patch with a handkerchief. "The River's cast up two corpses. With no heads. A man and a young boy. Lying there side by side on the sand, they were. What a thing to happen! There'll be an investigation all right and proper. I'm just taking them to the provincial center so they can be identified. Though the devil only knows how. I beg your pardon, that just slipped out."

Pelagia shrugged the devil off her shoulder so that he would not stick to her and crossed herself now, not the dead men.

"They're not ours," someone said in the crowd. "There's never been any such murdering around these parts."

"That's right," someone else agreed. "They must have floated down from Nizhny; there's plenty of brigands up there."

This opinion was greeted with universal approbation, because the Zavolzhians are not over-fond of the Nizhnegrodians, regarding them as thieving, good-for-nothing folk.

"Your Honor, why don't you show us what they look like? We might recognize them," asked a bearded man in a good knee-length coat—a respectable-looking man who was clearly not simply curious to gape at the dead bodies.

Many others supported this request and though the women gasped, that was mostly for appearances' sake.

The police officer put on his peaked cap, thought for a moment, and acceded to the request.

"Very well, I will show you. What if you really—"

Pakhom Sergeevich pulled back the cover and Pelagia immediately turned away, because the corpses were completely naked, and it was not decent for a nun to look at such things. All she had time to see was that the left arm of the large, hairy body ended in a stump of raw meat where the wrist should have been.

"Oh, dear Lord, the boy's only a little mite," one of the women keened. "My Afonka's just the same."

Pelagia did not look any more after that, because a work of penance is a work of penance, and she strode off along the country road toward Drozdovka.

The air was getting rather muggy, and there were bright shimmers rippling up from the ground, as happens on a hot day before rain. Pelagia quickened her stride, glancing up every now and then at the sky, where a round, tightly stuffed storm cloud was swelling rapidly as it rolled along. Ahead of her she could see the railings of the park, and the green roof of the manor house rising up above the trees, but she still had a fair distance to cover to reach it. Sister Pelagia felt herself being overcome by an unworthy feeling—envy. "Now, that is really serious business," she thought, remembering the consequential air with which Pakhom Sergeevich had pronounced the appetizing word "investigation."

Some people had fearful mysteries to untangle, and others had to investigate how an old woman's slack-lipped darling had died. A fine work of penance His Grace had given her!

# CHAPTER 2

# Storm Clouds Over Zavolzhsk

LET US LEAVE Sister Pelagia to continue on her way toward the gates of the Drozdovka park under a rapidly darkening sky while we digress briefly to explain certain mysteries of our provincial politics and also to introduce the individuals who are destined to play a key role in this somber and tangled tale.

As we have already said, the province of Zavolzhie is extensive, but it is located far from the seat of central government, and in recent times it had been, if not entirely abandoned to its own devices, then at least very little honored by attention from higher spheres. There was nothing that these spheres desired in Zavolzhie—for the province is nothing but forests and rivers and lakes and, in particular, a great many swamps, such huge ones that during the Time of Troubles an entire Polish wagon train perished somewhere in the quagmires around here when it was sent by the Pretender in search of the magical Golden Stone.

It is a back-of-beyond sort of place, fit for wolves and bears—and in some ways the local inhabitants themselves are not unlike bears, no less sluggish and shaggy. The lively Novgorodians and shrewd Kostromians have invented a stupid saying: "The Zavolzhians are born with lazy bones." Well, indeed, the Zavolzhians are not fond of fuss and bustle, they are none too quick on the uptake, and they will probably never invent the *perpetuum mobile*. And yet who can tell? Several years ago in the village of Rychalovka, just a hundred and twenty miles from Zavolzhsk, there was a sexton who invented a hoist for getting up the bell tower. He was tired, you see, of running up and down eighty steep steps every day. He fixed a chair on long trace lines, stuck on some cogs and pinions and little levers, and what do you know? He could soar up into the heavens in just two minutes. His Grace himself came to take a look at this great wonder. He marveled, nodded his head, took a ride on the miracle chair, and then another one, and then he ordered the entire construction to be dismantled, because a church bell should be rung with humility, with reverent puffing and panting, and apart from that it was an unnecessary temptation to young boys. Mitrofanii sent the sexton to Moscow to study mechanics and sent another, with less supple wits, to replace him as sexton. But this glimmer of native genius is the exception rather than the rule. Let us admit quite frankly that as a group the Zavolzhians are slow-witted and suspicious of anything new.

Even our present governor, Anton Antonovich von Haggenau, was initially received with disapproval because, thoroughly imbued as he was with the spirit of beneficial reforms, he set about trying to stand the entire province entrusted to him on its head, while claiming that he was doing the very opposite and standing it on its feet. However, the Lord spared us Zavolzhians any excessive cataclysms. The young reformer fell under the influence of Mitrofanii, humbled his pride, and settled down, especially after he had married the most eligible bride in the entire locality with the bishop's blessing. For this, of course, the baron had to convert from Lutheranism to Orthodoxy, and his new spiritual father was none other than His Grace himself. Von Haggenau put down such deep roots here that, for his exemplary administration of the province, he was summoned to manage a ministry in the capital. He refused, judging that he was better off where he was. Generally speaking, he used to be a German, but he completely recovered. It used to be that in the evenings he would drink mulled wine from a little china mug and play the cello by himself, but now he has become extremely fond of home-made cranberry vodka, and at Epiphany he bathes in a hole in the ice on the River and afterward stays in the steam room for three hours at a time without once coming out.

And just as a genuine Russian ought to be, the governor is under his wife's thumb. But then, to be under the thumb of a lady like Ludmila Platonovna is both a joy and a pleasure; there are many people who would positively desire such enslavement. She was born one of the Cheremisovs, the very foremost family in Zavolzhie, elevated from merchant rank to the title of count by Peter the Great himself. As a girl Ludmila Platonovna had been slim and delicate, but after four little barons had been born, her constitution changed, and she acquired a most agreeable luxuriance, which only enhanced her beauty. Clear-eyed and rosy-cheeked, with plump hands, after she passed the age of thirty the baroness came to represent an absolutely perfect example of that genuinely Russian beauty for which skinny and bald Germans (among whom Anton Antonovich was numbered) have since time immemorial evinced an enthusiasm of both spirit and body. Ludmila Platonovna very quickly realized what power she held over her husband and began exploiting it entirely as she wished, but for the time being this did not result in any damage to the province because, as a woman of feeling and sensitivity, Madame von Haggenau devoted her inexhaustible energy to charitable and godly activities, so that even His Grace found her influence on her husband to be useful, in the sense that it softened the Prussian rigidity from which the baron suffered to some extent in his relations with other people. It is true, of course, that as a result of recent events Mitrofanii has been obliged to change his views on the subject of female dominance, but we shall come to that a little farther on.

Perhaps the only individual whose influence the governor's wife had not been able to manipulate, despite all her efforts (not counting His Grace, naturally, whose authority Ludmila Platonovna never once thought of assailing), was the baron's trusted adviser, Matvei Bentsionovich Berdichevsky, who held the post of assistant procurator at the Chamber of Justice. The story of this official is somewhat unusual and deserves to be related in some detail.

Matvei Bentsionovich was a former Jew and, like the governor, one of His Grace Mitrofanii's godchildren. Before entering into the bosom of the Orthodox Church, he bore the inharmonious name of Mordka, which in Russian signifies "little snout," and this is still used to this very day with gleeful malice by his enemies—behind his back, of course, because Matvei Bentsionovich's intimacy with the authorities is no secret to anyone. The governor's future confidential adviser made his appearance in the world in the poorest family one could possibly imagine. Then he was orphaned at an early age, as a result of which, according to the custom that has been in force in these parts for some time, he was accepted on a public scholarship at the four-year primary school, and then, in view of his exceptional abilities, for the grammar school as well. Mitrofanii kept an eye on the gifted youth from early on, and when he graduated from his studies at the grammar school sent him to St. Petersburg University. Berdichevsky did not disgrace himself in the capital, either, graduating with distinction, first in his year, and was granted the right to work anywhere he chose, even the Ministry of Justice, and yet he chose Zavolzhsk. And why not? He was a highly intelligent man, and he had not miscalculated in the least. Who would he have been in St. Petersburg? A provincial, a plebeian of the Jewish tribe, which, as everyone knows, is worse than having no tribe at all. But here we greeted him with affection. We gave him a good job and married him to a fine bride. Mitrofanii always used to say that the wife makes the man, and he illustrated his idea with a mathematical allegory. A man, he would say, is like the number one while a woman is like a zero. When they each live apart, his value is not great, and she has no value at all, but when they enter into a marriage, then a certain new number is created. If she is a good wife, she stands behind the one and multiplies its strength tenfold. If she is a bad wife, then she pushes her way in front of it and weakens the man by the same number of times, reducing him to a mere tenth part of a whole.

For Matvei Bentsionovich the bishop selected a good girl who could keep house from among the children of a subaltern. From the beginning their life together was one of love and harmony and they set about propagating with such dedication that during the first ten years of their marriage, which have just expired at the beginning of our narrative, they produced twelve offspring of both sexes (but primarily girls).

If he had so wished, Berdichevsky could have occupied some other, more prestigious position, including even the chairmanship of the Chamber of Justice, but by virtue of his character and innate reticence he preferred to remain in the shadows: He gave his advice to the authorities not in the office and not at public meetings, but for the most part *in camera,* over tea or a quiet game of preference, of which Anton Antonovich was very fond. Nor did Matvei Bentsionovich like to appear as prosecutor in court cases, for which his excuse was his nasal voice and unfortunate appearance. He was indeed far from handsome—he was nervous and twitchy, with a crooked nose and one shoulder noticeably higher than the other. His nominal superior, the provincial procurator Silezius, a man of impressive appearance but very stupid, frequently earned stormy ovations in court by reading speeches written by Berdichevsky, leaving Matvei Bentsionovich to merely sigh and feel envious.

The position of this latter-day *éminence grise* was founded on support from two of the pillars of Zavolzhsk society, His Grace and the governor, but the third, the beautiful Ludmila Platonovna, did not favor the crafty Jew. However, the tension between Berdichevsky and the baroness was not by its nature a violent enmity, but rather a jealous rivalry, so that on Forgiveness Sunday both parties would always confess to each other and forgive each other wholeheartedly—which did absolutely nothing to prevent the rivalry from continuing after Easter.

Unfortunately this idyllic or, as Matvei Bentsionovich himself referred to it out of a certain tendency toward cynicism, herbivorous opposition came to an end when a thundercloud appeared on the peaceful horizon of Zavolzhsk, borne by a westerly wind from the direction of sly, ominous St. Petersburg.

ONE EVENING THREE weeks before, the police sentry who stands at the entrance to the town of Zavolzhsk to maintain order, who by old habit is known in these parts as the "dutyman," saw an apparition. Far down the Moscow highway, above which the thunderclouds were swelling in dense purple billows, a small cloud of dust appeared, approaching Zavolzhsk at a speed quite without precedent in our local customs. Some time later the dutyman heard a loud guttural screeching and whooping that was quite clearly not Christian, and already at that point he felt the desire to cross himself, but was too idle (let us add, for our own part, that this was a mistake). Soon thereafter, from out of the sphere of dust tumbling smartly along the highway, there erupted a pair of lathered raven horses, their crazed eyes bulging out of their heads from strain, and standing above them, whistling his whip through the air, a black-bearded bandit in a shaggy astrakhan hat and patched Circassian coat, screeching like an eagle and furiously rolling eyes that were as bloody as the horses'. The dutyman's jaw dropped at such a sight, and he even forgot to ask for the warrant for post horses. He only caught a quick glimpse through the small window of some gray-haired, respectable-looking man who nodded to him graciously and an even vaguer glimpse of a second man in the depths of the carriage—nothing more than a sharp-nosed profile and an eye that glinted with an intimidating gleam. The carriage rumbled over the cobblestones of Moscow Street, a mile and a half long, cut across Cathedral Square, and turned in at the gates of the finest hotel in Zavolzhsk, the Grand Duke. There are those who say that at the very moment when the carriage hurtled past the episcopal see, there was a sign: a flock of black crows flew up out of nowhere and drove the peaceful gray pigeons off the crosses of the bishop's church, which exalted position they had always regarded as their own inalienable private domain. But this attack by crows is most probably a lie, because in our town people in general lie with inspired fluency.

The following day it was already known that an inspector from the Holy Synod had arrived in Zavolzhsk, Chief Procurator Pobedin's very own assistant for special assignments. Pobedin was known throughout the empire simply by his first name and patronymic. If they said: "Konstantin Petrovich gave the emperor another talking-to yesterday" or, for instance: "Konstantin Petrovich's health is on the mend," no one would even ask who this Konstantin Petrovich was; it was already perfectly clear.

Informed individuals in higher political circles immediately stated with confidence that Konstantin Petrovich was displeased with the province, which augured serious unpleasantness for both the bishop and Anton Antonovich. They also immediately named the reason: The rulers of Zavolzhie were not demonstrating sufficient zeal in the extermination of alien creeds and the propagation of Orthodoxy.

The personal identity of the inspector also became known. Our town may be far away from Russia's capital cities, but we do not, after all, live on the moon. We have our own high society and our aristocracy takes its daughters to St. Petersburg for the season and receives letters from its friends. And so all the noteworthy and merely curious events that take place in their high society reach even as far as Zavolzhsk.

Vladimir Lvovich Bubentsov turned out to be a most interesting individual indeed. Prior to a scandal the previous year, which was described in great detail not only in private letters from St. Petersburg but also in the newspapers, he had served in the Guards and had the reputation of being one of those dissolute and dangerous men who are not infrequently encountered among our brilliant Guard officers. He received his inheritance at an early age, rapidly dissipated it in revels and binges, then grew rich again playing cards, and he played with such truly remarkable success that duels were even fought, but without any consequences. Our army command takes an indulgent view of duels between officers if the business goes off without a fatal outcome or severe injuries, and it even encourages them to some extent, believing that these jousts reinforce the spirit of chivalry and soldierly honor. And, as they say, a pleasurable habit becomes second nature.

In addition to cards, Vladimir Lvovich had another passion— women, and he had a reputation as one of the capital's leading ladykillers. Then he seduced a woman from a family that was not noble, but perfectly respectable, and treated her especially cruelly, so that the poor creature even tried to hang herself. Bubentsov had many similar stories to his name, but this time he did not get away with it. The seduced woman had protectors in the persons of her two brothers, an officer and a student. Everyone knew that Vladimir Lvovich's skill as a marksman was God-given or, more likely, inspired by the devil, and he had no fear of duels, since he could quite easily shoot his opponent's pistol out of his hand and had done so more than once. A duelist who lives by gambling at cards needs a reputation of that kind—it is excellent protection against suspicions of cheating and unnecessary scandals.

Realizing that in this case satisfaction could not be gained simply by issuing a challenge, the girl's brothers decided to settle accounts with the offender in their own way. They were both bold young men with powerful physiques who went bear hunting with a forked stick. One morning they lay in wait for Vladimir Lvovich at the entrance to his apartment as he was returning home from his usual game. They deliberately chose a time when he would be wearing civilian clothes— otherwise they could not have avoided being charged with insulting the honor of the uniform. One of them, the student, grabbed Bubentsov's shoulders from behind and lifted him up off the ground, because he was much taller, and the other, the dragoon, lashed Vladimir Lvovich across the face with his hunting crop. And all this in the open street, where passers-by could see. At first Bubentsov kicked out with his feet and tried to break free, but when he realized that he wasn't strong enough, he only squeezed his eyes tightly shut so that they would not be put out. When the brothers had had enough of their amusement and tossed him on the ground, the beaten man, speaking in a voice that was quiet but clearly audible, told them: "I swear by the devil: I shall put an end to your family line." That was exactly what he said.

At dawn the following day he fought them both, something that is supposedly not customary here in Russia, but this was a special case, and the seconds had to agree.

According to the agreed-upon terms, Vladimir Lvovich first exchanged shots with the elder brother. Beginning at thirty paces, with an approach to the deadline. Bubentsov gave his opponent no chance to advance even an inch, but fired immediately. The bullet struck a place that it is shameful even to name. The dragoon was a genuinely strong man and no weakling, but he rolled about on the ground, howling and shrieking and weeping floods of tears. And it was quite clear that the bullet had struck the very spot at which Bubentsov had been aiming with his diabolical precision.

He immediately went on to exchange shots with the younger brother, who was trembling and whose face was whiter than a sheet, because his elder brother was still screaming and would not let a doctor near him. In his nervousness the student fired first without taking proper aim and, of course, he shot wide. Then Vladimir Lvovich mocked and humiliated him. He set him right on the deadline, at ten paces, and took his time aiming his pistol. The seconds were already thinking that he would take pity on the boy, and just frighten him by shooting into the air. But Bubentsov had other ideas.

The student was standing sideways to him, and covering his loins with the pistol to protect them. His knees were giving way, the cold sweat was running down his face. Only his head kept twitching back and forth, from the black mouth of Bubentsov's pistol to his wounded brother. And so Vladimir Lvovich timed his shot for the moment when the student was perfectly in profile—and took his jaw clean off with the heavy bullet.

He didn't kill the brothers, but he did put an end to their line as he had threatened to do. From that time on the elder brother could not have any issue, and who would marry the younger now, when the bottom of his face was covered with a foulard, his saliva drained into a small tank, and he spoke so indistinctly that it required long practice to understand him?

The incident of the double duel provoked a great furor, and Bubentsov was given a severe sentence—ten years in prison. He ought to have rotted away in his stone cell, but somehow this cruel avenger managed to attract the attention of Konstantin Petrovich. The chief procurator visited the prisoner in his prison not once or twice, or even ten times, but many more times than that, holding quiet heartfelt conversations with him about the human soul, about the true meaning of Orthodoxy and Russia's way of the cross. And these conversations had such a great effect on Vladimir Lvovich that he saw his sinful life in an entirely different light and he took fright. They said that through this revelation he was granted the gift of tears and it would often happen that he and Konstantin Petrovich did not speak of anything at all, but simply wept and prayed together. The prisoner began inclining toward the idea of taking monastic vows and, in all probability, strict ascetic vows as well, but Konstantin Petrovich would not permit it. He told Bubentsov that it was too soon, that he was not worthy to serve the Ruler of Heaven until he had atoned for his guilt before his earthly ruler. He told Vladimir Lvovich first to serve in an inconspicuous, modest, unprofitable capacity, to learn humility and piety. Bubentsov was willing to agree even to this in order to please his mentor. And so the chief procurator then petitioned and obtained the emperor's pardon for the convicted prisoner and took him into his own department as a trusted official.

It is well known that those we love best are not those who have done good to us, but those to whom we ourselves have been benefactors and who we, in our eternal error, believe must feel a boundless gratitude to us. Evidently, this is the very reason why Konstantin Petrovich loved with all his heart the sinner whom he had saved, and began entertaining considerable hopes for him, especially since Bubentsov was universally acknowledged to have demonstrated that he was a talented and indefatigable worker. They say Vladimir Lvovich was genuinely completely transformed, absolutely abandoned his dueling, and began behaving toward the fair sex with the most circumspect discretion. He managed his first responsible mission—the eradication of the self-castrating Skoptsy sect in one of the northern provinces, so decisively and energetically that he earned praise from the emperor himself as well as his benefactor and was even granted an audience by the ruler. But it is only natural that vicious tongues will always be found to slander anyone favored by Fortune. It was said that the chief procurator's new favorite was concerned not so much for the great future of Russia as for his own future within that of Russia, but is this not a reproach that can ultimately be leveled at all servants of the state, with only extremely rare exceptions?

Such was the unusual envoy despatched by the supreme church authorities to the sleepy realm of Zavolzhie, in order to provoke revolution and upheaval in it. And the method to which Vladimir Lvovich had recourse in order to achieve his as yet not entirely clear goals was so original that it deserves to be described in detail.

THE EMISSARY OF the Holy Synod began by making a series of visits, beginning with the governor himself, as required by common courtesy and the official nature of his visit.

Anton Antonovich, already apprised of all the information given above concerning his visitor from the capital, expected to see a neophyte, a sort of Matthew the Publican, that most dangerous variety of the tribe of guardians of the faith, and therefore adopted an attitude of extreme caution in advance. However, Ludmila Platonovna, whose imagination had been caught not so much by this bandit's spiritual rebirth as by his previous transgressions, was inclined decisively and irreconcilably against him, although inwardly she was also a little fearful. The governor's wife pictured the appearance in her drawing room of an infernally handsome devil, a devourer of innocent maidens, a wolf in sheep's clothing, and she readied herself, on the one hand, not to submit to his satanic charms, and, on the other, to put the upstart in his place from the very beginning, for Zavolzhsk was not debauched St. Petersburg, where the women were immoral and loose.

It need hardly be said that in such an empty provincial backwater any man with a reputation like Bubentsov's, even though his appearance might not be particularly advantageous, would have every chance of appearing to be, if not strikingly handsome, then at least an "interesting character."

Even so, at first the governor's wife felt a profound disappointment. The gentleman who entered the drawing room with a bow was frail, not to say puny. He appeared to be about thirty years of age, with extremely mobile joints ("wobbly," thought Ludmila Platonovna, who was fond of simple, sweeping definitions). To be fair, however, she did acknowledge that her visitor had a good figure, and the elastic flexibility of a rapier blade could be sensed in his narrow frame, but that merely lent Vladimir Lvovich a disadvantageous similarity to the local dandy Monsieur Dudeval, the dance teacher at the Zavolzhsk boarding school for noble girls. Nor did Bubentsov prove to be handsome of face: sharp features, somewhat predatory, a beak of a nose, bright unblinking eyes somehow reminiscent of an owl's. A certain attractiveness was lent to this physiognomy only by the sweeping eyebrows and long, soft eyelashes. Ludmila Platonovna supposed that these must be what he had used to seduce his unfortunate victims. But winning the favor of the mistress of the governor's mansion required rather more substantial qualities, as she gave him to understand by not proffering her hand for a kiss.

At the beginning of the conversation she liked the St. Petersburg fop even less. His voice proved to be low and lazy, and he drawled his vowels carelessly. A smile of bored politeness wandered listlessly over his face.

Subsequently, when the Zovolzhians had had an opportunity to get to know Vladimir Lvovich better, it became clear that such was his usual manner when he first spoke with people new to him, if he had not set himself the goal of producing a particular impression on the other party. This rendered even more powerful the effect of the sudden metamorphoses, when listlessness and idle talk were replaced by force-fulness and the unexpected *touché*—for Bubentsov was a perfect mas-ter of this technique.

With the baron and baroness he began a conversation about all sorts of inconsequentialities having nothing at all to do with the pur-pose of his visit: about how tiring his journey had been, about the lat-est fashions, about the advantages that English horses possessed over Arabian ones. Anton Antonovich listened attentively, agreeing with everything and trying to gauge how dangerous this windbag was. At the same time, he himself affected a well-intentioned dullness of wit, in which, let us note, he was remarkably successful. The conclusion reached by the baron was not reassuring: Bubentsov appeared to be dangerous, and even extremely so.

As a matter of principle, Ludmila Platonovna did not take part in the worldly conversation, but sat with a severe expression on her face, examining with distaste the remarkably small, elegant hands of this dangerous official as they toyed with a lace fan (the evening had proved muggy) and thinking that here they had a would-be Count Nulin.

It took the visitor only five minutes to realize which of them was the more important and he almost completely stopped looking at the gov-ernor, directing his words exclusively to the governor's wife. This gave the impression that he was taking pleasure in irritating Ludmila Platonovna with that bored, condescending glance from under his su-perb lashes. This outrageous inspection made her feel very uncomfort-able, as if she had received her visitor in an incomplete state of dress.

Toward the end of the half-hour visit the following incident occurred. The secretary looked into the hall and the baron apologized and walked across to the desk to sign some important document (in fact, we even know which document it was—the removal of excise duty from the book trade). Immediately Bubentsov inquired in the same lazy manner, without changing his tone of voice or expression: "I have heard, my dear Ludmila Platonovna, that you are extremely active in charity work? They say that you are quite indefatigable? Praiseworthy, most praiseworthy . . ."

Stung by the tone in which these words were spoken, the governor's wife replied dryly, even acidly: "And what pastime, pray, could possibly be more worthy for a woman in my position?"

An eyebrow so regular that it seemed painted rose in astonishment, and one glinting eye gazed straight into Ludmila Platonovna's soul, while the other, on the contrary, shrank and became almost invisible.

"Why, what a question. One can see immediately that you have never loved and, I think, do not even have any idea of what love is."

His hostess blushed, but could not think of anything to say, and in any case she felt doubtful whether she had heard right, because the strange words had been pronounced without the slightest expression. At this point Anton Antonovich returned, so that the moment for a rebuff was in any case lost.

For another five minutes or so after that the visitor chatted about some nonsense or other, but now the governor's wife watched him differently, with an air of either fright or anticipation.

And as he was already taking his leave and stepping up to her hand (this time for some reason Ludmila Platonovna offered no resistance to the kiss) the inspector whispered: "The whole of life will slip through your fingers like that. It's a sin."

He was an adroit man—he took advantage of the fact that just at that moment the governor was engrossed in a yawn that was cracking his jaw, delicately covering his mouth with his skinny hand, and was therefore unable to hear the impertinent words.

That was all that happened. But to the surprise of everyone, and above all of Anton Antonovich himself, from that day Ludmila Platonovna began to favor the visitor from Petersburg—one might even say that she took him under her wing. He took to visiting her apartments frequently, entering unceremoniously, quite unannounced. And then the governor's house rang with the sounds of the piano, two voices singing duets, and happy laughter. At first Anton Antonovich attempted to join in with the merrymaking but, tormented by his own obvious superfluousness, he would leave, supposedly to deal with some urgent matters, and then suffer even greater agonies in the quiet of his study, wringing his dry white hands. There were also picnic outings with a narrow circle of friends and boating trips and other forms of amusement allowed by the proprieties. Perhaps Vladimir Lvovich was motivated by a genuine liking for the baroness, who, as we have already mentioned, possessed a brilliance both of beauty and of qualities of the heart, but one other thing is certain: A close friendship with the most influential woman in the province was also required by the synodical inspector for other purposes.

THE NEW ARRIVAL set out directly from the von Haggenaus' to visit the postmaster's wife, Olympiada Savelievna Shestago, the mistress of a salon run in opposition to that of the governor. At that time Zavolzhsk society was divided into two secret parties that might provisionally be defined as conservative and progressive (out of old habit the latter was also referred to as liberal, although in present-day Russia this word is decidedly going out of fashion). Both camps were headed by women. The conservative party was, as it ought to be, the ruling party, and its true leader was Ludmila Platonovna. This was the banner toward which the majority of state officials and their wives were drawn, by virtue of position, occupation, and natural conviction.

The party of opposition consisted for the most part of young people and the bolder individuals among the teachers, engineers, and telegraph or postal workers; moreover the political orientation of the latter was determined by their being members of a department that was headed by Olympiada Savelievna's husband, who was totally enslaved by his better half. In the town Madame Shestago was considered a beauty, but in a completely different style from the governor's wife: She did not captivate with her stateliness and sweetness of character but, on the contrary, with her leanness and sharpness of tongue, or, as Olympiada Savelievna herself defined these qualities, her grace and intellectualism. This lady came from a family of merchant millionaires and she had brought her husband a dowry of three hundred thousand, a fact she never forgot to remind him about at the slightest sign of clouds on the vault of their domestic sky, which for the most part remained quite cloudless. In her rich and hospitable home, customs that were exotic for Zavolzhsk were encouraged, such as atheism, the reading of prohibited newspapers, and free discussion of parliamentarianism. Anybody was free to turn up at Olympiada Savelievna's Thursdays without ceremony, and very many did come, because, as we have already noted, the fare was notable for its abundance and by provincial standards the conversations were interesting.

Since Bubentsov's first day of visits happened to fall on a Thursday, he made an appearance in the progressives' camp without concerning himself about being invited, which testified—as did the very fact that he visited the postmaster's wife at all—to his thorough knowledge of the customs and balance of forces in the province.

The appearance of the St. Petersburgian provoked a genuine furor among the liberals, since they had already agreed among themselves that this agent of reaction had been sent because of them, in order to eradicate freethinking and sedition in Zavolzhsk society. On one hand, this was alarming, but on the other hand it was really rather agreeable (just imagine the chief procurator himself feeling concerned about the Carbonari of Zavolzhsk), though on the whole it was more alarming.

The "agent of reaction" proved not to be frightening at all, however. In the first place, he demonstrated a total absence of any obscurantism whatever and spoke quite freely about the latest literature—about Count Tolstoy and even about the French naturalist school, which was known in the town mostly from hearsay. The guest also produced quite an impression with his razor-sharp tongue. When the inspector of public schools, Ilya Nikolaevich Fedyakin, reputed among the progressives to be a notably acerbic wit, attempted to put the overconfident speaker in his place, it became clear that Vladimir Lvovich was a mouthful too large for the native-bred carper to chew.

"It is agreeable to hear such bold judgments from the lips of a servant of pious humility," said Ilya Nikolaevich, squinting ironically and stroking his beard, which signaled his serious irritation. "I suppose you often discuss physiological love in Maupassant with the chief procurator?"

" 'Physiological love' is a mere tautology," Bubentsov interrupted his opponent sharply. "Or is the romantic view of relations between the sexes still predominant here in Zavolzhsk?"

Olympiada Savelievna even blushed, she felt so embarrassed that this intelligent man should see Fedyakin sitting at the head of the table, in the place of honor in her home, and she hastily expressed her opposition to all hypocrisy and dissembling in sexual partnership.

With the postmaster's wife the expeditious Petersburgian acted even more decisively than with the governor's. As he was leaving—earlier than all the other guests, as if giving them an opportunity to gossip about him—Olympiada Savelievna, by this time absolutely blinded by his metropolitan brilliance, came out to see her dear guest to the hallway. She extended her hand to be shaken (naturally, kissing was not the accepted manner among the progressives), and instead of her hand, Bubentsov took her elbow. With a gentle but astonishingly powerful movement, he pulled his hostess toward him and, without saying a word, kissed her full on the lips with such force that poor Olympiada Savelievna, who in all her twenty-nine years of life had never been kissed like that by anyone, felt her legs turn to cotton wool and began seeing stars. She returned to her guests quite pink and cut off the vengeful Ilya Nikolaevich's attempts to denigrate the departed visitor in a most energetic fashion.

Thus on his very first day in the province, Konstantin Petrovich's envoy had established friendly relations with both queens of Zavolzhsk, and his friendship with Olympiada Savelievna was especially agreeable, since this lady's house directly adjoined the building of the post office, the director of which was her husband, with whom Bubentsov was very soon also on a friendly footing, so that he could enter his office without ceremony and had unlimited access to the only telegraph apparatus for the whole of Zavolzhie. Vladimir Lvovich made assiduous use of this privilege and even managed without the services of a telegrapher, since it turned out that he knew how to use the cunning Baudot apparatus quite splendidly. And so it sometimes happened that the synodical inspector would enter the post office after midnight, despatch something, receive something, and generally behave quite as if he was at home.

. . .

BUT WHILE THIS Baltic Varangian's triumphs among the local ladies were overwhelming and undisputable, with the men things did not go so smoothly.

Bubentsov's only clear conquest in this field (the postmaster Shestago does not count, because he is not an independent individual) was his alliance with the police chief, Lagrange.

There were specific reasons for this. Felix Stanislavovich Lagrange was a man new to the town, sent to replace the recently deceased Lieutenant-Colonel Gulko, who was for many years a faithful helper of Anton Antonovich and His Grace Mitrofanii in all their undertakings. Everybody here had loved the dead man, they were all used to him, and they greeted the new ministerial appointee with caution. The new police chief was a large, handsome man with hair neatly trimmed at the temples and a picturesquely waxed mustache. He seemed to be obliging, and deferential to his superiors, but the bishop did not like him— he had asked to be allowed to take confession with His Grace, but the words he spoke were insincere and he tried far too hard to make a show of his piety.

Zavolzhsk was not to the police chief's liking, either, primarily because it was a very quiet and uneventful town. Fortunately, the province was entirely uninfected by the revolutionary plague, because before Mitrofanii and the baron's time it had not managed to gain a foothold, and after that it had no opportunity. We have no large factories or universities, nor are there any particular social injustices to be observed here, and, it being possible to complain to the authorities about those that do exist, there does not really seem to be any point in rebelling. Contrary to normal state practice, there is not even a department of gendarmes in the province, because when there used to be one, idleness drove the men to drink, or they lapsed into melancholy. In Zavolzhie the police chief is also in charge of all gendarme business, a fact that had initially tempted Felix Stanislavovich into accepting this appointment. It was only afterward that he realized what a cruel joke fate had played on him.

The circumstances under which Bubentsov and the chief of police struck up a friendship remained unknown to the local inhabitants, although there is generally little that escapes their attention, and this close relationship developed with such rapidity that it gave rise to a rumor: Supposedly the inspector's visit was not routine, but had been prompted by secret information passed on by Lagrange, who had decided that he would attract the attention of higher authorities to his own person by hook or by crook. In any case, following the arrival of the synodical inquisitor, Felix Stanislavovich made a demonstrative gesture by ceasing completely to attend confession with His Grace.

And so in the space of a mere few days Bubentsov effected a genuine *coup d'état* in Zavolzhsk, seizing almost all the strategic positions: the administration in the person of Ludmila Platonovna, the police in the person of Felix Stanislavovich, and public opinion in the person of Olympiada Savelievna. It only remained for him to take in hand the church and judicial authorities, but here his plans misfired.

THE BISHOP, TO whom Bubentsov presented himself on Friday, on the morning following his first visits, was cool to his uninvited visitor. Avoiding making any empty conversation, he immediately asked what exactly the purpose of the synodical emissary's visit was and what authority he possessed. Vladimir Lvovich thereupon changed his manner (he had begun in a tone of mellow piety, with quotations from Holy Writ) and expounded the essential core of his mission briefly and succinctly.

"Your Grace, as you are well aware, the present state policy in relation to the religious situation in Russia consists in strengthening in every possible way the leading and guiding role of Orthodoxy as a spiritual and ideological bulwark of the empire. Ours is a great power, but an unstable one, because some believe in Christ with three fingers, some with two fingers, and some from left to right, while others acknowledge Jehovah but reject Christ and others again even worship Mohammed. People can and should think differently, but a multinational people that wishes to remain united must have a single faith. Otherwise we shall face discord, internecine war, and the total breakdown of morality. Konstantin Petrovich's credo consists in this, and the emperor is of the same opinion. Hence the urgent demands addressed by the Holy Synod to the bishops of those provinces where followers of other faiths and schismatics are numerous. Every month, from the western, the Baltic, and even the Central Asian provinces the bishops report thousands and tens of thousands of conversions. From Zavolzhie alone, where both schism and Mohammedanism flourish, no joyful news is received. I declare quite openly that I have been sent here first and foremost to clarify whether the reason for this passivity is lack of ability or lack of will."

Vladimir Lvovich paused in a fashion appropriate to these words and then continued in a significantly softer tone: "Your inactivity is damaging to the monolithic unity of the empire and the very idea of Russian statehood; it sets a bad example for the other bishops. I am entirely open with you, Your Grace, because I can see that you are a practical individual and by no means the starry-eyed dreamer you are represented as being by certain people in St. Petersburg. So let us speak without equivocation and to the point. You and I have a common interest. It is essential that the true faith win a genuine victory here in Zavolzhie—complete conversion of all Old Believers to the bosom of Orthodoxy, the baptism of thousands upon thousands of Bashkirs, or something equally impressive. This will be salutary for you, since your bishopric will no longer be listed among those that are out of favor, and extremely useful to me, because these accomplishments will be the direct result of my visit."

Seeing the displeasure on the bishop's face and mistakenly taking this grimace for doubt, Bubentsov added: "Is Your Grace uncertain how to go about the business? Please do not be concerned. That is why I have been sent. I shall arrange everything, only do not stick any spokes in my wheel."

The bishop, being a genuinely straightforward man, did not beat about the bush, but replied in the same tone: "This credo of yours is pernicious nonsense. Konstantin Petrovich was not born yesterday and he knows as well as I do that you cannot win anyone over to a different faith by coercion. It is only possible to speak of the observance of one religious rite or another, and as far as the monolithic unity of the state is concerned, that is of no significance whatever. I believe that the chief procurator is pursuing some other goals that have nothing to do with faith. For instance, the introduction of police methods of management into the spiritual sphere."

"Well, and what of it?" said Bubentsov with a cool shrug. "If this empire of yours and mine holds firm, it will only be due to the effort of will demonstrated by the powers that be. Every dissenter in thought and faith must remember at every moment that he is under close observation, that he will not be indulged and given a totally free rein. Freedoms are for Gauls and Anglo-Saxons, but our strength lies in unity and obedience."

"You speak to me of politics, but I speak to you of the human soul." Mitrofanii sighed and then went on to say something that he should not have done. "I do not have many new conversions in my diocese, because I do not see any point in enticing schismatics, Muslims, and German colonists into Orthodoxy. I say let everyone believe as he wishes, as long as he believes in God and not in the devil. As long as people behave in a godly manner, that is all that is necessary."

Bubentsov's eyes glinted and he spoke in a voice that was ingratiating but conveyed an unconcealed threat: "An interesting opinion for a provincial bishop to hold. And far from coinciding with the opinion of Konstantin Petrovich and his majesty the emperor."

By this point everything had become clear to Mitrofanii, both about his visitor and about his probable subsequent course of action, and His Grace therefore rose unceremoniously to his feet to indicate that the conversation was over.

"I know. That is why I inform you of my opinion with no witnesses present, so that everything will be perfectly clear between us."

Bubentsov also rose and said briefly, with a bow: "Well, then, I thank you for your frankness."

He left and did not darken the door of the episcopal see with any further visits. The declaration of war had been made and accepted. The lull that is common before the beginning of a general engagement had set in, and, at the time our tale begins, it was not yet over.

THE UNSUCCESSFUL SALLY against the fortress of faith was followed in short order by a foray against the bulwark of jurisprudence. Enlightened by his well-wishers, who by this time were already numerous, Bubentsov did not make his approach to the chairman of the

Chamber of Justice or the provincial procurator, but the latter's assistant, Matvei Bentsionovich Berdichevsky.

Their conversation took place in the Nobles' Club, into which Matvei Bentsionovich had been accepted immediately after he was elevated to the personal nobility on the basis of a recommendation from Baron von Haggenau. Berdichevsky dropped into the club quite frequently, not out of the snobbishness typical of parvenus, but for a more prosaic reason: The procurator's assistant had many children, and his house was filled with such chaotic toing and froing that even this home-loving *paterfamilias* sometimes needed to take a break. In the evening Matvei Bentsionovich usually sat on his own in the club library and played himself at chess—our town could offer him no worthy opponent for that abstruse pastime.

Vladimir Lvovich walked up, introduced himself, and suggested a game. He was granted the right to make the first move and for a certain time there was complete silence in the library, with only the malachite chess pieces occasionally tapping against the board. Berdichevsky discovered, to his surprise and delight, that he had a serious opponent and he was obliged to make some effort, but even so little by little the black pieces won the upper hand.

"Oh, for a little trial," Bubentsov suddenly sighed, breaking the silence.

"What was that?"

"You and I are berries from the same field," Vladimir Lvovich said amiably. "We climb upward, tearing our nails, with everyone around us only trying to knock us back down. You are a converted Jew; it is hard for you. Your only support comes from the governor and the bishop. However, I assure you that neither the one nor the other will remain in his post for long. Then what will become of you?" He set down a rook and declared: *"En garde."*

"A little trial?" asked Matvei Bentsionovich, looking intently at the board and twisting the tip of his long nose with his fingers (a rather unpleasant habit of his).

"Exactly. Of schismatics. Some acts of sacrilege or other, or better still of savagery. Mockery of Orthodox sacred objects isn't bad, either.

We need to start with some merchant or other, one who is particularly respected. A rich man's purse always comes before his faith. Press him hard enough, and he will soon realize where his best interests lie and back down, and many others will follow him. As things are, no doubt the police and the consistory staff and your court officers all receive bribes from the Old Believers, but we won't make them pay with money, only by making the sign of the cross with three fingers, them and every last member of their households. How's that?"

"They don't receive anything," Matvei Bentsionovich replied, figuring out some baffling sequence of moves.

"How do you mean?"

"From the schismatics. The police and the consistory staff. Or the court officers, either. That is not the practice in our province. I'll take your pawn."

"What about your queen?" Bubentsov asked in surprise, but immediately took the queen with no hesitation. "Your protectors will be gobbled up in exactly the same way, and in the very near future, too. I shall be needing an experienced man of the law, Mr. Berdichevsky, someone well acquainted with the local conditions. Think on it. This has the whiff of a great career about it, even perhaps not purely in the field of jurispridence, but that of canon law. Even your Jewishness is no hindrance there. Many pillars of ecclesiastical law have been drawn from your nation, and even now the converted Jews include some of the most zealous propagators of Orthodoxy. And give some thought as well to the consequences of stubbornness." He waved the captured queen eloquently. "After all, you have a family. And I have heard that another addition is on the way."

Desperately afraid, and therefore avoiding raising his eyes from the board, Matvei Bentsionovich mumbled: "I beg your pardon, sir, but, first, you are in checkmate. And second"—he spoke these words almost in a whisper, with a powerful tremor in his voice—"you are a scoundrel and a base individual."

As he said it he squeezed his eyes tightly shut, recalling all at once the double duel, and his twelve children and the addition that was on the way.

Bubentsov laughed as he looked at this brave soul's pale face. He glanced around to make sure that there was no one nearby (there was not), gave Matvei Bentsionovich's long nose a highly painful tweak, and left. Berdichevsky twitched his nostrils, depositing two cherry-red drops on the chessboard, and made an unconvincing attempt to overtake his insulter, but the tears welling up in his eyes veiled everything in a rainbow-colored mist. Matvei stood there for some time and then sat back down.

AND NOW ALL that remains is for us to tell you about the retinue of the unusual synodical inspector, for in their own way this pair were no less colorful than Vladimir Lvovich himself.

As his secretary he had with him Provincial Secretary Tikhon Ieremeevich Spasyonny, the same respectable-looking gentleman who had nodded so amiably through the window of the black carriage. From this official's surname, which means "saved," and even more from his behavior and conversation it was clear that he came from the priestly estate. They said that Konstantin Petrovich had moved him close to his own person by advancing him from the rank of simple sexton— evidently he had spotted something exceptional in this modest junior clergyman. In the synod Tikhon Ieremeevich held a low, insignificant, and poorly paid post, but he was frequently honored with confidential tête-à-têtes with the chief procurator himself, so that there were many, even among the hierarchs, who were a little afraid of him.

This lowly official, as quiet as a mouse, had been attached to Bubentsov as the eye of the church authorities, who preferred to keep a check even on those they trusted. At first he had performed his duties conscientiously, but by the time the aforementioned carriage arrived in Zavolzhsk, he had fallen completely under the spell of his temporary superior and become his unquestioning minion, evidently having come to the conclusion that no man can serve two masters. How Vladimir Lvovich won him over we do not know, but we imagine that for such an inventive and talented man it was not a very difficult task. Tikhon Ieremeevich remained true to his trade, only instead of spying on and nosing things out against Bubentsov, he now did so exclusively for his benefit—it is quite possible that being a man of farseeing intelligence, he had identified some advantage to himself in such a change of vassalage. Though he was short, with a habit of constantly pulling his head down into his shoulders, Spasyonny possessed clawlike hands on unnaturally long arms that hung down almost as far as his knees, and therefore Vladimir Lvovich had at first called him "Orangutang," but later awarded him the less offensive nickname of "Undershirt." (The point was that Tikhon Ieremeevich was distinguished by such genuinely fervent piety that his every second word, whenever it was appropriate and also when it was not, was a citation from Holy Writ, and he had once been incautious enough to mention to his suzerain that for protection against the devil he wore beneath his frock coat a special shirt, which he called a "blessed baptismal shirt.") Like a good Christian, Spasyonny did not take offense at his master's jokes and merely repeated briefly: "Sprinkle me with hyssop and I shall be pure, wash me and I shall become whiter than snow."

The provincial secretary followed Bubentsov everywhere like a shadow, and yet despite this he also somehow managed to pop up in the most unexpected places, since he had familiarized himself with Zavolzhsk amazingly quickly. He was seen either in the cathedral, singing along in the choir, or in the market, haggling over the price of honey with the Old-Believer beekeepers, or in Olympiada Savelievna's salon, conversing with the attorney Korsh, who is regarded as the leading expert on investigative matters in our province.

It is astonishing how a person like Spasyonny was able to associate and even be on friendly terms with Bubentsov's beastlike driver. This Murad was a genuine Abrek, a true highway bandit. In Zavolzhsk he was dubbed "the Circassian," although he had no Circassian blood and came from a quite different mountain tribe. But who can tell all these blackbeards apart? Murad was not only Vladimir Lvovich's coachman, but also his valet and servant, and when occasion demanded his bodyguard. No one really knew for certain why he evinced such doglike devotion to his master. All that was known was that he had followed Bubentsov around since his childhood and been inherited by him from his father. A long time before that, Bubentsov senior, one of the Caucasian generals, had rescued the young Murad Djuraev from enemies seeking blood vengeance and carried him away to Russia. Perhaps there were some other special circumstances involved, but that was something the Zavolzhians had not been able to discover, and they lacked the courage to ask Murad about it. He looked far too frightening for that, with his shaved head and his face completely overgrown by a thick black beard that grew right up to his very eyes and those teeth—he could bite your arm off at the elbow and spit it out. Murad spoke little Russian and even that badly, although he had lived among the Orthodox for many years. He had also retained his Mohammedan faith, for which he was subjected to onslaughts of missionary zeal by Tikhon Ieremeevich, but so far without any result. He dressed in Caucasian fashion: in an old *beshmet* and patched soft-leather shoes, with an immense silver-bound dagger at his belt. Murad's bandy-legged, swaying walk and broad shoulders signaled brute strength, and men felt themselves constrained in his presence, while women of the simpler classes experienced a swooning sense of fright. Strangely enough, among the cooks and the maids Murad had the reputation of a paramour, although he treated them roughly and even violently. During the second week of Bubentsov's stay the firemen of Zavolzhsk conspired with the butchers of the town to teach the infidel a lesson and stop him from despoiling other people's girls. But Murad scattered his dozen "teachers" and then pursued them through the streets for a long time. He overtook the butcher Fedka and would surely have beaten him to death had Tikhon Ieremeevich not come upon the scene in time.

Things did not go as far as murder, but in view of this scandal, and especially the fact that the police had not dared to halt the ruffian, several of the more far-seeing among the townsfolk began to take stock, sensing the approach of troubled times. And they were right, for there was a rumbling of thunder in the atmosphere above our province and the black sky was ominously illuminated by flashes of lightning.

HOWEVER, HAVE WE not perhaps deviated too far from the central theme of our tale? Sister Pelagia has long since passed in through the wide-open gates of the Drozdovka park, and now we shall have to catch up with her.

# CHAPTER 3

# Dear People

THE RAIN OVERTOOK Pelagia at a distance of fifty paces from the gates. It came in a concerted, copious, merry downpour, instantly making clear that it intended to soak every last thread, not only of the nun's habit and headscarf, but also of her undershirt, and even of the knitting in the bag at her waist. Pelagia took fright. She glanced around to make sure that no one was coming, hoisted up her habit, and set off sprinting along the road with a quite remarkable alacrity, in which she was assisted by the English gymnastics that, as we have already said, the sister taught at the diocesan school.

Having attained the sanctuary of the avenue, Pelagia leaned back against the trunk of an old elm that offered her the secure protection of its dense crown, wiped the drops of water from her spectacles, and turned her gaze to the sky.

Her gaze was well rewarded. The nearer half of the high, arching firmament had turned a blackish hue of violet—not that murky, somber color of gloomy overcast days, but with an oleaginous shimmer, as if some mischievous heavenly schoolboy had overturned a bottle of purple ink onto a light-blue tablecloth. The stain had not yet spread to the firmament's more distant half, where the sun still reigned unchallenged, but two rainbows had sprung up there, arching from one side of the sky to the other, one brighter and smaller, the other dimmer but larger.

A quarter of an hour later everything had changed: The nearer half of the sky had become bright and the more distant half dark, which indicated that the cloudburst was over. Pelagia offered up a prayer of thanks for her safe deliverance from the torrential downpour and set out along the interminably long avenue that led up to the manor house.

The first of the inhabitants of the estate to greet the traveler was a snow-white pup with a brown ear who came bounding out of the bushes and immediately, without the slightest hesitation, sank his teeth into the edge of the nun's habit. The pup was still at an infantile age, but his character was already most determined. He tugged at the dense fabric, twisting his bulbous head this way and that and growling, and it was clear that he would not easily abandon this occupation.

Pelagia picked this bandit up and saw a pair of mischievous blue eyes, a pink nose speckled with black, and two little velvety cheeks drooping at the sides, which were for some strange reason smeared with earth, but she was unable to observe any other details, because the pup thrust out a long red tongue and licked her nose, forehead, and spectacles with quite exceptional dexterity.

Temporarily blinded, the nun heard someone forcing his way through the bushes. A breathless male voice said: "Aha, now you're caught! You've been eating soil somewhere again, you devil's spawn! Pardon me, sister, for mentioning the Evil One. It's this foolish creature's pa and grandpa as got him into that habit. Oof, thank you for catching the pest; I just can't keep up with him. He's cunning, the little devil. Oh, beg your pardon again."

Pelagia pressed the warm, resilient body against herself with one hand and removed her slavered spectacles with the other. The bearded man she saw standing in front of her was dressed in a collarless cotton shirt, velveteen trousers, and a leather apron—he looked like the gardener.

"Take your Zakusai," she said. "And hold him tight."

"How do you know what he's called?" the gardener asked, amazed. "Or have you been here before? Somehow I can't recall."

"Many things unknown to ordinary people are revealed through prayer to us persons of the monastic class," Pelagia said in a didactic tone of voice.

Whether the unknown man believed her or not was not clear, but he took a fifteen-kopek coin out of his pocket and bowed as he thrust it into the nun's bag.

"Take it, sister, it's given with a pure heart."

Pelagia did not attempt to refuse. She herself had no need of money, but even the smallest of gifts to God was a joyful thing if the intention was truly pure.

"Don't you go on up to the house," the gardener advised her, "don't go wearing your legs out in vain. Our masters here don't give charity to God's people, 'on prinsipul,' they say."

"I'm on my way to see Marya Afanasievna, with a letter from His Grace Mitrofanii," said Pelagia, declaring her credentials, and the denizen of Drozdovka respectfully doffed the cap from his head, bowed, and switched from calling her "sister" to "mother."

"You should have said straightaway, mother. And me pressing my money on you like a stupid fool. Follow me. I'll take you there."

He led the way, clutching Zakusai in both hands as the puppy wriggled and squealed in frustration.

To their right an odd-looking gentleman wearing a wide-brimmed hat and a cloak with a cape was strolling about on a grassy plot beside a pavilion of white stone. He was holding a small box of black lacquered wood under his arm and he had a long tripod with sharp, iron-tipped points in his hand. He thrust the tripod into the ground, then set the box on top of it, and it became clear that it was a photographic apparatus such as have ceased to be a rarity even in our remote province. The gentleman looked around, glanced briefly at the nun with no interest, and said to the gardener, "Well, Gerasim, so you've captured the fugitive, then? I'm just wandering through the park, photographing the way the steam rises from the ground. A rare optical effect."

The gentleman was handsome, with a well-kempt beard and long wavy hair, and it was clear immediately that he was not from these parts. Pelagia liked the look of him.

"He's an artist, makes photographic pictures," Gerasim explained to his companion when they had walked on a little way. "All the way from Pettersburk. He's staying here, a friend of Stepan Trofimovich, our manager. Arkadii Sergeevich his name is, Mr. Poggio."

They walked on for another hundred paces, but there was still a lot of walking to do to reach that green roof. Suddenly there was a clopping of hooves against the dampened surface of the driveway behind them and, looking around, Pelagia saw a light gig and a rosy-cheeked gentleman in a fluffy white hat and linen frock coat sitting in it.

"Good health to you, Kirill Nifontovich," said Gerasim, bowing. "Would you be hurrying on your way to supper?"

"And where else? Giddy-up, giddy-up!"

The small, faded eyes that radiated a childishly naïve curiosity lighted on Pelagia, the round cheeks set into the folds of a good-natured smile.

"Who's this you're escorting, Gerasim? Oho, and you have the royal infant, too."

"The sister's taking a letter from the bishop to the mistress."

The man in the gig assumed a respectful expression and raised the hat off his steaming bald head.

"Allow me to introduce myself. Kirill Nifontovich Krasnov, local landowner and neighbor. Get in, mother, I'll drive. Why should you have to be put to such trouble? And let's take the little doggie along with us; I expect Marya Afanasievna's missing him, all right. Peering from the porch on high for her dear herald drawing nigh."

"Is that from Pushkin?" asked Pelagia, taking a seat beside this likeable chatterbox.

"I'm flattered," he said with a bow and a crack of his whip. "No, I compose my own verse. The lines simply pour out of me of their own accord, whatever the occasion or even without any occasion at all. The only problem is that they don't add up to poems, otherwise I'd be every bit as famous as Nekrasov and Nadson."

Then he declaimed:

> "My verses are as light as fleas.
> Believe me when I say that these
> Are poems not designed to tease,
> But only to delight and please."

A minute or two later they were already driving up to a large house adorned with all the attributes of magnificence in the style of the previous century—a Doric colonnade, disgruntled lions on pedestals, and even bronze Gross-Jägersdorf unicorns at the sides of the steps.

In the entrance hall Krasnov spoke in a whisper for some reason as he asked the pretty maid: "Well, Taniusha, how is she? You see, we've brought Zakusai back for her."

The blue-eyed and plump-lipped Tanyusha only sighed.

"Very bad. She's not eating or drinking anything. Keeps crying all the time. The doctor left not long ago. Didn't say anything, just shook his head like that and left."

THE SICK WOMAN'S bedroom was gloomy and smelled of lavender drops. Pelagia saw a wide bed, a corpulent old woman in a mobcap half-sitting and half-lying on a mound of fluffy pillows, and some other people whom it was awkward for her to study there and then, from the threshold, and it was a bit too dark anyway—her eyes would have to get used to the light first.

"My little Zakusai?" the old lady asked in a deep voice, half-rising and reaching out her plump, flabby hands. "So that's where he is, my little droopy-cheeked love. Thank you, dear neighbor, for bringing him back." (That was to Krasnov.) "Who's this with you? A nun? I can't see, come closer." (This was to Pelagia.)

She moved closer to the bed and bowed.

"Marya Afanasievna, I bring you a pastoral blessing and wishes for a most speedy recovery from the bishop. That is why he has sent me, the nun Pelagia."

"What do I want with his blessing!" the general's widow Tatish-cheva exclaimed angrily. "Why didn't he come himself? Would you believe it, fobbed a nun off on me. I'll strike out every damn thing I've left to the church in my will."

The puppy was already in her hands, licking her old, wrinkled face without encountering the slightest resistance.

There was a loud bark at Pelagia's feet, and a broad-chested, snub-nosed dog threw its front paws on the bed, wrinkling up its large fore-head in annoyance.

"Don't you be jealous, little Zakidai," the sick woman said to him. "He's your son, a little drop of your own blood. Come on then, let me pet you, too."

She patted Zakusai's parent on the broad nape of his neck and started scratching him behind the ear.

Meanwhile Pelagia examined the other people who were in the bedroom with a surreptitious sideways glance.

The young man and young woman were probably the widow's grandson and granddaughter. His name was Pyotr Georgievich, and she was Naina Georgievna, both with the surname Telianov, from their father. They were surely the ones who would benefit most from the will.

Pelagia tried to imagine this man with clear eyes and dark hair, who was shifting from one foot to the other, in the act of sprinkling poison into the poor dogs' food. She failed. Nor did she wish to think evil of the young woman, who was a striking beauty—tall and haughtily majestic, with the corners of her mouth turned down capriciously.

There was also a man in a jacket and Russian shirt, with a simple, open face, whose pince-nez and short little reddish-brown beard suited him remarkably badly. It was not clear who he was.

"His Grace has sent you a letter," said Pelagia, holding the missive out to Tatishcheva.

"Why didn't you say so? Give it to me."

Marya Afanasievna took a closer look at the nun. Evidently taking note of her spectacles and her composed demeanor, she rephrased her request.

"Let me have it, mother, I'll read it. And you all go and have supper. Stop hanging around me pretending to be concerned. Let the holy mother have supper, too. Tanya, you make up a room for her, the corner room where that Spasyonny stayed just recently. That will be quite neat, his name meaning 'saved' and her being saved too because she's a bride of Christ. If Vladimir Lvovich comes as he threatened to, put that Spasyonny in the empty wing. He won't be missed, the repulsive man."

AS SHE SETTLED Pelagia into the bright, tidy room on the ground floor with a window looking out onto the garden, the garrulous Tanya told the guest about this person Spasyonny who had stayed here earlier. Pelagia knew about Spasyonny (how could she not have known about him, when in recent weeks all the talk in the episcopal see had been of nothing but the synodical inspector and his associates?), but she listened attentively. Then Tanya moved on almost immediately to talk about Bubentsov's Circassian—how frightening he looked, but how he was still a human being after all and really all he wanted was a kind word.

"When I met him in the yard that evening, it made me shudder. And he looked at me with those black eyes of his, and suddenly grabbed me right here. I went weak all over, and he . . ." Tanya said, holding a half-fluffed pillow in her hands and speaking in a half-whisper, then she suddenly recollected who she was talking to. "Oh, holy mother, what am I saying! You can't listen to such things, you're a nun."

Pelagia smiled at the sweet girl. She washed after her journey and cleaned her habit with a damp brush to remove the dust of the road. Then she stood at the window for a while, gazing out into the garden. It was quite wonderfully lovely, even though it was neglected. Or perhaps it was lovely because it was neglected?

Suddenly she heard voices somewhere nearby. First a man's voice, muffled and choking with powerful emotion: "I swear I will do it! After this it will be impossible for you to live here in any case! I shall make you go away!"

The number of amorous speeches that Sister Pelagia had heard in her life was very few, but still it was enough for her to tell immediately that this was the voice of a man madly in love.

"If I do go away, then it won't be with you," said a girl's voice, even nearer than the first one. "And we'll see whether I go away at all."

You poor thing, Pelagia thought about the man, she doesn't love you.

Beginning to feel curious, she gently pushed the window frame open and cautiously stuck her head out.

Her room was at the end, and the corner of the house was just to the right of the window. The girl was standing right on the very corner, only half-visible from the back. From the pink dress Pelagia realized immediately that it was Naina Georgievna. But it was a pity that the man was out of sight around the corner.

Just at that moment she heard a bell ring—the summons to supper.

THE TABLE WAS laid on the spacious veranda, with a balustrade and steps leading down into the garden with its trees, beyond which she could divine the wide expanse of the River, bearing its waters past the high bank at Drozdovka.

Pelagia saw quite a number of new faces and could not immediately make out who was who, but the meal and the tea-drinking that followed it lasted for a long time, so that little by little everything became clear.

In addition to those already known to the nun (the brother and sister, the photographic artist Arkadii Sergeevich Poggio, and the neighboring landowner Kirill Nifontovich Krasnov), also sitting at the table were the man in a Russian shirt she had seen earlier (that same one, with the plain yet somehow attractive appearance), another bearded man with a face like a peasant's, but wearing a tweed suit, and a shriveled creature of the female sex in a clumsy hat decorated with imitation paradise apples.

The plain-looking man turned to be the manager of the estate, Stepan Trofimovich Shiryaev. The bearded man in tweed was Donat Abramovich Sytnikov, a well-known rich businessman from a long line of Zavolzhie Old Believers, who had recently bought a summer house quite nearby. In total contrast, not only was the shriveled creature not from Zavolzhie, she was not even Russian, and her name was Miss Wrigley. What role she filled at Drozdovka was not entirely clear, but it seemed most likely that Miss Wrigley belonged to that extensive estate of French, English, and German women who have raised their Russian charges, taught them what they were able, and become permanent residents under their masters' roofs because it has simply become impossible to imagine the family without them.

At the beginning of supper an unpleasant shock awaited Sister Pelagia.

Marya Afanasievna came out to dine, leading Zakidai and Zakusai on a leash and leaning on Tanya's shoulder. The bishop's letter had evidently brought the general's widow some relief, but her mood was not in the least improved. His Grace always said that what some sick people needed was not to have medicines stuffed into them, but to be made thoroughly angry. We must assume that this was the method he had applied in this particular case.

Father and son were led off to one side, where a bowl of marrow bones stood waiting for the former and a bowl of goose liver for the latter. There was a sound of crunching and champing and the two rumps, large and small, began rhythmically wagging their white stumpy tails.

"Tell me, Miss Wrigley, why are you wearing a conservatory on your hat?" Tatishcheva asked, looking around the table, clearly in search of someone with whom to find fault. "A fine ingénue she makes. But then she's a rich heiress now, isn't she? Time to be thinking of fiancés."

Pelagia pricked up her ears and examined the Englishwoman more closely than before. She noted the vivacity of her expression, the thinness of her lips, the cunning wrinkles around her eyes.

Miss Wrigley was not at all cowed by this sudden attack and parried the thrust without the slightest servility, speaking Russian with hardly any accent at all.

"It is never too late to be thinking of fiancés. Even at your age, Marya Afanasievna. You spend so much time kissing that Zakidai of yours, you really ought to have legitimized your relations long ago. What kind of example is that to set little Naina?"

From the laugh that ran rapidly around the table, Pelagia realized that their hostess's bark was worse than her bite and her tyranny more appearance than substance.

Having been rebuffed by the Englishwoman, the general's widow turned her wrathful gaze on the nun.

"A fine bishop you have, and I a fine nephew. I could die here; the whole thing's no more than a joke to him. Why are you gaping like that, mother?" she asked Pelagia furiously, speaking once more in a familiar tone. "Allow me to introduce you, gentlemen. You see before you a latter-day Vidoq in a nun's habit. She's the one who is going to save me, she is going to unmask the criminal. My thanks to my nephew Misha for going to so much trouble, I'm so grateful. Just listen to what he writes here."

Marya Afanasievna took out the ill-starred letter, put on her spectacles, and began reading out loud: ". . . And in order that you, dear aunt, might feel completely reassured, I am sending to you my trusted assistant, Sister Pelagia. She is an individual of acute intellect and will quickly discover the truth concerning whoever it is that finds your dear dogs a hindrance. If any of those close to you truly wish you harm, which I should prefer not to believe, then Pelagia will expose and denounce the wretch."

The table fell quiet, but Pelagia did not see whose face bore what expression, for she was sitting there utterly mortified and bright red, with her nose stuck into her plate of burbot soufflé.

She continued to feel embarrassed for a long time, and tried to attract as little attention as possible. But in any case, no one attempted to strike up a conversation with her. Her only confidant in the ostracism to which she was subjected, either deliberately or by chance, was the impudent Zakidai, who crept under the table and stuck his wrinkled nose out from under the tablecloth straight onto Pelagia's knees. Zakidai had already emptied his bowl of marrow bones and now he had determined with unerring precision who among the diners at the table was the most vulnerable to extortion.

The eldest of the breed of white bulldogs gazed up unblinkingly at the nun, inclining his round head slightly to one side and wrinkling his Socratic brow. Although Pelagia was hungry, she felt guilty eating while facing this stare that pierced her very soul. She slyly removed a piece of soufflé from her fork and lowered her hand under the tablecloth. Her fingers were enveloped in a mist of hot breath and tickled by a rough tongue. The fish disappeared.

Meanwhile the conversation around the table had moved on to an interesting topic, the subject of talent and genius.

"Ever since I was little, what people have always said about me is 'he is a talent, a talent,'" Poggio said, narrowing his eyes wryly. "When I was still young and foolish, it used to make me feel proud, but when I grew wiser, I started thinking it over: Only a talent? Why is Raphael a genius and I am only a talent? What is the difference between him and me? I went to Italy and saw Raphael's *Madonna*—he is obviously a genius. But then I look at my canvases, and everything seems to be as it should. Original, and subtle, more subtle than Raphael's work, far more subtle. And you can see straight off that it's very talented, begging your pardon for my immodesty, but not work of a *ge-ni-us,*" he said, pronouncing the syllables separately, and he made a sound with his lips, as if he had let the air out of a balloon. "That is why I gave up painting, because I had talent but not genius. I make photographic pictures now, and they say that they are good ones, *talented.* But that is all right. There are no geniuses in photographic art as yet, and Raphael will not be standing in my light." Arkadii Sergeevich gave an ironic laugh. "But take Styopa here, when we were at the academy together, I should say that he showed signs of genius. You ought not to have given up painting, Stepan. I saw you make a quick watercolor sketch only recently. The technique was rusty, of course, but such boldness of attack. Little pieces like that go for big money in the Parisian salons now, and you saw the way things were going twenty years ago. Tell me, when you took up the brush again after all those years—did it not make your heart sing?"

Stepan Trofimovich Shiryaev answered moodily and unwillingly, looking down at the tablecloth: "Whether it did or it didn't—what's the difference? I just dashed off the watercolor for want of anything else to do. We've already mown the hay, and it's too soon to reap . . . What's the good of remembering the past? Things worked out as they did, and so be it. Talent or genius, it makes no damned difference. You have to do the task that you're set to do. And the more diligently you do it, the better."

Pelagia thought that Shiryaev seemed to be angry with Poggio about something, and the latter did seem a little put out by this rebuff. Attempting to move the conversation on to humorous ground, he turned to the nun and asked with exaggerated politeness: "And what does the holy church have to say on the matter of genius and talent?"

The theme of the conversation was one that the nun found interesting, and she liked the parties involved in discussing it, so she did not try to avoid an answer.

"Concerning the church's position, it would be better for you to ask one of the hierarchs, but to my own humble understanding the entire meaning of life on earth lies in discovering the genius in oneself."

"Life's meaning lies in that?" Arkadii Sergeevich asked in surprise. "And not in God? This is a fine holy sister."

"I think that there is genius hidden in everyone, a little hole through which God is visible," Pelagia began to explain. "But it is rare for anyone to discover this opening in themselves. Everybody gropes for it like blind kittens, but they keep missing. If a miracle occurs, then someone realizes straightaway that this is what he came into the world for, and after that he lives with a calm confidence and cannot be distracted by anybody else, and that is genius. But talents are encountered far more frequently. They are people who have not found that little magic window, but are close to it and are nourished by the reflected glow of its miraculous light."

To add conviction to her words, she swept her hand through the air to point up at the heavens, but so clumsily that her wide sleeve caught on a cup, spilling tea all over the leg of Kirill Nifontovich's trousers.

The poor man leapt up on one foot, it was so hot. He hopped about, gasping and misquoting Pushkin's *Golden Cockerel* as he intoned,

> "Then this maiden lost to shame,
> Black, but nun in only name,
> Said to that king, 'You shall not thrive,
> I'll boil you while you're still alive.'"

Pelagia felt so ashamed that she wished the earth would open and swallow her up—she almost burst into tears. And now she could not finish what she had been saying about talent, everybody was laughing so hard.

Stepan Trofimovich, certainly, did try to continue the conversation, looking closely at the nun and asking: "And what do you think of genius?"

But Marya Afanasievna, who had become very bored in the course of this theoretical discussion, broke into the conversation unceremoniously.

"Instead of discoursing on high matters and scalding people with boiling water, holy mother, you would do better to get on with solving the mystery of who poisoned Zagulyai and Zakusai for me."

Just then Gerasim carried in a bowl of apples, pears, and plums from the orchard. The gardener's appearance had an unexpectedly rousing effect on Miss Wrigley, who had so far been sitting there indifferently, smoking a cigarette.

"You've all gone crazy over those bulldogs of yours! Nothing but gluttonous beasts, always running around in the orchard, and they've taught the little puppy to do the same. But there's all sorts of filthy garbage in the garden. Yesterday with my own eyes, I saw a dead raven, on my word of honor! The best thing you could do, dear holy sister, would be to investigate who trampled my lawn."

A sound halfway between a sigh and a groan ran around the table, and Pelagia realized that Miss Wrigley's lawn must be proverbial among the natives of Drozdovka.

"But then, I can tell you myself the name of the person who trampled it," the Englishwoman said, raising one finger in a bellicose gesture. "You just help me to find the clues, because everyone here refuses to believe what is perfectly obvious."

"What would we want with her ladyship's lousy lawn?" Gerasim said, speaking to one side as he arranged the fruits to look their best. "Why would we want to go trampling on it?"

"This is an ancient jihad between him and Miss Wrigley," Pyotr Georgievich explained to the nun, wrinkling up his reddish nose merrily. "She accuses Gerasim of laziness and for educational purposes she has laid out nine square yards of genuine English lawn over there, beside the cliff. She is trying to show him how the grass in a park ought to look. But Gerasim doesn't want to learn, and he has apparently even resorted to sabotage. In any case, two days ago, someone gave the precious lawn a thorough trampling."

"You're the last one I'd expect that from, Pyotr Georgievich," Gerasim said in an offended tone. "It would make me sick to step on that shaven stubble—I wouldn't even spit on it. Nature shouldn't be defiled like that; let all the green things and the trees grow tall, the way the Lord intended."

"And he even calls God to witness!" was Miss Wrigley's comment on this doctrine. "Men are only interested in finding excuses for not doing anything."

The quarrel, however, was a rather lazy one, with no true heat to it, and in any case the close August evening was not conducive to anger.

There was a lengthy pause, perfectly relaxed, and then Naina Georgievna suddenly spoke, not entirely to the point and addressing no one in particular: "Yes, men are cruel and criminal, but without them there would be absolutely nothing in the world to do."

Throughout the meal the general's granddaughter had remained sad and thoughtful, not taking part in the general discussion and apparently not even listening to it. Pelagia had kept looking at her, trying to understand whether this was how she always behaved or if something special was happening to Naina Georgievna today. Perhaps the explanation for her strange aloofness lay in the conversation of which the nun had overheard a fragment just before supper?

And Pelagia marveled at the capricious way in which Providence had treated the brother and sister, arranging the same set of features quite differently. Pyotr Georgievich, still a young man (he looked about thirty years old), had black hair, eyebrows and eyelashes bleached by the sun, and a face as white as flour, with a large red nose stuck clumsily at its center. But in Naina Georgievna the distribution of colors was the precise opposite: golden hair, black brows and eyelashes, tender-pink cheeks, and a fine-chiselled, charmingly aquiline little nose. A beauty like that was certainly capable of turning a man's head and driving him to commit any act of insanity. From Pelagia's point of view, the young lady's looks were rather spoiled by the stubborn curve of her mouth, but it is very probable that this broken line was the feature that drove men out of their minds more certainly than all the others.

Naina Georgievna's position at Drozdovka appeared to be rather special—the incomprehensible phrase that she had dropped was followed by a tense silence, as if everybody was waiting for her to add something else.

And Naina Georgievna did add something, but since it followed the train of her own inner thoughts, it did not make things any clearer:

"Love is always an evil, even if it is happy, because that happiness is inevitably built on someone else's misery."

Shiryaev jerked his head as if he had been struck and Poggio smiled in a strangely forced fashion, while the rich man Sytnikov asked: "In what way do you mean, if I might ask?" And he gathered up his gray-streaked reddish beard between his strong, short fingers.

"There is no love without betrayal," Naina Georgievna continued, staring straight ahead, her black eyes wide. "Because the one who loves betrays his parents, betrays his friends, betrays the entire world for the sake of one person who is perhaps not worthy of this love. Yes, love is also a crime, it is absolutely obvious . . ."

"What do you mean when you say 'also'?" Sytnikov asked with a shrug. "What is this strange manner you have of not saying everything you mean?"

"She's just trying to sound interesting," the brother snorted. "She read somewhere that modern young ladies always speak in riddles, and she's practicing on us."

Just then Tanya came up to Pyotr Georgievich to pour his tea, and Pelagia noticed the young man give her fingers a momentary squeeze.

"Thank you, Tatyana Zotovna," he said affectionately, and the maid blushed, casting a rapid glance at Marya Afanasievna. "And what do you think about love?"

"It's not our place to think," Tanya babbled. "There are educated folk to do that."

"I must say, our nun has a quite excellent appetite," observed Krasnov, indicating the empty plate from which Pelagia had just taken the final slice of ham. "Is it permitted to eat meat, sister?"

"It is," Pelagia said shyly. "Today is the Festival of our Lord's Transfiguration; the rules allow it."

She pretended to be raising the ham to her mouth. Zakidai indignantly thrust his face against her knee to remind her not to forget her place. Pelagia dropped her hand without anyone noticing, thrust the ham into the extortionist's mouth, and patted her hand gently against the cold, wet nose: That's it, there's no more. Zakidai instantly disappeared.

"One thing I really love about the prescriptions of our Orthodox

Church," said Krasnov, "are its well-thought-out dietary arrangements. From a medical point of view, the entire system of fasts and the first meals that follow them regulates the working of the stomach and the intestines in an ideal fashion. No, really, why are you laughing, I'm serious! The autumn and winter periods when meat is allowed are designed to maintain the necessary level of nutrition during the cold part of the year, and the Lenten fast provides excellent cleansing of the intestines before the largely vegetable diet of spring and summer. Timely evacuation of the intestines is the cornerstone of intellectual and spiritual life! I, for instance, compensate for my non-observance of the fasts by taking enemas of infusion of chamomile every evening and I recommend everyone do the same. I have even composed a quatrain on the subject:

> Sleep not, sweet maid, tarry a while,
> Or you may err in your confusion,
> Omitting to take your infusion
> Of purifying chamomile."

"Why, get away with you, Kirill Nifontovich," exclaimed Marya Afanasievna, gesturing with a laugh. "Don't you listen to him, holy mother, he's our local agent of progress. He rides around the meadow on a bicycle, frightening the cows. And don't you ever think of visiting him without advance warning; he often sits up on the roof naked— taking sunbaths. Bah, for shame! And you see that hedgehog stubble around his bald patch? At the beginning of every summer he shaves all his hair off; that way he lets the back of his head breathe, you see. Just recently he remortgaged his estate to have a telegraph wire installed from Zavolzhsk to his house. And why, do you think? So that he can play checkers with the postmaster. It wouldn't be so bad if only he were a good player, but he keeps losing all the time."

"And what of it?" asked Kirill Nifontovich, not in the least offended. "I don't play out of vanity, but to teach our Zavolzhsk savages a thing or two. Let them know what progress is. Why, in Europe there are new discoveries and inventions every day. In America they build houses that reach right up to the clouds, but our two-fingered reactionaries in long coats even shy away from a steam engine, they close their eyes when they see a gas lamp in the street, to avoid being defiled by Satan's flame."

"It's true that our Old Believers are mistrustful of things that are new, but not all of them," said Sytnikov, intervening on behalf of his own. "When the young ones grow up, everything around here will change. Why, only a few days ago a merchant from the priestless Old Believers, Avvakum Silych Vonifatiev, came around to see me and made a deal to sell me some forest. Surely you should remember it— just before I went to meet him, we were having tea here and I was telling you how he was married off to a bride of thirty at the age of fifteen. You weren't here, Pyotr Georgievich, you'd gone into Zavolzhsk."

Stepan Trofimovich nodded.

"Of course, a picturesque story in the spirit of the local customs. Bubentsov also said that the reason the authorities wish to eradicate your wild schismatic ways is to put an end to that kind of barbarism. And you, Donat Abramovich, quarreled with him."

"Yes, that's it—it was that Vonifatiev."

"Well, then, did he sell you the forest?" asked Shiryaev. "What kind is it? How many acres?"

"Good forest, nothing but pine. Very nearly eight thousand acres, only it's a fair distance away, on the upper reaches of the Vetluga. He took a pretty high price for it, too, thirty-five thousand. But that's all right, I'll give that forest another five or ten years to grow. They're going to build a narrow-gauge railway all the way to it, and then I'm bound to get a good three hundred thousand out of it. But that's not what I was talking about. Vonifatiev had his son with him, an amusing little lad. While his father and I were behaving the way people do around these parts, agreeing on a price, disagreeing, spitting and agreeing on a new one before we shook hands on a deal, I sat the lad in the library with some apples and spice cakes so he wouldn't get bored. I glanced in to see if he'd gone to sleep, and there he was reading my textbook on electric motors (I ordered it recently from Moscow, it's an interest of mine). I was amazed. I asked him what the fascination was. And he said to me: When I grow up, mister, I'm going to drive an electrical road through the forest. Clearing a road and laying rails takes a long time and costs a lot of money. And so, he says, I'll set up strong pillars and run cable cars along them. That way it will be cheaper, quicker, and more convenient. And you and Bubentsov call them savages—"

"Zakidai!" Marya Afanasievna suddenly screeched, fluttering her hands in sudden alarm. "My little Zakidai! Where's Zakidai? I haven't seen him in ages."

Everyone began gazing around and Sister Pelagia even glanced under the table. There was no bulldog on the terrace. Little Zakusai was snoring peacefully with his paws spread out beside his empty bowl, but his father had vanished.

"He's run off into the woods," declared Miss Wrigley. "That's not good. He'll go guzzling more garbage now."

The general's widow clutched at her heart.

"Oh, I can't bear it . . . Oh, God . . ." and she gave a heart-rending shriek. "Zakidai, my love! Where are you?"

Pelagia watched in amazement as the large, hysterical tears welled up out of Tatishcheva's eyes. The mistress of Drozdovka attempted to stand up, but she could not manage it and slumped back helplessly into her wicker chair.

"Dear people, good people . . ." she muttered. "Run, quickly . . . Find him. Gerasim! Oh, be quick! Get away, Tanya, you and your drops. Run with the rest of them, look for him. The holy mother here can give me the drops, she doesn't know the park anyway . . . Find him for me!"

The terrace emptied in an instant—everybody, even the shrewish Miss Wrigley and the capricious Naina Georgievna dashed away to find the fugitive. The only ones left were Marya Afanasievna and Sister Pelagia.

"Twenty's not enough, put in thirty . . ."

Tatishcheva took the glass of heart drops with a trembling hand and drank.

"Give me Zakusai!" she demanded and took hold of the puppy, clutching the warm, sleepy little body to her breast.

Zakusai almost opened his little eyes, he gave a shrill yelp, but then thought better of waking up. He floundered about for a while, working his way in deeper under the old woman's ponderous bust, and then lay still.

From beyond the trees came the sound of voices and laughter as the searchers called to one another after spreading out across the extensive park, and poor Marya Afanasievna sat there more dead than alive, talking on and on, as if she was trying to drive away her alarm with words: "Ah, holy mother, don't you pay any attention to me having a house full of people here, when it comes right down to it I'm terrible lonely, nobody really loves me except for my little children."

"Is that not enough?" Pelagia tried to comfort her. "Such fine young people."

"You mean Pyotr and Naina? I meant my little dogs. As for Pyotr and Naina . . . I'm no more than a nuisance to them. The Lord has gathered in all my children. The youngest, Polina, lasted the longest of all, but even she had a short life. She died in childbirth, when Naina arrived. She was wonderful, so full of life, with a passionate heart, but a total fool of a woman, and Naina takes after her. Polina went and got married against Apollon Nikolaevich's will and mine to a mangy little Georgian princeling who was good for nothing but cutting a dashing figure. I didn't even want to know him, but when our Polina passed on, I felt sorry for the orphans. I bought them back and took them into my own home."

Pelagia was astonished.

"How do you mean, you bought them?"

The general's widow waved her hand in a disparaging gesture.

"It's very simple. I promised that father of theirs that I'd pay his debts if he signed a paper promising never to come near his son and daughter again."

"And he signed it?"

"What else could he do? He either signed or ended up in debtor's prison."

"And so he never showed up again?"

"Oh, yes, he did. About fifteen years ago he sent me a tearful pleading letter. Not pleading to be allowed to see his children, but looking for financial support. And after that, they say he left and went away to America. I don't know if he's alive or dead. But he spoiled my grandchildren with his coxcomb's blood. Petya's grown up into a good-for-nothing, the clumsy oaf. He was thrown out of grammar school for his pranks and excluded from university for sedition. I barely managed to get the minister to agree to send him here and leave him in my care; they wanted to send him straight off to Siberia. He's a kind-hearted boy, sensitive, but far too . . . stupid. He has no character and there's nothing he's any good at. He tries to help Stepan Trofimovich, but he's about as good for that as a nun is for breeding."

Pelagia coughed to indicate that she found this comparison infelicitous, but such subtleties were beyond Marya Afanasievna. She exclaimed in a voice filled with torment: "Lord, what can be taking them so long? What if something's happened?"

"And what about Naina Georgievna?" Pelagia asked, wishing to distract Tatishcheva from her troubled thoughts.

"Takes after her mother," her hostess snapped. "Just as capricious, only she inherited a passion for fashion from the prince as well. Wanton petulance, to use the good old Russian phrase. First she wanted to be an actress and kept declaiming monologues, then suddenly she was going to be an artist, and now there's no telling what she's jabbering about—she just rambles. And I'm to blame for it; I spoiled her far too much when she was a little girl. I felt sorry for her, being so young, and an orphan. And she was very like my little Polina . . . What's that, are they bringing him?"

She half-rose out of her chair, listened, and sat back down again.

"No, I only imagined it . . . What's going to happen to them when I die, God only knows. Stepan's my only hope. He's honest, devoted, decent. Now that's the kind of husband Naina needs, and he loves her, I can see that, but what does she understand about a man's value? Styopa's our ward. He grew up here, went off to the academy to study to be an artist, and then Apollon Nikolaevich passed away. So even though he was only a boy then, Stepan gave up his studies, came back to Drozdovka, and took the estate in hand, and he manages the whole business so well that I'm the envy of the entire province. His heart's not in the work, though, I can see that. But he sticks with it and doesn't grumble, because he knows where his duty lies. I'm guilty before him, old sinner that I am. I quarreled with him the day before yesterday, and with my grandchildren, I was out of sorts after Zagulyai. I changed my will, and now my conscience is bothering me . . ."

Pelagia almost opened her mouth to ask what changes had been made in the will, but she bit her tongue and said nothing, for something peculiar was happening to Marya Afanasievna.

The general's widow opened her mouth wide, her eyes bulged wildly, and the folds of flesh under her chin began shuddering rapidly.

A stroke, the nun thought in fright. It could easily be—in someone so stout, apoplexy was always a risk.

But Tatishcheva showed no signs of paralysis; on the contrary, she flung one hand up in the air and pointed her finger at something behind the nun's back.

Turning around, Pelagia saw Zakidai come crawling out of the garden toward the steps, leaving a scarlet trail on the ground. Protruding from the white, bumpy head was the handle of a firmly embedded hatchet, which was painted blue, so that the red, white, and blue combination precisely repeated the colors of the Russian flag.

Zakidai was using his last ounces of strength to crawl along with his tongue lolling out and his eyes fixed on a single point—the spot where Marya Afanasievna was sitting, frozen in horror. He did not whine, he did not whimper, he simply crawled. At the edge of the veranda his strength deserted him; he thrust his head against the bottom step, twitched twice, and lay absolutely still.

Tatishcheva's dress rustled as she heeled over sideways, and before Sister Pelagia could catch hold of her, the old woman had slumped to the floor and struck her head against the pine boards with a resounding smack. Ejected from his cradle, little Zakusai went tumbling across the veranda like a soft white ball and yelped plaintively, still half-asleep.

# CHAPTER 4

# A Nest of Vipers

THE DOCTOR FOUND no sign of a stroke, but neither did he hold out any great hope. A nervous fever, he said; there was nothing that medical science could do about it. It sometimes happened that a perfectly healthy person would be completely consumed in only a few days as a result of some shock, and this case involved advanced age, a bad heart, and a naturally hysterical temperament. When he was asked what could be done, how she should be treated, he gave a strange answer: "Distract her and cheer her up."

But how were they to distract her when she only talked of one thing all the time? How were they to cheer her up when the tears were flowing unceasingly from her eyes? And she would not even allow any members of her family to come near her, shouting: "You're all murderers!"

The doctor departed, taking the prescribed fee for his visit, and the family council decided to ask Sister Pelagia to assume responsibility for the spiritual care of the sick woman. Especially since Marya Afanasievna herself, while refusing to see her grandchildren or neighbors, or even her manager, kept asking after the nun all the time and demanding that she come to the bedroom almost every hour.

Pelagia came when she was summoned, sat at the head of the bed, and listened patiently to the widow's feverish talk. The curtains in the room were drawn, a lamp was lit under a green shade on the side table, there was a smell of aniseed and mint lozenges. Tatishcheva either sobbed and pressed her face into the pillow in fright, or flew into a sudden fury, but that soon came to an end, because she no longer had the strength to remain angry for long. Zakusai lay close at her side almost constantly. Marya Afanasievna stroked him, called him her "orphan," and fed him with chocolate. The poor creature was completely worn out with all this immobility and from time to time he rebelled, barking and squealing. Then Tanya would put him on his lead and take him out for a walk, but the lady of the house was ill at ease all the time they were absent and kept glancing constantly at the large clock on the wall.

Of course, Pelagia pitied the old woman for her suffering, but at the same time she was amazed that there could be so much spite in someone so weak that she could barely even control her tongue.

As she kissed Zakusai on his wrinkled little face, Marya Afanasievna said: "Dogs are so much better than people!"

She listened to the soft voices rising from somewhere in the depths of the house and whispered venomously: "This is no home, it's a nest of vipers."

Or she would simply fix her eyes on the nun's hands as they clattered away nimbly with the knitting needles and make a horrified face: "What's that you're knitting, holy mother? It's disgusting. Throw it away immediately."

Most unpleasant of all, however, were the fits of suspicion that came over the general's widow several times a day. Then the servants would go rushing off to seek out Sister Pelagia. They would find her in her room, or in the library, or in the park, and bring her to Marya Afanasievna, who would already be huddled up under the blanket so that only her frightened, glittering eyes could be seen, whispering:

"I know, it's Petya, it couldn't be anyone else! He hates me, he wants to do away with me! He's being held here against his will, and I'm responsible for him to the police officer. He called me a 'Benckendorf' and all kinds of other names. It's him, he's the one, that spawn of Telianov's! I'm always getting in his way. He wanted to teach the village children and I wouldn't let him, because he wouldn't teach them anything worthwhile. I don't give him any money, either—he'd send it to those nihilists of his. And now he's gone completely out of his mind and decided he wants to marry my Tanya. Marry the maid! 'Don't you dare be so dismissive of her, grandmother,' he says, 'you have to see the human being in her.' That would be a fine thing now, eh? If my grand-son marries the estate flirt! If only he was madly in love with her, any-thing's possible, after all, but he isn't. It's an idea he has—to sacrifice himself on the altar, to turn a common, semiliterate girl into an edu-cated woman. 'Great works,' he says, 'are for great people, but I'm a small man, and my work will be small, but it will be good. If every one of us can make at least one other person happy, then his life has not been lived in vain.' I said to him: 'You won't make the girl happy with-out love, not even if you shower her with gold, not even if you read every book in the world out loud to her. Why fill Tanya's head with nonsense? I've already picked out a groom for her, a cattle dealer's son, he'll be a perfect match for her. But all you're doing is giving her point-less ambition; you want her to suffer the rest of her life for things that could never be.' And you know, the most shameful thing is that he's not even sleeping with her, he's such a sissy! I've no doubt if he was to go to her at night, he'd work it out of his system soon enough and start to see reason. Now why are you giving me that reproachful look, mother? I've seen life; I know what I'm talking about."

But an hour later her head would be full of other ideas.

"No, it's Nainka. The idleness has driven her mad. I know her kind, I was the same myself. I remember the way it is, you just can't wait to get your fill of life, I could have strangled my parents with my own hands, I wanted my freedom so much. Especially when I was stupid enough to fall in love with the parish priest at the age of seventeen. He was so handsome and young, with such a velvety voice. I almost ran off with him—it was lucky my dear late papa caught me, gave me a sound beating, and locked me in the shed. Now Nainka's fallen for somebody, just look how many of those men she has circling around her. Her granny's in her way now, spoiling her happiness. She's chosen someone or other for herself that I'll never agree to while I'm alive and she's de-cided to take what she wants over my dead body. She could, she has the character for it. Ah, Nainka, Nainka, didn't I love you, didn't I give you my heart and soul . . . Zakusai, my little love, my angel without wings, you're the only one who won't betray me. You won't, will you, my sweet?"

And then, a little while later, Pelagia found Marya Afanasievna in a state of conciliatory self-reproach. Sobbing at her own nobility, the general's widow said: "Sit down, mother, listen. I've had a revelation: It's Stepan, and I don't blame him. How long can I go on making his life a misery? He's been stuck here with me for nigh on twenty years as it is. He gave up his dream, buried his talent in the ground, and at the age of forty he's still single. All I do is just sponge off all his hard work. Without him I'd have frittered away my husband's legacy long ago, with my foolish character, but he's preserved it and increased it. But he's a living human being, too. He must be thinking: 'You've lived long enough already, old woman, time to do the right thing.' That Poggio has turned his head by coming here, that's as clear as day. Styopa got his easel down out of the attic, brought some paints from the town, and the look in his eyes completely changed. It's all right, I understand, I don't judge him . . . although he could have told me straight out. This is the way it is, Marya Afanasievna, I've done enough work for you, now I'm asking you to let me go. But he won't say it, he's not like that. He feels ashamed. It's easier to do away with the old woman than appear ungrateful to her. I know that breed well enough, it has its fair share of pride and passion . . . Ah, no, how could I be so blind! It's not Stepan, it's Poggio!" She reached upward, struggling to raise herself up off the pillows. "Perhaps in secret Stepan wishes I would croak soon, but he wouldn't poison the poor defenseless dogs. But Poggio would! Just for amusement's sake, or out of friendship, to free his friend from slavery! He's depraved, a devil! He tried to seduce Naina, making drawings of her and photographing her. And he's leading Stepan astray . . . I noticed him looking daggers at me a long time ago. It's him! Look how long he's stayed, over two months already. And at first he said, 'Just for a month or so.' He won't go away now until he's driven me into my grave!"

Very soon after this a new conviction, no less unshakable, appeared.

"Sytnikov! He's a terrible man, give him profit at any price, he's sold his soul to the devil for it. It's true what they say, that he married for money and then poisoned his wife. And the reason I'm an obstacle to him is clear enough, too! The Goryaev wasteland! He's been badgering me for ages to let him have it, wants to set up a commercial wharf there—it's a very convenient spot. But I told him I wouldn't sell. I won't have him ruining my view with his barges! But he's not one just to let something go. His law is that everything has to be the way he wants. Otherwise he thinks life isn't worth living. He finished off his wife and now he wants to finish me off, too! Once I'm gone, Petka and Nainka will sell him everything here, let alone the wasteland, and they'll be up and off to the big cities and foreign parts. So Donat has good reason to despatch me to the next world as soon as possible. Well, curse the lot of them!" The old woman raised a feeble hand in a gesture of disdainful dismissal. "I was right to change my will two days ago. I left everything I have to the Englishwoman. I only wanted to give them a scare, but now I'll leave it like that. If they don't want me around, then they can have Janet for their mistress. She'll keep them all on their toes."

At first Pelagia listened very attentively to the sick woman's confused talk, comparing it with her own thoughts and observations, but every new hypothesis was even more outrageous than the ones before it.

The final one completely abandoned the ground of common sense.

"Kirya Krasnov," Marya Afanasievna rapped out as soon as Tanya brought the nun to the bedroom for another visit. "Cunning, the devil, but makes himself out to be a fool. Why does he come trailing around here every day? He wants money from me. This autumn his estate's going under the hammer, with all his wonderful telegraphs. He says: 'I'll die then.' And he will die, he will for sure. What will he do with himself without Krasnovka? He goes around moaning all the time. Give him one and a half thousand to pay his interest! I told him: I won't give it to you. I've already given you money more than once. That's enough. So he's decided to take his revenge on me. I know what he's thinking: If I'm going to die, then you're not going to live, either, you old witch!"

Pelagia began admonishing the sick woman—to bring her back to her senses and also in case, God forbid, she might really go and die, it was sinful to leave the earth in a state of such bitterness.

"Marya Afanasievna, perhaps if you lent Kirill Nifontovich the money, he would calm down? What do a thousand and a half rubles mean to you? You can't take them with you to the next world; money will be no use there."

This simple argument had its effect on Tatishcheva.

"Yes, yes," she muttered, looking at Zakusai as he slept, and the fevered look in her eyes softened. "What good is it to me; it will all go to Miss Wrigley anyway. I'll give it to him. Let him carry on with his foolish pranks for one more year. I'll give him two thousand."

"And this business with the will is wrong," the nun continued, encouraged by her success. "Miss Wrigley is a worthy individual, of course, but would it be fair to treat Pyotr Georgievich and Naina Georgievna like that? After all, they are not to blame that you raised them in idleness and did not teach them to do anything useful. And you would be ashamed to look Stepan Trofimovich in the eye in the next world. All those years he devoted to you, all of his best years. And you say yourself that he has greatly increased your fortune. Surely it is a sin?"

"It is, mother," Tatishcheva confessed in a pitiful voice. "You're quite right. I was angry, I got carried away. And I ought to leave something to my other relatives as well as my grandchildren. Hey, Tanya! Go and call her . . . Tanya, have them send to the town for Korsh. I want him to come to change my will."

DURING THE INTERVALS between summonses to the widow's bedroom, Pelagia spent most of her time strolling in the park. She also spent quite a lot of that time in a plank hut that stood not far from the edge of the cliff. Here there were mattocks, spades, saws, rakes, hoes, and other garden implements from Gerasim's arsenal, all of them painted blue. This was where the unknown villain had found the hatchet. Pelagia picked up some lumps of dried earth from the floor and rubbed them in her fingers, squatted down and crept around outside the little building, but she did not discover any clues. The hut did not have a lock; anyone at all could have taken the little axe, and there were no tracks to be found either outside or inside. There was nothing to be done but wait to see what would happen next.

In two days she walked the entire length and breadth of the park.

She also came across the famous English lawn, a little square of neatly trimmed grass that someone really had trampled very thoroughly only recently, but the short, springy stems had already begun to straighten up and it was clear that this oasis of civilization would soon be restored to its former glory. From here it was only a stone's throw to the River, there was a fresh breeze blowing, and beside the lawn a little aspen tree that was withering away swayed branches that were still green but no longer alive. The nun came here often—as she sat in the white arbor above the high, steep bluff, finishing the belt for Sister Emilia, she would freeze motionless for long moments, looking at the wide River, at the sky, at the marshes on the far bank. And it was good to wander through the clearings, along the overgrown pathways, where the air trembled with the humming of bees and the rustling of leaves.

But the calm was false, not genuine; in the electrified air of Drozdovka the nun could sense turmoil and hear a subtle ringing tone, as if somewhere someone were plucking a string stretched to its very breaking point. It was surprising that on the first day the estate had seemed almost like the Garden of Eden to her. Though Pelagia did not deliberately spy or eavesdrop on anyone, every now and again she found herself an inadvertent witness to certain scenes that were difficult to understand and the perplexed observer of the obscure relationships between the locals. It was obvious that the nervous conversation she had partly overheard by chance from her window was entirely in keeping with the order of things here.

On the morning of her third day, Pelagia was slowly wandering at random through the bushes, screwing up her eyes against the sunlight filtering through the foliage, when she suddenly saw a clearing ahead of her, and Shiryaev and Poggio standing in it, their backs to the bushes. They were both wearing wide-brimmed hats and canvas smocks and holding sketchbooks. She didn't want to distract them from their artistic endeavors by calling out, but she wanted to take a look, especially after what had been said the previous day about Stepan Trofimovich's talent.

The sister raised herself up on tiptoes, sticking her head out of the raspberry thickets. On Arkadii Sergeevich's sheet of paper she saw a sketch of the old oak that towered up at the far end of the clearing, and it was an amazing likeness, a real pleasure to look at. But, alas, she found Stepan Trofimovich's work a disappointment. The colors were simply dashed on any old way: It could have been an oak, or it could have been some wood goblin with a huge, overgrown head covered in shaggy hair, and Shiryaev handled his brush in a peculiar fashion, as if he was simply playing the fool, dabbing aimlessly again and again. Poggio painted with fine strokes, taking great care. The nun liked his work much more. Only it was boring to look at—Stepan Trofimovich's daub proved far more interesting to study. In general it was a rather touching scene: old friends immersing themselves in the pastime that they loved and not even talking, because they already knew all they needed to know about art and about each other.

Suddenly Shiryaev swung his hand through the air more boldly than usual and a shower of green blots spattered across his sketch.

"This is intolerable!" he exclaimed, turning toward his friend. "Pretending, discussing the play of light and shade, talking about nature, when all the time I hate you! I hate you!"

Poggio turned toward him just as sharply, and the old comrades suddenly looked like two cocks squaring up for a fight.

Horror-struck, Pelagia squatted down on her haunches in fright. It would be just too shameful for a nun to be caught spying.

She stopped watching, but she listened—she could not help it, she was afraid of rustling the leaves if she backed away.

"Have you been with Naina?" (That was Stepan Trofimovich.) "You have, admit it!"

The word "been" carried the force of a special meaning that made Pelagia blush and regret very much her impetuous decision to look at the sketches.

"Such questions are not asked and such admissions are not made," Arkadii Sergeevich answered in the same tone. "It is none of your business."

Stepan Trofimovich choked: "You destroyer, you devil! You pollute and defile everything with your very breath! All these years I have loved her. We talked, we dreamed. I promised her that when . . . when I was free, I would take her away to Moscow. She would become an actress,

I would take up painting again, and we would know what happiness is. But she no longer wishes to be an actress!"

"But she does wish to be an artist!" Poggio said mockingly. "At least, until just recently she did. What it is she wants now, I do not know."

Shiryaev was not listening, he was shouting incoherently about something that had clearly been bothering him for some time.

"You're a scoundrel. You don't even love her. If you did, I would be hurt, but I would put up with it. But you did it because you were bored!"

There was a loud noise, a crack of fabric tearing. Pelagia parted the bushes with her hands, afraid that matters might go as far as murder. They were very close to that: Stepan Trofimovich had grabbed Arkadii Sergeevich by the collar with both hands.

"Yes, because I was bored," Poggio wheezed in a strangled voice. "At first. But now I have lost my head. She doesn't want me anymore. A week ago she was imploring me to take her away to Paris, she was talking about a studio in an attic with a view of the Boulevard des Capucines, about sunsets over the Seine. Then suddenly everything changed. She became cold and strange. And I am going out of my mind. Yesterday . . . yesterday I said to her: 'Fine, let's go. To hell with everything. Let it be Paris, the attic, the boulevard—everything just as you wish.' Let go of me, I can't breathe."

Shiryaev unclenched his fingers and asked in torment: "And what did she say?"

"She burst out laughing. I . . . I was beside myself. I threatened her. I have something to threaten her with . . . You do not need to know about it. You'll find out later, when it makes no difference anymore." Poggio gave an unpleasant laugh. "Oh, I understand perfectly well what's going on. You and I, Styopa, are no longer required, we've been retired without a pension. A more interesting character has turned up. But I won't let myself be treated like some snot-nosed schoolboy! If she only knew what women have thrown themselves at my feet! I'll trample her into the mud! I'll make her come away with me!"

"You villain, don't you dare threaten her! I'll squash you like a worm!"

So saying, Stepan Trofimovich took his former classmate by the throat again, this time more firmly than before. The easels went flying to the ground, the men grappled with each other and tumbled over into the thick grass.

"Lord, Lord, do not allow this," Sister Pelagia began intoning quietly and jumped to her feet, since under the circumstances there was no need to be afraid of any rustling, then ran about twenty steps away and began shouting: "Zakusai-ai! Is that you making that noise over there? You naughty boy! Running off like that again!"

The commotion in the clearing ceased instantly. Pelagia did not go in that direction—there was no point in embarrassing people—but she carried on shouting for a little while and stamped her feet as she moved away through the bushes. It was enough that those two gamecocks had come to their senses and reassumed their human form. For sin had been very close.

She decided not to walk around the park anymore, but sit quietly in the library instead.

But would you believe it, she had merely leaped out of the frying pan into the fire . . .

NO SOONER HAD she made herself comfortable in the spacious, empty room with the tall bookcases crammed full of gold-tooled spines, pulling her feet up into the immense leather armchair and opening a volume of Pascal's *Lettres provinciales* that smelled deliciously of olden times, when the door creaked and someone came in, but who exactly she could not see, because of the tall back of her chair.

"We can say what we have to say here," said Sytnikov's calm, confident voice. "In this house hardly anyone ever looks into the library; we shan't be disturbed."

Pelagia was about to clear her throat or stick her head out, but she was not quick enough. Another voice (it was Naina Georgievna) spoke words in the wake of which she could only have placed everyone in an awkward position by revealing her presence.

"Are you going to offer me your hand and your heart again, Donat Abramovich?"

She has bewitched everyone here, thought Pelagia with a shake of her head, feeling sorry for the staid, composed industrialist who, if the mocking tone of the question was anything to go by, had no reason to expect his feelings to be reciprocated.

"I am afraid not," said Sytnikov, no less calmly than before. There was a leathery creak—they had obviously sat down on the divan. "Now I can only offer you my heart."

"How am I to understand you?"

"Let me explain. During the last few days I have come to understand you rather better than all these months that I have been turning up here because of your black eyes. I see now that I was mistaken. You are not suited to be my wife, and you yourself have no interest in that. I am not a man of idle words, I do not beat around the bush. I have not made any secret of my feelings for you, but neither have I tried to impose myself on you. I have given you enough time to realize that other than me there is no suitable match for you here. Stepan Trofimovich is a dreamer, and he is boring, too; with your character, after six months with him you would either put a noose around your neck or launch into a life of debauchery. Poggio—well, he's really only good for amusement. You didn't really take him seriously, did you? A petty little man, shallow. And now there is this new infatuation of yours. I don't really have any objections. Have your fling; I can wait until your whimsy passes. Only this time you are playing with fire; this gentleman has great big teeth. And he really has no need of you—his interests lie elsewhere. Just at the moment you are not yourself, my words are no more than an annoyance to you, but even so, listen to what Donat Sytnikov has to say. I am like a stone wall, you can lean against me, and you can hide behind me. There is only one thing I ask, when this project of yours collapses—do not throw yourself headfirst into the millpond. Such a shame to waste beauty like that. Come see me instead. I will not take you as my wife now, there would not be any point, but as a mistress—with great willingness. Stop flashing your eyes at me and listen; I am talking sense. As a mistress you would enjoy yourself more and feel more at ease—no domestic cares, no childbearing, and you will not be afraid of gossip. And what gossip could there be, in God's name? I have just made plans to move my head office to Odessa. The River is too limited for me; I'm moving out into the sea lanes. Odessa is a jolly southern city where the morals are freer.

You will be whoever you want to be. Paint pictures if you like—I'll find you the finest teachers, ones your Arkasha could never match. If you want, I'll give you a theater. You'll decide for yourself which plays to put on, hire any actors you like, even from St. Petersburg, and all the finest roles will be yours. I have enough money for all that. And I'm a good man, reliable and not dissipated, like your chosen favorite. That is all I have to say."

Naina Georgievna listened through to the very end of this incredible speech without interrupting even once. Of course, few would have dared to interrupt someone like Sytnikov—he was such an imposing man.

When he stopped speaking, however, the young woman laughed. Not loudly, but so strangely that Pelagia felt the frost creep across her skin.

"You know, Donat Abramovich, if my 'project,' as you call it, really does fail, I would sooner throw myself in the millpond than come to you. Only it will not fail. I hold a winning ticket. There are abysses here so deep that they take your breath away. I have had enough of being a rag doll that you all fight over and tear to shreds. I am going to grasp my own fate by the tail! And not only my own. I want to live life to the full. Not as its slave, but as its mistress!"

There was another creak of leather—Sytnikov had stood up.

"What you mean by this, I do not understand. I can only see that you are beside yourself. Therefore, I am leaving now, but you think about what I said. My word can be trusted."

The door opened and closed, but Naina Georgievna did not leave immediately. For another five minutes, or even longer, Pelagia heard inconsolable sobbing filled with bitter despair and a determined sniffing. Then there was whispering in a tone of mixed spite and passion. Listening closely, the nun heard the same thing repeated over and over:

"Well, let him be the fiend incarnate, let him, let him, let him. I don't care . . ."

When the way was clear, Pelagia went out into the corridor and set out for her room. As she walked along, she shook her head anxiously. That whisper was still echoing inside it.

. . .

THE NUN NEVER reached her room, however, for she met Tanya on her way there. The maid was carrying a bundle in one hand and dragging Zakusai along on his leash with the other. He was resisting stubbornly with all four paws.

"Mother," she said joyfully, "wouldn't you like to come with me? Marya Afanasievna has fallen asleep, so I'm on my way to the bathhouse; it's been heated since this morning. You can have a wash while I stay with the little dog. And then you can keep an eye on him. It would be a great help to me. I can't get into the suds with him, can I? The slobbery pest gives me no peace as it is."

Pelagia smiled amiably at the girl and agreed. At least in the bathhouse there was no one to eavesdrop or spy on.

The little bathhouse stood behind the house—a squat hut of amber-yellow pine logs with tiny windows right up under the eaves. A trickle of white smoke was rising from the pot-bellied chimney.

"You get washed; I'll sit here," the nun said in the small, clean changing room, lowering herself onto the bench and picking up the puppy.

"Oh, thank you, you've really saved me, you have, I've been running around all the time and I'm all sweaty, and I couldn't get a wash or run down to the River," Tanya jabbered, hastily undressing and unloosing her light brown hair from its tight bun.

Pelagia admired her finely molded, swarthy figure. A genuine Artemis, goddess of the forest; all that was lacking was a quiver of arrows over her shoulder.

No sooner had Tanya disappeared behind the rough wooden door than there was a gentle knock from the outside.

"Tanechka, my little Tanya," a man's voice whispered through the crack of the door. "Open up, sweetheart. I know you're in there. I saw you carrying your little bundle."

Was that really Krasnov? Pelagia jumped to her feet in consternation, and her habit made a rustling sound.

"I hear your dress rustling. Don't put it on, stay just the way you are. Let me in, no one will see. Come on—what have you got to lose? I've written a little poem in your honor:

> Like to a little, rain-filled cloud,
> Longing to pour its droplets down,
> Like to the bright moon's yellow face,
> E'er yearning for the earth's embrace,
> So I, consumed by passion's flame,
> Have breathed my darling Tanya's name
> And ached to have my love away
> Since chill December's seventh day.

"See, I even remembered the date when we went sleigh riding together. I've loved you ever since that day. Stop running away from me, my little Tanyushenka. Pyotr Georgievich won't write any poems about you, will he? Open up, eh?"

Tanya's admirer froze, listening, then half a minute later continued with a threat:

"Come on, open up, you little flirt, or I'll tell Pyotr Georgievich what you were up to with the Circassian the other day. I saw! He'll soon stop being so polite to you then. And I'll tell Marya Afanasievna, and she'll send you packing, you wanton. Open up, I say!"

Pelagia opened the door with a sudden jerk and folded her arms across her chest.

Kirill Nifontovich froze on the threshold just as he was, in his long white blouse and straw hat with his arms flung out wide and his lips pursed into a heart shape in anticipation of a kiss. His little blue eyes gaped in blank bewilderment.

"Oh, holy mother, it's you. . . . Why didn't you say so straightaway? Did you want to have a laugh at me?"

"To laugh at some people is no sin," Pelagia replied severely.

Krasnov's eyes flashed with a glitter in which there was not a trace of his usual childish naïveté. He swung around, darted around the corner of the bathhouse, and was gone.

This really is a nest of vipers, thought Sister Pelagia.

AFTER THE BATHHOUSE, they strolled unhurriedly through the cool of the evening, pacified by their steaming, their wet hair tightly bound up in kerchiefs (Tanya's white and the nun's black). They had given Zakusai a wash too, despite all the yelping and squealing. Now he was whiter than ever and his short coat was sticking out like the down on a duckling.

There was a black carriage covered in dust standing by the stable. A sullen, black-bearded man in a dirty Circassian coat and a round felt cap was unharnessing the black horses.

Tanya seized hold of Pelagia's elbow and sighed in a swooning voice. "He's here. . . . Mr. Bubentsov is here."

But she gazed as if spellbound at the Asiatic leading a horse into the stable.

Pelagia remembered Kirill Nifontovich's threat and looked at her companion more closely. Her face was quite still, with a strange dreamy expression; her pupils were dilated and her full pink lips slightly parted.

The Circassian cast a brief glance at the women. He did not greet them or even nod as he led the second horse in by the bridle.

Tanya walked over to him slowly, bowed, and said in a quiet voice: "Good day, Murad Djuraevich. Back to see us again?"

He did not answer. He stood there, looking gloomily off to one side, winding the patterned bridle around his broad, hairy wrist.

Then he went back to the carriage and began brushing off the dust. Tanya trailed after him.

"Are you tired after the journey? Would you like some cold milk? Or some kvass?"

The Circassian did not turn around; he did not even shrug his shoulders.

Pelagia merely sighed, shook her head, and continued on her way.

"Your clothes are all dirty," she heard Tanya's voice say behind her. "Why not take them off, and I'll wash them? They'll be dry by tomorrow. Are you staying the night?"

Silence.

At the door of the house Pelagia glanced back and saw Bubentsov's driver, as gloomy as ever, walking toward the open gates of the stable, leading Tanya by the hand—exactly as he had just led the horse. The girl was moving her feet obediently in quick little steps, and Zakusai was trailing along behind her just as submissively on his lead.

STANDING MEEKLY OUTSIDE the widow's bedroom was a man who had gray hair but was not yet old, with a very creased, smiling face, a black frock coat buttoned all the way up, and equally black trousers of fine wool worn to a shine at the knees. The hands at the end of his long arms were clasped almost halfway down his thighs and in them he was holding a plump prayer book.

"Give me your blessing, holy mother!" he exclaimed in a thin voice the moment he spied Pelagia, blocking her way. "I am Tikhon Ieremeevich Spasyonny, a most unworthy worm. Allow me to kiss your blessed hand." He reached out with a grasping, long-fingered hand, but Pelagia hid her own hands behind her back.

"We are not allowed," she said, examining the humble supplicant. "The statute forbids it."

"Well then, without the hand, simply make the sign of the cross over me," said Spasyonny, readily consenting. "I shall be blessed in any case. Do not refuse me, for it is written: 'Despise not my sinful sores, but soothe them with the unction of thy grace.'"

Having received his blessing, he bowed from the waist, but still did not clear the way.

"You must surely be Sister Pelagia, the envoy of His Grace, the most honorable and greatly hallowed Mitrofanii? I am informed that you have been accommodated in the chamber formerly occupied by myself, and am extremely glad of it, for I see you are a most worthy lady. I myself have been quartered in the other wing, among the slaves and the servants, as if it had been said unto me: Get thee hence from this place, for unworthy art thou to be here. I do not complain and I submit, recalling the words of the prophet: 'Should they persecute you in one city, hie thee to another.'"

"Why do you not go in to Marya Afanasievna?" the nun asked, confused by what she had heard.

"I do not dare," Spasyonny said briefly. "I know that the sight of me is repulsive to that noble lady, and my venerable superior, Vladimir

Lvovich Bubentsov, has ordered me to wait here at the gates of the chamber. Permit me to open the door before you."

He finally stepped aside, opening one side of the door for Pelagia, and nonetheless somehow managed to press his wet lips against her hand.

In the room a slim, elegant gentleman was sitting beside the bed with one leg crossed over the other, swaying the small, narrow foot at the end of it to and fro. He glanced around at the sound but, seeing that it was a nun, immediately turned back to the woman lying in the bed and continued speaking where he had left off.

"As soon as I learned, aunty, that your condition had worsened, I said to hell with all state business and came rushing to see you. Korsh told me, the attorney. He intends to be here with you tomorrow morning. Well, what has made you decide to lose heart like this? For shame, to be sure. I was planning to marry you off; I've already picked out a bridegroom, a most placid old gentleman. You won't hear a peep out of him, he'll toe the line for you, all right."

It was amazing—the reply was a weak sound, but it was quite clearly a laugh.

"Get away with you, Volodya. What old gentleman is that? Someone really decrepit, I'll be bound."

"Aunty"? "Volodya"? Pelagia could not believe her ears.

"Very far from decrepit," laughed Bubentsov, with a glint of white teeth. "And a general as well, like my deceased uncle. Huge long mustache, with a barrel of a chest, and when he starts skipping the mazurka, there's no way to stop him."

"Oh, you're full of lies," Marya Afanasievna exclaimed with a quavering laugh, then she was immediately overtaken by a fit of coughing, and it was a long time before she could catch her breath. ". . . Oh, you prankster. You deliberately invent things just to distract an old woman like me. And I really do think I'm feeling a bit better."

Bubentsov's presence was clearly good for the patient—she did not even ask Pelagia where Zakusai was.

It seemed that the pernicious inspector about whom Pelagia had heard so many bad things, even from the bishop himself, was not such a great Satan after all. The nun actually found Vladimir Lvovich quite likeable: a pleasant person, easygoing and good-looking, especially when he smiled.

Let him sit with Marya Afanasievna a little longer. He would distract her from her dark thoughts.

Bubentsov began an extremely amusing account of Spasyonny agitating the wild Murad to take up the Christian cross at the expense of the Mohammedan crescent moon, and Pelagia backed quietly away toward the door in order not to bother them.

She pushed the door and it struck against something yielding that immediately moved away. Tikhon Ieremeevich was standing in an awkward pose in the corridor, bent over double. He had been eavesdropping!

"Guilty I am, holy mother, guilty of the sin of wanton curiosity," he muttered, rubbing his bruised forehead. "Most soundly stung and sadly shamed. I take my leave."

Two spies under one roof was perhaps too many, thought Sister Pelagia as she watched him go.

THAT EVENING THEY gathered around the samovar on the terrace as usual. Vladimir Lvovich behaved quite differently from the way he had in Marya Afanasievna's bedroom. He was unsmiling, reserved, dry—in short, his manner was that of someone whose opinion of himself sets him much higher than those around him. Pelagia found him much less agreeable now. One might even say that she did not like him at all.

The only person missing was Tatishcheva herself, who was brought tea in her bedroom by Tanya, and from among the regular guests Sytnikov was absent—he had left as soon as the black carriage appeared. He had taken his hat and stick and set off for home—the summer house was a three-mile walk away, through the park and then across the meadow and the fields. At first Pelagia was surprised, but then she recalled the disagreement that Donat Abramovich and Bubentsov had had concerning the backwardness of the Old Believers, and the industrialist's behavior became clear. Sytnikov's place was occupied by Spasyonny, who took almost no part in the conversation.

Only at the very beginning, as he took his seat and surveyed the abundant display of spice cakes, sweets, and jams, did he remark severely: "Overeating is harmful to purity of the soul. Saint Cassian taught the avoidance of much food and an excess of victuals, as also of overindulgence in the satiety of the belly and the sweet pleasure of the throat."

Vladimir Lvovich, however, snapped: "Be quiet, Undershirt, and know your place."

Tikhon Ieremeevich meekly fell silent, and immediately began energetically partaking of the victuals displayed on the table.

The line of conversation was very quickly determined. Bubentsov captured the attention of all present by beginning to tell them about the astonishing discoveries that had already horrified Zavolzhsk, that would set the entire province buzzing tomorrow and shake the entire empire to its foundations the day after that.

"You have probably heard about the two headless corpses cast up on the riverbank in the Chernoyarsk district," Vladimir Lvovich began, knitting his handsome eyebrows. "The police investigation has failed to establish the victims' identities, for without a head that is almost impossible. It has, however, been established that the bodies are quite fresh, no more than three days old, which means that the crime was committed somewhere within the bounds of the province of Zavolzhsk. When I learned this, I began pondering on why the criminal or criminals would have wished to decapitate their victims."

At this point Bubentsov paused and glanced mockingly around his audience, as if offering them the opportunity to guess this riddle.

No one spoke, they all gazed fixedly at the narrator, and Naina Georgievna actually leaned far forward, piercing him with her blinding black eyes. Indeed, for the entire remainder of the evening she had eyes only for Vladimir Lvovich and made no great attempt to conceal it. It was a strange look: At times Pelagia imagined that she could see something akin to revulsion in it, but there was also passionate interest and a species of astonishment that was more than merely passionate, even morbid.

The nun observed that Stepan Trofimovich and Poggio, who were sitting far apart as if they had deliberately arranged it, constantly turned their heads, glancing alternately at the young woman and the object of her rapt attention. Shiryaev had two crimson scratches on his cheek (quite definitely left by fingernails), and there was white powder under Arkadii Sergeevich's right eye.

Yet Bubentsov appeared to regard Naina Georgievna's glances as entirely insignificant. Up to this point he had not addressed her even once, and if he had glanced at her occasionally, then it had been with lazy indifference.

Since the pause in the narrative dragged on somewhat, and she wanted to hear what would come next, Sister Pelagia suggested: "Perhaps the heads were removed precisely in order to make it impossible to identify the dead men?"

"I rather think not." Vladimir Lvovich's lips stretched briefly into a smile of satisfaction. "Local killers would not have thought of anything so artfully cunning. Especially since the dead men are clearly not local people; had someone local gone missing, they would have been identified anyway. This is a different case."

"But what?" asked Pyotr Georgievich. "Don't tantalize us so!"

"Ropsha," replied Bubentsov, folding his arms across his chest and leaning back in his chair, as if he had given an exhaustive explanation of everything.

There was a jangling sound—Sister Pelagia had dropped her spoon on the floor and she gasped, covering her mouth with her hand.

"What's that?" said Kirill Nifontovich, who had misheard. "Are the Polish convicts taking to highway robbery? Why, all of a sudden? They're too old for that already."

"Ropsha?" Pyotr Georgievich echoed, perplexed. "Ah, yes, just a moment now . . . that's from the chronicle! The Novgorodian merchant who had his head cut off by the pagans in these parts during Ivan the Fourth's time. I beg your pardon, but what has Ropsha got to do with it?"

The synodical inspector's nostrils flared rapaciously.

"Ropsha has nothing to do with the case, but the pagans have a great deal to do with it. We have been receiving reports for a long time that the local Zyts, while formally observing the rites of the Orthodox Church, secretly worship idols and perform all sorts of loathsome rituals. And, by the way, in Ropsha's time, the very same tribe lived here, and their gods were the very same."

"It's not likely," said Shiryaev with a shrug. "I know the Zyts. They're a quiet, peaceful people. True, they have their own customs, their own superstitions and festivals. It is possible that something of the old beliefs might still remain. But killing people and cutting off their heads? Nonsense. Why on earth would they have taken a break of five hundred years after Ropsha?"

"That is the very point," said Bubentsov, gazing triumphantly around the table. "The inquiries I have made have revealed a most interesting little fact. A rumor has recently spread among the forest Zyts that in the near future the god Shishiga will come sailing down the Heavenly River in his sacred bark after sleeping on a cloud for many centuries, and Shishiga must be offered his favorite food if he is not to grow angry. And this Shishiga's favorite food, as the chronicle makes clear, is human heads. Hence my assumption (indeed, more than a mere assumption, I am absolutely certain of it) that Shishiga's bark has already reached the Zyts, and he is damnably hungry."

"What on earth are you talking about!" exclaimed Stepan Trofimovich, growing furious. "These are quite absurd conjectures!"

"Alas, they are not conjectures," said Vladimir Lvovich, assuming a severe expression, one might even call it an official state expression. "Tikhon Ieremeevich has wasted no time here in acquiring people of his own, including in the most remote districts. And his informants report that an incomprehensible ferment and agitation are to be observed among the Zyt youth. We have information that somewhere in a remote thicket an idol representing the god Shishiga has been erected in a clearing, and severed heads have been brought to that place."

"Bravo!" Naina Georgievna suddenly threw up her hands and began to applaud. Everybody looked at her in bewilderment. "Shishiga and human sacrifices—that is absolutely brilliant! I knew that I was not mistaken about you, Vladimir Lvovich. I can just imagine the sensation you will make with this story throughout the length and breadth of Russia."

"I am flattered," said Bubentsov, inclining his head with seeming astonishment as he met her gaze, which had changed from disgusted amazement to adoration. "A scandal on a genuinely nationwide scale. To have wild pagans running riot is a disgrace for a European power, and the guilt lies fairly and squarely with the local authorities, above all the church authorities. It is a good thing that I happened to be here. You may be sure, ladies and gentlemen, that I shall investigate this incident with great thoroughness, seek out the guilty parties, and return the forest savages to the bosom of the church."

"I do not doubt it," chuckled Poggio. "Oh, you are a fortunate man, Mr. Bubentsov, to have drawn such a lucky ticket."

But Vladimir Lvovich had apparently entered completely into the role of the man of state and inquisitor, and he was not inclined to joke.

"Your comedy is misplaced, sir," he said in a stern voice. "This is a terrible business, even monstrous. We do not know how many such headless bodies are lying on the bottom of the rivers and lakes. And it is also quite certain that there will be more victims. We already know from reliable sources how the ritual of murder is performed. The servants of Shishiga creep up on a lone traveler from behind in the night, throw a sack over his head, tie it tight around the neck with a string, and drag their victim into the bushes or to some other secluded spot, so that the unfortunate cannot even call out for help. There they cut off the head, throw the body into the swamp or the water, and carry their booty off to the heathen site of worship."

"Oh, my God!" Miss Wrigley said, crossing herself.

"We must locate this site of worship and send for the experts from the Imperial Ethnographical Society," Kirill Nifontovich suggested enthusiastically. "Idol worship and headhunting—those are extremely rare phenomena in this part of the world!"

"We are looking," Bubentsov said ominously. "And we shall find it. I have already been granted all the necessary authority by telegraph from St. Petersburg."

"Do you remember?" Naina Georgievna exclaimed, once again apropos of nothing. "Do you remember that place in Lermontov?

> Ruling this paltry realm of earth,
> He sowed his evil far afield,

No opposition did he meet,
All to his artful wiles did yield.

"Gentlemen, why are you all so glum? Look what a moon there is, how much mysterious, evil power there is in it! Let us go walking in the park. Really, Vladimir Lvovich, let us go!"

She jumped to her feet and dashed impetuously over to Bubentsov, holding out her slim hand to him. Something had happened to Naina Georgievna, and it seemed to be something good—her face was shining in ecstatic happiness, her eyes sparkling, her finely molded nostrils flaring passionately. No one was particularly surprised by the extravagant young woman's sudden outburst—they were evidently all accustomed to her wild changes of mood.

"A short walk would be welcome," Krasnov said complacently, getting to his feet. "Here is my arm, miss." And he offered the Englishwoman his arm, poised in a gallant curve. "Only mind you do not leave me, or they will jump on me from behind and throw a sack over my head, ha-ha."

Naina Georgievna remained standing in front of Vladimir Lvovich, holding out her hand to him, but Bubentsov made no movement in reply and only surveyed the beautiful woman from her feet up to her head with a calm and confident glance.

"I have no time, Naina Georgievna," he said finally in an even tone of voice. "I have to sit with my aunt for a while. And before going to bed I was also intending to compose a memorandum for the police guards. Petersburg has sent instructions for me to be placed under protection. This is a serious matter. Today I have already received my first threat in written form—it has been added to the case file."

The young woman spoke tenderly to him: "Ah, dear Vladimir Lvovich, the best protection is love. That is where you should place your trust, not in the police."

If Bubentsov's refusal had upset her, she gave no sign of it.

"Well, as you wish." With a meek smile she turned to the other men and announced in a different voice, imperious and demanding: "Let's go into the park. But each of us on our own, to make it more frightening, and we'll call out to one another."

She ran down the steps and melted into the darkness. Shiryaev, Poggio, and Pyotr Georgievich followed her without saying a word. Except that the latter looked back and asked: "What about you, Sister Pelagia? Come on. It's a truly wonderful evening."

"No, Pyotr Georgievich, I shall also pay a visit to your grandmother."

Pelagia set off after the formidable inspector, and the only person left behind on the terrace, which a moment ago had been full of people, was Spasyonny, heaping raspberry jam into a dish.

"TOMORROW MORNING YOU will be much better, aunty, and we shall go for a ride," said Bubentsov in a tone of confidence that brooked no denial, holding Marya Afanasievna by the wrist and looking her straight in the eyes. "But first let us settle this little business with the attorney. It really is very good that you have summoned him, you did the right thing. Truly, it is a shameful kind of joke—to leave Drozdovka to a household retainer. It is just the same as if Elizabeth of England had left the throne to the court jester. That is not the way things are done, aunty."

"But who should I leave it to? Petka and Nainka?" Tatishcheva objected in a barely audible voice. "They'll fritter away the lot. They'll sell the estate, and not to some decent person, because nowadays the nobles have no money, but to some moneybags. He'll tear up the park and turn the house into a factory. But Janet won't change anything, she'll leave everything the way it is. She'll give Pyotr and Naina money, they're like family to her, but she won't allow them to play the fool."

"Queen Elizabeth acted differently—she made James Stuart her heir, although she had closer relatives than he. And all because she was concerned for the welfare of her realm. Stuart was a man of genuine stately intellect. The queen could be certain that he would not only preserve her realm, but also strengthen it several times over. She also knew that in his eternal gratitude to her, he would glorify her memory and would not mistreat the associates who were dear to her heart."

What astounded Pelagia most of all was the fact that Vladimir Lvovich was not in the least embarrassed by the presence of outsiders. Tanya, of course, was dozing, draped across her chair, drained of all her strength—she had exhausted herself in the course of the day—but

Pelagia was sitting close by, at the foot of the bed, and deliberately clicking her knitting needles as loudly as she could to bring the shameless villain to his senses.

Much chance there was of that!

Bubentsov leaned down closer, looking into Tatishcheva's eyes again.

"I know how to perpetuate your memory. What you need is not a headstone of Carrara marble, or a chapel. All that is nothing but dead stone. What you need is a memorial of a different kind, one that will spread out from Drozdovka through the whole of Russia, and then through the whole world. Who will continue your noble labors in the effort to breed the white bulldog? For all of them it is no more than a foolish caprice, an absurd whim. Your Miss Wrigley cannot stand dogs."

"That's true," squeaked Marya Afanasievna. "Last year she even dared to get herself a cat, but Zagulyai and Zakidai tore him in two."

"There, you see. But I have been a dog-lover since my childhood. My father had excellent borzois. You could say that I was raised in the kennels. It will take another ten years for this sturdy chap"—Vladimir Lvovich fondled the ear of the puppy, who was snoring sweetly close beside the general's widow—"to father a firm, stable breed. I shall call the breed the Tatishchev bulldog, so that a hundred and two hundred years from now . . ."

At that very moment Zakusai, awoken by this touch and closely observing the hand that was absentmindedly tousling his ear, took decisive action and snapped at the pampered finger with his sharp little teeth.

"Ah!" Bubentsov cried briefly in surprise and jerked his hand away, sending the puppy flying head over heels to the floor. Not offended in the slightest, Zakusai gave a joyful bark and suddenly darted straight for the door, which had not been completely shut, leaving just a crack open.

"Catch him!" cried Marya Afanasievna, started up from her pillow in a panic. "Tanya, Tanya, he's gone again!"

The maid jumped up from her chair, still half asleep and totally bemused, and Vladimir Lvovich stood up as well.

The round white rump stuck in the narrow crack of the door, but not for long. The fat little legs scraped rapidly at the floor, the door opened just a little wider, Zakusai broke through and was free.

"Stop!" shouted Bubentsov. "Don't worry, aunty, I'll catch him soon enough."

The three of them—Vladimir Lvovich, Pelagia, and Tanya—ran out into the corridor. The white pup was already at its far end. Seeing that the enormity of his daring had been duly appreciated, he yelped in triumph and disappeared around the corner.

"He'll run out into the garden," gasped Tanya. "The doors are wide open!"

Zakusai ran quicker than his pursuers—as she bounded out onto the veranda, Pelagia was barely in time to see the little white blob leap friskily from the step straight into the darkness.

"We have to catch him quickly, or aunty will go out of her mind," Bubentsov said anxiously, and he began issuing commands in military style: "You, whatever your name is, to the left, the nun to the right, I go straight on. Shout to the others and tell them to search, too. Forward!"

A moment later the drowsy calm of the park was shattered by numerous voices calling to the fugitive.

"Zakusai! Here, boy, Zakusai!" called Pelagia.

"Zakusai, come here, you damned pest!" Tanya's shrill voice called out somewhere behind the raspberry patch.

"Gentlemen, Zakusai has run off!" Bubentsov's brisk cavalryman's tenor informed the others who were wandering about the park.

And they were also quick to respond.

"Hey there!" Pyotr Georgievich responded from somewhere in the distance. "He won't get away, the little tormentor! We'll find him and punish him!"

"Tally-ho, tally-ho!" Kirill Nifontovich hallooed from the birch grove. "Miss Wrigley, I'll go to the clearing, and you go over that way!"

And now on all sides there were branches cracking, merry voices calling, laughter rippling. The customary game, by now already a ritual, was beginning.

Sister Pelagia gazed hard into the darkness and listened for that familiar squealing coming from any direction. And only a little while later, after about ten minutes, when she was already close to the river-bank, she finally saw something small and white ahead of her. She quickened her stride—it was definitely Zakusai. Exhausted from all the running, he had laid down to rest under the withered aspen, two steps away from the Englishwoman's lawn.

"So that's where you are," Pelagia sang quietly, thinking only of how to avoid startling the little scamp—then she would have to spend half the night searching all the thickets for him.

There was a rustling of rapid footsteps in the bushes at one side—evidently someone else was hurrying to the same spot.

The nun crept up to the puppy, bent down over him, and with a tri-umphant cry of "Got you!" seized hold of his plump white body with both hands.

Zakusai did not make a sound, he did not even stir.

Pelagia squatted down quickly. Her heart gave a tight shudder, as if refusing to pump any more blood, and she had a tight, hot feeling in her chest.

The puppy's head was strangely flattened and lying beside him was a big flat stone, still with a lump of wet earth clinging to it and gleam-ing in the moonlight. And there was the hole out of which the stone had been tugged.

In death Zakusai's little face had become long and sad. Now he re-ally did look like a little angel.

The steps were still rustling through the bushes, but not moving closer, on the contrary, they were farther away and less distinct now. And then Pelagia finally realized: Whoever it was, they were not hurry-ing to the spot, but away from it.

# CHAPTER 5

# A Terrible Fright

MARYA AFANASIEVNA WAS dying. At the very beginning of the night, when she guessed what had happened from Tanya's heartrending wailing, she lost the power of speech. She simply lay on her back, wheezing, her eyes gaping wildly up at the ceiling as her plump fingers fiddled and fidgeted with the edge of the blanket, shaking and shaking it, brushing at something that would not be shaken off.

The doctor was brought from the town in the very fastest carriage-and-three. He felt the patient here and there, kneaded her a little, listened to her through a stethoscope, gave her an injection so that she would not choke, and then came out into the corridor and said with a dismissive wave of his hand: "She's going. She should be given the sacraments."

Then he sat in the drawing room, drank tea with cognac, and talked in low voices with Stepan Trofimovich about the prospects for the harvest, glancing into the bedroom once every half-hour to see if she was still breathing. Marya Afanasievna was breathing, but ever more weakly as time passed, and she was oblivious to her surroundings for long periods at a time.

Long after midnight the rural dean was brought, having been roused from his bed. He arrived disheveled and not yet fully awake, but in full vestments and with all the gifts of the Holy Sacrament. However, when he entered the dying woman's room, she opened her eyes and mumbled implacably: "I don't want him."

"Don't you want the sacraments, granny?" Pyotr Georgievich asked in fright. He had been affected very powerfully by the dramatic events.

Tatishcheva nodded her head very weakly.

"What is it, then?" asked Sister Pelagia, leaning down to her. "You don't want the holy father?"

The old woman slowly lowered her eyelids, then raised them again and pointed upward and off to one side.

Pelagia followed the line of her finger with her eyes. There was nothing special up there on the left: the wall, a lithograph with a view of St. Petersburg, a portrait of the deceased Apollon Nikolaevich, a photograph of His Grace Mitrofanii in full bishop's vestments.

"You want the bishop to administer the sacraments?" the nun guessed. The general's widow closed her eyelids again and lowered her finger. Apparently that was it.

They sent to Zavolzhsk again, to the episcopal see, and began waiting for Mitrofanii to arrive.

No one slept all night long, but everyone scattered throughout the house. Here and there groups of two or three talked quietly among themselves, while others, in contrast, sat in silent solitude. Pelagia had no opportunity to observe the way in which everyone behaved, which was unfortunate, for many things might have been revealed. Who knows, poor Zakusai's killer might even have given himself away somehow or other. But Christian duty comes before worldly concerns, and the nun remained constantly at Marya Afanasievna's side, reading prayers and whispering words of consolation that in all likelihood the sick woman could not even hear. It was not until dawn that Pelagia finally ventured out into the garden for some reason and returned after an absence of about half an hour in a state of great thoughtfulness.

The sun rose and began clambering higher and higher; it was already past noon, and still His Grace was not there. The doctor merely shook his head and said that the patient was clinging on out of sheer stubbornness: She had got it into her head that she must hold out until her nephew arrived, no matter what, and now there was no way she would go until she had seen him.

The attorney Korsh arrived. Bubentsov put Pelagia out of the room so that she would not interfere with the rewriting of the will. Spasyonny and Krasnov were summoned to be witnesses, because Naina Georgievna would not leave her room, Pyotr Georgievich asked to be excused, and Stepan Trofimovich merely frowned fastidiously. How could he think of wills at such a moment!

Pelagia found all this very unpleasant, but there was nothing that she could do. Donat Abramovich Sytnikov appeared, but did not wish to interfere in other people's family affairs—let things take their own course, he said, from which it followed that he was not after all quite as interested in the Goryaev wilderness as the mistrustful Marya Afanasievna had fancied.

Bubentsov's efforts over the dying woman were in vain; there was no rewriting of the will. An hour later Korsh emerged from the bedroom, wiping away the sweat with his handkerchief, and asked for some kvass.

"It is not customary to attempt to guess a person's last wishes from inarticulate mumbling," he explained angrily to Sister Pelagia. "I'm not some fairground clown, I am a member of the notary's guild." And he ordered the horses to be harnessed to his britzka, even refusing the offer of dinner.

Vladimir Lvovich darted out after him with a face darker than thunder. Overtaking the obdurate Korsh, he took him by the elbow and said something in a loud whisper. What he said is not known, but Korsh left in any case.

What was heard, however, was Bubentsov's shout from the courtyard after the departing britzka: "You'll be sorry!"

The attorney drove away, but a stream of new guests kept arriving, having learned of the sad event. There were neighboring landowners, and many of the province's notables, including even the marshal of the nobility. It is unlikely that so great a crowd would have come to bid farewell to the general's widow Tatishcheva if not for the rumors that had spread rapidly through the territory of Zavolzhie. The faces of those gathered together expressed, in addition to the mournful anticipation appropriate to the occasion, a strange excitement, and the words "will" and "puppy" were spoken frequently in low, hissing whispers.

Miss Wrigley was enveloped in a strange agitation that became ever more noticeable as things went on. When it finally became clear that the will remained in force, the Englishwoman was entirely engulfed in something very much like a whirlpool. Ladies and gentlemen whom she scarcely knew, or did not know at all, approached her and spoke words filled with the most fervid sympathy, glancing curiously into her eyes. Others, in contrast, demonstratively avoided the heiress, their entire demeanor expressive of condemnation and even contempt. Poor Miss Wrigley lost her bearings completely and every now and then went dashing impulsively to seek out Pyotr Georgievich and Naina Georgievna, desperate to explain herself to them.

However, Naina Georgievna still did not come out of her room, and Pyotr Georgievich had been appropriated by Bubentsov. When she went out into the courtyard to see if the bishop was coming at last, Pelagia saw Vladimir Lvovich rapidly leading the confused Petya as far away as possible from the general crowd, holding him by the shoulder with one hand and gesticulating with the other. She caught a brief snatch of a phrase: ". . . investigate the circumstances and appeal, you absolutely must appeal."

Moreover, the public servant had plenty of other business in hand as well. In the morning an express courier came galloping out to him from the town at breakneck speed, and in the afternoon there was another. On both occasions Vladimir Lvovich shut himself away in the library with the messengers for a long time, after which the mysterious riders hurtled off no less recklessly in the opposite direction. The investigation into the case of the missing heads was clearly being conducted in earnest.

MITROFANII ARRIVED WHEN it was almost evening, after they had already given up hope.

Approaching to be blessed, Pelagia said reproachfully: "Marya Afanasievna will be happy now. She is worn out with waiting, poor woman."

"Never mind," replied His Grace, absentmindedly crossing everyone who had come out into the yard to meet him. "It is not her, but death who is tired of waiting. And there is no harm in taunting the grim reaper a little."

He seemed somehow brisk and businesslike, not solemn at all. As if he had not come to give a dying woman the last sacraments but to inspect the local deanery or on some other important but routine matter.

"Air the carriage, it's rather stuffy in there," he said for some reason to the lay brother who was sitting beside the driver on the coachbox.

To Pelagia he said: "Come on, then, take me to her."

"Your Grace, what about the gifts of the Holy Sacrament?" she reminded him. "You have to administer extreme unction."

"Extreme unction? Why not, I can give the last rites; unction is good for the health too. Father Alexii!"

A subdeacon in a brocade surplice clambered ponderously out of the carriage, carrying a portable tabernacle.

They walked along the dark corridor where the walls were lined with people bowing as their voices rustled: "Bless me, Your Grace." Mitrofanii gave his blessing, but he did not seem to recognize anyone and he had an abstracted air. He turned everybody out of the bedroom, allowing only Father Alexii and Pelagia to enter with him.

"What's this, handmaid of the Lord, have you decided to die?" he asked the woman in the bed severely, and it was clear that this was not the nephew Mishenka talking, but the strict pastor. "Are you yearning so greatly to join our Heavenly Father? Has He called you, or are you imposing yourself on His hospitality? If it is your will, then it is a sin."

But the stern words produced no effect on Marya Afanasievna. She gazed fixedly at the bishop with a severe look in her eyes and waited.

"Very well," sighed Mitrofanii, and he pulled his black traveling cassock up over his head, revealing the gold chasuble beneath it, with the precious episcopal panagion on the chest. "Make ready, father."

The deacon placed a small silver dish on the bedside table and sprinkled grains of wheat onto it. He set an empty censer at its center and laid out seven candles. Mitrofanii blessed the unction and the wine, poured them into the censer, and lit the candles himself. As he anointed the dying woman's forehead, nostrils, cheeks, lips, breast, and hands, he began reciting a prayer with quiet feeling: "Holy Father, Healer of spirit and of body, Who didst send Thine only Son, our Lord Jesus Christ, Who does heal all ills and free us from death: Heal likewise this Thy handmaiden Marya of the bodily and spiritual ailments that do oppress her and return her to life through the grace of Thy

Christ and the prayers of Mary, Most Glorious Ever Virgin, Mother of Christ our God. . . ."

Seven times the bishop performed the appointed rite and prayer, each time extinguishing one of the candles. Marya Afanasievna lay quietly, gazing meekly at the flames of the candles and moving her lips soundlessly, as if she was pronouncing the words: "Lord have mercy."

When the supplication concluded, Mitrofanii moved a chair up to the bed, sat down, and said in an everyday voice: "We'll wait a little while to administer Holy Communion. I think the anointing will be enough for now."

Tatishcheva twitched the corner of her mouth in annoyance and gave a pitiful groan, but the bishop merely held up his hand.

"Lie still and listen. You didn't pass on yesterday evening, so now you can wait a little longer while your prelate talks to you. And if you decide to die it will be out of sheer obstinacy."

After this preamble His Grace fell silent for a moment and then he began speaking differently, less loudly but with an earnest sadness.

"You often hear people say, even those who do not believe blindly, but with open eyes, that life is a precious gift from God. But it seems to me that it is not a gift at all, for a gift is intended to bring only plea- sure to the heart and the body, while the life of mortal men contains little that is pleasurable. Bodily and spiritual torment, sin and vice, the loss of loved ones—that is our life. A fine gift, is it not? Therefore it seems to me that life should not be understood as a gift, but as a cer- tain work of penance, such as is given to monks, and always his own work to each man, to the limit of his strength, no more but also no less. Each of us possesses a different spiritual strength, and so the sever- ity of the work of penance is different. And likewise each of us has his own appointed term. Those on whom God takes pity He gathers to himself when they are children. For others He appoints a middling term, and those He wishes to test most of all He burdens with long years. The gift will come later, after life. Foolish sinners that we are, we fear it and call it death, but this death is the long-awaited meeting with our All-Merciful Father. The Lord tests each one of us in our own way and in His infinite ingenuity will never repeat Himself. However, it is a great sin and a grievous offense to our Heavenly Father if anyone should seek to shorten the appointed term of his work of penance illegitimately. It is not man who appoints this meeting, but God alone. Therefore is the church set so adamantly against suicide, regarding it as the worst of all sins. Though you may be suffering, in pain and despair, endure it. The Lord knows how much strength each of us has in his soul, and He will not lay an excessive burden on His offspring. What is required is to endure all things with patience so that through this your soul will be cleansed and you will be exalted. But what you are doing is straightforward suicide," said Mitrofanii, growing angry and departing from his tone of confidential intimacy. "A strong, healthy old woman! What are you doing playing out this comedy? Offending the Lord for the sake of some white bulldog, trying to destroy your very soul! You shall not have deathbed absolution from me, I tell you, because the holy church does not connive with suicides! And if you remain stubborn, I shall have you buried outside the cemetery wall, in unhallowed ground. And I shall lodge objections against your will with the secular authorities, because under the law of Russia the wills of suicides have no validity!"

The dying woman's eyes glinted briefly with bright fury, and her lips smacked against each other without producing a single sound. But the hands folded piously at her breast trembled, and the hand on the top, the right, struggled to set the thumb between the fingers in a gesture of defiance.

"Very good, very good," the bishop said gleefully. "Depart this life with the sign of the devil. That will be just perfect for you. When you die, I shan't allow them to straighten out your fingers. Lie there in the coffin making that gesture, let everybody take a good look at it."

The widow's fingers unclenched themselves and straightened out; the palm of her right hand settled gracefully on top of her left.

His Grace nodded and began speaking humanely again, as if he had never lost his temper.

"See, Marya, how deep you have drunk of bitter grief in your life. You have buried your beloved husband and outlived four children. But still you did not die. Are these flat-faced dogs really more dear to you than the people you loved? Truly, for shame!"

Mitrofanii waited to see if there would be any sign, but Marya Afanasievna merely closed her eyes.

"But then I know that there is still much life in you, you have not yet lived out your term, you have not yet become ripe and full of years like the patriarchs of the Old Testament. And here is something else for you to think about. Those for whom the Lord has appointed long life bear the greatest suffering of all, because their ordeal is so very long. But their reward is also a special one. The longer I live in this world, the more it seems to me that the infirmity of old age is not even a test, but rather an expression of special grace from God. And this gift is truly a gift. It is only in the wisdom of advanced age that man is freed from the fear of death. The withering of the flesh and the fading of the mind itself—these are a blessed preparation for another life. Death does not scythe your legs from under you with no warning, but enters slowly, a drop at a time, and in this there is perhaps even a certain sweetness. It is no wonder that in their declining years so many of the venerable secluded ascetics who have lived to a great age are less here, in this life, than there, in a state of heavenly bliss. There are times when their very flesh becomes incorruptible at death, and people are astounded. But why do I speak of the venerable saints? It is the same for anyone who is very old, all those he has known—those he has loved or hated—are already there, waiting for him, he is the only one who has tarried, and therefore he is not afraid. He knows with certainty that people of every kind—both cleverer and more stupid than he, both crueler and kinder, both braver and more cowardly—have crossed this terrible threshold safely. And that means it is not so very terrible after all . . ."

At this point Marya Afanasievna, who had been listening to the bishop's sermon intently, smiled rapturously and Mitrofanii knitted his black brows, because he had anticipated a different effect. He sighed, crossed himself, and abandoned all attempts to remonstrate with her.

"Well then, if you feel that your time has come, if you are being called—I shall not try to detain you. I shall administer the Last Sacrament and conduct your funeral and lay you in hallowed ground in the proper fashion. I frightened you because I was angry. Die, if your mind is made up. If life no longer has any hold on you, if it has lost its attraction, how can a weak soul such as I am keep you here? Only there is one thing . . ." He glanced around and spoke to the deacon: "Bring it in now, father."

Father Alexii nodded and went out of the door. Silence fell in the bedroom. Marya Afanasievna lay with her eyes closed, and her face already looked as if she were not lying in bed, but in the center of a church, in an open coffin, and from under the tall vaults the angels were singing their sweet song of greeting to her. Mitrofanii got up, walked across to the lithograph hanging on the wall, and began studying it intently.

But shortly the door opened and the deacon and the lay brother carried in a closed wicker box with a small opening in the top. They set it down on the floor and, with a bow to the bishop, withdrew to the wall.

Inside the box something rustled strangely and there was a sound that could almost have been squealing. Sister Pelagia craned her neck and stood up on tiptoe in her curiosity as she tried to glance in through the little opening, but Mitrofanii had already thrown back the lid and thrust both his hands into the basket.

"Here, aunty," he said in his ordinary, non-churchman's voice. "I wanted to show you this before you die. That's why I was a little late. On my instructions, messengers combed the entire district; they even made use of the telegraph, although, as you know, I am not fond of such novelties. In a litter at retired major Sipyagin's house they found a white bulldog, a female, and her ear is just right, too, take a look. And just two hours ago the express steam launch from Nizhny brought me a gift from first-guild merchant Saikin, a little white male, a month and a half old. And he's a perfect specimen in every respect. The bitch is not white all over—she has brown socks—but she is exceptionally bandy-legged. Her name is Musya. Sipyagin almost refused to let her go—his daughter didn't want to part with her at all. I had to threaten him with excommunication for the death of a Christian soul, which was actually unlawful on my part. The little dog doesn't have a name yet, though. Just look at his brown ear. His nose is pink, just as it is supposed to be, and speckled, but most important of all, his little face has quite remarkably droopy cheeks. When the pups are a little older, we can start breeding again. And in no time at all, in no more than two or three generations, the white bulldog will be restored."

He extracted two fat-bellied puppies from the basket. One was a bit bigger than the other, it yelped angrily and kicked out, the other hung there in meek silence.

Glancing around at the dying woman, Pelagia saw that a magical transformation had taken place and she was quite clearly no longer ready for the grave. She was gazing intently at the bulldog puppies, and the fingers lying on her breast were stirring feebly, as if attempting to catch hold of something.

A trembling voice, just barely audible, asked: "But are they slobbery?"

His Grace whispered to Pelagia: "The doctor!"—and he himself went up to the bed and set both puppies down on the widow's chest.

"There, take a look for yourself. It's positively streaming off them."

Pelagia darted out into the corridor with such an expression on her face that the doctor, who was standing not far away, nodded sympathetically.

"Is it over?" he asked.

She shook her head, her wits still stunned by the miracle that God had just manifested, and without speaking gestured for him to go in.

The doctor stuck his head out two minutes later. His manner was simultaneously perplexed and brisk.

"Never anything like it in twenty-seven years of practice," he told the people who had gathered at the door, and shouted, "Hey, anybody there? Maid! Some hot broth, and make it strong!"

WHEN THE BISHOP greeted Pelagia he was already refreshed and cheerful, having had time to get washed, change into a light-gray cassock, and drink a glass of cold kvass.

"Well, what do the Orthodox faithful make of it?" he asked with a cunning smile. "I suppose they're talking about miraculous deliverance?"

"Almost everyone has left," Pelagia reported. "I should think so, after an event like this. They are all impatient to tell their families and friends all about it. But the marshal of the nobility is still here, and so are Bubentsov and his secretary."

"With his tail between his legs now, is he, the devil?" asked Mitrofanii, growing serious. "While you, Pelagia, have been idling away the time here, in Zavolzhsk we've had serious business to deal with."

The nun accepted the reproach without a murmur, bowing her head. After all, she was at fault, she had failed to protect little Zakusai, and if Marya Afanasievna was on the road to recovery, it was none of her doing.

"Bubentsov has become very strong; he has concocted such a pack of cock-and-bull stories and raised such a clamor throughout the whole of Russia, that I simply don't know if I'll be able to hold him off."

And His Grace told Pelagia what she had already heard from Bubentsov himself, except that Mitrofanii's interpretation of the murders proved to be quite different.

"All these fantasies about the god Shishiga are simply stupid nonsense. Some evil people took the lives of a couple of souls, undressed them, and cut their heads off, either out of idle mischief or malicious spite, or something else. There are all sorts of vicious monsters in this world. And Bubentsov is delighted; he's already spun an entire web out of it. That antediluvian chronicle played right into his hands. I know myself that our Zyts are Christians largely in name only and many of them are infected with pagan superstitions, but they are a quiet, peaceful people. Never mind murder—they're not even in the habit of stealing. But it has only taken this devil a few days to stir up the dregs of darkness from the bottom of people's souls and plant his whisperers and slanderers. As it says in the Gospel: 'And then shall many be seduced, and shall betray one another, and shall hate one another.' Ugh, such vileness! Now many people are afraid to leave their houses in the evening, and they close the shutters across their doors at night—we've had nothing so shameful around here for ten years at least, ever since we got rid of our bandits. Well, never mind, for Satan's suggestion, seek the Lord's protection. There's a stout stick for every dirty trick. Just as one has been found here at Drozdovka."

And with this return to a more pleasant theme, Mitrofanii's mood mellowed once again.

"What do you say, my little Pelagia?" he asked, narrowing his eyes in laughter. "Can I be forgiven the sin of feeling just a little proud?"

"Who would not be proud?" the nun replied sincerely. "The Lord will not be vexed. You saved Marya Afanasievna, and everybody saw it, everybody will testify to it."

"Indeed. And I am especially pleased to have ruined the game for that stealthy scoundrel who killed the dogs. The filthy villain must have been rubbing his hands in glee at having killed off the old woman, and then . . . take that." And the bishop set his fingers into the same gesture that only a little while before he himself had called "the devil's sign." "We're hearty stock. Aunty will live another ten years yet, or fifteen, God willing. And she'll breed her ugly, flat-faced monsters all over again."

Mitrofanii relished his pride for only a very short while, and then decided that was enough. He glanced quizzically at Pelagia and shook his head.

"Well then, has the work of penance turned out not to be so simple? You were probably thinking: This is nothing serious, a few funny-looking dogs, I've untangled tougher knots than this before? Only, you see, the entire business has resolved itself. When I said scoundrel and villain just now, I should have made it clear that it was a woman. After all, the picture is quite clear. Marya Afanasievna was angry with her legitimate heirs, and just to spite them she drew up her will in favor of this Englishwoman. She wasn't serious, of course, she just wanted to give them a fright. But the Protestant woman's reason was clouded, which is quite understandable in her situation. From being a household retainer suddenly to become a rich woman in your old age—it's enough to addle anyone's brains."

"Miss Wrigley is not old," said Pelagia. "I should say she is no more than fifty."

"All the more reason, then. The very age when strength begins to desert the human frame and tomorrow becomes something to be afraid of. They'll turn her out of the house now, and quite right, too. Ingratitude is a serious sin, and betrayal is the worst of all."

"They must not be allowed to throw her out," Pelagia declared resolutely. "Miss Wrigley did not kill the dogs. When the poison was put in Zagulyai's and Zakidai's food, the will had not yet been changed in her favor. I think that the inheritance has absolutely nothing to do with all of this."

"Nothing to do with it? Then what need was there to drive the old woman into her grave? And whose plot was it, if not the Englishwoman's?"

Mitrofanii stared at his spiritual daughter in amazement, and she raised and lowered those ginger eyebrows that had been bleached by the sun before taking the plunge—straight off the cliff into the River.

"What need there was, I do not understand, but I do know who killed the dogs."

There was a polite but insistent knock at the door—very ill-timed, indeed. The subdeacon put his head in.

"Your Grace, everyone is assembled in the drawing room and they are asking for you. I said you were resting after the journey, but they begged me to supplicate you for them. The marshal is only waiting for you; the horses are already harnessed to his carriage, but he just won't go without your blessing. Perhaps you might come?"

The bishop transferred his gaze from Father Alexii back to Pelagia. Three deep creases had appeared right across his forehead.

"I think, Pelagia, that our conversation will be a long one. Let us go to the drawing room. I shall observe the necessary proprieties, and afterward we shall continue."

EVERYBODY WAS INDEED gathered in the drawing room, where they greeted the bishop with a rapturous murmur, and would certainly have broken into applause if not for their respect for his high church rank. Even Bubentsov himself came up to Mitrofanii and said with feeling: "I am eternally grateful to you, Your Grace, for saving my aunt."

And why should he not be grateful—now he could continue with his scheming about the will. For a moment the expression of pleasure on Mitrofanii's face was darkened by a shadow (evidently due to precisely this thought), and the pastor turned away from this disagreeable young man as if he had simply forgotten to bless him.

But Spasyonny was already creeping up to him from the other side, intoning tearfully: "For such is our life: verily as the flower and the smoke and the morning dew. Your hand, let me kiss your holy hand."

"Gentlemen! Gentlemen!" Krasnov announced. "A poem has just been born. Listen to my improvisation, gentlemen. In the style of the great Derzhavin! 'An Ode on the Miraculous Deliverance of the Tsaritsa of Drozdovka, Marya Afanasievna, from Mortal Danger.'

> For all the joyous Russian nation
> I take my flute to sing of this.
> The cause of our exultant bliss,
> Our much beloved queen's salvation.
>
> Thy angels white as eiderdown,
> Stung by the venom of the serpent,
> By thy black-hearted, thankless servant
> Were most perfidiously cut down.
>
> But Providence would not be mocked
> By such perverse malevolence,
> And by our Lord's own trusty hand
> The loathsome sting was safely plucked—"

"Kirill Nifontovich!" Miss Wrigley cried out in a trembling voice, interrupting the declamation and holding her skinny arms out to the poet. "Surely you have not also deserted me?"

Vladimir Lvovich smiled spitefully: "Excellent! Now we can truly see how the cap fits!"

The Englishwoman somehow suddenly found herself at the center of an empty circle, as if she were being deliberately displayed for public inspection.

"Miss Wrigley certainly did not like granny's bulldogs, but to assume that she . . . No, no, it's unthinkable," said Pyotr Georgievich with a shake of his head. "You do not know her at all, Vladimir Lvovich. That is, of course, to external appearances the circumstances might seem, and probably cannot help but seem, suspicious in the highest degree. However, as a person who has known Miss Wrigley since my early childhood, I can vouch for her completely and assure you that this speculation has no—"

"She's the one, the Englishwoman, no one else would have done it," exclaimed one of the guests, interrupting these faltering assurances. "Why, the very idea isn't even Russian, somehow. Not just to take someone and kill them, but to break the person's heart. Too tricky altogether for a true Orthodox believer. What's the point of talking—the business is clear enough."

To which Spasyonny added: "They have eyes and they do see, they have ears and they do hear."

"Oh, stop all this nonsense!" said Naina Georgievna, going up to Miss Wrigley and taking her by the hand. "Don't listen to them," she said in English. "They don't know what they are saying." The young woman glanced around, surveying everyone present with hatred in her eyes. "You've already condemned her! I won't let you lay the blame on Janet!"

The Englishwoman sobbed and pressed her forehead against her pupil's shoulder in gratitude.

"Come now, Naina Georgievna, it does not lie in your power to forestall the investigation required by law," remarked the marshal. "Naturally, we understand and respect your feelings, but leave it to the police to determine whether any crime has been committed in this business and who must bear responsibility. I am profoundly convinced that we are indeed dealing with a crime and that it must be treated as attempted murder. And I am sure that a trial by jury will reach the same conclusion."

"Does it mean hard labor?" Miss Wrigley squeaked in terror, glancing all around her like an animal at bay. "Siberia?"

"Well, certainly not Brighton," the marshal replied ominously—he prided himself on his knowledge of the European resorts.

The Englishwoman hung her head and began crying quietly, clearly having abandoned all hope. Naina Georgievna, who had turned bright pink with indignation, hugged her around the shoulders and began whispering something reassuring, but Miss Wrigley only repeated bitterly: "No, no, I'm a foreigner, the jury will condemn me . . ."

Sister Pelagia, whose heart was breaking at this pitiful spectacle, cast an imploring glance at His Grace. He nodded reassuringly, tapped his crook on the floor, and cleared his throat, and everyone immediately fell silent and turned toward him respectfully.

"Leave that woman alone," the bishop thundered. "She is not guilty."

"But what about the will, Your Grace?" asked the marshal, spreading his arms wide in protest. "The first principle of investigation is *cui prodest.*"

"Count Gavriil Alexandrovich," said the bishop, wagging a finger at him in admonishment, "pies should be baked by the pie-man; your job is to take care of our nobility and not to concern yourself with legal inquiries, for which you do not in any case—no offense intended—even possess the prerequisite qualities."

The marshal smiled in embarrassment, and Mitrofanii continued equally unhurriedly.

"You should not have dismissed the assurances of this young man and woman, who have known this person almost since the day they were born. And if that is not enough for you, then consider this: The first dog was killed before the will had been changed in Miss Wrigley's favor. And just where, tell me, Gavriil Alexandrovich, does that leave your *prodest,* eh?"

"Hmm, that's right," said the disrespectful Poggio, snapping his fingers. "His Grace is very sharp."

Now totally disconcerted, the marshal spread his arms even wider.

"But wait, then who killed the dogs? Or is that to remain a mystery and a secret?"

The silence was so tense, the gazes focused on the bishop from all sides so full of anticipation, that Mitrofanii was unable to resist the temptation.

"A mystery to men, but known to God," he said impressively. "And through Him to His servants."

Instantly the least movement in the drawing room ceased. The maid Tanya froze by the door, clutching the ribbons of her white apron with both hands. Bubentsov inclined his head skeptically. Miss Wrigley, about to wipe her eyes with a handkerchief, froze with her hand in midair. Even the haughty Naina Georgievna stared at the bishop as if spellbound.

Mitrofanii took Pelagia by the hand and led her into the center of the room.

"On my instructions, Sister Pelagia, my ever-vigilant eye, has spent several days here. I order you, my daughter, to tell these people what you have discovered. This affair has agitated minds and troubled hearts too profoundly for you and me to keep it our secret."

Pelagia lowered her eyes and shifted her spectacles up and down her nose, which was a sign that she was annoyed, but it was not her place to be angry with the bishop. There was nothing for her to do but obey.

"If you bless the deed, father, I will tell them," she said, overcoming her quite understandable nervousness. "But first let me confess and ask pardon. I should have solved the matter sooner. The innocent little creature would still be alive, and Marya Afanasievna would have been spared the terrible shock that almost sent her to the grave. I was too late; it was not until this morning that certain things became clear to me, and even then not completely clear."

Everybody listened to the nun very attentively, with the sole exception of Vladimir Lvovich, who stood there, arms akimbo, gazing at Pelagia in amused surprise. And his minion Tikhon Ieremeevich, infected by his master's example, took advantage of the pause to declare in a low voice, seemingly to himself: "Let your womenfolk hold their peace for they are bidden not to speak but to obey as the law says . . ."

"Do not pervert the Sacred Writ, it is a great sin and also punishable by law," said Mitrofanii, refusing to let him get away with this low trick. "The holy apostle wrote 'let them hold their peace in the churches,' meaning that during the service the long-tongued women should keep quiet, but the Christian law does not stop the mouths of women. You have evidently confused it, my dear sir, with Mohammedanism."

"Apologies, Your Grace, I have become feeble of memory," Spasyonny responded humbly, and bowed low before the bishop, almost down to the very ground.

Pelagia crossed herself, knowing that in a very short while the quiet of this hall would be shattered by the howling of Sodom and Gomorrah, but there was nothing to be done, and so she began: "Here at Drozdovka three murders have been committed. One five days ago, another two days ago, and the last one yesterday evening. They are truly murders, even though no people were killed. The first murder was planned in advance, with careful forethought. Someone wished to poison Zagulyai and Zakidai together. On the second and third occasions, things turned out differently: The murderer made no preparations at all, but acted in haste, killing with whatever came to hand. When Zakidai was killed, it was with an axe taken from the garden shed. Yesterday an ordinary stone was sufficient. How much is needed for a little puppy? I dare say he had no time even to squeal. . . ."

The nun crossed herself again, although she was not supposed to do so for a dog. But never mind that, it could do no harm.

"One thing is clear: The murder of the dogs is not connected with the will in any way because, as His Grace has pointed out, the change in the will had no effect on the dog-killer's evil intent. This person carried his dark plot through to the end. Either he wished in this way to do away with Marya Afanasievna, or he was pursuing some other goal unknown to us. But in the latter case the actions of the murderer are doubly repulsive, because of the indifference with which this person regarded the unfortunate woman's suffering. The murderer could not have failed to understand that he was destroying her mental and physical well-being. . . . And the most mysterious thing about this business is this . . ." Pelagia pushed up the spectacles that had slipped down her nose. "Why was such haste necessary with Zakidai and Zakusai? Why did the murderer have to take such risks? On both occasions there were people walking in the park. They could have seen him, exposed him. Yesterday, for instance, I very nearly came upon the criminal at the scene of the crime, I even heard steps, but, may God forgive me, I was afraid to run in pursuit, and by the time I screwed up my courage, it was already too late. The callousness and daring of the criminal indicate some exceptional passion. Either hatred, or fear, or something else. I do not know and I do not undertake to guess what our killer feels. I can only hope that he, or rather she, will tell us that herself."

"She!" gasped Shiryaev. "You mean to say, sister, that the killer is female?"

Everybody began talking at once and Mitrofanii glanced at Pelagia with a doubtful air, seeming already to regret that he had authorized her denunciation.

"So it is the Englishwoman after all?" said the marshal, totally confused.

Naina Georgievna threw up her finely sculpted chin defiantly. "No, you were told it was not her. The hint is obvious. Apart from Miss Wrigley, there is only one other woman here—me."

"And is Tatyana Zotovna not a woman, according to you?" asked Pyotr Georgievich, offended for the honor of his Dulcinea, but, realizing immediately that his intercession was not entirely appropriate, he added in confusion, "Oh, I'm sorry, Tanya, that was not what I meant at all. . . ."

Recovering his wits, he bounded across to the nun like an enraged cockerel.

"What sort of hysterical nonsense is this! What makes you think that it was a woman? Have you had a revelation or something of the sort?"

Tikhon Ieremeevich, clearly still not having forgiven Pelagia for his exile to the other wing, cited an appropriate dictum: "The lips of the foolish do speak forth foolishness."

He looked around at his master for support, but Bubentsov did not even glance at him; he was watching the nun, not in the way that he had been before, but with obvious interest. Vladimir Lvovich was behaving oddly today: He was usually expansive in company and could not bear it when people listened to anyone else, but this evening he had hardly even opened his mouth once.

"There was no revelation," Pelagia replied calmly, "and there is no need of one, when ordinary human reason will suffice. At first light I visited the spot where Zakusai was killed yesterday. The earth around it had been thoroughly trampled; someone had walked around the spot for quite a long time. Beside the hollow that was left by the stone was a deeper print of a right foot, as if someone had put their weight on it as they bent down, and another one, exactly the same, where the killer bent over to hit the puppy on the head. It is a woman's shoe, with a high heel. Only two people in the house wear shoes with high heels—Miss Wrigley and Naina Georgievna." Pelagia took a sheet of paper with the outline of a shoe traced on it out of her waist bag. "This is the footprint; the length of the foot is nine and a half inches. We can measure it against their feet to make quite sure."

"My foot is not nine and a half inches long, but eleven," Miss Wrigley declared in fright, having fallen under suspicion for the second time that evening. "Here, gentlemen, look."

In confirmation of her words the Englishwoman lifted her foot in its lace-up boot high in the air, but nobody looked—they had all dashed to drag Naina Georgievna away from Sister Pelagia.

Enraptured, the young woman was shouting and shaking the nun by the collar.

"You sniffed and spied me out, you little black mouse. Yes, it was me, I did it! But why is nobody else's concern!"

The spectacles fell to the floor, fabric tore, and when they finally managed to detach Naina Georgievna, there was a serious scratch oozing blood on the nun's cheek.

That was when the howling of Sodom and Gomorrah that Pelagia had foreseen began.

Pyotr Georgievich laughed uncertainly. "No, Naina, no. Why are you talking such nonsense about yourself? Are you just trying to appear interesting again?"

But Shiryaev's voice was louder. Stepan Trofimovich cried out in torment: "Naina, but what for? Why, it's appalling! It's base!"

"Appalling? Base? There are limits beyond which neither fear nor baseness exist!"

Her eyes glinted with a frenzy in which there was not a trace of guilt, repentance, or even shame—only ecstasy and a strange triumph. One might even say that something majestic was revealed in Naina Georgievna's character at that moment.

"Bravo! I recognize that. *Macbeth,* act two and scene two, I think," said Arkadii Sergeevich, pretending to clap his hands. "The same and Lady Macbeth:

> My hands are of your color: but I shame
> To wear a heart so white.

"The audience is ecstatic, the entire stage is strewn with bouquets. Bravo!"

"You pitiful jester and talentless dauber," the dangerous young lady hissed. "They threw you out of art, and that little wooden box of yours won't save you for long. Soon anyone who feels like it will be a photographer, and the only path left for you to follow will be playing living tableaux at the fairground!"

Pyotr Georgievich took hold of his sister's hands.

"Naina, Naina, stop it! You are not yourself, I will call the doctor."

The next moment a furious shove almost sent him tumbling head over heels and the wrath of the enraged fury was unleashed on her brother: "Petenka, my darling brother! Your Excellency! What are you frowning at? Ah, you don't like being called 'Excellency'! You're our little democrat, you're too good for titles. That's because you're ashamed of your family name, my fine little cockerel. Prince Telianov has a dubious ring to it. What sort of princes are these, that no one has ever heard of? If it were Obolensky or Volkonsky, you wouldn't be so squeamish about your 'Excellency.' Get married, go on, marry Tanyusha. She'll be just the right sort of princess for you. Only what are you going to do with her, eh, Petya? Read clever books? That's not enough for a woman, it's nowhere near enough. But you're not capable of anything else. Thirty years old, and still a boy. She'll run away from you to some other fine young man."

"What on earth is going on here!" the marshal exclaimed in outrage. "Such indecent talk in the presence of the bishop, in the presence of all of us! Why, she's having hysterics, a perfectly obvious fit of hysterics."

Stepan Trofimovich pulled the violator of the proprieties toward the doors.

"Come on, Naina. You and I need to have a talk."

She burst into spiteful laughter: "Oh yes, of course, we absolutely must have a talk and wash ourselves clean with our pure tears. How sick I am of all of you and your heart-to-heart talks! Boo-hoo-hoo, goo-goo-goo," she mocked, "our duty to mankind, the fusion of souls, in a hundred years the world will be transformed into a garden. You can't just simply put your arms around a girl and kiss her. You idiot! You couldn't see what was there for the taking."

Sytnikov had already opened his mouth to say something, except that after the retribution meted out to his precursors, he thought it wiser to hold his peace. But his turn still came.

"And you, Donat Abramovich, why are you looking at me so reproachfully? Do you disapprove? Or do you feel sorry for the little dogs? Is it true when they say that you killed your gross wife with poisonous mushrooms? To leave the vacancy open for a new wife? Not for me, was it? Of course, I was still running around in short skirts at the time, but then you're such a thorough man, you plan so far ahead!"

Naina Georgievna began gasping for breath, choking on short, muffled sobs, and suddenly dashed toward the door. She stopped in the doorway and looked around the hall, her glance lingering for an instant on Bubentsov, who was standing there with a wide smile on his face, clearly savoring the scandal, and said: "I'm moving out. I shall live in the town. Think what you will of me, that does not concern me in the least. But as for all of you, including the sneaky little nun and the most gracious Mitrofanii, I curse and ana-them-at-ize you."

And with this final bad joke, she ran out, slamming the door loudly in farewell.

"In olden times they would have said the devil had got into the girl," Mitrofanii concluded sadly.

The insulted Sytnikov muttered: "In our merchant community they would have whipped her with birch rods and the devil would have left her in a moment."

"Oh, how can we tell granny?" said Pyotr Georgievich, taking his head in his hands.

Bubentsov started: "Aunty must not be told! It would kill her. Later, not just now. Let her recover a little."

The marshal was concerned by something else.

"But why this strange hatred for dogs? Probably this is really some kind of insanity. Is there such a psychological illness as cynophobia?"

"This is not insanity," said Pelagia, inspecting her handkerchief to see if the scratch on her cheek had stopped bleeding. At least her spectacles had not been broken. "There's a mystery here that still needs to be unraveled."

"And is there anything to go on?" asked the bishop.

"If we look, something will turn up. The thing that bothers me—"

Shiryaev did not let the nun finish what she was saying.

"Why am I standing here rooted to the spot like this!" He shook his head as if he were driving away some hallucination. "Stop her! She will lay hands on herself! She's delirious!"

He ran out into the corridor. Pyotr Georgievich dashed after him. Arkadii Sergeevich hesitated for a moment, shrugged, and followed them.

"All still chasing after her," declared Sytnikov.

ALTHOUGH THE MOON was already waning, it was still pleasantly round and shone as bright as a crystal chandelier, and like little lampions the stars did their best to light up the blue ceiling of the sky so that the night was not much darker than the day.

His Grace and Pelagia walked along the main alley of the park and behind them the horses drowsily set one hoof in front of another and jangled their harness as they pulled along the carriage, which seemed almost to merge into the trees and the bushes.

"Ooh, that vulture," said Mitrofanii. "Did you see the way he sent for Korsh? He won't back down now until he gets what he's after. That disturbed girl has made his job easier for him—that's one heir less. Pelagia, here is what I would like you to do. Prepare Marya Afanasievna so that the news won't distress her so badly again. It is not easy to discover something like that about your own granddaughter. And stay here for a little while longer, be near my aunt."

"She won't be distressed. It seems to me, father, that Marya Afanasievna is far less interested in people than in dogs. Of course, I shall sit with her and console her as best I can, but for the sake of the investigation it would be best for me to come back to town."

"What investigation do you mean?" His Grace asked, surprised. "The investigation is concluded. And you wanted to find out why this Naina killed the dogs."

"That's what's on my mind. There is something unusual here, Your Grace, something that makes my skin crawl. What you just said about the devil getting into her was very much to the point."

"That's just superstition," said Mitrofanii, even more surprised. "Surely you do not believe in satanic possession? I was speaking metaphorically; it was a figure of speech. There is no devil, but there is evil, formless and ubiquitous, and that is what seduces the soul."

Pelagia's spectacles glinted as she looked up at the bishop.

"But the devil does exist! Who was that grinning at the sight of human vileness all evening?"

"You mean Bubentsov?"

"And who else? He is the very devil incarnate. Spiteful, venomous, and fascinating. I am sure he is the key to all this, father. Did you see the looks that Naina Georgievna was giving him? As if she was expecting him to praise her. It was for his benefit that she played out her drama with all that wailing and gnashing of teeth. The rest of us are nothing to her, a mere theatrical backdrop."

The bishop said nothing, because he had not noticed any such special looks, but he had more faith in Pelagia's powers of observation than in his own.

They came out of the gates of the park into open space. Here the alleyway became a road that stretched out across the countryside to the Astrakhan highway. The bishop halted to allow the carriage to reach them.

"But why do you need to come to town? Naina will not stay there for long, surely she will go away. As soon as the news of her antics gets out, nobody will want to have anything to do with her. And she has nowhere to live there. She is bound to go away, to Moscow or St. Petersburg, if she doesn't leave the country entirely."

"Not for anything. Wherever Bubentsov is, that is where she will be," the nun declared confidently. "And I need to be close by as well. As for the public condemnation, in her present bitter mood Naina Georgievna will only savor it. And she does have a place to live. I heard from the maid that Naina Georgievna has a house of her own in Zavolzhsk, she inherited it from some female relative. Not a large house, but in a lovely setting, with an orchard."

"So you believe that Bubentsov is involved in all this?" the bishop asked, setting his foot on the step, but still in no haste to get into the carriage. "That would be most opportune. If he were caught out in some villainy, then the synod would have less faith in him. Otherwise I'm afraid I shall be no match for his zeal. In all probability the worst ordeals are yet to come. Return to the see tomorrow, then, and the two of us will put our heads together and think out our problems. I can see that we shall be requiring Miss Lisitsyna's services in this matter."

These mysterious words had a strange effect on the nun, who seemed at once delighted and dismayed.

"It's a sin, father. And we vowed not to—"

"Never mind, this is important business, far more important than the previous cases." The bishop sighed as he took his seat in the carriage opposite the father subdeacon. "It is my decision and my responsibility before God and man. Well, then, my blessings, my daughter. Farewell."

And the carriage moved off, picking up speed and darting away almost soundlessly along the dust-covered road, while Sister Pelagia turned back into the park.

She walked along the alley with the sky bright above her, but the trees on both sides fused into dark, solid walls, so that the nun seemed to be moving along the bottom of a strange, luminous ravine.

Lying ahead of her in the middle of her path she saw a white square of some kind, with another little black square at its center. When she and the bishop had walked by here only five or ten minutes earlier there had not been anything of the kind in the alley.

Pelagia quickened her stride in order to reach this curious phenomenon and examine it more closely. When she reached it, she squatted down.

Strange: It was a large white handkerchief with a book in a black leather binding lying on it. She picked it up—it was a prayerbook. A perfectly ordinary prayerbook, the kind that could be found anywhere. What strange goings-on were these?

Pelagia was about to check whether there was anything between the pages when suddenly she heard a rustling sound behind her. Before she had a chance to turn around someone had thrown a sack over her head, scraping her cheeks. Not understanding what was happening, the nun tried to cry out, but her cry was choked off in a hoarse whisper as a loop of rope was drawn tight around the sack. And then a dark, feral terror rose up inside her. Pelagia began struggling, scrabbling with her fingers at the sackcloth and the coarse rope. But strong hands seized her and would not let her break free or loosen the stranglehold. Someone was panting behind her, breathing noisily into her right ear, but she could not even catch her breath.

She tried striking backward with her fist, but it was too awkward—there was no way to get a good swing going. She kicked out with her foot and hit something, but probably not hard enough to hurt—her habit cushioned the blow.

Feeling the ringing in her ears grow louder and the call of the deep, comforting black millpond grow stronger, the nun tore her knitting out of her waist bag, took a firm grasp of the needles, and jabbed them hard into something soft—and then again.

"U-u-ugh!"

A hollow, snarling grunt, and the grip slackened. Pelagia swung the needles again, but this time into emptiness.

There was no longer anyone holding her, no elbow pressing against her throat. She slumped down to her knees, tore off the cursed noose, pulled the sack off her head, and began gasping hoarsely at the air with her mouth, muttering: "Most . . . Ho . . . ly . . . Mo . . . ther . . . of . . . God . . . preserve me . . . from my enemies . . . visible . . . and invisible . . ."

As soon as the darkness cleared from her eyes a little, she gazed around keenly in all directions.

Nobody. But the points of her knitting needles were dark with blood.

# PART TWO

# And Beware of Evildoers

# CHAPTER 6

# A Soirée

AND NOW WE shall omit a period of something rather more than a month and move directly to the denouement of our tangled tale, or rather, to the commencement of this denouement, which coincides with a party for select guests that took place at the home of Olympiada Savelievna Shestago. The postmaster's wife herself preferred, in homage to contemporary art, to honor this festive occasion with the grand title of "soirée," and so let it remain, especially since *this* soirée will not soon be forgotten in Zavolzhsk.

As for the month omitted by our narrative, one could not say that nothing at all had happened during its course—on the contrary, things had happened, a great many things, but these events had no direct connection to the main line of our narrative and we shall therefore skip through them briefly, "with a light step," as the ancients used to say.

The modest name of our province thundered resoundingly throughout the length and breadth of Russia, even echoing beyond its borders. The newspapers of Petersburg and Moscow took to writing about us almost every day, separating into two camps, with the supporters of the first asserting that the Zavolzhsk region was the location of a new Battle of Kulikovo Field, a holy war for Russia, our faith, and the church of Christ, while their opponents, in contrast, characterized the events that were taking place as medieval obscurantism and a new Inquisition. Even the London *Times* wrote about us, although not, we admit, on the front page or even the second, saying that in a certain remote corner of the Russian Empire by the name of Zavolger (sic!) instances of human sacrifice had been uncovered, resulting in a tsarist commissioner's being despatched to the area from St. Petersburg and the entire province being placed under his emergency administration.

Well, as far the emergency administration was concerned—that was something of an exaggeration on the part of the English, but events did nonetheless come thick and fast enough to make your head spin. Vladimir Lvovich Bubentsov, having been vouchsafed the complete support of the higher echelons, proceeded with his investigation into the case of the heads (or, rather, of their absence) with truly Napoleonic panache. A special commission was set up to deal with the case under Bubentsov's chairmanship, with a membership consisting of special investigators sent from St. Petersburg, and also a few local investigators and police officials—each of whom was selected by Vladimir Lvovich himself. The commission was not subordinated to either the governor or the district procurator and it did not have to report to them about its activities.

Fortunately, no more bodies were discovered, but the police carried out several arrests among the Zyts and one of the prisoners had supposedly admitted that in the dark forests beyond the remote Volochaisk swamps there was a certain clearing in which on Friday nights fires were lit to Shishiga and sacks containing offerings were brought, but as for what was in the sacks, only the elders knew.

The gallant Vladimir Lvovich equipped an expedition and led it himself. He prowled through the swamps and thickets for a number of days and finally discovered a certain clearing that appeared suspicious because, although there was not actually any stone idol, there were the remains of campfires and animal bones. He arrested the headman of the nearby Zyt village, as well as another old man who, according to information in Bubentsov's possession, was a shaman. They put the prisoners in a cart and set out with them through the wet bog, but on an island in the middle of it the convoy was attacked with clubs and knives by the men of the Zyt village, who were attempting to free their elders. The police guards (there were two of them attached to Bubentsov) took to their heels and Spasyonny was so frightened that he jumped into the swamp and almost drowned, but the inspector himself proved to be made of sterner stuff: He shot one of the attackers dead, the Circassian hacked another two to death with his terrible dagger, and the other rebels fled in all directions.

Vladimir Lvovich later returned to the village with a military detachment, but the houses were all empty—the Zyts had upped and moved away deeper into the forest. Bubentsov's heroism was written about in all the newspapers, even the illustrated ones, where he was depicted as a fine, upstanding young man with a dashing mustache and an aquiline nose. The hero's courage earned him an Order of Saint Anne from the emperor and also praise from Konstantin Petrovich—a fact to which the well-informed accorded greater significance than the decoration from the sovereign.

The entire province seemed suddenly to have nearly lost its mind. The forest Zyts had never been known to commit any audacities of this sort. Even during Pugachev's time they had not rebelled, but served Mikhelson as guides, so what on earth could have got into them now?

Some said that it was Bubentsov who had driven them to it by the disgraceful way in which he shackled their venerable elders and tossed them into a dirty cart, but there were many, very many, who thought differently: The perspicacious inspector had been proved right— something sinister had begun to stir in the depths of those still waters.

The province of Zavolzhie was uneasy. No one traveled the forest roads alone any longer, only in groups—and this in our quiet province, where nobody had even given a thought to such precautions in recent years!

Vladimir Lvovich rode about with an armed guard, paid visits to the various districts as and when he chose, demanding explanations from town governors and military commanders and district police officers, and they all submitted to his authority.

Thus dual power was established in these parts. And after all, what was so surprising about that? In the eyes of the church authorities the bishop had been discredited by all these pagan outrages, and many respectable folk who liked to trim their sails to the wind took up the habit of calling to pay their respects not at the episcopal see, but at the Grand Duke, where Bubentsov lived. The administrative authorities became less conscientious than formerly. The chief of police, Lagrange, for instance, did not actually stop taking orders from the governor completely, but he went running to the synodical inspector for approval of every instruction he received from Anton Antonovich, even the most petty, such as the introduction of numbers for horse cabs. Felix Stanislavovich told everyone that the baron was simply serving out his final days as governor, and in the company of his friends and subordinates he even expressed the expectation that the person appointed as the next governor of Zavolzhsk would be none other than himself, Colonel Lagrange.

In the course of this month the entire edifice of our province's life had been twisted awry, although it had appeared to be soundly and intelligently constructed, not having been built from the roof down, as in the other Russian provinces, but from the foundation up. Perhaps, though, this image is overly abstruse and requires some clarification.

Some twenty years or so ago, ours was a province like any other: poverty, drunkenness, ignorance, arbitrary rule, brigands on the roads. In a word, we had the ordinary Russian life, more or less the same as in every part of the vast empire. In Zavolzhie it was perhaps somewhat smoother and calmer than in other regions, where people are led astray by the prospect of easy money. In these parts everything was sedate and patriarchal, life following a set of rules that been established once and for all.

Let us say a merchant wanted to float his goods down the River or transport them through the forest. The first thing he did was go to the right man (he already knew who that was, every district and every *volost* had its own), pay his respects, and offer him a tenth of everything, and then he carried blithely on about his business, nobody would touch him or bother him—neither evildoers, nor the police, nor excise agents. But if you didn't pay your respects and placed your trust in reliable guards or simply trusted to luck in the slapdash Russian fashion, you only had yourself to blame if anything happened. You might get through the forest or you might not. And on the River, too, anything could happen, especially at nighttime, somewhere on the rapids.

If someone wanted to open a shop or a tavern in the town, it was the same thing. Have a word with the right man, show him some respect, promise him a tenth, and may God grant you every possible success. The public health inspector would not bother you because there were flies on the counter, or rats in the basement, and the tax inspector would be satisfied with a small bribe.

Everybody knew about the right man—the district police officer, the procurator, and the bailiff—but nobody hindered him in going about his business, because the right man was everybody's friend; he might even be your relative or your godfather.

There were times when honest senior officials were appointed from the capital, or they might even send someone who was not just honest but also took a determined and workmanlike approach, who firmly intended to unmask everyone and immediately establish the rule of justice and order—even that kind of eagle soon found his wings clipped in Zavolzhie. If possible it was done through kindness, by means of presents or favors of other kinds, or, if he was absolutely incorruptible, then by means of calumny and slander. Fortunately there would be no shortage of witnesses; the right man only had to whistle and they would slander anyone at all.

But thirty years or so ago a new chief of police arrived in our town, before the late Gulko. He was a real terror, absolutely inflexible. He raked the entire police force over the coals: Some he sacked, some he sent to trial, and the rest he reduced to a state of constant trepidation. The unrest that this stirred up disrupted certain long-established, tried-and-true relations between serious people. And in the meantime this Robespierre was recklessly edging closer to the right people. That was when his outrageous activities were terminated. One day he went duck-hunting with his own colleagues, and all of a sudden the boat overturned. Everybody else managed to swim to safety; only the chief was unlucky. He had been creating uproar in these parts for only six months or so. And that was the chief of police, an important man! But if it was some ordinary district police officer or investigator who proved stubborn, he was dealt with far more simply, bludgeoned over the head or shot from the bushes in the night, and that was the end of the matter. It was put down to the bandits who roamed our forests in such abundance. For the sake of appearances the police would search for a while and then close the case because it was impossible to solve. But what point is there in telling you all this? It is a sheer waste of time. Every province has a plentiful store of such stories.

And then Mitrofanii was appointed from St. Petersburg to be our bishop, for the second and final time. That was very nearly twenty years ago. He already knew the local ways and customs, and so he didn't go running at things pell-mell. He began with his own quiet area of jurisdiction: He took the priests in hand, so that they would not practice extortion; he introduced a strict regimen in the monasteries. He removed some of the rural deans and pricked the consciences of others, and he also brought with him from the capital clergy and monks who were young graduates of the ecclesiastical academy.

In the churches and parishes, things also changed. The priests and deacons were sober, they led the services in a dignified manner, their sermons were moral and comprehensible, they did not accept any offerings over and above what was prescribed. But, of course, all this was not achieved immediately. Rather, it took two or three years. And at first no one was alarmed by this quite unprecedented novelty, neither the right people nor the light-fingered high officials. If the priests no longer wished to eat well and sleep soft, that was their business. They had started talking a lot about honesty and the love of virtue from the pulpits, but that was what they were supposed to do. And anyway, who was going to take what the longhairs said seriously? But meanwhile the authority of men of the church increased gradually and imperceptibly, and the churches were far more crowded than they had been.

And at this point, through Mitrofanii's still-reliable connections in the capital, the old governor, with whom the bishop had fallen out seriously more than once, was retired. The new one sent to replace him was Anton Antonovich von Haggenau, who was barely thirty years old at the time. He was energetic, indefatigable, European, and quite ferociously devoted to justice.

The baron struggled for a while with the local mores, butting his head against this stone wall and breaking his horns, and in his despair he began seeking refuge in administrative severity, which, as everyone knows, only aggravates all manner of misfortune. But, thank God, he proved to be a sensible man, even though he was a German—he had the wits to turn to His Grace for advice and guidance. What sort of miracle was this, he asked? How did Mitrofanii manage his spiritual domain so that everything in it was decorous and sedate, not like the other provincial bishops?

His Grace replied that it was very simple: What was needed was less management, and then things would manage themselves. One needed only to lay a firm foundation and everything else would follow of its own accord.

How would it follow, the young Anton Antonovich protested passionately, if the local folk were such worthless villains?

People are different, there are good ones and bad ones, His Grace taught him, but for the most part they are neither one thing nor the other, like frogs that take on the temperature of the air around them. If it was warm, they were warm. If it was cold, they were cold. What was needed was to act so as to make the climate in our province warmer, then the people would become warmer and better. That was the authorities' only responsibility—to create the correct climate— and as for the rest, the Lord would concern Himself with that, and people would do the right thing.

"But just how is it kept warm, this climate of yours?" the governor asked, struggling to understand.

"One has to cultivate and foster the dignity in people. So that people will respect themselves and other people. A man who understands dignity will not steal, act meanly, or live by deceit—that will seem dishonorable to him."

This almost made the baron feel disillusioned in the bishop and dismiss him as a hopeless case.

"Ah, but you are an idealist, Your Grace. We are in Russia, not Switzerland. How long is it since peasants were sold here by the head, like cattle? Where are you going to find dignity here? It takes centuries for such a tender plant to grow."

Mitrofanii, who was younger at the time and therefore had a weakness for verbal theatrics, replied with a curt, didactic phrase, in the manner of the ancients.

"Legality, satiety, education. And nothing more, my good sir" (at that time he would still occasionally employ such apostrophes for rhetoric purposes).

"Ah, Your Grace, look how hard I struggle in the cause of legality, and what comes of it! No one, high or low, wishes to live according to the law."

"And they will not want to. People only follow those laws that are rational and beneficial to the majority. A wise legislator is like an experienced gardener in a public park. When he has sown the lawns, he does not lay the paths immediately; he waits first to see which route people find it most convenient to follow—and that is the one he paves. So that afterward people will not trample their own paths through the grass."

"Those are the wise laws," said Anton Antonovich, lowering his voice in order to speak sedition. "But here in Russia we have all sorts of laws. You and I do not invent them; there are higher authorities for that. But I am the one charged with ensuring the observance of these laws."

The bishop smiled.

"There is the law of God and the law of man. And only those human laws should be observed that do not contradict the laws of God."

The governor only shrugged.

"I beg your pardon, but that I cannot understand. As you know, I am German. For me the law is the law."

"That is why I am appointed to guide you," Mitrofanii told the uncomprehending governor amiably. "You ask me, my dear sir, which law is from God and which from the devil. I will explain."

And he did explain, only this explanation took not just an hour, or even two, but a great deal longer, and in time long conversations with His Grace became something of a habit for the young official. . . .

## THE CONVERSATIONS
## OF HIS GRACE MITROFANII

### A brief interpolation

For those who are following our tale only in order to discover how it concludes, and who have no interest in the history of our region, it is permissible to omit this brief section completely. No damage will be caused to the elegant line of the narrative as a result. Here we adduce no more than brief excerpts from some of the intellectual dialogues between the bishop and the governor (only three, in fact, although there were many more than that), for these conversations had the most decisive consequences for Zavolzhie. At the same time, in the commentaries that follow each of the conversations, we shall indicate in brief which of these idealistic teachings were put into effect, and which were not.

### On the pecuniary greed of officials

"Do you agree, my son, that no ruler, no matter how well-intentioned, can implement his beneficial ideas unless he possesses a sound and reliable set of tools in the form of capable and honest assistants, those self-same tools that in your bureaucratic dialect are referred to as 'personnel'?"

"I entirely agree."

"And what is to be done if this personnel is mired in base greed?"

"I do not know, father, that is why I have come to you. But the main problem is that all the officials are like that and there is nowhere to get any others from."

"What do you mean, nowhere? In part you can invite high-minded individuals from St. Petersburg, and they will come, because they wish to apply their knowledge and convictions in practice. And honest officials can be found here; it is simply that at present they have no chance of advancement."

"How am I to identify these honest men if they are not in open view?"

"I have been here for several years now, I know which men are worth something, and I will name them. But that is only a quarter of the job, because any man is corrupted by power if the wrong practices are established. And for the most part bureaucrats take to extorting money from people, not out of their own innate viciousness, but because that is the established practice, and if anyone does not extort, then he is regarded with suspicion by his superiors and his subordinates."

"But how can the correct practices be established so that extortion becomes unfashionable?"

"Are you familiar, my son, with the saying according to which a fish rots from the head? This actually is the case, and medicine also affirms that all illnesses start in the head. To which I can add that in the reverse case the recovery of a sick person starts in the head. Before anyone can start to get better, he must wish to recover and believe in his own recovery."

"But where should I begin? The most important thing here is to make a good beginning!"

"Choose yourself honest and efficient people to be your closest aides: the vice-governor, the manager of state property, the heads of the excise and provincial administrations, and also the chairmen of the chambers of justice, supervision, and the treasury. And, of course, the top people in the police, that is absolutely essential. For a start, that will be enough. We have already talked about where to find the people; we can find a dozen or so who will suit from around the province and across Russia. And the very first thing to do is to conclude a covenant among yourselves: We are not harnessing ourselves to this carriage in order to enrich ourselves, but in order to get things done. And if anyone feels that he has a weak spot, let him leave, or at least not take offense if he is asked to leave. Let every one of your close colleagues make a public declaration of his property and henceforth not conceal his income or his expenditures from anyone. In general, Anton Antonovich, I hold fast to the hope that Russia's salvation will not come from its capital cities, but from its provinces. This also follows from common sense. It is easier to establish order in a single room than in an entire house, easier in one house than in an entire street, easier in one street than in an entire town, and easier in one town than in an entire country."

"All right, then, let us assume that the head is honest, but lower down, what about lower down? I shall be delivering beautiful flowery speeches to my circle of friends, and we shall start admiring one another because we are so proud and incorruptible, and all through the province the bribe-takers will continue to run amok, just as they always have done. You cannot catch everyone in the act and hand them over for trial."

"You don't need to catch the thieves; you need to act so that the thieves do not appear in the first place."

"That's easy to say!"

"And not so difficult to do. Let your closest assistants, each of whom is responsible for an important area of activity, select his own deputies according to the same method—those who agree to accept the covenant. Here it is possible to leave some of the present officials in place, even if they have taken bribes, only not out of cupidity or malice, but because that has been the custom since olden times. And as for the most rabid extortioners and reprobates—whom I know, and you also know—of course, they should be handed over to the court and judged with all severity, that is absolutely essential."

"Very well, let us assume that my deputies do not steal and neither do their deputies, then what?"

"Then this. It is called psychology, Anton Antonovich. The man at the top has nothing but his salary; he does not take bribes because he is afraid or feels ashamed. But his subordinate rides around in a carriage and four and his wife orders fine outfits from Paris. Will any normal man stand for that? Never. And his wife will not allow him to, because she has no outfits from Paris, while the wife of his subordinate Ivan Ivanovich does. And the boss will apply pressure to Ivan Ivanovich and tell him: You either live like I do, brother, or get out of the job. Ivan Ivanovich, if he stays on in the job after that, will start looking daggers at his bribe-taking subordinate Pyotr Petrovich, although formerly he connived with him and protected him. Why should Pyotr Petrovich have what he does not? And so on all the way down from the top to the very bottom of the pyramid. You will be amazed at how quickly our official will develop the habit of austerity and learn to love righteousness."

*Commentary.* That, of course, was not the way things turned out, although Anton Antonovich invested a lot of time and effort in the construction of this ideal pyramid. Well, people are only people. Although Christ told us to love all alike, that is something of which only the holy hermits are capable, but ordinary mortals have friends and relatives—and one good turn always deserves another. There has never been an entirely just and impartial bureaucracy, and one did not take root in Zavolzhie, either. In these parts, too, people "look after their own" and oppress their enemies when they get the chance, and scratch the back of the person who has scratched theirs.

But at the same time it could not be said that His Grace's theory proved a total failure. The national tradition, universal and even hallowed in Russia, of the "sealed envelope" fell into total desuetude here, although it was replaced in part by Gogol's notorious "borzoi pups," which are less easily detectable and yet still, let us agree, represent undoubted progress by comparison with the taking of direct bribes. Such direct bribes, and even more so extortion, came to be considered shameful by the Zavolzhie bureaucracy, which is to say that the "incorrect practices" of which the bishop spoke were changed after all. So that, although the kingdom of justice was not established and total equality of all before the law was also not achieved, shameless abuses, while not disappearing totally, were certainly greatly reduced. And until very recently our police also had the reputation of being honest, and the courts, too, and even the excise department, which is something that might have seemed quite impossible anywhere at all. But the matter of taxes forms the subject of the next conversation.

### On obedience to the law

"Your Grace, I have thought a great deal about our previous conversation, and I cannot help but feel concerned about the following. You say that a fish rots from the head and that healing should also start from the head. That sounds reasonable, but in my opinion, the social order is less reminiscent of a fish than of a building of some kind."

"Truly that is so."

"But if that is so, will a house turn out well if it is built from the crown downward?"

"It will turn out badly, my son, and I am very glad that you have reached this conclusion yourself, without any prompting from me. With nothing but personnel, no matter how wonderful they might be, you can never make the crooked straight. The majority have to want the same thing that you want, and then your efforts and those of your aides will not encounter resistance, but support."

"But what each man wants differs, and each man's advantage is different. Many people, very many, find it more convenient and less trouble to carry on living as they do now—obeying the right people instead of the legal authorities. That makes things simpler and cheaper for both the merchants and the tradesmen, and for the factory owners, and for the general population. How can you change all of their minds? They will never listen."

"One need not try to change their minds. Here in Russia no one has any faith in words, especially if they come from the top. The foundation of a sound social order, my son, consists in voluntary observance of the law."

"Oh, Your Grace! What are you talking about? What voluntary observance of the law can there possibly be in Russia?"

"Why, the same as there is in this Switzerland that is so dear to your heart!"

"Please, father, do not be angry, only I would prefer us not to talk about ideal schemes, but about steps that can have practical consequences."

"That is the subject of my exposition. Voluntary observance of a law is not a consequence of the advanced social consciousness of the average citizen, it is merely a sign of the fact that it is in people's interest to keep this law rather than to break it. And if you think about it for a moment, you will see that in Russia it is by no means all the laws that are broken, but only certain of them. Is that not the case?"

"I suppose it is. Before the abolition of the state monopoly trade in vodka, many people distilled homebrew and sold it secretly, but now there is none of that. However, one area in which nine out of ten Russians are crooked is the payment of taxes and duties. You cannot argue about that, father."

"Of course I cannot, my son, but I can tell you that you have unerringly defined the very source of this sickness known as lawlessness. Murderers are isolated individuals, and there are not many thieves, either, but no one wishes to pay all of the countless levies, duties, and taxes, many of which are both absurd and exorbitant. This is what causes all the harm:

the bribery and corruption, the impoverishment of the treasury, and the appearance of these so-called right people against whom neither you nor your predecessors have ever been able to bring effective justice to bear. And the very worst harm of all is caused by the fact that, as you so rightly remarked, nine people out of ten feel themselves to be lawbreakers. This signifies that they feel the law is not there to protect them but to frighten them, and they themselves are not respectable members of society but petty thieves who can be called to account at any moment by the courts and the police. This is where the right people draw their support: They know precisely how much everyone has failed to pay the treasury. They charge less for their knowledge than the state takes, and they protect the transgressors from the servants of the law. And so it comes about that our society consists entirely of petty thieves who are governed by bandits. Is a man going to have any respect for himself when he knows that he is a thief and giver of bribes? No, Anton Antonovich, he is not, neither for himself nor for the laws."

"But there is nothing one can do about this!"

"I hear despair in your voice, but it is entirely unfounded. What needs to be done is the following: For every taxpayer, no matter who he is, establish a single tax, not too great, which is known in advance and collectable immediately from all payments, deliveries, transactions, and income. And this tribute must not exceed one tenth part, because the holy church has tested this since ancient times and learned from its own rich experience that a man will agree to pay a tenth part of his wealth, but no more, not even out of fear of our Father in Heaven. And this means that there is no point in tempting him. Let him pay you his tenth part. If a man is poor and barely has ten rubles a month, take a ruble from him, and if someone earns a million, take a hundred thousand from him, but such a man should be given special thanks and respect, because the state is founded on his enterprising spirit and thrift."

"All this is very fine, but it is not the governor who sets the taxes and duties. You know perfectly well, Your Grace, that the rates at which all kinds of duties are levied are determined in St. Petersburg, and I am powerless to change them. For that they will throw me out of my job and take me to court."

"They will not take you to court. Because you will go to St. Petersburg and conclude an agreement with the government. Never once has it happened that the province of Zavolzhie paid all its prescribed taxes to the treasury in full, because the people here avoid paying and try not to pay anything at all. Nothing but shortfalls in these parts, just as in most of the other provinces. But you will guarantee them that you will return the prescribed sum on time, only you will collect it in your own way, and explain to them exactly how, so that they don't see you as a tax farmer. And I for my part will vouch for you and explain to those who need to know exactly what your idea consists of. They will agree, because it is in the treasury's direct interest. They will want to try it in one insignificant province that is always in arrears, to see what might come of this experiment. Note also, my son, that as a result of this experiment you rid yourself at a stroke of the right people and most of the bribe-takers. Nobody will pay them any money, because it will be more profitable and safer to pay the state its due, and then demand protection by the law. Our Zavolzhie bandits will be left without any support from below, and your police will press them from above, because it will no longer be corrupt, as it used to be, but honest."

*Commentary.* In this case everything came about exactly as described, even exceeding what His Grace had promised. The bandits in the forests and the towns were all quickly caught, because this is not Moscow or Petersburg and what sort of man you are is well known to everyone. Of the right people, some moved to other provinces, some set out for penal servitude, and the cleverest ones kept their heads down and went in for some permitted form of trading or other legal business. The most remarkable thing is that after the establishment of a unified tax, for some reason all sorts of other crimes became much less frequent. Perhaps this was because the Zavolzhians all suddenly started putting on airs and became more grave in their speech, their actions, and even their movements? The number of bureaucrats we have here decreased somewhat, because many of those who collected, verified, and supervised became unnecessary, and an entire multitude of merchants and industrialists moved in from other provinces—they thought they saw an advantage in living in Zavolzhie and conducting their business here. Money appeared in the provincial treasury, so that in recent years a lot of new houses have been built, as well as hospitals and schools and roads, and we have even begun thinking about our own theater.

People have come from the capital cities and other regions to view our wonders and attempts have been made to introduce the same arrangements in other provinces, but somehow it has not worked out for them.

## On dignity

"But tell me, my son, in your opinion, what is the difference between pauperage and poverty?"

"Pauperage and poverty? Well, a poor man, as distinct from a complete pauper, has at least some sort of dwelling and food and he does not dress in rags, but respectably. Poverty can be noble, but pauperage is repulsive."

"Or, as the author of a certain novel that has been too highly praised expresses it, pauperage is already a vice, for which they drive you out of society with a stick."

"Pardon me, Your Grace, but do you really judge *Crime and Punishment* so harshly?"

"We will talk about literature, Anton Antonovich, another time, but at present I am addressing a different theme. To wit, that a hungry, homeless man with no clothes cannot be noble in his behavior, or elegant. And although in the Holy Writ we read a lot about holy fools and prophets who went around in rags and took no care at all for their sustenance and decent appearance, it is a fatal error for ordinary people to take their example from these holy saints, for it is frightening and unnatural to imagine a society composed entirely of individuals who mortify the flesh, are hung around with heavy chains, and proclaim prophecies. That is not what the Lord wishes from his children; he wishes them to conduct themselves with dignity."

"I am entirely in agreement with that, although it is somehow not an entirely Russian point of view, but I would still like to take Mr. Dostoevsky's part. What did you not like in the novel *Crime and Punishment?*"

"Ah, you and your Mr. Dostoevsky. Very well, so be it. I believe the author made his own task too easy when he had the proud Raskolnikov kill not only the repulsive old moneylender, but her meek, innocent sister as well. Mr. Dostoevsky took fright at the thought that his reader would not condemn the criminal for the moneylender alone. As if to say that a creature like that does not deserve any pity. But the Lord has no such creatures; all are equally dear to him. If the writer had managed to express how absolutely undignified murder is with just the old moneylender, that would be a different matter."

"Surely you meant to say impermissible?"

"Undignified. To pick up an axe or some other object and smash another person's skull is above all an act unworthy of being called human. After all, what is sin? It is an action through which a person betrays his dignity. Yes, yes, Anton Antonovich, I come back again to this theme, for the hundredth time, because the longer I live on this earth, the more convinced I become that a sense of dignity is the cornerstone of a just society and the very destiny of the human being. I have told you that dignity has three foundation stones, which are called legality, satiety, and education. Enough has already been said about observance of the law; you yourself have spoken most eloquently to me concerning the benefits of rational, God-inspired education, and I have nothing more to add. But these inspiring matters must not lead us to forget the most fundamental thing of all—the human belly, the word for which in our language also, most appropriately, means 'life.' If the belly is empty, that is already pauperage, and a pauper is like an animal, for he thinks only of how he can fill this belly, and he has no strength left for any other, higher aspirations."

"But why are you telling me all this, father?"

"Because you are the powers that be, and your primary responsibility is to ensure that every inhabitant of this province has a piece of bread and a roof over his head, since without these basic necessities man cannot have any dignity, and a man without dignity is not a citizen. Not everyone can be rich, and there would be no point in it, but everyone must be fed. Not only for the sake of the destitute, but for everyone else's sake as well, so that they do not have to hide away shamefacedly from the poor as they eat their fine white bread. Those who feast in the midst of wailing and misery will not be dignified."

"That is indeed the case, Your Grace. I have been thinking about this and I have even calculated that it would not require any truly great amount of funds to support the genuinely needy. Can it all really be that easy? Simply feed the hungry and the people will immediately develop *Selbstachtung*\*?"

"No, my son, not immediately, and a full belly is only the beginning. One also needs to eradicate insulting behavior to the individual, which by ancient custom we here in Russia do not regard as important. As you know, in this country abuse is like water off a duck's back, and the simple people regard punches and cuffs to the head from their superiors as fatherly reproofs. And flogging is also common everywhere. What *Selbstachtung* can there be if there is flogging? So let us agree that in our province nobody will ever be whipped for anything again, not even by a decision of the peasant assembly concerning its own people. Let it be forbidden once and for all. And I shall instruct the priests to preach in the churches that parents should not thrash their children, not even the absolutely wild ones who cannot understand a single rational word. Children who are thrashed do not grow up into citizens, but into serfs. It would be good to forbid bad language, too, but of course that is only a dream. I myself am guilty in that area."

"And it would also be marvelous, Your Grace, if everyone started speaking politely to people of lower status and addressing them as 'mister so-and-so.' That is very important for *Selbstachtung*. If the first name and patronymic were used, that would be good, too."

"It might be good, but is it not a little too soon? The peasants will take fright if everyone suddenly starts talking politely to them. They will suspect some sly trickery by their superiors, like the emancipation of the serfs in 1861. No, that will have to wait for a while, until a generation that has never been flogged grows up."

"Ah, father, but just imagine what blessed times they will be when our ordinary people will not be given cranks like me for their governor, but will be able to hold an election of their own free will and choose the most worthy person from among themselves, someone they know and respect! That is when a true paradise will be established in the land of Russia!"

"Only it would be better not to be in too much of a hurry. First, let our ordinary people acquire some dignity and become citizens, and then they

*Self-respect (German)

can have an election. Or else they'll elect some tavern-keeper to be their governor if he rolls a couple of barrels of green wine out into the square for them."

*Commentary.* On the matter of dignity, we do not know what to add, because it is a subtle subject that is not easily reduced to figures, and the amount of time that has passed is not yet very great—the generation of which the bishop spoke, one that has never been whipped, has not yet left the school bench. Of late we have had fewer people lying blind drunk in the gutters. And when they leave their houses and go out, people have begun to dress more respectably. But perhaps that is because poverty has decreased due to the aforementioned development of trade and various industries. We really cannot say . . . although just last year there was an incident in which the policeman Shtukin called the tradesman Selyodkin a "pig." Formerly Selyodkin would have taken such a form of address for a term of endearment, but this time he told the servant of the law: "It's you who's a pig." And the justice of the peace found nothing culpable in that.

Well, perhaps the Zavolzhians really do have more dignity now.

# CHAPTER 7

# A Soirée

(CONTINUED)

. . . AND THE GENERAL consequence of all these conversations was that, little by little, year by year, life in Zavolzhie began to change for the better, so that people in neighboring provinces started to envy us. Perhaps they were the ones who put the jinx on us; in any case, the Evil One must have begun to feel jealous of our prosperity.

The day after Vladimir Lvovich returned to the town like some Roman general in triumph, bringing with him the captured Zyt elders and greeted by massed crowds who had gathered to see this unprecedented sight—two servants of Shishiga in irons and three dead bodies in a cart—Mitrofanii gathered his closest advisers in an extraordinary meeting at the see, which with morose humor he dubbed "the council at Fili," and his introductory address began in a manner appropriate to this comparison.

"Field Marshal Kutuzov could abandon Moscow because he had territory into which he could fall back, but you and I, gentlemen, have nowhere to retreat. A capital city is not so much a local concentration of the life of society as a certain symbol of it, and a symbol may be abandoned temporarily. But you and I live in Zavolzhie; for us it is no abstract symbol, but our only home, and we do not have the right, nor even the opportunity, to allow it to be desecrated by the powers of evil."

"That is undoubtedly so," confirmed the agitated Anton Antonovich.

To which Matvei Bentsionovich Berdichevsky also added: "I cannot imagine myself living anywhere but in Zavolzhie, but if the practices that these inquisitors are introducing should prevail, then I shall not be able to go on living here."

Mitrofanii nodded, as if he had expected no other answer.

"At various times each of us has been invited to serve in a more prominent capacity in the capital, but we did not go. Why? Because we understood that the capital is the kingdom of evil, and anyone who goes there loses himself and places his very soul in danger. But our world here is simple and good, for it is far closer to nature and to God. In our province, if you use your authority for serious work, you can keep your soul alive, but in Petersburg you cannot. The capital is a source of nothing but harm, nothing but violence against the natural life. And it is our duty to defend the region entrusted to our care against this onslaught. The devil is powerful, but his power is not secure, because it is founded not on human virtues but on human vices, that is to say, it is based not on strength but on weakness. Evil usually destroys even itself, crumbling from within. However, we have no right to wait for this to happen, because too much that is good, that we have built up with such great effort, will be destroyed even sooner than the evil. We have to act, and I have gathered you together, gentlemen, in order to draw up a plan."

"Just imagine, Your Grace, I have been thinking about the same thing," said the baron. "And this is what has occurred to me. As you know, my older brother Karl Antonovich holds the position of equerry, and once a month he is invited to a small supper attended by the emperor, where our sovereign converses informally with him and asks him about all manner of business. I shall write Karl a detailed letter and ask for his assistance. He has a wise head and will certainly be able to present the matter in a way that will not leave the emperor indifferent to our plight."

"Unfortunately, my son, Konstantin Petrovich converses with the sovereign far more frequently than once a month," the bishop sighed. "We must assume that His Majesty is biased in favor of Bubentsov and that changing his opinion will not be easy. Alas, our scandal has advantages for far too many important individuals in St. Petersburg. They can use it to flog the whole of Russia."

"But we have to do something," Anton Antonovich said wearily. "I even dream about this synodical spider at night. I am lying there and I cannot move, and he goes on and on winding his sticky web around me. He has me bound in tight from every side . . ."

There was an oppressive, but brief, pause that was broken by Matvei Bentsionovich's declaring, pale-faced: "Gentlemen, I know what must be done. I shall challenge him to a duel, that's what! If he refuses to exchange shots with me, he will be disgraced in the eyes of the whole of society, nobody will ever allow him across their threshold again, and all the ladies of Zavolzhsk, who are presently so eager to dance attention on him, will turn their backs on him. But if he agrees to a duel, then the chief procurator will dismiss him from his post. One way or the other, we win."

The other two members of the council were dumbstruck by this original idea. The baron shook his head.

"But if he does accept, you really will have to exchange shots with him, and he will not forgive you for destroying his career. What will you do when you are standing on the deadline, Matvei Bentsionovich? I saw the way you shoot when we went hunting. You put a hole in my cap instead of in the gray hen. And think of your children."

Berdichevsky turned even whiter, because he had a very vivid imagination and he immediately pictured his wife in mourning, and the children in little black dresses and little black suits, but still he did not renounce his idea: "Never mind—"

"Ah, this is all stupid nonsense," the governor said dismissively. "You won't be able to challenge him; he won't give you any reason to."

At this point Berdichevsky's color suddenly changed from white to crimson and he confessed the shameful incident that had occurred some time before: "I have a reason. He tweaked my nose, and very painfully, too, so that it bled, but I did nothing. I was thinking of the children then as well . . ."

The baron explained matters to this titled gentleman of the personal nobility: "According to the rules of dueling, a challenge must be issued within twenty-four hours after the insult has been given, and not later. So I am afraid, Matvei Bentsionovich, that you are too late."

"Then I shall tweak his nose, too, he will know what for!"

"He might well know, but nobody else will," His Grace remarked. "And they'll take you away to the madhouse as a raving lunatic. No, it won't do. And a duel's not a Christian way of doing things. I will not give my blessing to something like that."

"Then how about this," said Berdichevsky, catching hold of his own nose and twisting it one way and then the other. "We can try a different approach, using a Trojan horse."

"How can we do that?" Anton Antonovich asked in surprise. "Who is going to be the horse?"

"Police Chief Lagrange. He has become Bubentsov's right hand, and Bubentsov entrusts a lot of business to him. But in my capacity as public prosecutor I possess certain information concerning our charming friend Felix Stanislavovich."

Berdichevsky spoke calmly and briskly now, with no trace of any trembling in his voice.

"Two days ago, Lagrange accepted a gift from the Old Believer merchant Pimenov. Seven thousand in bank notes. He extorted it himself by threatening to arrest Pimenov for speaking abusively about the rites of the Orthodox Church."

"What are you saying?" the baron gasped. "Why, that's unheard-of!"

(Anton Antonovich's amazement is quite understandable since, as we have already mentioned, in our province blatant bribe-taking, especially by highly placed officials, had been entirely banished to the realm of legend.)

"Nonetheless, he took it—no doubt in anticipation of changing times. I even have a statement from Pimenov. So far I have not done anything about it. I can have a word with Felix Stanislavovich. He is not a very intelligent man, but he will take my point. He will appear to remain Bubentsov's accomplice, but in secret he will report to me in detail about our dear friend's plotting and scheming."

Mitrofanii started groaning and sighing: "Oh, I don't know . . . I shall pray and ask the Lord whether such trickery is permissible. He does sometimes permit evil to be destroyed by evil means, but, even so, it is not good."

"It is even less good to sit here with our arms folded, doing nothing, but no matter what we suggest, Your Grace, you are not happy with anything," the governor rebuked the bishop.

"You are right, my son. It is better to sin than to turn a blind eye and connive spinelessly with evil. Anton Antonovich, write to your brother, let him have a word with the emperor. At least then the wind will not be blowing into His Majesty's ear from only one direction. And you, Matvei, act as you think best"—the bishop addressed Berdichevsky without ceremony because he had known him since he was a boy. "I do not need to tell you what to do. And, er, one more thing . . ." Mitrofanii cleared his throat. "Anton Antonovich, be sure not to tell your wife about what we are intending."

An expression of profound suffering appeared on the baron's long face.

"But what about you, father?" Berdichevsky put in hastily in order to leave this awkward moment behind. "What actions will you take?"

"I shall pray," the bishop declared solemnly, "and ask the Lord to grant us deliverance. And I also have high hopes of help from a certain lady unknown to you. . . ."

AND SO THE elders of the province spent the season of summer's decline in a state of alarm and turmoil, for which they had the most serious of reasons, although it is also true that our Zavolzhsk society had never found life quite so fascinating as it did during those August and September days.

And it was not just a matter of the political and religious convulsions that had made our region famous throughout Russia in a mere few days. Such events are capable of agitating minds, but they do not provoke any exceptional tingling of the nerves, and it was precisely nervous excitement that could be observed in these parts—excitement of that special quality that can only be generated by women tormented and driven half-crazy by curiosity. It is well known, after all, that the defining mood of society is determined by the members of the weaker sex. When they are bored and depressed, everything in the world shrinks, shrivels, becomes gray and colorless. But when, in the grip of excitement, they shake off their drowsiness, the pulse of life immediately quickens and blossoms, becoming filled with sound and color. In our capital cities the ladies are almost always either in a state of palpitation and Ecstatic Complicity with a Great Event or of anticipation of this delightful condition, which accounts for the eternal female yearning to escape from the provinces to St. Petersburg or, if that cannot be managed, to Moscow, to the bustle and lights and the constant, shimmering glow of an endless holiday. But in the backwoods the dreary peace and quiet reduce the ladies to a state of hysterical melancholy, which only renders the outburst of congested feelings all the more violent when a miracle occurs and the yawningly familiar native hearths are suddenly illuminated by the sun of a Genuine Scandal. Here is drama and passion for you, and such incomparably delightful rumors—and it is all so near, so close at hand, you are almost up on the stage itself, not gazing through a lorgnette from a chair in the fourth circle, as you would be in the capital cities.

At the very center of this fascinating life, for which our quiet Zavolzhsk had some time earlier become the arena, there stood, of course, Vladimir Lvovich Bubentsov, a former sinner, but now a hero, in other words a figure not merely doubly dangerous for the female heart but quadruply so. The synodical emissary's relations with the governor's wife, Ludmila Platonovna, the postmaster's wife, Olympiada Savelievna, and several other lionesses of our local society were the main subject of discussion in all our drawing rooms and salons. The most varied opinions were expressed concerning the nature of these relations, from the charitable to the extremely audacious, and it must be admitted that the latter clearly predominated.

The other, almost equally piquant, source of gossip was Naina Georgievna Telianova. After leaving her grandmother's estate, she had moved to Zavolzhsk and had not demonstrated the slightest desire to take refuge in flight to other parts—that is, things had happened precisely as the perspicacious Sister Pelagia had predicted. Naturally, everyone knew about the unseemly part that Naina Georgievna had played in the story of the unfortunate dogs, and there were few who were willing to associate with the crazy princess now, and yet the young woman was not embarrassed in the least by the general condemnation. The apprehension once expressed by Sister Pelagia concerning the desperate situation in which Naina Georgievna might find

154 / Boris Akunin

herself should she be left without any inheritance from her grand-mother had proved to be completely unfounded. In addition to the very fine little town house that Telianova had inherited from a recently deceased female relative, the princess proved also to possess her own capital—yet another inheritance, this time from some great-uncle or second cousin. God only knows how much it was worth, but it was at least quite sufficient for her to keep a maid and dress in the latest fash-ion. Naina appeared quite openly everywhere she wished, and in gen-eral her manner of behavior was such that at times her exploits even eclipsed the missionary and amatory conquests of Vladimir Lvovich.

How intriguing, for instance, were the young lady's daily rides in the early evening to St. Petersburg Boulevard, our very own Zavolzhsk Champs Élysées!

Decked out in a positively breathtaking dress (a new one every time), under an immensely wide hat with feathers, sheltering under a lace parasol, Naina Georgievna would ride unhurriedly along the esplanade in her carriage, boldly scrutinizing all the ladies walking toward her, and on Cathedral Square she would order her driver to halt in front of the Grand Duke hotel and gaze fixedly for a long time, sometimes even for as long as half an hour, at the windows of the wing in which Vladimir Lvovich had his lodgings. Aware of this custom of hers, at the appointed hour a small crowd would already be gathered in anticipation by the railings, ready to gape at the remarkable young woman. It is true that no one ever saw the door of the wing open and the inspector invite the princess to enter, but this standoffish response merely accentuated the scandalous nature of the entire situation.

On the eve of the Beheading of John the Baptist, the town was fra-grant with the scent of a new scandal, the precise content of which was not yet clear. But the scent was the same as ever, spicy and unmistak-able. And the same rumors, ripe with promise, were hovering in the air.

There was the prospect of a rare, indeed almost unprecedented event for Zavolzhsk—a public art exhibition. Not an exhibition of drawings by grammar-school pupils or of watercolors painted by members of the "Officials' Wives for Public Morality" association, but a display of photographic pictures by the Petersburg celebrity Arkadii Sergeevich Poggio.

The *vernissage* for invited guests—with champagne and hors d'oeuvres—was set for the same date as this doleful holy day, for which, as everyone knows, the observance of a strict fast is prescribed. In this alone a certain defiance of the proprieties could already be discerned. But even more remarkable was the suggestive air of mystery with which the patroness of the exhibition, Olympiada Savelievna Shestago, distributed the invitations to a narrow circle of friends and acquaintances. There were those who said that this small number of fortunates would be shown something quite exceptional, and tremulous apprehensions were even expressed that afterward the most interesting things would not be shown to the public or even that no public showing would take place at all.

The postmaster's wife luxuriated in the bright glow of this universal excitation. Never before had she received so many invitations at the same time for all manner of gatherings, name-day parties and open-house days. She did not go to all of them, but was very selective, affecting an air of intrigue and replying to direct requests for an invitation by saying that the hall was too small and the artist himself objected to a crowd, for that would make it difficult to view his works. But as of the day after the *vernissage,* everyone would be most welcome.

THE EXHIBITION WAS located in a separate wing of the postmaster's house, with a door that opened straight onto the street. Arkadii Sergeevich had been living in this comfortable apartment for an entire month, ever since he moved out of Drozdovka. The reason for his move was not entirely clear, because no one had observed that Poggio had quarreled about anything with the inhabitants of the estate, though certain of the more perspicacious female commentators did remark that the timing of the move had coincided with Naina Georgievna's emigration. On the first floor of the apartment there was a spacious salon, where the exhibition in question was sited, and before the salon there was also a drawing room. The second floor consisted of two rooms: one served Arkadii Sergeevich as his bedroom, and he had set up his photographic laboratory in the other, blacking out the windows completely with curtains.

The invited guests assembled only gradually, and therefore the hostess's foresight in providing a table of hors d'oeuvres in the drawing room was much appreciated.

Almost the first to arrive were Stepan Trofimovich Shiryaev and Pyotr Georgievich Telianov, which conclusively refuted speculation concerning a quarrel between Arkadii Sergeevich and the inhabitants of Drozdovka. Shiryaev was pale and tense, as though he foresaw some unpleasant consequences for himself arising from the exhibition, but his young companion was in a lighthearted mood, joking a great deal and repeatedly attempting to poke his nose into the locked salon when no one was looking, so that Olympiada Savelievna was obliged to keep a close eye on the mischievous prankster.

Also invited, from the artist's side, were Donat Abramovich Sytnikov and Kirill Nifontovich Krasnov. General Tatishchev's widow had recovered from her illness, but she was not yet traveling beyond the bounds of her estate, and if she was to have ventured out she would hardly have honored with her presence an exhibition by her much-disliked "nutcracker" (that was the name on which she had finally settled for Arkadii Sergeevich, apparently having in mind the clicking sound that his photographic apparatus produced when taking a picture).

A greater number of guests had been invited by the hostess: Vladimir Lvovich and his inseparable secretary, the provincial marshal of the nobility, Count Gavriil Alexandrovich (on this occasion with his wife), several of her most tried-and-true liberal friends, and also a newcomer from Moscow—a certain Polina Andreevna Lisitsyna, who, despite having arrived in Zavolzhsk only recently, was already on friendly terms with all the pillars of Zavolzhsk society. Olympiada Savelievna's husband had not been allowed to attend the soirée due to his lack of sensitivity to art and in general because it was obviously inappropriate if Bubentsov was to attend.

Everyone had arrived, and from one moment to the next they were anticipating the arrival of the most important guest—Vladimir Lvovich, who had been delayed somewhat by state business, but had promised that he would definitely be there. The guests had already bolstered their spirits substantially with champagne and were casting glances of mounting curiosity at the hero of the evening. Poggio moved from one group to the next, joking a lot and anxiously wiping his hands with his handkerchief, occasionally looking in the direction of the door—no doubt he was tormented by impatience and mentally urging the tardy Bubentsov to make haste.

And so Arkadii Sergeevich reached the spot where one of the local progressives was circling around the young woman from Moscow, and exclaimed with exaggerated gusto: "Yes, indeed, Polina Andreevna, you absolutely must permit me to make your portrait! The longer I observe your charming face, the more interesting it seems to me. And it would be even more wonderful if you were to persuade your sister to pose for me with you. It is simply astounding how great a difference there can be between faces that display all the features of a family likeness!"

Lisitsyna smiled and her lively brown eyes flashed, but she said nothing.

"Do not be angry, *Pauline*, when I say that such a double portrait would demonstrate to everyone in the most eloquent fashion possible what a crime it is when women decide to shut themselves away from the world. Your sister Pelagia is a little gray mouse, but you are a fiery lioness. She is like the pale moon, but you are the blinding sun. The nose, the eyebrows, the eyes all have the same form, but the two of you could never be confused. I suppose that she is much older than you?"

"Is that a compliment or an attempt to establish my age?" Lisitsyna said with a laugh, exposing her even white teeth and striking Arkadii Sergeevich jokingly on the hand with her black ostrich-feather fan. "And don't you dare abuse Pelagia in my presence. We see each other so rarely! I came to see her once ages ago, and they had sent her off to some remote monastery."

She fluttered her weapon of retribution, fanning air onto her naked shoulders with their charming sprinkling of bright-orange freckles. She tossed her luxuriant ginger coiffure and screwed up her eyes as she peered at the clock.

"Are you short-sighted?" asked the observant Poggio. "It is twenty minutes past eight."

"Short-sightedness runs in our family," Polina Andreevna confessed with a disarming smile. "And I'm too embarrassed to wear spectacles."

"Even spectacles could hardly spoil you," Arkadii Sergeevich assured her gallantly. "So, how about a portrait?"

"Not for anything. You'll only go and show it in an exhibition." Lisitsyna began speaking in a conspiratorial whisper. "What kind of surprise is it that you have in there? I bet it's something indecent, isn't it?"

Poggio gave a slightly forced smile and said nothing. The ginger-haired charmer gazed up at him, puckering her round forehead inquisitively, as if she were trying to solve some kind of riddle.

Ah, but why attempt to bamboozle the reader any longer, especially since he has already guessed everything for himself?

The woman standing before the nervous artist (wearing a low-cut velvet evening dress and white gloves up to the elbow, her face framed by those whimsically coiled copper-red locks) was not Polina Andreevna Lisitsyna at all, but . . .

That is to say, it is not exactly that she was not Polina Andreevna Lisitsyna, for at one time she really had been called precisely that, but then she had changed her first name, dropped her family name, and become simply Pelagia.

In order to understand how this incredible and even blasphemous transformation of a nun into a society lady had come about, we shall be obliged to go back two weeks in time, to those final lingering days of summer, when barges were sailing upstream along the River with watermelons from Astrakhan and Tsaritsyn, and bishop Mitrofanii had only just held his distressing "council at Fili."

"THIS IS DANGEROUS both for me and the governor. But that is not the worst thing, and not by a long way. Today our entire way of life is under threat. As a shepherd of the church I cannot just sit here while a ravenous beast devours my flock. I am in open view, my hands are tied, Bubentsov's spies are swarming all around me, I cannot tell who to trust. They have already reported that I was in conference with Anton Antonovich and Matvei yesterday, I know that quite certainly. Without you, Pelagia, I shall not be able to cope. Help me. We will try to extinguish the blaze from both sides. As we did last year, when you and I traveled to Kazan to look for the Icon of the Afon Virgin after it was stolen."

With that His Grace concluded his speech. Mitrofanii and his spiritual daughter were strolling together along the pathways of the bishop's garden, although the day was overcast and there was a fine rain sprinkling down from the sky. This was what things had come to—His Grace was afraid to hold a secret conversation in his very own chambers. There were too many stealthy ears listening.

"So I have to play Polina again?" sighed the nun. "We vowed that it was going to be the last time. I don't say that because I am afraid that I shall be exposed and expelled from the order. I actually enjoy this playacting. That is what I am afraid of. Worldly temptation. These masquerades make my heart beat faster. And that is a sin."

"The sin is not your concern," Mitrofanii said severely. "I set the work of penance and I bear the responsibility for it. The goal is a good one and the means, while not entirely legitimate, are not dishonorable. Go to Sister Emilia and tell her that I am sending you to the Efimiev Monastery. And then take the steamer as far as Egoriev, assume the appearance required, and be sure to be back here again the day after tomorrow. I shall introduce you to the houses that Bubentsov visits—the homes of Count Gavriil Alexandrovich, and the governor and his wife, and the others. After that, you know what to do. Here, take this." He handed Pelagia a large leather purse. "You will order some dresses from Leblanc, buy various perfumes and lipsticks and such—whatever is necessary. And have that ginger mop styled into a proper coiffure, like in Kazan, with those little curls. Well, go now, and God be with you."

PELAGIA—OR RATHER, not Pelagia, but the young Moscow widow Polina Andreevna Lisitsyna—took lodgings with the colonel's wife Grabbe, an old friend of Mitrofanii's. The old woman knew nothing at all about the masquerade, but she gave her guest a warm welcome and made her comfortable, and everything would have been quite wonderful, if only the kind-hearted Antonina Ivanovna had not got it into her head that she ought to find this dear, unhappy lady a husband as quickly as possible.

This caused the female conspirator numerous awkward moments. Almost every day the colonel's widow invited young and not-so-young gentlemen with the status of bachelor or widower to tea, and to the extreme embarrassment of Polina Andreevna (let us, after all, refer to her in that manner) almost all of them displayed a most lively interest in her white skin, bright eyes, and "bronze-helmet" coiffure: smoothly parted at the top and wavy down the back of the head, with three pendant coils at each side. Things even reached the stage of rivalry. For instance, the engineer Surkov, a very good man, would come to visit with a huge bunch of chrysanthemums, but then the grammar-school inspector Poluectov would show up with an entire basketful, and the former would spend the entire evening feeling envious of the latter.

Sister Emilia, who had been a bride three times before she took the veil and therefore regarded herself as a great expert in the area of male habits, taught that men pay attention of a certain kind (that was what she said: "attention of a certain kind") not to all women, but only to those who give them some kind of sign, sometimes even unintentionally. A glance, perhaps, or a sudden blush, or some kind of imperceptible odor to which men's noses are particularly sensitive. The meaning of this sign is: I am accessible, you may approach me. And as proof of this, Emilia, who was, among other things, a teacher of natural science, would adduce examples from the life of animals, for some reason most often dogs. Christina, Olympiada, Ambrosia, and Apollinaria would listen with bated breath, because they had left the world before they had a chance to become acquainted with male habits at all. Pelagia listened sadly, because from her experience in the role of Mrs. Lisitsyna, it was perfectly obvious that she gave signs of her own accessibility, she most certainly did. Either a glance or a blush or that thrice-cursed treacherous odor. And most disagreeable of all was the fact that the nun felt as much at home in the role of the flippant Mrs. Lisitsyna as a fish in water, and her customary clumsiness somehow completely evaporated. Her manner became assured, her movements graceful, and even her hips began to behave in the most treacherous manner as she walked along, so that some men even turned to look. After each reincarnation it required the performance of several thousand bows and the reading of a hundred prayers to the Virgin Mary to restore her to a state of blessed calm.

So far it seemed that on this occasion Pelagia had taken the burden of sin on her soul almost completely in vain. In two weeks of following a virtually uninterrupted round of private parties, dinners, and balls she had succeeded in discovering very little. Bubentsov did not visit Naina Georgievna's house, nor did she visit him. If they were meeting anywhere, then it was in secret. That, though, was unlikely, if one took into account Princess Telianova's daily demonstrations in front of the wing of the hotel. Once, when she and the postmistress called at Vladimir Lvovich's apartment, she had seen an envelope on the table with the letters NT written at the bottom in a crooked hand, but the envelope was lying there unopened, and apparently not for the first day.

Mrs. Lisitsyna's efforts in the matter of the Zyt case had been somewhat more successful.

A curious circumstance had emerged from a conversation with the pathologist Wiesel, one of the soft-hearted Antonina Ivanovna's protégés. Apparently Bubentsov had brought back from the sinister clearing, which was presumed to be the bloodthirsty Shishiga's site of worship, certain samples of soil impregnated with some fluid similar to blood, and the task of analyzing this trophy had fallen to Wiesel. Laboratory tests had shown that it was indeed blood, but not human—it had come from a moose. This was reported to Chief of Police Lagrange. However, this important piece of news had not been brought to the attention of the newspapers and the public.

The gendarmes captain Prishibyakin, commandeered from St. Petersburg to assist the Extraordinary Commission, had breathed hotly into her ear and tickled her with his pomaded mustache as he told her in secret about shrunken human heads that had supposedly been found at the Zyt shaman's house, and promised to show them to Polina Andreevna if she would visit him at the hotel. Lisitsyna believed him and went—and what do you think? Prishibyakin didn't show her any shrunken heads at all, but instead popped a champagne cork and tried to press his embraces on her. She had been obliged to strike him in the groin with her elbow as if by accident, following which the inventive captain had become pale and taciturn—he merely groaned and gazed at his guest with an air of suffering as she flitted out of the door.

She had more luck with the investigator Borisenko, also from the Extraordinary Commission. During a ball at the Nobles' Club, in a flagrant attempt to impress the inquisitive beauty, he had complained that the arrested Zyts were stubborn and would not give candid testimony, and the ones who did say anything about Shishiga and the sacrifices kept getting confused all the time and losing the thread, so that afterward the minutes had to be corrected and written out again.

This was all noteworthy, but insufficient for the Zavolzhsk party to be able to launch a decisive counterattack against the Petersburg invasion. That was why Polina Andreevna attached such importance to the opening of the photographic exhibition: It highlighted the Drozdovka connection once again, and this time it seemed as if something might become clear. Was not this the mysterious threat with which Arkadii Sergeevich had sought to frighten Naina Georgievna? And then again, Bubentsov would be there. Taking everything together, Polina Andreevna absolutely had to get her hands on an invitation to the *vernissage,* and she had eventually succeeded in this by dint of immense ingenuity and unflagging persistence.

On the eve of the longingly anticipated soirée, Mrs. Lisitsyna had experienced serious difficulties in connection with an instruction given in the invitation: "Ladies in open dresses." Even at the balls, Polina Lisitsyna had made her appearance with her shoulders, breasts, and back covered by a filmy gauze, which the local ladies of fashion had taken for the latest Moscow chic and had already ordered the same for themselves from Leblanc. However, to ignore the hostess's strict instruction would have seemed an affront, all the more noticeable because, as far as she could tell, the visitor from Moscow was almost the only lady to have been honored with an invitation to the *vernissage* from Olympiada Savelievna. To provoke the displeasure of Bubentsov's main confidante and female ally would be unwise, to say the least.

Poor Pelagia sat in front of the dressing-table mirror in her room for almost half a day, pulling the low neck on the shameless velvet dress almost right up to her chin, then once again lowering the light fabric to the limit prescribed by Monsieur Leblanc.

It should be noted that the décolleté really did not look bad at all, for by the autumn her freckles had almost completely disappeared at the front, but they had clambered up onto her shoulders—evidently as a consequence of her swimming lessons—and, in Polina Andreevna's opinion, they lent these two elements of her anatomy a likeness to two golden oranges. Everybody was bound to stare.

It was terrible, but she had no choice.

THE LITTLE BRONZE bell tinkled—someone had come into the entrance from the street—and Lisitsyna saw Arkadii Sergeevich raise himself up high on tiptoes and crane his neck.

It was Vladimir Lvovich and his inseparable Patroclus, Spasyonny, who had arrived. Polina Andreevna noted the expression of disappointment that distorted the artist's mouth, and then turned with everyone else to face the new arrivals.

Bubentsov nodded curtly to the guests, not feeling any necessity to apologize for his lateness. He shook their hostess's hand, detaining her long pale fingers for just a moment, and Olympiada Savelievna immediately flushed and became radiant.

"Well, now everybody's here!" she exclaimed happily. "All right, then, Arkadii Sergeevich—Open sesame?" And she pointed to the closed door of the salon.

"That's not right. We have to give the latecomers a chance to have a glass of champagne," the artist objected, glancing at the entrance door again. "Really, the champagne is far more interesting than my boring landscapes."

"Today is a fast day," Tikhon Ieremeevich rebuked him sternly. "And Vladimir Lvovich and I are godly people. So do come on and show us your pictures."

Bubentsov did actually take a sip from a glass, but immediately set it down. Raising his eyebrows in anticipation, the servant of the state said: "Yes, indeed. Do open the exhibition. Let us see what it is that you have been teasing us all with."

Poggio turned pale. Eventually, having overcome his agitation and even seeming rather annoyed with himself, he started speaking rapidly.

"Very well, so be it. And so, ladies and gentlemen, as some of you are already aware, I came here to make a series of works for an exhibition in Moscow, at the Rumyantsev Museum. The title is *The Disappearing Russia*. The poetic world of the old noble's estate, the image of the neglected garden, the bowers covered with climbing ivy, the early-evening mists, and other romantic nonsense. Ah, but what point is there in describing it—see for yourself."

With a gesture that seemed somehow excessively abrupt, almost despairing, he pushed open the doors, inviting people into the salon.

The small exhibition—perhaps no more than thirty works in all—was hung simply but artfully. The slightly flickering light from the gas lamps did not spoil the impression with its glare; on the contrary, it lent the black-and-white pictures an air of living reality. Hanging along both side walls were charming landscapes and studies that captured the unpretentious but captivating beauty of the Drozdovka park, the broad expanse of the River, the decaying mansion house. The viewers passed slowly along the line of photographs, nodding their heads in approval, until they reached the wall opposite the door and froze, moving no farther, so that quite soon a rather substantial obstruction had formed there.

Polina Andreevna was among the first to find themselves at this enchanted spot, and she gave a quiet gasp, pressing her hands to her heart. Three large works, each almost a yard across, hung above a single title: "By the curving shore." Each of them showed a female nude, apparently the same person in every case. We say "apparently" because the face of the sitter was hidden. In the photograph on the left she was squatting close to the edge of the water, her head lowered and her long hair hanging loose with waterweed twined into it. In the picture on the right the model was lying with her back to the viewer, with her hands extended above her head: the foreground was sand, the backdrop all glimmers of sun on water. But hanging in the center was a half-length portrait *en face*: The woman was standing in water up to her hips, covering her face with her hands; the wet, light-colored hair was crowned with a garland of lilies, the laughing eyes sparkled through the gaps between the parted fingers. One had to admit that the works had been executed most skillfully, but that, of course, was not the reason why everybody crowded around them.

So this was it, that wonderful, terrifying, unprecedented scandal, the approach of which Zavolzhsk had detected in advance with its sensitive nose! And the point was not at all that the model was naked. This may be a remote backwater, but it is not Persia, and our lovers of art cannot be embarrassed by a nude, not even by a photographic one. No, the whole catch here lay in the identity of the model, whose lineaments the viewers studied with avid interest. Was it her or was it not?

Donat Abramovich grunted hoarsely, grabbed hold of his beard with one hand, and shook his head in condemnation, but he was in no hurry to move aside—most definitely not. On the contrary, he put on the pince-nez that did not suit him at all and began studying the details as if he was evaluating a consignment of goods.

Shiryaev was a pitiful sight. He blushed bright red to the roots of his hair, his chest began heaving, and his fingers worked convulsively, alternately opening and clenching into fists. Poggio was also strange. He gazed at his own works with a vague, pained smile, seeming to have completely forgotten about his audience.

Bubentsov was the last to come up. He surveyed the triptych with the air of a connoisseur, inclined his head to one side, and asked with a laugh: "Who is this nymph?"

Arkadii Sergeevich roused himself and said with a careless wave of his hand, "Oh, just one of the local girls. Pretty, is she not?"

At that moment a loud, mocking voice spoke behind them.

"What is that you are all looking at, gentlemen? It must be quite a masterpiece."

Standing in the doorway was Naina Georgievna, looking inexpressibly beautiful in a white dress girded around with a broad scarlet belt and a velvet hat with a veil, through which they could see her huge black eyes glittering.

Apparently the major scandal was yet to break.

"You came after all!" exclaimed Arkadii Sergeevich, taking a step toward her. "Too late! Or did you think I was only joking?"

"That was deliberate," she replied, approaching the group of guests. "I was curious to find out what kind devilment you are capable of."

She walked around the landscape section of the exhibition with studied slowness, even stopping in front of one rather unremarkable little study—probably simply in order to make a greater impression. Finally she reached the knot of people clustering around the triptych. They all hastily made way to allow her to the front.

There was complete silence while Telianova looked at the seditious photographs. Polina Andreevna noticed that several men were studying the line of the dangerous young lady's neck from behind with especial interest, comparing it with the model as shown *de derrière*. It looked similar—very similar in fact.

When Naina Georgievna finally turned around, it was evident that her initial bravado had diminished somewhat, and the eyes behind the fine mesh had begun to glitter almost too brightly—could it be because of tears?

"And what has the curving shore got to do with all this?" Kirill Nifontovich Krasnov asked in a loud voice, evidently wishing to smooth over the awkward moment. "That is a motif from Pushkin, *Ruslan and Ludmila.*"

"Precisely," replied Poggio, looking at Naina Georgievna with red, inflamed eyes.

"So you have depicted the mermaid, that's it! 'There be marvels, there the forest goblin wanders and a mermaid in the branches sits.'"

Extending his red lips into a pitiless smile, Arkadii Sergeevich drawled: "Perhaps. Or something else from the same work, from *Ruslan.*" And, emphasizing every word, he added, "'Oh, knight, that was Naina.'"

Without saying anything at all (that was the most terrifying thing about it), Stepan Trofimovich launched himself at his old classmate and punched him viciously in the face, sending the artist sprawling back against the wall with the red blood gushing out of his broken mouth onto his beard.

"Stepan, what are you doing?" Pyotr Georgievich exclaimed in horror, grabbing Shiryaev by the shoulder from behind. "What's wrong with you?" And then he suddenly realized—"You thought it was Naina?"

The scene that ensued was perfectly outrageous, with several men restraining Stepan Trofimovich, who tried to break free, but still said nothing at all and merely wheezed hoarsely. Pyotr Georgievich covered his face with his hands and sobbed loudly. Poggio, who looked like a vampire with his bloodied mouth, was choking on his own coughing or hysterical laughter.

Naina Georgievna suddenly swung around sharply to face Bubentsov, who was observing the battle with a carefree smile, and asked in a ringing voice: "Well, are you enjoying yourself?"

"But of course!" he replied softly.

"The Prince of Darkness," whispered Naina Georgievna, stepping away from him in fright, and then, speaking even more quietly, she added the following incomprehensible words: "The Prince and the Princess, how fitting . . ."

And without waiting for the end of the altercation, she went dashing headlong out of the salon.

"Princess Telianova has not quite mastered the art of leaving the stage," Vladimir Lvovich remarked ironically, addressing his hostess. "She cannot make a simple exit; she always has to run."

Olympiada Savelievna looked like a triumphant Nike—the soirée had exceeded all her expectations.

"That's enough, gentlemen!" she announced loudly. "Really, what sort of childishness is this? It's all that champagne that's to blame. Come to the public opening tomorrow. I think it will be interesting."

ONLY THERE WAS no public opening the following day, because there was nothing to open.

And no one to open it.

# CHAPTER 8

# The Same Characters, Almost

LET US TAKE everything in the right order, however, because here every little detail is important, even if at first sight it seems absolutely insignificant.

When Arkadii Sergeevich failed to appear for his breakfast at half past nine, Olympiada Savelievna thought nothing of it at first because, as might naturally be expected from a member of an artistic profession, the guest from St. Petersburg was not notable for his punctuality. However, a quarter of an hour later, when the omelette could wait no longer, she sent a manservant. He went around via the courtyard and the street, since there was no other way to gain admission to the separate wing, rang the bell, and then, just to make sure, knocked at the door. There was no reply.

At this the postmaster's wife became concerned that Arkadii Sergeevich might be feeling unwell after the harrowing experiences of the previous day and the blow to the face he had received from Stepan Trofimovich Shiryaev. The manservant was despatched for a second time, this time with a key. But the key proved not to be necessary because, in his usual absentminded manner, Poggio had left the door unlocked. The messenger entered the apartment and a few moments later his piercing screams were heard resounding through the house.

AT THIS POINT we ought to explain that murders had become extremely rare events in our town in recent years. To be specific, the last time this sin had been committed was in the summer of the year before last, when two carters got into a quarrel over some local Carmen from the market, and one struck the other too lustily over the head with a thick billet. And the murder before that one had taken place an entire five years earlier, again not with any malice aforethought, but out of love: Two sixth-form grammar-school pupils took it into their heads to fight a duel. One of them—at this point there is no way to tell which—intercepted a love letter addressed to the pretty young daughter of our municipal archivist, Benevolenksky. The boys did not have any pistols, so they fired at each other with shotguns, and both of them were killed outright. All the newspapers wrote about that incident, although not as sensationally, of course, as in their articles about the current Zyt case. And the poor girl who had been the unwitting cause of a double murder was sent away from Zavolzhsk forever to live with relatives in some distant province almost as remote as Vladivostok itself.

But on this occasion it was not a case of a drunken brawl or youthful extremism. This instance displayed all the signs of a premeditated, carefully planned murder, and one that was aggravated by exceptional brutality. Headless bodies that belonged to people whom nobody knew and had been dragged here from some remote thicket or other were all very well and good. But it was quite another thing when such an appalling incident occurred in Zavolzhsk itself, on the very finest street, and to a celebrity from the capital who was known to every member of good society. But the most terrible thing of all was that the crime had been committed—and of this no one had the slightest doubt—by someone from that very society and, in addition, for motives that were highly inflammatory to the imagination (we hardly need mention that the whole town had learned about the scandalous finale to Olympiada Savelievna's soirée that very same evening).

These motives were the main subject of popular discussion, but there were various suggestions as to the identity of the murderer, and at least three different parties were formed. The most numerous was the Shiryaev party. The next in size consisted of those who saw the culprit in the insulted and humiliated Naina Georgievna, from whom it was possible to expect anything at all after the story of the dogs. The third party directed its suspicions at Pyotr Georgievich, citing his nihilist convictions and Caucasian blood. We said "at least three," since there was also a fourth party, which was not very numerous, being formed in circles close to the governor and Matvei Bentsionovich Berdichevsky. These people whispered that Bubentsov must have been involved in some way or another—but this was only too clearly a case of wishful thinking.

It is hardly surprising that by midday the whole of Zvolzhsk had learned about the terrible event. Our townsfolk were in a strange condition, both excited and subdued at one and the same time, and the general state of mind was so apprehensive that His Grace ordered services of lustration to be held in the churches and he himself delivered a sermon in the cathedral, speaking of the heavy trials that had been visited upon the town, by which he most certainly did not mean only the murder of the photographer.

JUST AS MITROFANII was about to leave to give his sermon he was visited at the episcopal see by the assistant provincial prosecutor, Berdichevsky, who had been summoned to the bishop by special messenger.

"Do this for me, Matiusha," said His Grace, already arrayed in his purple mantle and cuffs, but still without his miter and panagia. "Do not entrust this case to anyone else; deal with it yourself. I cannot exclude the possibility that something might be discovered here that will lead straight to a certain individual well known to us." Mitrofanii glanced around briefly at the firmly closed door. "Judge for yourself. The murdered man and the young woman whom he apparently wished to hurt are both very well known to our clever friend, and he is bound to the latter by some very unusual relationship. And in addition he was present in person, one of only a small number of people, at yesterday's bout of fisticuffs—"

Matvei Bentsionovich threw his hands up in the air and actually interrupted what the bishop was saying, something he had never done before: "Father, I simply cannot do it! In the first place, I shall have to visit the site of the murder, and I am afraid of dead bodies."

"Come, now," said Mitrofanii, wagging his finger at him "you must overcome this weakness of the heart. Are you a public prosecutor or aren't you. I'll take you along with me to the Starosvyatskoe cemetery, where all the coffins are being moved because the River has completely undercut its bank there. I shall read prayers, as is only appropriate, and I shall set you to manage the exhumation of the remains. It will help to strengthen your nerves."

"Ah, but it is not just a matter of the dead body," said Berdichevsky, glancing into the bishop's eyes imploringly. "I have no gift for investigation. When it comes to drawing up a bill of indictment or even conducting an interrogation, I can manage very well, but as a criminal investigator I am quite useless. You are the one with the talent for solving riddles, father. It is a pity that you cannot go there yourself, it would be inappropriate."

"I shall not go, but I shall give you my eye. Come in, my daughter," said the bishop, turning toward the small door that led into the inner chambers.

A thin nun in a black wimple and *kamilavka* entered the study where the bishop and the assistant prosecutor were conversing and bowed without speaking. Berdichevsky, who had seen Pelagia on numerous previous occasions and knew that she enjoyed Mitrofanii's special confidence, rose and replied with an equally respectful bow.

"Take Sister Pelagia with you," the bishop instructed him. "She is observant and sharp-witted and will be a great help to you."

"But the police will certainly be there already, and Lagrange himself," said Matvei Bentsionovich, throwing up his hands again. "How shall I explain such a strange companion to them?"

"Tell them that after his sermon the bishop will come to sanctify this house against defilement, but he has sent the nun on ahead to prepare and bring the place into a seemly condition, so that His Grace's sight will not be offended. And as for Lagrange, as far as I understand matters, you now have that scoundrel on a leash." And, flashing a rapid glance at Pelagia, he added: "Tell him the nun is meek and humble; she is feeble-minded and will not hinder the investigation."

NEITHER OF THEM spoke as they rode along Dvoryanskaya Street, because Pelagia felt a little timid in the company of such a highly intelligent and well-educated companion, and Matvei Bentsionovich was not accustomed to associating with ecclesiastics in holy orders (Mitrofanii did not count; he was a special case) and he simply did not know how to conduct a conversation with the nun.

Eventually, having hit upon a felicitous subject in his mind, he opened his mouth and said: "Mother . . ." But then he faltered, because it occurred to him that a woman who was not yet old at all, even if she was a nun, was unlikely to find it pleasant to be addressed in such a fashion by a bald, already slightly flabby gentleman who was well past thirty.

He had always had difficulties in talking with Pelagia, albeit their occasions for conversation had not been many. To Matvei Bentsionovich's way of thinking, the nun had an extremely discomfiting manner of appearing at times like a mature and worldly-wise woman and at others like a perfect little girl, as she did now, for instance.

"I mean, sister," he corrected himself, "you are after all the sister [this sounded perfectly stupid now] of Polina Andreevna Lisitsyna?"

The nun nodded in a rather indefinite manner and Berdichevsky felt afraid that he might have broken some unknown rule of etiquette that forbade talking to nuns about the relatives whom they had left behind in the outside world.

"I only asked . . . she is a very intelligent and likable person, and a little bit like you." He glanced politely at his companion, swaying beside him on the leather seat of the carriage, and added: "Just a tiny little bit."

We do not know what direction this not entirely comfortable conversation might have taken had the carriage not driven on to Cathedral Square, the main public space of our town, where the cathedral itself is located, as well as the governor's house, and the main administrative buildings, and the see and the Grand Duke hotel, where Grand Duke Konstantin Pavlovich really had stayed one hundred years previously while making his journey of familiarization with the eastern provinces of the empire.

There in the square, right beside the cast-iron railings of this finest hostelry in Zavolzhsk, there was a noisy, jostling crowd of people, and police caps could be seen in among them. Some outrage was clearly being committed, and in close proximity, moreover, to the seats of spiritual and temporal authority, and by virtue of the power invested in him Matvei Bentsionovich had no right to ignore it and simply ride on by. And if the entire truth was told, he also had a certain weakness for situations in which he could give free rein to the more commanding side of his character.

"You sit here, sister," he told Pelagia with a grand air, then he ordered the coachman to stop and set off to sort this business out.

The high-ranking official was allowed through without any resistance to the very center of the crowd, where it turned out that everyone was staring at an individual of eastern appearance—Bubentsov's Abrek.

The Circassian, dead drunk, was performing some kind of insane dance with himself, from time to time uttering guttural exclamations, but for the most part in silence. He stamped on the spot and took tiny steps with his large feet in their tattered soft-leather shoes, occasionally springing up to his toes in an extremely agile manner and tracing out rapid, glittering circles above his shaven head with a dagger of monstrous size. It was immediately obvious that he had already been dancing like this for a long time and intended to devote his energies to this same occupation for a long time more to come.

"And what do we have here?" Berdichevsky asked the police officer with a frown.

"You can see for yourself, your honor. He's been defying us like this without a break for nigh on an hour now. And before that he smashed all the mirrors in the Mirror Tavern and gave the waiters a good kicking. Before that he was creating uproar at the Samson Inn as well, but he was already completely drunk when he got there."

"Why haven't you stopped him?"

"We tried, your honor. But he beat constable Karasiuk here's face to a pulp and very nearly stabbed me with that cutlass of his."

"We ought to shoot him before he does someone in," raged a constable who was holding a bloody handkerchief over his face—we must assume that he was Karasiuk. "There's nothing else left to be done."

"Sure we'll shoot him," the officer yelled back. "He's Vladimir Lvovich Bubentsov's own man!"

"And why aren't you doing anything?" Berdichevsky asked Tikhon Ieremeevich Spasyonny, who was right beside him at the front of the crowd. "Take your savage away from here."

"Why, I've been following him all night," Spasyonny declared plaintively. "Stop drinking, I told him, stop drinking. But do you think he would listen? He shouldn't drink, not at all. He's not a Russian, so what can you expect? Either he doesn't touch a drop or he downs half a pailful and then goes on a rampage. Some wicked person must have been feeding him liquor. Now he'll keep dancing until he collapses."

Sensing that the eyes of the entire crowd were now turned in his direction, Matvei Bentsionovich declared in a peremptory tone: "It's not allowed. This is not just anyplace, this is Cathedral Square. The bishop will be arriving soon to give his sermon. Take him away immediately!"

There were shouts from the crowd (so much for that sense of dignity): "If you're so smart, you take him away, you great hero!"

And at this point Matvei Bentsionovich realized that he had fallen into a trap entirely of his own making. What on earth could have possessed him to stop the carriage like that? But there was no turning back now. And he could not expect any support from the police officer or the bloodied constable.

Tensing his jaw muscles to screw up his courage, Berdichevsky took one step, then another, moving closer to the terrifying dancer. The Abrek suddenly broke into some wild song that was rather tuneful in its own savage way and began waving his knife around faster and faster.

"Stop that immediately!" Matvei Bentsionovich barked as loudly as he could.

The Circassian merely looked at him with eyes crimson from drink.

"I'm talking to you!"

Berdichevsky took another step forward, and then another.

"Just look at that bold devil," someone said in the crowd behind him.

It was not clear who was meant—the Circassian or the assistant prosecutor, but Matvei Bentsionovich took it as intended for him and his spirits rose somewhat. He reached out his hand to grab the mountain tribesman by the sleeve, and suddenly—whoosh!—the arc of steel glittered as it swept past just above Berdichevsky's fingers, and two buttons bearing the official coat of arms fell to the ground, neatly pruned from the cuff of his frock coat.

Matvei Bentsionovich leapt aside with an involuntary cry and, infuriated at such a loss of face, shouted to the police officer: "Get Bubentsov immediately! If he can't tame his Abrek, I order you to shoot him in the legs!"

"Vladimir Lvovich is still asleep, and he gave orders not to be woken," Spasyonny explained.

"Right, I'll wait ten minutes by my watch," said Berdichevsky, gesturing angrily with his small silver sphere. "Then I'll give the order to fire!"

Tikhon Ieremeevich set off at a rapid waddle in the direction of the wing of the hotel, and a curious silence fell over the square.

The Circassian merely carried on with his unique and inimitable dance. Berdichevsky stood there, holding his watch in his hand, feeling extremely stupid. Karasiuk loaded cartridges into his revolver with obvious pleasure.

When only a minute remained until the ultimatum expired, the police officer said nervously: "Your Excellency, you'll testify that I had nothing to do—"

"He's coming! He's coming!" someone started shouting in the crowd.

Vladimir Lvovich came strolling out through the gates of the hotel, wearing a silk dressing gown and a Turkish fez with a tassel. The crowd parted to let him through. He halted, set his hands against his sides, and for a while simply looked at his half-crazed janissary. Then he yawned and began advancing slowly straight toward him. One of the women gasped. The Circassian did not appear to be looking at his lord and master, but nonetheless, even while continuing to dance, he backed away a little toward the wall of the hotel. Bubentsov continued his advance in the same lazy fashion, without saying a single word, until the Circassian ran up against the wall and froze on the spot. His eyes were completely still, almost as if he were dead.

"Done dancing, you oaf?" Vladimir Lvovich asked in the silence that had fallen. "Come with me and sleep it off."

And so saying, the inspector turned on his heels and set off toward the wing of the hotel without a backward glance. Murad strode obediently after him, with Spasyonny mincing rapidly alongside.

Everybody followed the departure of the picturesque threesome.

A sexton crossed himself and intoned in a deep bass: "Grant unto them power over evil spirits."

Pelagia also crossed herself, and, as we already know, she never made the sign of the cross in vain.

ANOTHER DENSE CIRCLE of curious people was standing at the entrance to the apartment that had been occupied until only recently by poor Arkadii Sergeevich, and a police constable glared down menacingly from the porch. Before she went in, Pelagia crossed herself once more, and again for good reason.

The drawing room looked almost exactly as it had the day before, except that the tables on which the wine and hors d'oeuvres had stood during the soirée were now bare. All the more terrible, therefore, was the scene that met the nun's gaze in the salon. All the photographs had been ripped off the walls and, worse even than that, torn into tiny pieces that were scattered all over the floor. Someone in an absolute frenzy had taken considerable time and trouble to destroy Poggio's exhibition absolutely and utterly.

Chief of Police Lagrange came running briskly down the stairs toward Berdichevsky, his face lighting up in an ingratiating smile at the sight of the assistant prosecutor.

"Matvei Bentsionovich, you have come? Decided to deal with it yourself? Well, that's right."

He bowed as he shook Berdichevsky's hand and glanced in bewilderment at Pelagia, but was completely satisfied by Matvei Bentsionovich's explanation and thereafter paid not the slightest attention to the nun. Felix Stanislavovich was clearly in a quite excellent mood.

"Not much to see here," he said, gesturing dismissively at the havoc in the salon. "But come upstairs. That's where the real scene is."

There were only two rooms upstairs—the bedroom and one other, in which, as we have already mentioned, Arkadii Sergeevich had set up his photographic laboratory. They glanced into this room first, since it was the first one they came to.

"Take a look at that," Lagrange declared haughtily as he showed it to them. "Everything totally shattered."

And, indeed, the laboratory looked even more terrible than the salon. The Kodak camera was lying in the middle of the room, either smashed by a crushing blow or trampled flat, and scattered around it were the glittering icicle fragments of photographic plates.

"Not one left intact; they're all smashed to smithereens," the police chief explained as cheerfully as ever, as if he were boasting about the unknown criminal's talents.

"Any clues?" inquired Berdichevsky with a glance at the two police officers crawling across the floor, clutching magnifying glasses in their hands.

"What clues could there be here?" replied the one who was slightly older, raising a crumpled face haggard from drink. "You can see for yourself, it's like a herd of elephants has run through here. We're just wasting our time on nonsense, assembling the fragments. At the bottom of every plate there's a paper label with the title—'The White Arbor,' 'Sunset over the River,' 'The Mermaid.' We're putting them together from corner to corner, like doing a children's jigsaw. Maybe we'll turn up something useful. But, of course, that's not very likely."

"I see." Speaking in a low voice, Berdichevsky asked Lagrange: "And where is . . . the body?"

"Come this way," said Felix Stanislavovich with a laugh. "You won't be able to sleep tonight after this. It's quite a still-life."

Matvei Bentsionovich wiped his forehead with his handkerchief and followed his blue-jacketed Virgil along the corridor. Pelagia walked softly behind.

Poggio was lying on the bed, staring solemnly up at the ceiling as if he were pondering something very significant; in any case, certainly not the tripod that had pinned him to the bed and remained stuck there, protruding from his ribcage.

"Killed immediately, of course," said the police chief, pointing with a white-gloved finger. "Please note that the blow was struck from directly above. And so the victim must have been lying down; he didn't even attempt to get up. Obviously he was asleep. He opened his eyes, and at that very moment—off to his eternal reward. And the killer started wrecking and smashing everything afterward."

Matvei Bentsionovich forced himself to look at the three tightly bunched wooden legs thrust deep into the dead man's body. Their lower sections were bound in brass, no doubt with sharp points.

"A powerful blow," he said, pretending to be unruffled, and tried to clasp his fingers around the top of the tripod. He could not—his fingers did not reach around it. "A woman could not have done that. It's too heavy, and she couldn't get a proper grip."

"Yes, I agree," said Lagrange. "Which means that it's not Princess Telianova. Basically, this case is about as complicated as a boiled turnip. I was just waiting for the inspector, and my men have carried out a complete search. Do you think you could sign the report?"

Berdichevsky frowned at such a flagrant breach of procedure—the report of the search ought to have been drawn up in the presence of the prosecutor's representative, and therefore he set about reading the document with deliberate slowness.

"Any ideas?" Matvei Bentsionovich asked.

"Why don't we go downstairs to the salon, while they're clearing all this away," Felix Stanislavovich suggested.

And so they did.

They stood in the corner of the empty salon. The chief of police lit his pipe and Matvei Bentsionovich took out a little notebook. Sister Pelagia positioned herself nearby: She crawled across the floor as if picking up rubbish, but in actual fact she was gathering fragments of pictures and matching them up with one another. The men talked without paying any attention to her.

"Go ahead," said Berdichevsky, ready to start taking notes.

"The number of people involved in the case is small. The number of those who might have had some motive for murder is even smaller. We need to establish which member of the last group has no alibi, and the case is closed."

Lagrange was quite magnificent now; his eyes glowed like fire, the ends of his mustache quivered triumphantly, his hand sawed the air vigorously, he rolled specialized terms around his tongue as if they were sugarplums. One imagines that during the preceding weeks Felix Stanislavovich had changed his mind about Zavolzhie being boring and lacking in prospects. Why, just take the Zyt case, if nothing else! But there all the plaudits and public acclaim had clearly gone to Bubentsov, while here, in the investigation of this most appetizing murder, no one else could cut across the police chief's bows. And then again, it was an opportunity to demonstrate his own indispensability to the crafty and dangerous Mr. Berdichevsky, for indispensability was currently under a dark cloud of doubt in connection with Felix Stanislavovich's blunder with the bribe.

"Judge for yourself, Matvei Bentsionovich," said Lagrange, brushing a little feather off the assistant prosecutor's sleeve. "The link between the murder in the night and the scandal of the previous evening is clear, is it not?"

"That would seem to be the case."

"There were ten people at Olympiada Savelievna's soirée, not counting the ladies. We shall omit the synodical inspector and the marshal of the nobility, because they are quality, and in any case there is no indication of any motive. In addition, those invited by the deceased included: the estate manager Shiryaev, Prince Telianov, and merchant of the first guild Krasnov. The hostess's own guests included the headmaster of the grammar school, Sonin, the barrister Kleist, and the architect Brandt. And Vladimir Lvovich also brought his secretary, Spasyonny."

"That would seem to be the case," repeated Berdichevsky, scribbling away rapidly with his pencil. "And, of course, in the first instance you suspect Shiryaev and in the second Telianov?"

"Not so fast," said Felix Stanislavovich with a rapturous smile. "At this stage of initial approximation I am not inclined to narrow the circle of suspects too far. Take the ladies, for instance. Princess Telianova was the main target of yesterday's scandal. If she did not kill him herself, she could be the mastermind or an accomplice, and I shall have more to say about that. Now for Mrs. Lisitsyna."

Pelagia froze, with the photograph of the nude on the sand still not completely assembled.

"A very unusual lady. It's not clear what exactly she has been doing in Zavolzhsk for all this time. I made inquiries, and apparently she came to visit her sister, a nun. Then why is she making the rounds of all the balls and the salons? She gets everywhere; everybody knows her. She's lively and flirtatious, and she turns men's heads. All the signs suggest that she's an adventuress."

Berdichevsky squinted sideways at Pelagia in embarrassment, but she did not seem to be listening any longer; she was fiddling intently with her scraps of paper.

"Today I inquired by telegraph whether Polina Andreevna Lisitsyna had figured in any other cases. And what do you think? She had, in three of them! Three years ago in Perm, in the case of the murder of the ascetic monk Pafnutii. Last year in Kazan, in the case of the theft of a miraculous icon, and again in Samara, in the case of the sinking of the steamer *Svyatogor*. In all three cases she testified as a witness at the trials. How do you like that?"

Berdichevsky gave the nun another glance, not embarrassed this time, but quizzical.

"Yes, that is curious," he admitted. "But we have already established that a woman could not have committed this murder."

"Even so, this Lisitsyna is damned suspicious. But never mind her, we'll sort that out later. And now let us move on to the prime suspects, meaning those who have known Poggio for a long time and had, or could have had, reasons for killing him." Lagrange extended his index finger. "Number one, of course, is Shiryaev. He is insanely in love with Telianova and tried to kill Poggio right there at the opening. They barely managed to pull him off. Number two is the princess's brother, Pyotr Telianov." The chief of police extended his middle finger as well. "Here the matter of wounded vanity could also well play a part. Telianov was the last one there to realize that his sister had been insulted, and that made him look like either a fool or a coward. An unstable young man of unsavory character. He is under open surveillance, and I regard these nihilist types as capable of any kind of abomination. When someone has raised his hand against the foundations of the state, what can one man's life mean to him? But in this case it is even excusable in a certain sense—he was standing up for his sister. But that is still not all." His ring finger, still half-bent, was added to the other two. "Sytnikov. A secretive gentleman, but also not without his passions. According to my information, by no means indifferent to Telianova's charms. So there's your motive—envy of a more successful rival. Donat Abramovich would not go skulking around at night like a bandit himself, but he could well have sent one of his fine young fellows. All of his employees are Old Believers to a man. Morose types with long beards who regard the authorities with hostility." Felix Stanislavovich seemed to find the idea that the murderers were Old Believers to his liking. "Why not, it would certainly be easy enough. I'd better inform Vladimir Lvovich . . ."

"And by the way, about Vladimir Lvovich," Berdichevsky remarked with an innocent air. "Not everything is clear there, either. They say that Telianova didn't simply drop Poggio, she dropped him for Bubentsov."

"Rubbish," said the police chief, waving the hand with the extended fingers dismissively. "Women's tittle-tattle. Telianova, of course, might well be pining for Vladimir Lvovich. Nothing surprising in that—he's a most exceptional man. But Vladimir Lvovich is absolutely indifferent to her. And even if there had been something between them before, where's the motive? Jealousy for a lover you don't care for and don't know how to get rid of? Murder somebody because of that? That sort of thing doesn't happen, Matvei Bentsionovich."

He had to admit that Lagrange was right.

"Then what are we going to do?" asked Berdichevsky.

"I think that for a start it would be a good idea to question all three of them. . . ."

The chief of police did not finish what he was saying—he had noticed the nun standing to one side not far away. Scraps of photographs, neatly assembled into rectangles, lay on the floor along the walls.

"Why are you still nosing around?" Felix Stanislavovich exclaimed irritably. "Finish tidying up and get out. Or even better, sweep all this litter out of here."

Pelagia bowed without speaking and walked upstairs to the second floor.

The police officers who had carried out the search were sitting in the laboratory, smoking cigarettes.

"What do you want, little sister?" the one she already knew, with the crumpled face, asked in a jolly voice. "Forget something?"

The nun saw that there were no more fragments of glass lying on the floor—they had all been collected and laid out, just like the photographs in the salon. Following the direction of her gaze, the jolly fellow said: "There's some there as wouldn't be recommended for your eyes. He was quite an interesting gentleman, was our Poggio. A shame; no way to restore anything now."

Pelagia asked: "Tell me, sir, is there a plate here with the title 'Rainy Morning'?"

The detective stopped smiling and raised his eyebrows in surprise.

"Strange you should ask that, sister. There's a 'Rainy Morning' here in the list, but we didn't find any plate. Not a scrap. He must have been unhappy with it and decided to throw it out. And what do you know about it?"

Pelagia said nothing, knitting her ginger brows in a frown. She was thinking.

"So what about this 'Rainy Morning' then?" the detective with the crumbled face persisted.

"Do not distract me, my son, I am praying," the nun replied absentmindedly, and then she turned and went back downstairs.

The whole point was that the photograph with that title was also missing from the salon. All the pictures assembled from fragments corresponded to the titles remaining on the walls—even the three of the unknown nude that had provoked the scandal. But she had not discovered a single fragment, even the tiniest, of "Rainy Morning."

". . . But still, Bubentsov should also be questioned!" she heard as she entered the salon.

Matvei Bentsionovich and Felix Stanislavovich were apparently unable to agree on the list of suspects.

"You can't insult a man like that by suspecting him! Think again, Mr. Berdichevsky! Of course, I am entirely in your power, but . . . Well, now what do you want?" the chief of police barked at Pelagia.

"We should gather everyone who was here yesterday and all pray together for the soul of the recently departed servant of God," she said, glancing meekly at him with her radiant brown eyes. "Who knows; perhaps the monster might repent?"

"Get out, at the double!" barked Lagrange. "Why on earth did you have to bring her with you?"

Matvei Bentsionovich nodded imperceptibly to Pelagia and took the chief of police by the elbow.

"I'll tell you what we need to do. Praying, of course, is a waste of time, but it would not be a bad idea to arrange a confrontation, as a kind of investigative experiment. We'll gather together everyone who was here yesterday, on the pretext of establishing who was where at any given moment, and who said—"

"Excellent!" exclaimed Felix Stanislavovich, catching on to the idea. "You have a genuine talent for criminology! And we must bring in Telianova. The mere sight of her will send all these gamecocks into a frenzy, and the killer is bound to give himself away. After all, it's perfectly obvious that this is no cold-blooded killing, it's a crime of passion. How will a man in the grip of passion be able to restrain himself? We'll gather them together this very evening. And in the meantime I'll check the alibis of everyone involved."

"And make sure Bubentsov comes; he has to be here."

"You are destroying me, Matvei Bentsionovich; do you wish to ruin your most devoted servant?" Lagrange complained bitterly. "What if Vladimir Lvovich gets angry at me?"

"Better take care that *I* don't get angry at you," was Berdichevsky's quiet reply.

EVERYTHING WAS ARRANGED precisely as it had been during the ill-starred soirée, even with hors d'oeuvres and wine (although not, of course, champagne, because that would have been excessive). The hostess, Olympiada Savelievna, had conceived the happy thought of transforming the humiliating police procedure into a memorial evening for Arkadii Sergeevich, and now she felt even more like the hostess at her own name-day party than she had the previous day. That is to say, in the morning, when she heard about the murder, she had been frightened at first, and her woman's heart had even ached with pity for poor Poggio. She had cried a little, but sometime later, when it emerged that the scandalous fame of the soirée had exceeded her very wildest hopes and that even more sensational events might still be to come, the postmaster's wife had completely shaken off her dejection and spent the entire second half of the day refurbishing a black shot-silk dress that had been lying in mothballs in the cupboard since the last funeral.

For this new soirée the list of participants—on this occasion summoned rather than invited—was almost identical with that for the first. For obvious reasons, Arkadii Sergeevich was absent, but his vengeful spirit was represented by the assistant prosecutor and the chief of police. In addition, in contrast with the previous day, Naina Georgievna was present from the very beginning, for, having been officially notified of the investigative experiment, she arrived promptly at the appointed time of nine o'clock, although Felix Stanislavovich had expected that she would have to be brought under armed escort.

Once she arrived, the party responsible for this calamity (for that was how the majority of those present regarded her) instantly eclipsed their hostess, relegating her to the background. Today Naina Georgievna was more beautiful than ever. She looked quite exceptionally good in the lilac mourning dress and long black gloves that emphasized the elegant lines of her arms, and her black velvet eyes glowed with a special, mysterious light. There was not a trace of embarrassment in her manner; quite the contrary, she carried herself like a genuine queen, the guest of honor for whom this entire funeral feast had been convened.

The prime suspect was quiet, taciturn, and quite different from the way he had been the previous day. Polina Andreevna was surprised to note that, in total contrast with yesterday, his face bore an expression of appeasement, even contentment.

Pyotr Georgievich, however, was as prickly as a hedgehog, repeatedly making impertinent remarks to the representatives of authority, proclaiming in stentorian tones that it was disgraceful to arrange such a show, and demonstratively turning his back on his sister to indicate that he did not wish to have anything to do her.

Among the other participants, Krasnov attracted attention to himself by sobbing interminably and blowing his nose into a truly immense handkerchief. At the beginning of the evening he expressed a desire to recite an ode dedicated to the dead man's memory, and had read the first two verses before Berdichevksy called a halt to the recital as inappropriate. The two verses were as follows:

> He perished in his very prime,
> This sorcerer of lens and light.
> Fate's bloody sword cut short his time,
> A murderous blow struck in the night.
>
> His flame of heavenly inspiration
> No longer now lights up the room.
> In disarray and consternation
> The world is plunged in deepest gloom.

Vladimir Lvovich again arrived later than everyone else and again dispensed with all apologies—why indeed should he bother when Lagrange was showering him with verbose justifications and begging forgiveness for distracting a busy man from state business?

"No matter, you are doing your duty," Bubentsov commented drily, taking a file of documents from his secretary and settling himself in an armchair. "I only hope that this will not last long."

"For that yesterday I did speak unto you and suddenly the terrible hour of death came upon me, for all of us do disappear, all of us do die, both kings and princes, both rich and poor and the whole of humankind," Tikhon Ieremeevich declaimed with feeling, and following these doleful words the experiment began in earnest.

Felix Stanislavovich immediately took center stage.

"Ladies and gentlemen, please come into the salon," he said, pushing open the double doors that led into the adjoining room.

Just as on the previous day, the guests left the drawing room and moved into the exhibition hall. Of course, there were no pictures this time; all that was left were the lonely little strips of paper with the titles of the works that had been irretrievably lost.

The chief of police halted beside the title "On the Curving Shore."

"I hope that everyone remembers the three pictures showing a certain lady in the nude that were hanging here, here, and here," he began, jabbing his finger three times at the empty wallpaper.

The only response was silence.

"I know that the model's face was not fully visible in any of the photographs, but I would like us to make a concerted effort to restore certain features. It is extremely important for the investigation to establish the identity of this woman. Or perhaps someone here present already knows it?"

The chief of police glared hard at Princess Telianova, but she failed to notice his piercing glance because she was not even looking at the speaker, but at Bubentsov. He was standing slightly apart from everyone else, closely studying a sheet of paper.

"Very well, ladies and gentlemen," Lagrange drawled ominously. "Then we shall follow a slow and indelicate route. We shall establish the identity of the model one part at a time and, moreover, by those parts that are usually concealed under clothing, for we are hardly going to learn much about the face. But we shall in any case start with the head. What color was the hair of the lady in question?"

"Light, with a golden shimmer to it," said the marshal's wife. "Very thick and slightly wavy."

"Excellent," said the chief of police with a nod. "Thank you, Evgenia Anatolievna. More or less like this?" He pointed to the coils of hair dangling from under Naina Georgievna's hat.

"Very possibly," the countess stammered, blushing.

"And the neck? What can you tell me about the neck?" Felix Stanislavovich asked, sighing with the air of a man whose patience is almost exhausted. "And then we shall discuss in the greatest possible detail the shoulders, the back, the bust, the stomach, the legs. And other parts of the body, including the thighs and the buttocks—we shall certainly have to do that."

Lagrange's tone of voice had become threatening, and he pronounced the awkward word "buttocks" with especial emphasis, almost chanting it.

"Or perhaps we might just be able to manage without that?" he asked, this time addressing Naina Georgievna directly.

She smiled calmly, evidently enjoying all the glances directed at her and the general embarrassment. She did not betray the slightest sign of the offended modesty that had almost reduced her to tears the day before.

"Well, let us suppose that you can define the breasts and the buttocks," she said with a shrug. "What then? Are you going to strip all the female inhabitants of the province naked and hold a parade?"

"Why all of them?" Felix Stanislavovich hissed through his teeth. "Only those who are under suspicion. And no parade will be required; what would we want with a scandal like that? It will be quite sufficient to verify certain specific features. I am actually conducting this interrogation to maintain formal procedure and for the sake of later record-keeping, but in actual fact I have already spoken with some of those now present. I know, specifically, that the lady in whom we are interested has two noticeable moles on her right buttock and that just below her breasts she has a light-colored birthmark the size of a fifty-kopek piece. You have no idea, princess, how attentive the male eye is to small details of that kind."

Even the indomitable Naina Georgievna was stung by that—she blushed and was at a loss for words.

Lisitsyna came to her aid.

"Ah, gentlemen, why do we keep talking about the same photographs all the time?" she twittered, trying to divert the conversation away from this indecorous theme. "There were so many wonderful landscapes here! Over there, for instance, there was an absolutely marvelous work—it impressed me so much that I simply can't forget it. Don't you remember? It was called 'Rainy Morning.' Such expression, such subtle play of light and shade!"

Matvei Bentsionovich gave this lady who had spoken out of turn a look of clear dissatisfaction and Lagrange even knitted his brows and frowned menacingly, intending to call the idle prattler to order, but Naina Georgievna was clearly delighted by the turn of conversation.

"Yes, indeed, if we are going to talk about anything, then it ought to be that curious picture," she exclaimed with an evil-sounding laugh that seemed to contain a hint of mystery. "I also paid particular attention to it yesterday, although not because of its expressive qualities.

The most remarkable thing about it, Mrs. Lisitsyna, was not the play of light and shade at all, but a certain interesting detail . . ."

"Stop that," Felix Stanislavovich roared furiously, flushing bright red. "You will not succeed in diverting me from my line of inquiry! All this prevarication will get us nowhere; we are simply wasting our time."

"Precisely so," declared Spasyonny. " 'Blessed are they who do stop their ears, so that they shall not hear what they should not.' And it is also written: 'In the company of the unwise, guard your time well.' "

"Yes, Lagrange, you really are simply wasting time," Bubentsov said suddenly, raising his head from his documents. "Good Lord, I have a mountain of work to do, and you're playing out this foolish melodrama. In your report to me yesterday you said that you have a definite clue. Out with it, and the business is over and done with."

At these words Matvei Bentsionovich, who knew nothing about any "definite clue" or the very existence of any report to Vladimir Lvovich by the chief of police, peered angrily at Lagrange. In his embarrassment at not knowing to whom he ought to apologize first, Lagrange addressed both of his superiors at the same time by conflating their names: "Vladimir Bentsionovich, I was attempting to demonstrate everything absolutely as clearly as possible, to reconstruct the entire logic of the crime. And it is also a matter of charity; I wished to give the criminal a chance to repent. I thought that now we would establish that it was Princess Telianova in the photographs, Shiryaev would explode, start defending her and confess."

Everyone gasped and shied away from Stepan Trofimovich. But he stood there as if turned to stone, only turning his head rapidly first to the left and then to the right.

"Confess?" said Berdichevsky, pressing the chief of police. "So you have evidence against Shiryaev?"

"Matvei Bentsionovich, I had no time to report to you, or rather, it was not that I had no time," babbled Lagrange. "I wanted to create a dramatic effect; I'm sorry."

"What are you talking about? Get to the point!" the assistant prosecutor shouted at him.

Felix Stanislavovich mopped the sweat off his forehead.

"What can I say? Everything is quite clear. Shiryaev is in love with Telianova; he was dreaming of marrying her. And then this ladykiller from the capital appeared, Poggio. He enthralled her, turned her head, and debauched her. It's perfectly clear that she was the one who posed for those nudes. Shiryaev had known about, or at least suspected, the relationship between Poggio and Telianova earlier, but it is one thing to picture something in your mind, while this was proof positive, and such scandalous proof as well. I won't undertake to judge Poggio's motives for such disgraceful behavior, because they do not have any direct connection to the crime under investigation. Yesterday in front of everyone Shiryaev attacked the culprit with his fists and he would surely have killed him there and then had he not been pulled away. So he waited until night and crept into the apartment to finish the business. And afterward, not satisfied with his revenge, he destroyed all the fruits of his sworn enemy's work, as well as the camera with which Poggio had so mortally offended him."

"But we have been told all this before," Berdichevsky observed with annoyance. "It is a plausible account, but founded completely on suppositions. Where is this definite clue of yours?"

"Matvei Bentsionovich, I promised you that I would check the alibis of all the leading figures in the case. That is what my agents have been doing today. Yesterday Pyotr Georgievich got completely drunk, carried on shouting and weeping until late into the night, and then the servants fed him herbal infusions to sober him up. That is an alibi. Mr. Sytnikov went straight from here to Madam Gruber's establishment on Warsaw Street, and stayed there until morning in the company of a certain Zemphira, whose passport gives her name as Matryona Sychkina. That is also an alibi."

"A fine old two-fingered believer," said Vladimir Lvovich with a whistle. "I am prepared to wager that Zemphira Sychkina looks at least a little bit like Naina Georgievna—the honorable gentleman has been licking his lips over her for a long time."

Donat Abramovich held his peace, nonplussed at such a turn of events, but the look that he cast at Bubentsov made it clear that the perceptive psychologist was correct in his supposition.

"But as for Mr. Shiryaev," said the chief of police, claiming his dramatic effect after all, "he has no alibi at all. Furthermore, it has been established beyond all doubt that he did not return to Drozdovka for the night, nor did he stay in any of the hotels in the town or go to any of his friends here. Permit me to ask you, sir," he said severely, addressing Stepan Trofimovich, "where and how did you spend last night?"

Shiryaev hung his head and gave no reply. His chest was heaving strenuously.

"There is your definite clue, as good as a confession."

Lagrange directed Berdichevsky's and Bubentsov's attention toward the exposed criminal with a picturesque gesture. Then he clapped his hands loudly three times.

In came two policemen who had obviously been informed about everything in advance, because they immediately walked across to Shiryaev and took him by the arms. He shuddered, but even now he still said nothing.

"Take him to the station," ordered Felix Stanislavovich. "Put him in the nobles' cell. Mr. Berdichevsky and I will arrive soon to interrogate him."

They led Stepan Trofimovich to the door. He kept turning around to look at the princess, and she looked back at him with a strange smile, unusually gentle and almost affectionate. Not a single word passed between them.

When the prisoner had been taken away, Spasyonny crossed himself and declared: "Suffer not for long the doers of evil, for they shall fall into profound torment."

"As you see," Lagrange said modestly, addressing primarily Bubentsov and Berdichevsky, "the investigation really did not take very long. Ladies and gentlemen, I thank you all for your assistance and I beg your forgiveness if I have caused you any unpleasant moments."

These restrained and noble words were pronounced in a stately manner appropriate to the occasion, and when Naina Georgievna started speaking, everyone assumed at first that she was talking about Felix Stanislavovich.

"Now there is a truly noble man for you, not like all the rest," the young lady said thoughtfully, as if she was talking to herself, and then suddenly raised her voice. "Alas, dear gentlemen guardians of the law.

You will have to release Stepan Trofimovich. I deliberately tried to test him, to see if he would tell you. But just imagine—he didn't! And I'm certain that he will accept hard labor without giving me away. . . . Stepan Trofimovich did not commit any murder, because he spent the whole of last night at my house. If my words are not enough for you, then question the maid. The way he intervened to defend my honor yesterday touched some chord inside me . . . But that is of no interest to you. What are you all gawping at?"

She gave a most disagreeable laugh and cast a strange glance at Vladimir Lvovich—challenging and imploring all at once. He smiled without saying anything, as if he was waiting to see if there were any more confessions to come. But when it became clear that everything had been said, the investigative experiment was a categorical failure and Lagrange had been reduced to total confusion, even seeming to have lost the power of speech, Bubentsov turned to the representatives of authority and inquired mockingly: "Well, then, is the evening's program over? May I go? Undershirt, fetch me my cloak."

The secretary slithered out of the salon without a murmur and came back half a minute later, already wearing his peaked cap. He handed his lord and master a light velvet cloak with a cape and a uniform cap.

"Good day to you," Bubentsov said sardonically. He bowed and walked toward the door.

In his foppish outfit he looked from behind exactly like some dandified Guards officer, which, strictly speaking, was exactly who he had been until quite recently.

"The same cloak," Naina Georgievna declaimed in a loud voice. "The same cap. How it gleamed in the moonlight . . ."

It was not clear whether the young woman was playing the part of the disconsolate Ophelia or she really had lost her wits and was raving.

"We shall leave your rotten little swamp. Perhaps we shall marry and I shall have children. Then I shall be forgiven everything," the princess continued with her gibberish. "But first all debts must be repaid, full justice must be established. Isn't that so, Vladimir Lvovich?"

Vladimir Lvovich stood in the doorway, looking back at her in bewildered amusement.

Then Naina Georgievna proceeded royally past him, brushing him gently with her shoulder, and disappeared into the drawing room. Apparently she had at last learned to make her exit not at a run, but a walk.

"A young lady of iron," Donat Abramovich drawled in evident admiration. "I do not know to whom she intended to pay back her debts, but I should not like to be in their place."

"Well, yes," said Berdichevsky, summing up. "Felix Stanislavovich, Shiryaev will have to be released."

The chief of police started muttering: "But it still doesn't mean a thing. They still absolutely must be interrogated. Shiryaev, and Telianova, and the maid. It could be a criminal conspiracy. Any kind of low trickery can be expected from a perverse and hysterical creature like that."

But no one was listening to him. One by one the participants in the experiment made their way the door.

POLINA ANDREEVNA LISITSYNA returned to her lodgings with the colonel's widow in a state of profound preoccupation. The venerable Antonina Ivanovna took to her bed immediately after supper and at this late hour she was already dreaming serenely, and so there was no one to distract the houseguest with conversations and questions.

Once in her room, the ginger-haired lady quickly undressed, but she did not proceed with her bedtime toilet, as might have been expected; instead she took a bundle of black robes out of her travel bag and in less than a minute she had transformed herself into the meek Sister Pelagia. Treading softly, she walked along the corridor and slipped out through the kitchen into the street.

The moonless, windy night eagerly accepted the black-robed nun into its equally black embrace, and the nun flitted past the sleeping houses like a faint shadow.

From Pelagia's point of view, Police Chief Lagrange's investigative experiment had proved very useful indeed—so useful, in fact, that it had become a matter of urgency for her to talk to Naina Georgievna face-to-face straightaway, without waiting for tomorrow to come. The mysterious photograph entitled "Rainy Morning" had left no impression whatever in Polina Andreevna's memory, and yet her intuition told her that it might well hold the key to this entire unpleasant episode. Of course, it would have been simpler to go straight to the princess's house in the character of Mrs. Lisitsyna, but respectable ladies did not go driving around the town alone at night, and they certainly did not wander about on foot—that would attract far too much attention. But who would take any notice of a humble nun?

It was quite a long walk, all the way to the bank of the River, where the old house that Naina Georgievna had inherited stood. It was getting near midnight. At that time of night in Zavolzhsk the only people not sleeping are lovers and police constables on guard duty (although the latter are probably also asleep, in their little booths), and so the nun did not encounter a single living soul along her way.

Our town has a strange appearance on a wet and windy autumn night. It is as if the entire population has been spirited away to a distant, unknown land by some mysterious magical spell, leaving behind only the dark houses with their black windows, the streetlamps with their flames burning low, and the foolish bell towers with their orphaned crosses. And if someone who cannot sleep because his nerves are on edge should start to get frightening ideas into his head, it would be very easy indeed to imagine that power has changed hands in Zavolzhsk and that until the sun and the daylight return, the town will be ruled by the powers of darkness—from whom any kind of foul nastiness may be expected.

In general, the town was a bad place to be out in. Deserted, lifeless, frightening.

# CHAPTER 9

# Night. The River

WHEN PELAGIA TURNED off into Varravkin cul-de-sac, which led to Naina Georgievna's house, the sky suddenly lit up without the slightest sound—which made the sight all the more eerie—with a blindingly bright sheet of lightning, and the darkness that followed seemed so dense that the nun was forced to stop, no longer able to make out the outlines of the houses. No sooner had she grown accustomed to it and taken a few more steps than there was another white flash and again she was obliged to wait with her eyes squeezed tightly shut until her pupils, violently assaulted by this atrocious glare, had expanded once more. But this time she could hear a slow, distant rumble of thunder.

And so it went: a dozen or so steps in pitch-darkness, then a momentary orgy of satanic brightness, then again blackness, filled with the low growling of the storm advancing on the town.

The house proved easy to find. Varravkin cul-de-sac ran right to it. Another blaze of lightning lit up the little house with its dead, boarded-up attic floor, the wooden fence, and the leaves of the trees behind it, with their whitish undersides all turned upward by the gusty wind. When the peal of thunder died away she could hear the agitated River roaring in indignation somewhere behind the house and the trees. The bank here rose up especially high, and the channel was narrowed by almost six hundred yards, so that even on the most tranquil of days the confined torrent seethed in anger as it went rushing past the steep cliff, and in bad weather the River grew so furious that it seemed enraged with the town for pressing it so hard and strove to wash away the hateful bank and bring Zavolzhsk tumbling down into its foaming waters.

The orchard that began immediately behind the house merged almost imperceptibly with a birch grove where the public of Zavolzhsk loved to stroll on fine evenings—from the top of the precipice the view across the open expanse of the River was so very fine. It was clear that this grove was already doomed, that in a year or two, or five at the most, the River would undercut it, tear it down, and carry it away downstream, all the way to the Caspian or even beyond. Some wave would cast up a sodden, salt-soaked birch trunk on a distant Persian shore, and swarthy-skinned people would gather around to behold this great marvel. After the high waters of spring one of the birches was already on the point of tumbling over the steep cliff, only clinging on with its final snag of root, dangling above the rushing rapids like a white finger pointing outward and upward. The wildest of the young boys were in the habit of rocking up and down on it, and many people said that the tree ought to be pushed over the edge out of harm's way before there was a tragic accident, but somehow no one had ever gotten around to doing it.

Pelagia shuddered in the wind as she stood for a moment at the gate, gazing at the dark windows of the house. It seemed as though she would have to wake Naina Georgievna. That was awkward, of course, but this was a serious matter.

The gate creaked in complaint as it opened and the steps of the old porch squeaked in different voices, like the keys on a broken old piano. The nun listened to see if she could hear any sound from inside the house. It was quiet. What if nobody was there?

Resolutely grasping the bronze knocker that took the place of a bell, she knocked loudly. And again she listened.

No, there was someone there after all—she thought she heard a voice say something, or was it the squeak of a door hinge?

"Open the door!" the nun shouted. "It is I, Sister Pelagia from the episcopal see."

Had she imagined it then? There was not a sound.

She pushed and pulled at the door—it was bolted on the inside. That meant they were at home, but asleep and so could not hear her. Or perhaps they could hear her, but they did not wish to let her in?

Pelagia knocked again, a little longer this time, to make it quite clear that she was not going to leave empty-handed. The echoing crash of the bronze knocker was so thunderous that someone—either the mistress of the house or the maid—was bound to wake up.

And once again, from somewhere deep inside the house, she heard a low voice calling, this time quite distinctly. As if someone had sung a few notes quietly and then fallen silent.

That was really strange.

Pelagia came down from the porch and walked around under the windows. As was only to be expected, they were slightly open—it had been muggy earlier in the evening, as the thunderstorm approached. Hoisting up her habit almost as far as her waist, the nun climbed onto the step in the wall, grabbed hold of the windowsill, and pushed the window frame.

But it was pointless—the darkness was absolutely impenetrable.

"Hey!" Pelagia called out fearfully. "Is anybody there? Naina Georgievna! Are you there? Naina Georgievna!"

No answer, only the squeak of a floorboard—either somebody taking a step or simply the house settling.

The sister crossed herself, and at that instant the sky was set aglow by a luminous discharge that lit up the room as brightly as the noonday sun. It was not long, just a second, but that was enough for Pelagia to make out the little drawing room and something long and white lying on the floor in the middle of it.

"Holy Virgin, Mother of God, save and protect us," Pelagia muttered, and she climbed in over the windowsill.

So much for the "young woman of iron." She had come home and fainted. Which was not at all surprising, after such a fraught evening, but what was the maid thinking? Pelagia took some phosphorus matches out of her waist bag and struck one.

It was not Naina Georgievna at all, but a round-faced girl she did not know—her hair loose, wearing her nightshirt, with a shawl thrown over her shoulders. She could only assume that it was the maid. The girl's eyes were closed, but her mouth, on the contrary, was slightly open. Her hair looked odd somehow—at the ends it seemed to be light-colored, but higher up, close to the forehead, it was black and shiny. Pelagia touched it and pulled her hand away with a shriek. It was wet. Her fingers had turned black, too. Blood!

At that moment the match burned out, and Pelagia started crawling, just as she was, on all fours, back toward the windows. Her spectacles clattered as they went tumbling to the floor, but she felt no urge to go back for them.

She had to tumble over the windowsill and run away from this terrible silent house as fast as her legs would carry her!

But then again she heard the same sound as before—quiet, like a voice calling. Only now she could tell that it was not a call and not singing, but a weak groan. It came from somewhere in the dark depths of the house, and that meant that she simply could not run away.

With a sinking heart the nun straightened, crossed the left half of her chest with small, rapid movements, and addressed a mental prayer to her patroness, Saint Pelagia, whom she only bothered in cases of extreme need.

"Supplicate God for me, holy Pelagia, most pleasing to God, hear my most fervent appeal to thee, who art quick to succor, intercessor for my soul."

And instantly there was help from her saint, the beautiful Roman girl who was burned alive in a bull of bronze. A feeble flare of lightning dispelled the gloom for a moment and Pelagia saw a candle standing in a copper holder on the windowsill. It was a good sign, strengthening the resolve of her soul.

Her fingers were trembling so much that the first match broke, and the second one likewise, but she lit the candle with the third, and now she could take a better look around.

The first thing that caught her eye was the clear print of a boot on the windowsill, with the toe pointing inward, into the house. Pelagia resolutely turned her back to the window and raised the hand with the candle higher. Now she could see that a dark puddle had spread out all around the maid's head. The spectacles that she had dropped glinted. Pelagia picked them up and saw that the left lens was cracked, but she was not upset—this was no time to worry about such things.

The picture that emerged was as follows. When everyone in the house had already gone to bed for the night, someone had climbed in through the window, evidently making a lot of noise about it. The maid had come to see what the noise was and the intruder had struck her over the head with some heavy object.

Pelagia squatted down and put her fingers to the temple, where the vein ought to be pulsating. The vein was not pulsating; the girl was dead. The nun murmured a prayer, but without any inspiration, because she was still listening.

Another groan. And close by—perhaps only ten steps away.

She took a first step, a second, a third, ready at the first sign of danger to drop the candle and dash back to the open window.

The dark opening of a door gaped ahead of her.

The corridor?

Pelagia took another step and saw Naina Georgievna.

The princess was lying on the floor in the corridor, very close to the drawing room.

She was wearing a peignoir and a lace cap, and a single backless embroidered velvet slipper was lying to one side of her. Farther along the corridor Pelagia could see a slightly open door that obviously led to the bedroom. But Pelagia was not concerned with the arrangement of the rooms just at this moment—Naina Georgievna's cap was completely soaked with blood, and her huge, beautiful eyes were gazing upward, absolutely motionless, with two little lights reflected in them. And the nun also spotted something black, a large stone, lying on the floor a short distance away. When she saw it, she could not help recalling Zakusai lying dead under the little tree, and she crossed herself.

Naina Georgievna was still alive, but her life was ebbing away—the nun realized that immediately, the moment her fingers felt the sharp edge of the shattered parietal bone. When Pelagia was undergoing her probation as a novice, her first work of penance had been working in the convent hospital, so that she had ample experience in the area of medicine.

The long eyelashes fluttered; the dying woman's gaze focused slowly and reluctantly on the nun.

"Ah, Sister Pelagia," said Naina Georgievna, without the slightest surprise, even seeming pleased, but not to excess.

Pronouncing her words clearly, but drawling very slightly (that was what happened with an injury to the skull), she declared: "I shall die now." Having said it, she seemed slightly surprised at her own words. "I can feel it. And it's quite all right. I'm not afraid at all. And it doesn't hurt."

"I'll run to get help," sobbed Pelagia.

"Don't, it's too late. I don't want to be alone in the dark again."

"Who did this to you?"

"I didn't see . . . There was a noise. I called—Dunyasha didn't answer. I came out to see, there was a blow. Then nothing. Then I heard a woman's voice, far, far away. Calling: 'Naina Georgievna.' It was dark. I thought: Where am I, what's happening to me . . ." The corners of the princess's lips twitched—she must have been trying to smile. "I'm glad that I'm dying. It's the best thing that could have happened. And you being here is a sign, a miracle from God. He is forgiving me. I am guilty before Him. I shan't have time to tell you, it's all slipping away. You just grant me absolution. It's all right that you're not a priest, you're still a cleric."

With her teeth chattering, Pelagia began reciting the requisite words.

"Like unto drops of rain, my evil and brief days do grow scant in the summer of life, disappearing little by little, Queen of Heaven, save me . . ."

Naina Georgievna repeated: "Have mercy, have mercy"—but more and more quietly. Her strength was fading with every moment that passed. When the nun had finished reciting the canon, the princess could no longer speak and only smiled weakly.

Pelagia leaned down over her and asked: "What was in the photograph? The one of the rainy morning?"

She did not think there would be any answer, but a minute later the pale lips stirred.

"An aspen . . ."

"What about the aspen?"

"A-live. And a mattock."

"Who's alive? What mattock?"

The floor squeaked behind her—not as quietly as before, but quite substantially, as if under the weight of someone's heavy tread.

Pelagia looked around and gasped. A black silhouette emerged from the doorway that led into the bedroom, moving slowly, as if it were not real, but part of some terrible dream.

"Ah-ah!" The nun choked on her own cry and dropped the candle, which immediately went out.

Clearly that was the only thing that saved her. In the ensuing pitch-black darkness she heard the sound of rapid steps and felt a draft of cold air on her forehead from something heavy that whistled past just above her head as she shrank down toward the floor.

Without standing up, the nun spun around and darted into the drawing room. It was absolutely black in there, too, with only the vague rectangular outlines of the three windows to be seen. Behind her she could hear hoarse breathing, the scrabbling of feet on the waxed floor. Neither Pelagia nor her pursuer could see each other. Afraid of giving herself away by making a sound, she froze on the spot, staring into the darkness. Boom-boom-boom, beat her poor heart, and it seemed to Pelagia that this drumbeat filled the entire drawing room.

Someone was moving there in the darkness, someone was coming closer down the corridor. The darkness whistled: whoosh-sh! And then again, closer now: whoosh-sh!

He's lashing out at random with his club or whatever he has, thought Pelagia. She could not stay where she was any longer. She swung around and dashed for the middle gray rectangle. On the way she knocked over a chair, cursing her own eternal clumsiness, yet somehow managed to stay on her feet. But whoever was dogging her footsteps seemed to stumble over the chair and go crashing to the floor. A normal person would have called out or cursed, but this one did not make a sound.

Pelagia climbed up into the window and the hem of her habit snagged on the projecting sill. She tugged as hard as she could, but the coarse material refused to yield. A hand clutched the nun tightly by the collar from behind, and at this touch the nun's strength seemed to increase tenfold. She jerked with all her might, the habit tore at the hem and at the collar—and, thanks be to God, Pelagia went tumbling out through the window. Not even knowing if she had hurt herself, she jumped to her feet, looking to the right and to the left.

To the right was the gate and the street. She couldn't go that way. Before she could get the gate open he would overtake her. And even if she managed to get out into the street, she still would not be able to run away fast enough in her habit.

This thought flashed through her mind in a fraction of a second, and in the next fraction of the same second Pelagia was already running to the left, around the corner of the house.

Without the slightest warning or preliminary sprinkling, the rain came lashing down in such a sudden torrent that the nun almost choked. Now it was absolutely impossible for her to make out anything at all. She ran through the orchard and then through the birch grove, holding out her hands in front of her to avoid running into a tree.

There was a flash of lightning somewhere nearby. Pelagia looked around as she ran and saw white tree trunks and a glassy wall of rain, and behind that, about twenty steps away, a black figure, moving with its arms outstretched.

She had absolutely nowhere to go. Another ten steps and she could feel the breath of the chasm in her face. Pelagia did not see the cliff edge, she inhaled it. The deafening lashing of the rain drowned out the sound of the rushing River.

The black chasm gaped in front of her, and footsteps splashed through puddles behind her—not too hurriedly, for her pursuer realized perfectly well that the nun had nowhere to run and he was evidently afraid that she might conceal herself under one of the bushes.

On her left she could just make out some vague white form through the gloom. Like a finger pointing outward and slightly upward to where the first star appeared in the evening sky.

A birch tree! The one that was dangling over the edge of the cliff!

Pelagia ran to the doomed tree, went down on all fours, and crawled along it, trying not to think about the eighty feet of emptiness below her. She reached the crown and stopped there, putting her arms around the trunk as tightly as she could and pressing her cheek against the wet, rough bark. Could she be seen from the bank or not?

Of course she could—black against white!

Pelagia jerked up into a sitting position and dangled her legs into empty air. She tore off her black headscarf and dropped it. She pulled the habit up over her head, but it was heavy and swollen with water, it didn't want to go flying down into the darkness, it caught at her elbows and her chin. When it finally yielded, it took its revenge by dragging her spectacles off with it. But what good were spectacles when she could not see anything anyway?

Pelagia turned to face the bank and sat with her back against the thick stump of a broken branch. She was left wearing only her linen shirt and was shuddering all over now, not from the cold, but from the icy terror that was piercing to the very marrow of her bones.

"Intercessor, Intercessor . . ." the nun whispered, but she simply could not remember what came next in the prayer to the Holy Virgin.

The rain was streaming down her face, the water lashed against the crookedly protruding tree trunk, the River rumbled far below, but Pelagia's straining ears also caught other sounds.

The blows of wood on wood. Steps. The crunching of twigs.

Soon this will come to an end, Pelagia told herself. It cannot go on forever. He will wander this way and that and then go away.

But time seemed to have stopped. Perhaps this is the end of the world, the nun suddenly thought. Perhaps this is how everything will end: darkness, the gates of heaven opened, heart-stopping horror, steps in the darkness—how could anything more terrifying possibly be imagined?

Ah, the lightning, the lightning—why did it have to choose that very moment to split the sky, just when the storm had almost moved away toward the forests beyond the River and only the rain and the wind were left!

But the birch grove was lit by one last flash, and Pelagia saw a black figure close by, standing among the bushes, gleaming wet with rain. And even worse than that was the fact that Pelagia had also been seen.

The steps came closer. The birch tree swayed as a foot was set on it.

Using her hands to help her along, the nun edged backward along the trunk on her buttocks. The trunk began to creak and sag. Now it no longer hung over the chasm at an angle, but level with the ground.

"You should leave, sir," Pelagia shouted in a trembling voice, because she could no longer bear the silence. "I do not know who you are, I have not seen you. And so you have nothing to be afraid of. Do not take another sin on your soul; you have done enough already. And you will not get me here, or we shall both fall together."

The black, silent figure seemed to have realized already that the tree would not support the double burden.

For about a minute there was silence. Then there were sounds that Pelagia could not understand at first. Squelching, champing, and knocking. The birch tree seemed to come alive; it started swaying and creaking.

He's digging out the root, Pelagia suddenly realized. And once she knew that, it was as if her fear had never existed. Suddenly it was clear that fear was another name for hope. And if there was absolutely no hope, there was nothing to fear.

And then she remembered the prayer: "Zealous intercessor, beneficent Mother of God, unto you do I appeal in my sinfulness, greatest of all sinners as I am, hear the voice of my prayer and attend to my wailing and lament . . ."

At the words "like unto a ship in an abysm, I do founder in the sea of my sins," the trunk began to fall in a rapidly accelerating movement and threw the nun off into the black, echoing space.

Throwing out her arms, Pelagia dived soundlessly and unhindered through the void toward the loud roaring and splashing.

". . . now and ever and into ages of ages. Amen."

The River accepted her with an unexpected, yielding softness. Pelagia did not feel any wetness, because she was already as soaked as she could possibly be, and she only guessed that she was no longer in the air but underwater because her downward movement was impeded and slowed.

The nun flapped her arms, pushed off with her legs and went darting upward, to where it was open and airy. But the water would not let her go; it kept pulling her away somewhere, spinning her around, and now there was absolutely no air left in her lungs. I'll count to three before I open my mouth and then come what may, the drowning woman thought. But she did not have the strength to hold out any longer. She parted her lips wide, ready to fill her lungs with the River, and her mouth drew in not water but air and flying spray, because at that very moment Pelagia's head surfaced among the foaming waves.

She drew in a breath greedily, and another, and another, forgetting to breathe out and making herself cough, but the underwater current was already drawing her back down, and the nun disappeared below the surface again.

This time it proved even harder to surface—her sodden, heavy shoes kept trying to straighten Pelagia's body out into a vertical line, to make it easier for the River to drag her to the bottom. She hunched over tight and tugged the weights off her feet, and it became easier to fight against the water. As she began floundering in the enveloping embrace of the rushing torrent, she pushed off with her feet and shot up, up, up.

Again she began gulping in air, but the River was intent on bearing its booty on and away into the darkness, and seemed to find it amusing to spin her around, first clockwise and then counterclockwise. Nearby, too far away for her to touch it, but close enough to be seen, there was something light-colored sticking up out of the water and trembling as it moved in the same direction and at the same speed as herself. Pelagia could not so much see as guess at the outlines of the broken branches, and she realized that it was the birch tree, her companion in misfortune.

Crossing the gap of a mere eight feet that separated the nun from the tree proved very difficult. The River seemed to imagine that Pelagia wanted to play with it, and accepted the invitation gladly. The moment the nun came close enough to the birch tree to touch the slippery bark with her fingers, the current gently tossed the trunk aside with ease, as if it were a mere splinter of wood. Once it dragged it a long way from her and Pelagia lost sight of the outline that promised salvation. She herself could not remain afloat for very much longer—she was being tossed about too hard to the right and the left, spun around too fast, and from time to time a wave broke over her head, so that she could easily have choked on the water.

But when Pelagia had already resigned herself to the tree's disappearance, it swam out of the gloom unseen and hit her on the back of her head with one of its branches.

At first the exhausted nun simply clung to the submerged trunk, delighted that she need no longer flounder and struggle. After resting for a moment, she began clambering onto the tree. She slipped off several times and scraped her shoulder, but she still managed to climb up and sit on the log, straddling it with her legs.

Once, a long time before, in a different life, Pelagia had been a capable horsewoman, and she loved to race through the meadow early in the morning at a speed that set everything inside her quivering. She felt something of the same kind now, but she could only guess at her own movement from the wind blowing in her face, for the River had suddenly stopped moving. Pelagia had become fused with it, a single particle of it. She was simply sitting on an uncomfortable wooden bench that was no longer rushing anywhere, merely rotating slowly in one place.

Not only had time disappeared, so had space. But there was a chill cold that Pelagia had noticed before. She could feel the rain once again, beating heavily against her forehead and cheeks.

First her teeth began chattering, then her shoulders began shuddering, and things became really bad when she lost the feeling in her hands. She could tell quite clearly what would happen next: Her fingers would open, releasing their grasp on the trunk, and the unfortunate rider would be thrown into the River, but this time she would have no strength left to struggle against the current.

That was exactly the way things would happen, because no other outcome was possible.

There was only one decision she could take, a terrifying one. Throw herself into the water and try to reach the bank before her muscles stiffened completely. But which way should she swim—to the right or to the left? She had fallen into the River from the high left bank, but how much time had passed since then she could not tell. She could easily have been carried out into midstream, or all the way over close to the right bank. She would not be able to swim for long. If she chose the wrong direction, it was the end; her soul would join the saints in heaven. Well, then, if that was the way things were, the Lord must have decided to summon his handmaiden Pelagia. It was shameful for a nun to be afraid of death. If the grim reaper suddenly leapt out from around the corner like a thief in the night and blew his hot, stinking breath in one's face—then it was forgivable to feel frightened. But if one had time to prepare oneself and gather one's courage, then to be afraid of death was a foolish sin.

The nun slid resolutely into the water on the left side of the tree trunk and pushed off hard from it with her feet. The current here was not so furious—obviously the narrow channel had been left behind and the River had emerged onto the flat plain. Swimming in total darkness without knowing where she was going felt strange, and soon Pelagia could not tell if she was maintaining the correct direction or had gone astray. Her arms and legs performed their work rhythmically, but the long shirt was a terrible hindrance, clinging to her knees. Should she remove it? Pelagia imagined the River casting her body up on the bank: naked, with her hair loose. Oh no. If she was to drown, she would drown in her shirt.

All the signs were that she was going to drown. Her arms barely obeyed her any longer, and still there was no shore to be seen. Forgive me, Lord, Pelagia thought wearily. I honestly did everything that I could. She turned over on to her back and surrendered to the will of the current. Her only regret was that she could not look up at the sky—it would have been good to see at least one little star before she went, but that was impossible.

When her head and shoulders ran up against something unyielding, Pelagia did not immediately realize it was sand.

SHE COULD NOT see the bank, but she could touch it with her hands.

And that was what Pelagia did: She went down on her knees and stroked the cold, sodden ground with her palms. After praying in thanks for her miraculous deliverance, she wrung out her shirt and sat down, hugging her shoulders. It was still not clear where she was and which way she ought to walk. The rain continued for a while and then stopped. The nun wrung out her shirt again and in an attempt to get warm began jumping up and down on one leg and then on the other. She sat for a while, hopped about for a while, sat, hopped about—and her shirt was a vague white silhouette, stretched out on a snag embedded in the silt.

As she jumped up and down yet again, slapping her sides loudly, the nun suddenly noticed that the darkness had grown less dense. There was the edge of the water, and a dead seagull on the sand, and if everything beyond that was fused into a single mass, it was not because of the night but because of the tall cliff that towered up above the narrow strip of water. If she strained her eyes she could make out the top of the cliff and the gray sky above it.

Pelagia squatted down in fright. God forbid that some insomniac should come out for a stroll in the cool freshness before dawn, look down from the bank, and see this scene: a naked witch with her hair loose jumping up and down and waving her arms in the air. It would be absolutely dreadful.

As she pulled on her cold, wet shirt, she thought for the first time about her situation. First, she had no idea where the current had carried her—perhaps there was no human habitation here at all. And second, even if the area was inhabited, everything was still far from simple. It was hardly appropriate for a nun to appear in front of people like this.

She walked to and fro under the cliff and spied out a faintly visible path that led upward. The incline was steep and every now and then her feet trod on sharp stones, so that Pelagia looked down more than up, but when she did throw her head back to check whether she still had far to go, she gasped. There was a strange white object standing at the top of the cliff, something she had not been able to see from below: tall, elegant, static. The nun thought that the shape of this strange object seemed familiar. She walked a little higher, looking upward now instead of down at her feet.

A pavilion. With short white columns, decorative iron railings, and a rounded top. A familiar pavilion—the same one from which she had so enjoyed observing the River from the Drozdovka park.

Pelagia could not decide immediately if it was a good thing that the current had carried her to Drozdovka. Of course, people whom she knew would be more willing to help than strangers, but the shame she would feel in front of them would be even greater.

The trees standing in the park were soaking wet and dismal. There was a white mist floating up from the ground, still quite thin, but gradually thickening. It was chilly and damp. And there was still a long time left before the real dawn came. What should she do?

Pelagia ran, hopping and skipping, toward the house, her teeth chattering. She could wait it out somehow until the morning, and then Tanya or one of the other women servants would come out of the house, and she could call them quietly. There was nothing else that she could do. She couldn't go bursting into the house of the general's widow in the middle of the night in such a dreadful state, with her ginger hair all matted and tangled.

She squatted down beside the bathhouse. She tugged at the door—a pity, it was locked, it would have been a lot warmer inside. Out in the open air she had become completely chilled, and her jumping had not helped.

And then the nun remembered about the gardener's hut. That definitely could not be locked.

She ran back along the alley. Her damp shirt clung repulsively to her legs.

There was the little house. And yes—the door was not locked.

Pelagia went into the dark shelter. Treading cautiously so as not to step on anything sharp, she made her way into a corner and sat down. At least it was dry; for that, many thanks, Lord.

Little by little it grew light. She could see the cracks in the planking walls, the tools: rakes, spades, hoes, an axe, mattocks.

Mattocks? What had Naina Georgievna said? A live aspen and a mattock?

What did it mean?

Since she had nothing else to do, Pelagia began turning the strange words over and over in her mind. It must mean that the photograph called "Rainy Morning" showed some kind of mattock and an aspen tree. Alive. But what other kinds of aspens were there—dead ones?

The young woman must have been raving as she died. But no—the words had been spoken in reply to a question asked by Pelagia.

There were plenty of aspens in the park, every one more alive than the last.

But again, no! The nun whistled out loud. One was certainly not alive—the one beside which poor innocent Zakusai was lying after he was murdered. Perhaps the princess had been talking about that little tree? Had she been saying that in the photograph it had still been alive? But what was so unusual about that, and what had the mattock to do with it?

Pelagia could not go on sitting there, consumed as she was by a fever of speculation. And why should she stay where she was, if she could go and look?

She clambered out of the hut and trotted to where the withered little tree protruded from the ground. Everything was familiar in the park, the twilight and the mist were no hindrance to her, and a minute later the nun was standing beside the memorable English lawn, with the dead aspen cringing beside it.

What was its secret?

Pelagia squatted down and touched the wrinkled leaves, ran her palm down along the smooth trunk. What was this disturbed earth here, by the roots? Ah, yes, that was where Zakusai had been scraping at it with his paws.

But no, surely a puppy could not have dug up so much earth?

The nun put her nose down close to the earth as she examined the hollow.

She remembered how on the very first day the gardener Gerasim had said that the little scamp Zakusai had been taught to eat earth by his father and grandfather. Could that have been here?

If one looked closely, even the grass on this side of the aspen was different from the grass all around—shorter and sparser.

What could the dogs have been interested in here?

Pelagia took a splinter of wood and started scrabbling at the earth—it yielded reluctantly. The work would go quicker if she ran back to the hut for a spade.

And that was what she did, except that she did not take a spade, but a mattock; it would be handier to dig with.

She spat on her hands the way that the workmen had done when they laid the water main to the episcopal see, then swung, hit, and scraped. Then again, and again. The work went quickly. By about the tenth stroke, Pelagia stopped shivering—she had warmed up. The mist swirled above the grass, rising from her ankles up to her knees.

The blade sank into something crunchy, like a cabbage. Pelagia tugged the blade out, and hanging on it was something round and dark, about the size of a child's head. Because her wits were numbed and there was a strange ringing sound in her ears, the nun did not immediately realize that it was precisely that—a child's head: yellowish-purple, with the light hair clumped and the eye sockets sunken in mourning.

With a sudden gasp, Pelagia flung the mattock and its nightmarish prize away so abruptly that she slipped on the damp earth and tumbled into the pit that she herself had dug. As she climbed out, wailing softly, she grabbed hold of a cold, slimy root, which promptly slid smoothly out of the earth.

And then Pelagia saw that it was not a root at all, but a hand—hairy, with blue fingernails and a little stump where the ring finger ought to have been.

At this everything went dark before the poor nun's eyes, because there is, after all, a limit to human endurance and, thanks be to God, Pelagia did not have to suffer any more frights—she suddenly went limp and slid down onto the bottom of the pit in a dead faint.

# CHAPTER 10

# A Borzoi Pup

WHEN SHE OPENED her eyes, Pelagia saw the vault of heaven hanging low above her, dark blue, studded with faint, motionless stars and supported, as described in the ancient books, on four pillars. This confirmed that Corpernicus had been wrong, which did not surprise the sister in the least, but even made her feel rather glad. Suspended above where she lay was the immense face of His Grace Mitrofanii— gray-bearded, handsome, and sad. Realizing that he was actually the Lord God of Hosts, Pelagia felt even more delighted, and yet she was surprised at her own blindness: How could she have failed to realize something so simple and obvious earlier? It was also suddenly clear that all of this was a dream, but it was a good dream that boded well. Perhaps it was even prophetic.

"What are you gawking at, you scandalous creature?" asked the Lord of Hosts, in the way that God was supposed to talk, with apparent strictness but with love, too. "You have profaned the most honorable episcopal bed with female flesh, such as it has never known in all its days, and you lie there smiling. How am I going to sleep now? I shall probably be tormented by worse temptations of the flesh than Saint Anthony. Look out, Pelagia, or I shall hand you over to the consistory court for indecency—that will teach you. A fine bride of Christ: Lying there covered in mud, soaking wet, almost naked, and in a pit with those revolting objects! Would you be so kind as to explain to me, your foolish pastor, how you ended up there? How did you guess that the heads of the murder victims were buried at that very spot? You can talk, can you?" Mitrofanii leaned down lower in alarm and set a pleasantly cool hand on Pelagia's brow. "If it is hard for you, then do not talk. Your forehead is all wet. The doctor says it is the fever following a severe shock. You have been unconscious for more than a day. You were carried in people's arms and driven in a carriage, and all the while you were just like Sleeping Beauty. What on earth happened to you, eh? You can't say? All right, don't talk, don't talk."

It was only then that the nun guessed the riddle of the pillars and the vault of heaven. It was the canopy above the old bed in the bishop's bedchamber: brocade stars sewn on the blue velvet.

Pelagia felt very weak, but not all unwell—the exhaustion was a pleasant sensation, like after swimming for a long time.

But I was swimming, she remembered, and for a really long time, too.

She moved her lips and tried her voice. It came out slightly hoarse but clear: "Ah-ah-ah."

"What, what's that you say?" the bishop fussed. "Tell me, what shall I get for you? Or shall I call the doctor?"

And he leapt to his feet, ready to run for help.

"Sit down, Your Grace," Pelagia said to him, cautiously feeling her aching shoulder muscles. "Sit down and listen."

And she told the bishop about everything that had happened, beginning with the "investigative experiment" and right up to her terrifying excavation, the mere memory of which set her voice trembling and brought tears to her eyes.

Mitrofanii listened without interrupting, only intoning "Lord God in Heaven" or "Son of God" and crossing himself at the most critical points.

But when the nun had finished her account, the bishop went down on his knees before the icon of the Savior hanging in the corner and recited a brief but fervent prayer of thanksgiving.

Then he sat on the bed and, with his eyelashes fluttering rapidly, said: "Forgive me, my little Pelagia, for sending you into such horrors. But I shall never forgive myself, power-loving tyrant that I am. No intentions of good stewardship supported by a bishop's crook can justify laying such a burden on any Christian soul, let alone upon the weak shoulders of a woman."

"It offends me to hear talk of the weak shoulders of a woman," said the nun angrily. "I should like to see what man could swim that far along the River in such a storm, and at night, too. And as for those good intentions and the crook, you should not be so free with them, either. Where in the Scriptures does it say that we should yield to the evil spirit without a battle? I think that would be the worst possible thing. You would do better, Your Grace, to tell me what you have discovered here, while I was lying in a faint. You said 'heads'? Are they the same ones that were supposedly carried away as a gift to Shishiga? I really only saw one, and a severed hand as well. Where did the hand come from?"

"Wait, wait, don't hurl so many questions at me all at once," said Mitrofanii, putting his open hand over her mouth. The bishop's fingers had a pleasant smell of book bindings and incense. "There was a second head in the pit; you did not dig quite far enough to find it. There was clothing, too. Yes, the heads are the same ones, from the bodies cast up by the River last month. And the identities have now been established—from the hand with one finger missing. Do you remember that the dead man's arm was cut off at the wrist? Evidently it was cut off deliberately in order to make identification difficult, because it bore too distinctive a feature."

"Ba boo ad dy?" Pelagia lowed through his palm, meaning, "But who are they?"

The bishop understood her.

"The merchant Avvakum Vonifatiev from the Glukhov district and his nine-year-old son, the boy Savva. The merchant came to see Donat Abramovich Sytnikov to sell a stretch of forest and disappeared. He was not missed at home, because he had told his wife that he was leaving her forever and would not be coming back. They did not get along; she was a lot older than he was. Apparently Vonifatiev wished to use the money he received to start a new life somewhere else. But things did not work out that way . . . It has been established that Sytnikov bought the forest for thirty-five thousand and paid Vonifatiev on the spot, in cash, after which the father and son set out on foot, even though the hour was late. Sytnikov says that he offered them his britzka, but the merchant refused. He said that he would take a troika at the coaching inn in the nearby village of Sholkovo, but no one at Sholkovo ever saw Vonifatiev. Of course, the police took Sytnikov in for questioning, but I think that he is innocent. He is too rich a man to take such a sin on his soul for the sake of thirty-five thousand. Or perhaps he was tempted by the devil of greed—anything can happen. But that is not the point . . ." Mitrofanii's eyes glittered ardently. "The important thing about all this is that . . ."

He removed his hand from Pelagia's lips in order to raise a finger in triumph, and the nun immediately made use of the freedom of speech that this gave her: ". . . that Inspector Bubentsov is in a fine mess," she said, concluding the sentence for Mitrofanii.

The bishop smiled. "I was about to say 'the satanic machinations have been confounded,' but you, my daughter, have expressed it more precisely. The Vonifatievs were killed for money, there was no human sacrifice involved, and there is no site for the worship of Shishiga. Bubentsov had no reason to harass the unfortunate Zyts. His entire investigation and his Extraordinary Commission are not worth a bent penny. This is a gift from God to all of us. Manifested to us through you, through your talents and your bravery. Our imp of mischief has been undone. Now he will go away empty-handed and receive a severe reprimand from his protector for such an embarrassing fiasco."

"He will not leave," Sister Pelagia declared with quiet resolution. "And he will not receive any reprimand."

Mitrofanii clutched his pectoral cross in his hand.

"What do you mean, he will not leave? And he will not get any reprimand? Why not? What is he going to do here now?"

"Sit in a prison cell," the nun snapped. "And he will not get off with just a reprimand. This is a question of hard labor, father. Twenty years' worth. For a double murder committed out of greed, and the killing of a boy, the court will not give him any less."

"Vengefulness is a grave sin," the bishop said in a didactic tone. "You must not give way to that feeling. Bubentsov is a scoundrel, of course, but such a crime would be too monstrous even for him: to kill two innocents, one of them a child, and cut off their heads, and all in order to further his own career? No, that is going too far, my daughter. Of course, I must admit that I also became incensed when the same idea occurred to me, but then I cooled down. No, my little Pelagia, our overweening braggart did not kill anybody, he simply chose to exploit a convenient event. And then there was the mention in the ancient manuscript of a severed head and the god Shishiga. All extremely plausible. What do we know about the murder of the Vonifatievs? Very little. That they were killed somewhere close to Drozdovka, so they had not yet gone very far from Sytnikov's summer house. The money was taken, the bodies were thrown over the cliff into the River and they were cast up farther downstream. The heads, the hand, and the clothing were buried in the garden, under the aspen. And now it is impossible to find the culprit (or culprits). Too much time has passed."

Pelagia was not listening. She exclaimed, "Ah, that's why she killed the dogs!"

The nun sat up suddenly on the bed, but the sharp movement set the room swaying and shifting around her, and she lay back down. After waiting for the dizziness to pass she continued, "Now I understand. Of course, the inheritance has nothing to do with it. It is all to do with the bulldogs themselves. They ran around wherever they wanted, chasing all over the park. They caught an interesting smell under the aspen and began digging, and Naina Georgievna saw them. No doubt the first time she simply drove them away, but they kept coming back again and again. Then she decided to poison them . . ."

"Wait, wait," said Mitrofanii, frowning. "That means it was Naina who killed the merchant and his son and cut off their heads? That's absurd!"

"No, she was not the killer. But she did know who it was, and she knew about the heads."

"An accomplice? The princess? But why?"

"Not an accomplice, more likely a witness. A chance witness. How could it have happened?" Pelagia was not looking at His Grace. She raised and lowered her eyebrows rapidly, wrinkling up her freckly forehead and gesturing with her hands—in a word, she was trying to think something through. "She often used to wander through the park in the evenings and even at night. Romantic young women are like that. She must have seen the killer burying the heads."

Mitrofanii shook his head doubtfully.

216 / Boris Akunin

"She saw that and said nothing? Such a heinous, satanic crime!"

"That's it!" exclaimed the nun. "It is precisely satanic! That's the point! She spoke some mysterious words about evil and about the devil. 'Love is always an evil'—that was what she said."

"What, you mean that she served the devil?" asked the bishop, astonished.

"Nothing of the sort, Your Grace, what devil? She served love."

"I don't understand."

"Why, of course," said Pelagia with a disrespectful wave of her hand, as if she were talking to herself. "A passionate young woman, imaginative, pining away with her unspent feelings. Spoilt ever since she was a child, exceptional and also cruel. She was living as if in a dream; she loved the only decent man in her circle, Shiryaev. She talked to him of beauty and things eternal. She dreamed of becoming an actress. She would have carried on living like that until she was an old maid, because Marya Afanasievna is a lady of sound health and Shiryaev would have stayed at Drozdovka until she died—he would never have left and never have asked for her hand. From his point of view that would have been immoral—to coerce those who are dependent on you. The problem is that he is too scrupulous a man. He loved Naina Georgievna passionately, but he made no attempt on her innocence. But he should have done," the nun added in a low voice. "And then she might still be alive."

"Now just you stop that propaganda for fornication," said the bishop, calling his spiritual daughter to order. "And don't get so distracted—talk to the point."

"Then suddenly Poggio appeared, a man from a different, more exciting life. And he had no scruples. He turned the young woman's head and seduced her. And I expect it was not difficult—she could hardly have been more ready for it. She forgot her dreams of acting and decided she wanted to be an artist. But by the time I arrived at Drozdovka, Paris and the palette had been forgotten, and Poggio had been dropped. Naina Georgievna was gloomy and taciturn, acting mysteriously and speaking in riddles. I even thought that she was not in her right mind. And in fact she was not. If she was prepared to kill the dogs, if she could decide to end her grandmother's life just like that—

and she really did almost send the old woman to her grave—that means she really had fallen in love, and her love had no bounds, it was so powerful that it displaced all her other feelings."

"With whom, Bubentsov?" asked the bishop, scarcely able to keep pace with Pelagia's fleet thought. "But he only paid passing visits to Drozdovka. Although, he is a past master when it comes to women. Of course, he could have debauched her, and apparently he did. But what has this to do with the Vonifatievs?"

"It is very simple. That evening, when the sale of the forest took place, Sytnikov had been at his neighbors' house first. He drank tea on the veranda and talked about the merchant and the forthcoming deal. At that time Bubentsov was staying there, and he and Donat Abramovich had a quarrel about the customs of the Old Believers— I was told about all of this. Then, after Sytnikov left, offended—"

"Yes, yes!" Mitrofanii interrupted her excitedly. "Of course, let me finish! The young girl, in love and most likely already seduced (Bubentsov had visited Drozdovka previously, after all), was strolling around the garden at night. Either her aroused passion would not let her sleep or she was waiting for the object of her adoration to return. She saw him disposing of the bodies and imagined it was some kind of satanic ritual, and Bubentsov was Satan himself. And since she loved him boundlessly, she decided also to join the army of Satan! She threw herself on this devil's chest and swore—"

"Oh, Your Grace, what sort of wild imaginings are these?" said the nun, fluttering her hands at him. "You should write novels for the magazines. She did not swear anything to him; I have no doubt she felt numb with horror and gave no sign that she was there. Many times she dropped hints to him in my presence—now I understand what they meant, but Bubentsov only smiled and shrugged. He evidently could not imagine that she knew everything. And she could hardly have taken him for Satan then, on the night of the crime. At first she was probably confused; she did not know what to think or what to do. But a woman's love is capable of justifying anything at all. I remember that Naina Georgievna said 'Love is also a crime,' emphasizing the word 'also.' That was what she was thinking of . . . She decided to protect the man she loved. That was why she put poison in the dogs' food. I saw when Bubentsov arrived, I was there at the time, I saw how she looked at him at first: very strangely, almost with loathing. But everything suddenly changed when he started talking about the Zyt case. I was amazed when I noticed it—Naina Georgievna seemed transformed. She grew lively, she blushed and started looking at Bubentsov in a different way—with pure, adoring admiration. She realized why it had been necessary to sever the heads. Instead of being terrified and recoiling from him in horror, she was enraptured. It turned out that her beloved was not a simple robber, but a man of ambition on a gigantic scale who toyed with people like a genuine demon. That was what she meant by the words: 'Vladimir Lvovich, I was not mistaken about you.' She even quoted from Lermontov's *Demon,* and when he started talking about the death threats and the police guard, she hinted to him: 'The best protection is love.' She was telling him that she would be his faithful helper and protector, but he did not understand her." Pelagia sighed sadly. "A woman, a real woman, self-sacrificing and impetuous in love."

"Don't you dare to sigh about a love of that sort," said Mitrofanii, frowning. "There is no such love for you anymore. It has died, your love. And in its place you have been given a different Love, a Love supreme. And you have a different Beloved, much finer than the former one. You are a bride of Christ. Remember that."

The sister smiled gently at His Grace's severe tone.

"Yes, I have been more fortunate with my Beloved than poor Naina. The fact that he is a villain, a criminal, the devil incarnate—she forgave him all that. But she did not forgive him what no woman can ever forgive: failure to love. Even worse than that—cold, insulting indifference. I am surprised at Vladimir Lvovich, Your Grace. It is quite clear that he is well used to exploiting the weaker sex in all his schemes, and we must assume that he understands the hearts of women very well. How could he have failed to spot the danger from Naina Georgievna and be so careless about it? At first he needed her for something— perhaps because of some complicated plans to do with the old widow's legacy. Then afterward he probably realized that he could manage without Tatishcheva's granddaughter. Or else he found Naina too exhausting, with her frenzied passion and love of histrionic declarations. But one way or another Bubentsov drove the young woman to the very edge. And that alone makes it clear that he did not suspect how much she knew and for the time being regarded her hints as no more than an expression of her love of melodramatic posturing. At Olympiada Savelievna's soirée, Bubentsov saw one photograph that alarmed him very seriously. Just another picture, it was called 'Rainy Morning.' A quiet corner of the park after the rain: grass, bushes, an aspen tree— nothing special. None of the other visitors to the exhibition even paid any attention to this unpretentious study; there were other pictures there that made far more of an impression. But what if sooner or later someone were to look more closely at this dangerous photograph? It had to be destroyed, and that could only be done by resorting to some diversionary maneuver to send the investigation off in the wrong direction."

"What was there in this picture that was so terrible?"

"I assume that it showed the same aspen under which the heads were buried, but photographed the morning after the double murder. The aspen was already doomed, because its roots had been severed by the sharp mattock, but it had not withered yet and still looked alive. But the most important thing is that the mattock itself was leaning against the little tree, where it had been forgotten by the murderer. Or perhaps it was lying in the grass nearby—I don't know. One of the inhabitants or long-term guests at Drozdovka could have noticed this strange detail, connected it with the unaccountable withering of the aspen, remembered about the trampled lawn and the way Zakusai was killed—and come to conclusions that were dangerous for the criminal."

"I see, I see," said the bishop with a nod of his head. "And what happened to the mattock afterward?"

"Perhaps the murderer came back for it that afternoon and put it back in its place. Or, even more likely, Naina Georgievna did it."

"And so Bubentsov killed Poggio and wrecked the entire exhibition all because of this photograph?"

"Yes, no doubt about it. Of all the pictures and the plates, the only one to disappear was 'Rainy Morning.' The scandalous pictures of Telianova naked were of no interest to the criminal. But the scandal was useful to Bubentsov: It cast clear and obvious suspicion on Shiryaev."

"Now I can see that that is exactly the way it all happened," said Mitrofanii, inclining his head to one side as he ran through everything to make sure that it all fitted and apparently satisfying himself that it did. "But in deciding to kill Telianova, Bubentsov was taking a tremendous risk. Shiryaev could not have been suspected of that murder—he was being questioned at the police station at the time."

"But Shiryaev had already been cleared of any suspicion of killing Poggio, when Naina Georgievna announced that Stepan Trofimovich spent the entire night with her. Bubentsov was obliged to take the risk, because during the experiment Naina Georgievna made it perfectly clear to him that she knew everything and would no longer protect him. Do you remember when I told you how she threatened to pay back her debts? And she would have repaid them, because she had freed herself of her demonic obsession and wished to serve the demon no longer. Either her patience was exhausted or her pride had been pricked. Or perhaps she had made a choice—for Stepan Trofimovich. But she had played with fire for too long. Bubentsov could not leave her alive, not even for one more day. So he killed her. And the maid with her. What does someone's little life matter to a 'spirit of exile' like that?"

"And he almost killed you, too," the bishop said in a low voice full of dread, and his gaze blazed brightly enough to light a candle from it.

"Yes. And not just once, but twice."

Pelagia sighed and told His Grace about the incident at Drozdovka after she had seen the bishop to the gates of the park and was walking back along the alley, when someone had tried to strangle her.

"I did not tell anyone about it at the time, since it would have just played into Bubentsov's hands. He would have blamed the Zyts again. What a perfect gift for the synodical investigators—an attack on a nun. Just the evening before, Bubentsov had been talking about how the Zyts threw sacks over their victims' heads on deserted roads. Now it is clear who attempted to strangle me and why. Do you remember when I exposed Naina Georgievna in front of everyone and I said that I would not stop there?"

"Yes, I remember," said the bishop with a nod. "You said that there was some mystery here that needed to be solved."

"That was stupid of me, careless," sighed Pelagia, and, lowering her eyes modestly, she added: "Apparently Bubentsov must have had a high opinion of my abilities, since he decided to remove the danger."

Mitrofanii thundered ominously: "God is merciful and he forgives malefactors all sorts of evil deeds far worse than this. But I am not God, only a sinful man, and for you I shall grind Bubentsov to dust. You just tell me, can we act according to the law here, or do we have to seek out other means? After all, you did not see who attacked you on either occasion, and so there is no proof."

"Only circumstantial evidence."

Pelagia felt sufficiently restored to sit up on the bed. The bishop put some cushions behind the nun's back.

"We have three crimes that are clearly connected: first Vonifatiev and his son were killed, then Arkadii Sergeevich Poggio, then Naina Telianova and her maid," the sister began explaining. "For reasons already mentioned, Bubentsov is among the suspects in all three cases. Correct?"

"He was not the only one involved in all these events," the bishop objected. "Also present at Drozdovka and the two gatherings at Olympiada Savelievna's house were Shiryaev, Pyotr Telianov, Sytnikov, and that other one, the rhymester, what's his name . . . Krasnov! They might have had reasons of their own for killing the Vonifatievs. And the other two killings were committed out of the fear of being discovered."

"Correct, father. Only Pyotr Georgievich cannot be included, because on the day when the man came to Sytnikov to sell him the forest, the young master was not at Drozdovka; he had still not come back from town. I remember that I was told that. As for Krasnov and Sytnikov, they could have killed Vonifatiev, of course. The former if only for the sake of the thirty-five thousand. The latter . . . Well, let us assume he quarreled about something with his guest. But that will not hold up, Your Grace, because the princess would not have protected either Krasnov or Sytnikov."

"Agreed. But what about Shiryaev?" the bishop asked, largely for form's sake.

"You have forgotten, father. We have already established that Stepan Trofimovich could not have committed the murders in Varravkin cul-de-sac because he was still under arrest."

"Yes, yes, that's right. And so no one apart from Bubentsov could have committed all three murders?"

"That is the conclusion. Only not three murders, but five," Pelagia corrected him. "The first and the last crimes were both double murders. After a careful analysis, the only person who remains under suspicion is Vladimir Lvovich. Remember also that on the night of Poggio's murder the inspector was entirely alone—Murad Djuraev was wandering around the taverns, completely drunk, and the secretary Spasyonny was trying to make the rowdy ruffian see reason. Might Bubentsov himself possibly have fed his servant drink, knowing what it would lead to?"

The nun spread her hands conclusively. "That is everything that we have to go on. Under ordinary circumstances this would be enough for an arrest on suspicion, but Vladimir Lvovich is a special case. Even if Matvei Bentsionovich issues a warrant, I am afraid that the chief of police will not obey his orders. He will say there are insufficient grounds. For him, Bubentsov is tsar and God in one. No, we won't be able to arrest him."

"But that is not for you to worry about," Mitrofanii said confidently. "You have done your part. Rest now and restore your strength. I shall give orders for you not to be disturbed, and if you need anything, just tug this velvet cord. A lay brother will come running and do whatever you ask."

And thereupon the bishop demonstrated how to tug on the cord, and indeed only a second later a glum-looking face with a sparse beard surmounted by a *kamilavka* appeared in the crack of the door.

"Patapii, tell them to send for Matvei Berdichevsky. And look lively about it, now."

. . .

MATVEI WAS FEELING very worried.

Not because of the chief of police—he was like putty in his hands. That is, at first, when he saw the arrest warrant, he had turned pale and broken into a sweat all over, right to the roots of his hair, but when Berdichevsky explained to him that after the collapse of the Zyt case the synodical inspector's goose was cooked in any case, Felix Stanislavovich had taken heart and set about the business at hand with quite exceptional despatch.

The assistant prosecutor's concern was not occasioned by doubts concerning the loyalty of the police, but by the supreme responsibility of his task, and especially by the somewhat shaky nature of the evidence. Strictly speaking, there was no evidence as such—nothing but suspicious circumstances, not enough to build a genuine case. Bubentsov had been in this place and that place, he could have committed this act and that act, but what of it? A good defense lawyer would rapidly demolish such speculative suppositions. A great deal of preparatory work was required here, and Matvei Bentsionovich was not certain that he could cope. For a moment he thought with envy of the investigators of former times. Life had been so simple and easy for them. Pick up a suspect, put him on the rack, and he would happily confess all on his own. Of course, Berdichevsky was a progressive and civilized individual and his thoughts about the rack were not really serious, but a confession was absolutely essential in this case, and Vladimir Lvovich Bubentsov was not the kind of man to provide testimony against himself. Berdichevsky was placing all his hopes in the interrogation of the inspector's henchmen, Spasyonny and the Circassian. He would work for a while with each of them separately, and who knew? Perhaps some inconsistencies, clues, or loose ends might turn up so that he could keep pulling at one of them and unwind the whole ball of thread.

If only there was some attempt to escape, or even better, to resist arrest, Matvei Bentsionovich daydreamed as they were on their way to detain Bubentsov.

To make quite certain of things—after all, this was the arrest of a murderer—the operation had been prepared by the book. Lagrange had gathered together thirty police constables and officers, ordered them to oil their pistols, and personally checked to make sure that they still remembered how to shoot. Before setting out, the chief of police had drawn out the entire plan on a piece of paper.

"This circle here, Matvei Bentsionovich, is the town square. The dotted line is the fence, with the courtyard of the Grand Duke behind it. The large square is the hotel itself, and the small one is the general's wing. Bubentsov is at home; my people have already checked. I'll set half the men around the edge of the square and order the others to conceal themselves behind the fence. You and I will go in with just two or three of them."

"No." Berdichevsky interrupted him. "I shall go into the yard alone. If we show up in a gang like that, they will see us through the window and, God only knows, they might lock themselves in and destroy the evidence. And I hope very much to find something useful in there. I'll go in quietly, as if I am just paying a visit. I'll invite Bubentsov to come for a talk—let's say at the governor's house. And as we come out into the yard, that's when we'll arrest our friend. If I get into any difficulties I'll shout to you for assistance."

"Why strain your throat?" the chastened Lagrange said with a reproachful shake of his head. "Here, take my whistle. Blow it, and I'll be right there, quick as a wink."

In actual fact, apart from professional considerations, Matvei Bentsionovich had personal reasons for wanting to take Bubentsov himself. He wanted very badly to get even with the base Petersburgian for that memorable tweak of his nose. With a feeling of anticipation unworthy of a Christian, but nonetheless sweet, he imagined how Bubentsov's haughty features would turn pale and distorted by shock when he, Berdichevsky, said to him: "Be so good as to put your hands behind your back. You're under arrest."

Or even better, in a more worldly tone: "You know, my good fellow, you are under arrest. What a very unpleasant surprise it must be."

BUT EVEN SO, as he crossed the courtyard alone, he began feeling unwell. His stomach knotted into cramps and his throat went dry.

Summoning up his courage, Matvei Bentsionovich stood on the

porch of the general's wing for a half a minute. This tidy little single-story house contained the very best suite of rooms in the entire hotel; it was intended for individuals of importance who visited the province on state business, as well as for rich people who regarded it as beneath their dignity to stay under the same roof as the other guests.

The windows of the wing were curtained over and Berdichevsky was suddenly afraid that Lagrange might have been mistaken. What if Bubentsov were not here?

His nerves suddenly calmed in the face of concern for the success of his mission. Matvei Bentsionovich did not even ring the bell as he had been intending to do—he simply pushed the door open and went in.

From the entrance hall he went through into a large room crammed full of open trunks and suitcases. Spasyonny and Murad Djuraev were sitting at the table, moving black and white stones around a board. Matvei Bentsionovich, who knew no games except for chess and preference, guessed that it must be backgammon.

"Inform Mr. Bubentsov that assistant provincial prosecutor Berdichevsky wishes to see him immediately," he declared in an icy tone, addressing the secretary.

Spasyonny bowed respectfully and disappeared through the door that led into the inner chambers. The Circassian cast a quick glance at the visitor and fixed his gaze on the board again, muttering something unintelligible under his breath. It was remarkable that even indoors this wild man never removed his astrakhan hat and his faithful dagger.

Spasyonny returned and said, "If you please, sir."

Bubentsov was sitting at a desk, dark-faced, writing something. He did not get to his feet or greet Berdichevsky. He merely tore his glance away from his papers for an instant and asked, "What do you want?"

This obvious insult finally soothed Matvei Bentsionovich's nerves completely, because everyone knows that he who barks loudly is unlikely to bite. Bubentsov had nothing to bite with—his teeth had been blunted.

"Getting ready to leave?" the assistant prosecutor inquired politely.

"Yes." Vladimir Lvovich threw down his pen angrily, sending splashes of ink flying across the green fabric. "After the governor, on your recommendation, ordered the investigation to be halted, there was nothing more for me to do here. But never mind, my dear gentle-man of Zavolzhsk, I shall go to St. Petersburg and then return. And after that I shall scatter this almshouse of yours to the four winds."

Matvei Bentsionovich had never seen the synodical inspector so irritated before. Where had that customary tone of lazy condescension gone?

"That will not be possible for some time," sighed Berdichevsky, as if he regretted the fact.

"What will not be possible?"

"Your leaving." Matvei Bentsionovich even spread his hands, entering completely into his role. "Anton Antonovich requests that you visit him immediately. He even orders it."

"Orders it?" exploded Bubentsov. "I don't care a damn about his orders."

"That is as you wish, but his excellency has ordered not to allow you to cross the boundaries of the province until you have provided a satisfactory explanation with regard to the unlawful arrest of the Zyt elders and the killing of three Zyts who were trying to free them."

"Rubbish! Everyone knows that the Zyts attacked representatives of authority while carrying weapons. They themselves are to blame. And as for the illegality of the arrest of the elders—we shall see about that. So you protect idolaters, do you? Very well, Konstantin Petrovich will see that you pay for that, too." Vladimir Lvovich stood up and put on his frock coat. "Damn you. I shall call in to see your Haggenau. Not for his sake, but for Ludmila Platonovna's. She is a real darling. I shall kiss her hand in farewell."

Bubentsov's eyes sparkled evilly—the inspector evidently had plans to play some humiliating trick on Anton Antonovich as a parting gift.

I rather think not, mused Matvei Bentsionovich, restraining a smile of triumph with some difficulty. Your reach is too short now, my good sir.

They walked through into the drawing room. The inspector's associates were no longer playing backgammon. Spasyonny was packing a travel bag, while the Circassian was standing beside the window, watching something in the courtyard.

Then suddenly something unexpected happened. Something, in fact, quite incredible, almost unimaginable.

In two catlike bounds Murad flew across to Matvei Bentsionovich and grabbed him by the throat with his short fingers of iron.

"Treason," the Circassian cried hoarsely. "Volodya, don't go! It's an ambush!"

"What nonsense is this?" asked Bubentsov, gazing hard at him. "Have you lost your mind?"

Berdichevsky pulled the whistle out of his pocket and blew it with all his might. That very second there was the sound of numerous feet tramping in the yard.

The Circassian knocked Matvei Bentsionovich to the floor with a blow of his gnarled fist, dashed across to one of the suitcases, and pulled out a long-barreled revolver.

"Stop!" shouted Vladimir Lvovich, but it was too late.

Murad smashed out the glass with the barrel of the gun and fired through the window three times. There was a howl and in the next instant a hail of shots was returned from the courtyard, so thick that chips of plaster flew off the walls and the ceiling, the carafe of water with the chrysanthemum on the piano shattered, and the wall clock suddenly burst into desperate chiming.

Spasyonny dropped flat to the floor and crawled toward the study. Bubentsov also squatted down on his haunches. When the firing eased off a little, he said disdainfully: "Murad, you're a blockhead. What a mess. You made it, now you can clear it up. I'm leaving by the back door and going to the stables. I'll ride to Peter. Don't you worry; I'll fix this. You keep firing for a while so that I can get away, and then surrender. I'll have you freed. Understand?"

Without waiting for an answer, still bent over double, he went out through the door. Spasyonny, still lying on his belly, crept out after him.

"I understand, Volodya, what's so hard about it?" the Circassian said in a soft voice. "Only Murad doesn't know how to surrender."

He put his hand out over the sill, aimed, and fired. Someone cried out again in the courtyard, and the volley of shots started up again.

Seizing his chance, the Abrek fired once more, but this time he was un-lucky. His astrakhan hat went flying to the floor, his blue-gray shaven head jerked, and a crimson furrow appeared on his cheek, blood in-stantly welling up out of it. Murad angrily wiped his face with the sleeve of his dirty *beshmet* and fired over the windowsill.

By this time Matvei Bentsionovich had been engaged in a tor-mented inner struggle with himself for about a minute. One side of his faltering scales held nothing but his duty, the other held his wife, his twelve (in fact, now almost thirteen) little children, and his own life thrown into the bargain. Unequal loads, it must be admitted. Ber-dichevsky decided that he would sit there quietly—after all, they could send a detail in pursuit of Bubentsov. But immediately after he had taken this salutary decision there was a lull in the firing and Matvei Bentsionovich crossed himself and shouted, "Lagrange, the back door!"

Murad swung around in fury and Berdichevsky saw an incredibly huge black hole staring straight at the bridge of his nose. The hammer gave a dry click, then again, and the Circassian swore in a style that was not Russian as he flung the useless revolver aside.

But Matvei Bentsionovich's miraculous deliverance was no more than a dream, because then the Circassian pulled out his monstrous dagger, bent over, and came rushing at the assistant prosecutor.

Berdichevsky struck the fearsome man with an unconvincing blow to the side of his head, but it was as if he were banging his fist against a stone. Matvei Bentsionovich froze, spellbound by the enigmatic gleam of that wide blade.

The Circassian put his arm around his prisoner's neck, pressed the cold steel against his throat, and spoke, breathing a smell of blood and garlic into Berdichevsky's face.

"I slit you later, not now. If I do it now they kill me straightaway. But this way we keep talking our talk a long time. When Volodya gets well away, then I slit you."

Matvei Bentsionovich squeezed his eyes tightly shut, unable to bear the closeness of the wild eyes, the black beard, and the bleeding cheek.

Outside, Felix Stanislavovich's voice called out: "Get a carriage on to Malaya Kupecheskaya Street! You three, to the gates, quick march. Lower the bars! Eliseev, take four men and go to the stables!"

Now Bubentsov cannot get away, Berdichevsky realized, but the thought brought him no comfort. It was difficult to breathe with the arm around his neck, the dreary terror was beginning to make him feel nauseous, and he even wished the Abrek would slit his throat there and then to put an end to his torment.

Lagrange's head peered up cautiously from behind the windowsill.

"Mr. Berdichevsky, are you alive?"

Murad replied.

"You interfere and he'll be dead."

Then the chief of police, growing bolder, raised up his hand, holding a revolver, and grinned, "Well now, Djuraev, shot all your bullets, have you? I counted them. You touch his excellency, and I'll shoot you like a mad dog. I won't take you alive, I swear by Jesus Christ I won't."

"Murad's not afraid of death," the bandit retorted contemptuously, protecting himself with Berdichevsky like a shield.

Felix Stanislavovich scrambled slowly up onto the windowsill.

"You're lying there, brother. Everyone's afraid of the old noseless reaper."

He cautiously lowered his feet to the floor.

"One more step and I slit him," the Circassian promised quietly but convincingly.

"I'm finished," the chief of police assured him, "see, I'm putting the revolver down.

"Now, Djuraev, let's talk peace terms." Lagrange took out his cigarette case and lit one up. "You've put holes in two of my men. For that I ought to drop you where you stand. But if you let his excellency go and surrender, I'll take you to prison alive. And we won't even beat you, on my word as an officer."

Murad snorted contemptuously.

"Well, have you caught him?" Felix Stanislavovich asked his subordinates, turning around to the window.

Somebody answered him, but the words could not be made out inside the room.

"Ah, you villains, you let him go!" the colonel roared menacingly and smashed his fist down hard on the windowsill, but so clumsily that it hit the protruding barrel of the revolver.

Following this blow, in perfect conformity with the laws of physics, the revolver described a complicated somersault through the air and landed on the floor with a clatter in the very middle of the drawing room.

Releasing his hostage, the Circassian was beside the gun in a single predatory bound.

And then it became clear that the trick with the flying revolver had been played deliberately by the crafty chief of police. From out of nowhere a second revolver, a little smaller, appeared in Felix Stanislavovich's hand and belched flame and smoke at Djuraev.

The bullets threw the Circassian back against the wall, but he immediately leapt to his feet and advanced on the colonel, waving his dagger.

Lagrange took good aim and fired three more shots—all on target—but Murad did not fall; each step simply cost him an ever greater effort.

When the Circassian was little more than a yard away from the windowsill the colonel jumped down onto the floor and set the gun barrel right against Djuraev's forehead. The top of the shaven skull shattered into flying shards.

The dead man swayed a little and finally collapsed onto his back.

"Damned hard to kill," said the chief of police, shaking his head in amazement as he leaned down over the body. "Some kind of werewolf. Just look, he's still batting his eyelids. If you told anyone, they'd never believe you."

Then he went over to Berdichevsky, who was more dead than alive after so many shocks to his nerves, and squatted down on his haunches beside him.

"Well, you're a brave man, Matvei Bentsionovich." He shook his head respectfully. "I'm amazed you weren't afraid to shout about the back entrance!"

"But it did no good," the assistant prosecutor said in a weak voice. "Bubentsov got away anyway."

Lagrange laughed, showing his white teeth.

"He got away, you say! We got him. Him and his nasty little secretary. Right there in the stables."

"But what about . . . ?" Matvei Bentsionovich asked, staring wildly. He no longer understood anything that was happening.

"I deliberately swore at my men like that, for the Circassian. So it would look more convincing when I tossed him the revolver."

Berdichevsky was so delighted and relieved that he couldn't find the right words to say.

"I . . . Really, Felix Stanislavovich, you are my savior . . . I shall never forget what you did for me."

"I hope very much that you will not," said the gallant chief of police, peering searchingly into his eyes. "I'll carry on serving you faithfully, on my word of honor. Only don't let the story about that blasted bribe get out. I was tempted by the devil. I've even given the merchant his money back. Put in a word for me with the bishop and Anton Antonovich, eh?"

Berdichevsky gave a heavy sigh, remembering how eloquently he had denounced the cupidity of officials that sprouted up like thistles through the very best of good intentions—if it was not money, then it was the notorious borzoi pups.

And wasn't a life saved just like a borzoi pup?

# CHAPTER 11

# The Trial

THE HEARING OF the Zavolzhsk murder case opened in the new provincial court building, which was remarkably spacious and elegant. Anton Antonovich von Haggenau had approved the architect's designs himself and personally supervised the construction work, because he regarded this building as being of great importance. He had always said that you could tell whether the people of any particular region respected the rule of law from the appearance of their courthouses. In Russia court offices were dirty, cramped, and shabby, and one saw every manner of injustice and abuse committed in them. But it was the governor's unshakable (although, perhaps, also naïve) conviction that if the courtroom possessed a distinct resemblance to a clean and beautiful church, then far fewer violations would be committed within its walls. And our local administrator also had another idea in mind when he gave instructions for such a substantial sum to be allocated to the building work: The new courthouse was to usher in a golden age in the history of Zavolzhsk, firmly established on the secure foundations of legality and justice.

The completion of the construction work could not have come at a better time, because previously the courtroom could not have held even the most distinguished guests who had arrived for the trial. But the new temple of Themis easily accommodated an audience as numerous as five hundred. Of course, even that was only a small portion of those who would have liked to attend the hearing of the celebrated case, but at least there were enough places for all those people who were indispensable (apart from official and honorary guests, those who were indispensable also included the cream of Zavolzhsk society, numerous journalists, writers from the capital cities, and representatives of the legal community who had descended like locusts from all over Russia for this courtroom jousting session). The particularly large numbers of legal men were accounted for by the fact that Gurii Samsonovich Lomeiko himself, the luminary of the Russian bar and a celebrity on a European scale, had agreed to act for the defense. Everyone still had fresh memories of Gurii Samsonovich's triumph of the previous year, when he achieved total acquittal for the actress Granatova, who had shot the wife of her lover, the entrepreneur Anatoliisky.

The feeble intellect of the provincial prosecutor could not, of course, be pitted against such a formidable opponent and, partly through persuasion and partly through coercion, the bishop and the governor had prevailed upon Matvei Bentsionovich to take on the courtroom duties of public prosecutor himself. This choice had been facilitated by the fact that Berdichevsky's behavior at the time of the dangerous criminals' detention had won him the glorious reputation of a hero—if not throughout the whole of Russia, then at least within the confines of the province.

Matvei Bentsionovich found the reputation of a bold man of action inexpressibly pleasant, for in the depths of his heart he knew perfectly well that he did not deserve it in any way. But the price to be paid for his fame was not cheap.

In his agitation the assistant prosecutor lost his appetite and the ability to sleep two weeks before the trial actually began. He himself could not tell what it was that he feared most: the formidable Lomeiko, the slanderous newspaper reporters, or the wrath of Konstantin Petrovich, who had sent an entire deputation to the court, led by Heller, the deputy chief procurator of the Holy Synod—after all, however one viewed it, the Zavolzhsk scandal was causing serious damage to the prestige of the empire's supreme agency for the protection of the faith.

It was not just that Berdichevsky was about to make his first appearance before a broad (and also very exalted) public. Well, what if he did stammer a little and tremble a bit—that was forgivable in a provincial prosecutor. Much worse than that was the fact that the case for the prosecution seemed rather fragile.

On the advice of his counsel, Bubentsov had not given any testimony to the investigators. He had remained defiantly silent, regarding the sweating Matvei Bentsionovich as if he were a mere wood louse, polishing his nails and yawning. On returning to his cell, he penned complaints to higher authorities.

Spasyonny, who had been arrested on suspicion of complicity, spoke a great deal, but communicated nothing of any use. Most of the time he complained of his health and discoursed on matters divine. It seemed that the facts of the case would only be revealed during the actual trial.

This was the state of affairs on the day when the tall doors of the new courthouse swung open to admit the fortunate possessors of guest tickets, and thus began a trial that was destined to go down not only in the annals of our provincial history, but also in the textbooks of jurisprudence.

THE SEATING ARRANGEMENTS in the hall differed from usual in that two additional rows of armchairs had been installed for the most distinguished guests behind the table for members of the court. In particular, these chairs accommodated the deputy chief procurator of the Holy Synod, with his two closest aides, the governor and the provincial marshal of the nobility, both with their wives, the governors of the two contiguous provinces (also, naturally, with their wives), and His Grace Mitrofanii, with a quiet little nun whom the public had not even noticed yet peeping out from behind his shoulder like a small black bird.

The chairman of the court was the most venerable and learned of our judges, with the rank of a general and a ribbon. Everybody knew that he had already applied to retire because of his advanced age, and therefore they expected absolute impartiality from him—after all, anyone would feel flattered to conclude a long and distinguished career with such an exceptional trial. The other two members of the court were highly authoritative justices of the peace, one of them by no means old as yet, the other perhaps of an even greater age than the chairman.

The public greeted the counsel from the capital with lively applause, at which he immediately seemed to become more dignified and taller, like dough inflated by yeast. He bowed with modest dignity to the court, the public, and, especially, with emphatic respect, to His Grace Mitrofanii, which was viewed in a most positive light by the local residents. Gurii Samsonovich himself somewhat resembled the bishop—he was so imposing and clear-eyed, with a thick, graying beard.

The prosecutor was also well received—admittedly, mostly by the local people, but they clapped even more loudly for him than for the famous figure from the capital. Berdichevsky, absolutely pale, his lips blue, bowed awkwardly and thumbed a thick pile of papers.

Then there began the lengthy procedure of presenting the members of the jury, during which the council for the defense displayed exceptional severity, decisively rejecting two Old Believer merchants, a Zyt elder, and also, for some reason, the headmaster of the grammar school. The prosecutor raised no protests against the predations of the defense, seeming to declare with his entire demeanor that the composition of the jury had no significance, since the case was clear anyway.

Matvei Bentsionovich's address was rendered in the same tone. He began, as was to be expected, incoherently and unimpressively, even managing to blow his nose during his second phrase, but afterward he grew more assured (especially when he won sympathetic applause in the hall) and thenceforth spoke animatedly, smoothly, and at times even with inspiration.

He had prepared thoroughly, and even learned the most important parts by heart. By the end of the second hour, the prosecutor was already able successfully to maintain an effective pause, direct an ominous finger toward the accused, and even raise his eyes in an expression of grief, something that very few public prosecutors are capable of doing without appearing ridiculous. On numerous occasions Berdichevsky's speech was interrupted by applause, and once he was even accorded a genuine ovation (when he described in the most moving terms the seduced and abandoned Princess Telianova—at this point many of the ladies made no attempt even to disguise their sobs).

It was a most excellent speech, replete with supremely subtle psychological nuances and crushing rhetorical questions. We would have preferred to relate it in detail, but that would take up too much space, because it lasted for more than three hours. And the speech did not contain anything fundamentally new as compared with the conclusions that Sister Pelagia had drawn, and which are already known to the reader, although in Matvei Bentsionovich's transcription the nun's hasty and raw conclusions acquired weight, conviction, and even brilliance. Regretfully omitting all the subtle psychology and rhetorical devices, we shall here expound only the main points of the accusation.

And so, Bubentsov was accused of the murder of the merchant Vonifatiev and his young son; the murder of the St. Petersburg photographic artist Arkadii Poggio; the murder of Princess Naina Telianova and her maid Evdokia Syskina; and finally of resisting arrest, with the result that two police constables had been wounded, one of whom had subsequently passed away. The prosecutor requested the court to condemn Bubentsov to hard labor for life and his accomplice Spasyonny, who could not have been ignorant of his superior's crimes and had also attempted to flee from arrest, to one year of imprisonment to be followed by internal exile.

Matvei Bentsionovich sat down, feeling thoroughly hoarse but pleased with himself. He was applauded heartily, even by the visiting men of law, which was an encouraging sign. Berdichevsky wiped the sweat from his brow and looked inquiringly at the bishop, who during the course of the speech had more than once supported his protégé by inclining his head and lowering his eyelids approvingly. And now once again the bishop replied to the prosecutor's glance with an encouraging nod. And indeed, Matvei Bentsionovich's speech really had been a success.

THE SESSION CONTINUED after a break during which a heated discussion took place among the visiting men of law concerning the prospects for the case. The majority inclined to the opinion that the accusation had been expounded in competent fashion and that the little prosecutor from the back of beyond had set Gurii Samsonovich quite a difficult task, but Lomeiko was not the kind of man to give up easily. He would most probably produce a flash of even more virtuosic eloquence and eclipse the silver-tongued provincial orator.

But the generally acknowledged genius of the great advocate consisted in his ability not to justify the expectations that people had of him—but to do so in a quite special manner, that is, by exceeding them.

The beginning of his speech seemed strange, to say the least.

Lomeiko stepped forward and stood with his back to the public and his side to the members of the jury, facing the members of the court, which was already unusual in itself. He spread his arms wide in a gesture expressive of either perplexity or distress and stood in that strange pose without moving, uttering not a single word.

The audience that had fallen quiet began whispering and scraping its chairs, but the defender still said nothing. He only began to speak when the puzzled chairman of the court began squirming on his chair and a tense silence once again descended on the hall.

"I simply do not know . . . I do not know what to say about the speech that the honorable prosecutor has delivered," Gurii Samsonovich informed the judges in a quiet, confidential tone of voice, and then suddenly, apropos of nothing, declared, "You know, I actually grew up not very far from here. My childhood was spent on the River. I breathed this air, I was raised on it . . . then I went away and was caught up in the vain tumult of life, but, you know, my heart was never parted from the River. I shall say what I think without any histrionics. Here, amid the thick forests and the modest, infertile fields, is where the very heart of Russia lies. That is why, gentlemen . . ." at this point the speaker's voice altered imperceptibly, acquiring a subtle resilience, strength, and even, perhaps, concealed menace, ". . . that is why, gentlemen, I feel genuinely ill when I learn of those instances of savagery and Asiatic barbarism that, alas, take place only too frequently in the depths of Russia. I have heard many good things about Zavolzhsk and the practices introduced here, and therefore I believe sincerely that the high court will not give any cause for it to be suspected of prejudice and local patriotism. I am sorry to say that I, and indeed many visitors to your town, have already caught a whiff of precisely that unappetizing aroma in the expressions employed by my learned opponent."

Such a beginning quite annoyed the judges on the one hand, but at the same time it set their nerves on edge, as though they were seeing for the first time the reporters scribbling in their notepads, and the newspaper illustrators, and the stern feature writers who represented the public opinion of the vast empire.

But the advocate had already turned away from the judges and trained his glance on the members of the jury. He spoke to them quite simply and without any undertone of menace.

"Gentlemen, I wish to point out once again something that you, of course, understand quite well without me. Today the most important event in your lives as citizens is taking place. There has never been a trial like this in your quiet town before and, God willing, there never will be again. I tormented you at length with questions and rejected many jurors, but I did so exclusively in the interests of justice. I understand perfectly well that you are all people with minds of your own. Each of you has almost certainly formed his own opinion, you have discussed the circumstances of the case with your relatives, friends, and acquaintances. There is just one thing I beg of you"—Lomeiko actually folded his hands together prayerfully. "Do not condemn these two men in advance. You are in any case already inclined against them, because for you they are the embodiment of an alien and hostile power, the name of which is the capital. You regard this power with suspicion and mistrust that is frequently, alas, unjustified. I allow that Bubentsov might have offended or angered some of you. He is a difficult, uncomfortable kind of man. Such men always become involved in unpleasant incidents—sometimes through their own fault, sometimes through the caprice of fate. If the gentlemen judges will allow me to deviate briefly from the case under consideration, I will tell you a little story about Vladimir Lvovich. But in fact, there will not be any real deviation, because you are deciding the fate of a man and you should know as much as possible about what kind of man he is."

The defender paused again, as if he was checking to make sure that people were listening to what he said. They were listening remarkably closely—there was total silence, broken only by the squeaking of chairs.

"It is possible that this story might display my client in an even less advantageous light, but even so I shall tell it—it illustrates his personality so very graphically . . . Well, then, at the age of fifteen years Vladimir Lvovich fell in love. Passionately, rashly, as these things happen in early youth. With whom, you will ask? Therein lies the rashness, for the chosen object of the young page's heart was a grand duchess. I will not give her name, because now this individual has become the wife of one of the crowned heads of Europe."

There was a murmur among the journalists as they tried to figure out who was meant and apparently quickly reached a conclusion.

"Vladimir Lvovich initially wrote her imperial highness a love letter, and then he was caught wandering at night beneath the windows of her bedroom. A most unpleasant scandal ensued. In order to remain in the Corps of Pages, the boy had to beg forgiveness from the administration. He absolutely refused to do this and was expelled, thereby closing off his own road to a brilliant career at court. I have mentioned this old story in order to give you a better understanding of the character of the defendant. He is a proud man, gentlemen, and there is nothing to be done about that. When monstrously absurd accusations are made against him, he does not condescend to justify himself. He maintains a proud silence."

One must assume that Gurii Samsonovich's "little story" was addressed not so much to the members of the jury, who were for the most part men no longer young and rather staid, as it was to the female half of the audience, whose mood usually determines the atmosphere at such proceedings. The women, who had already been glancing at Bubentsov with avid interest, were duly impressed by this anecdote, and their curiosity seemingly underwent a certain metamorphosis— from being primarily fearful, it became primarily sympathetic.

Having won this important, although hardly very striking victory, the adroit advocate immediately exposed his own cunning.

"Ah, what a pity it is that representatives of the fair sex are not allowed to be members of the jury," he sighed with absolute sincerity.

"They are so much more merciful than men. But, gentlemen of the jury, I am by no means asking you for mercy or even, God forbid, for condescension for Vladimir Lvovich."

Somehow it seemed that there was no specific mention made of the second accused. Either the supremely humble Tikhon Ieremeevich was of too little interest to the lion of the bar or Lomeiko rightly judged that the acquittal of the main suspect would naturally entail the withdrawal of the charges brought against his henchman.

"Your condescension would be a torment to this proud man. And especially because"—at this point the defender's voice suddenly acquired the resonance of a bronze bell—"*he has no need of your condescension!*"

Several of the jurors frowned at these words, and in a few supremely light steps Gurii Samsonovich flew across to the long table at which the twelve representatives of the people were seated and implored them in gentle, humane tones: "Do not pity him. Simply forget your irritation with him. After all, you are not judging him for his bad character, not for his dissoluteness or his vanity, but for terrible, blood-chilling crimes that, I assure you, Bubentsov did not commit. As I shall now prove to you."

All of the above was apparently no more than a prelude to the defense as such. The members of the audience murmured and seated themselves more comfortably as they prepared themselves for a long speech, but Lomeiko expounded his argument in less than a quarter of an hour.

"Gentlemen, you have heard the extremely lengthy speech of the prosecutor, which was more like the wailing of Hamlet's father than a serious legal discourse."

A brief laugh of approval was heard from the entourage of the deputy chief procurator of the Holy Synod.

"I saw, gentlemen, that this speech, unfortunately, influenced you. But it was constructed entirely on cheap effects. The lack of evidence was concealed by high-flown style and conjectures with nothing to back them up. I have no wish to offend anyone, but this was an example of provincial oratory at its very worst. In Moscow and St. Petersburg, grandiloquence of this sort passed out of fashion a long time ago.

There our prosecutor would simply be hissed at, exactly what poor acting deserves."

Matvei Bentsionovich blushed bright red and turned in outrage to the chairman of the court, but he appeared to be somewhat discomfited. The members of the jury were also clearly embarrassed.

"And now for the essence of the matter." The sorcerer's tone of voice had changed yet again, from caustically regretful to dry and businesslike. This was not the famous orator speaking, but the learned pedant, expounding scientifically proven facts that were obvious to any even slightly rational individual. "I shall tell you, gentlemen, how everything really happened. I have known the truth from the very beginning. However, I ordered the accused to hold their tongues because the local investigators are quite clearly not impartial; they thirst for vengeance and would probably have distorted the circumstances of the case, as pettifogging scribes have delighted in doing throughout the ages in our long-suffering Rus."

Gurii Samsonovich paid not the slightest attention to the applause awarded this remark by the liberal section of the audience. He simply waited until they had finished clapping and then continued.

"Night, an empty road. The moon gleams eerily through the gray clouds. There is a smell of rain in the air and the wind howls softly. Two people walk along the road: one with a beard and his hair trimmed evenly all around, the other still entirely a child. The man has his arm around the boy's shoulders, and the boy is leaning his light-haired head against his father's shoulder, half-dozing as they walk along. All around there is silence—not a soul, not a movement, only the mournful hooting of an owl from the forest . . ."

Lomeiko put his hand over his eyes, and one might have thought that there, on his palm, his sight beheld living pictures and he was merely relating what he saw.

"Suddenly a dim figure rises up at the edge of the road. The stranger raises his hand, as if he wants something. The merchant, suspecting nothing, asks: 'What do you want, good man?' And then the stranger strikes him in the throat with a knife and throws him to the ground and rips open a bloody wound from ear to ear. Paralyzed with fear, the child watches, sobbing, as his father is murdered. And then the stranger gets to his feet, seizes the boy by his thin shoulders, and, peering straight into the eyes gaping wide in terror, slits that thin throat with his sharp blade. The entreaty for mercy becomes a croaking wheeze, then a gurgle . . .

"But wait, that is not yet everything!" exclaimed the advocate, appealing to his hysterically sobbing listeners. "I have not yet described to you the greatest horror—how the murderer hacks into the lifeless bodies as he removes the heads. How the vertebrae crunch, how the black blood spurts up like a fountain . . . And now look at Vladimir Lvovich." A rapid turn, an extended arm. "Tell me, in all conscience, can you see a former Guards lieutenant, a synodical inspector, as such a butcher? But of course not! . . . And now for the murder of the photographic artist Poggio. Despite all the conjecture indulged in by the prosecutor, it is perfectly evident that this is a crime of passion. Vladimir Lvovich has spent a considerable time in your town and you have, of course, been able to study his character and his habits. You are familiar with his customary coolness, and his blasé manner that produces such an unpleasant impression on so many people. Can you really imagine this restrained, rational man swinging a tripod, ripping photographs to pieces in a frenzy, and trampling on photographic plates? Why, take a closer look at him! He is a slender man, of delicate physique, not broad in the shoulders. Would he really have had the Satanic strength to strike such a heavy blow with the tripod?"

After this first substantive argument (for everything else so far had been no more than psychology), Gurii Samsonovich returned to the realm of feelings, while continuing to speak in the same severe and far from sentimental tone.

"Very well, gentlemen, let us leave the conclusions of logic and reason aside. Let us turn to the heart, to the instinct that never misleads us. It sometimes happens that reason repeats insistently to us: This is black, black, and we begin to believe it is so, then the heart suddenly awakes and shakes its head"—the advocate's evocation of the heart shaking its head did not sit so very smoothly, but everyone was so carried away by his speech that they paid no attention to the dubious nature of the image—"and exclaims: 'What do you mean by saying it is black, when it is white?' I appeal to the ladies sitting in the hall. Many of you have joked, laughed, and—I beg your pardon—flirted with Bubentsov. You have made music with him, gone on picnics, and so on and so forth. Can you really imagine that this lover of female beauty was capable of smashing the Princess Telianova's head with a stone? Just look at this nightmarish, crude implement." Lomeiko pointed to the weighty cobblestone lying on the material evidence table. "Can you even imagine Vladimir Lvovich with such a weapon in his hand?"

"No! Never!" Olympiada Savelievna called loudly from the hall, and many of the ladies passionately supported her.

"You doubt it," stated the impassioned defender. "And you are right to do so, because this accused has not committed any crime. You will ask me, Who then killed these unfortunates? Who is this monster? And I shall answer you gladly. The gentlemen investigators have failed to see the forest for the trees, but to the unbiased eye of the unblinkered man the essence of the matter is perfectly clear."

The advocate set his hands on his sides, thrust out his beard, and advanced his main forces into battle.

"Yes, Bubentsov is guilty. Not of murder, but of pardonable blindness. Like many others present here, as it happens. He, like you, failed to recognize the savage monster who had long enjoyed his patronage. Yes, yes, you have understood me correctly. The murderer in every case was Murad Djuraev, it is absolutely clear. To a man like Djuraev, slitting the throat of the merchant and his son would have meant nothing. And the thirty-five thousand that Vonifatiev had on him was huge money for Djuraev. He was in Drozdovka that day, he learned about the purchase of the forest, and after that everything was very simple. It is far easier for a coachman to absent himself from the house than a guest, especially such a distinguished one. And as you can well understand, this bashi-bazouk would have had no problem with the severing of the heads."

This was a clear, indubitable *touché*, and the best possible confirmation of that was the low murmur that rippled around the hall.

"Now let us recall the circumstances of Poggio's death. On that night, Djuraev was behaving violently. He wandered around the taverns and inns, appearing and disappearing by turns. Nobody seems to have wondered why this non-drinking Caucasian had suddenly launched into a drunken debauch. But here again the case is quite clear. If there was anything human about Djuraev, it was his doglike devotion to his master. Djuraev knew that Bubentsov and Poggio had quarreled over a woman. In the Caucasus the attitude to conflicts of that sort is quite different from here, among us cynical and comfortable Europeans. Let us not forget that from Djuraev's point of view, Naina Telianova was not simply some infidel woman, but the daughter of a Caucasian prince. We must assume that Murad approved of his master's choice—apparently even more so than his master did." (This subtle comment was received with total sympathy by the female section of the audience.) "Mr. Spasyonny has informed me that he told the Circassian about the scandal that occurred at the *vernissage*—about how Poggio had attempted to shame Princess Telianova by exhibiting immodest photographs to public view. Those of us who have been to the Caucasus can imagine how insulting such an act is to a young woman's honor and the honor of all who are linked to her by ties of blood or in any other manner. The woman that the Circassian regarded as a bride worthy of his master—I beg the pardon of the ladies present—was exhibited naked for the amusement of the public."

Oh, what a tremor ran around the hall, how the reporters' pencils scraped!

"In the Caucasus, such insults are redeemed with blood. Hence the peculiar ferocity of the murder and the frenzied destruction of the pictures—every last one of them. Only the indomitable eastern temperament is capable of such frenzied violence. Those feeble speculations that we have heard from the prosecutor concerning the aspen and the mattock are good for nothing more than a crime novel. The investigation has attempted to construct the entire edifice of the accusation upon a coincidence that is entirely accidental. It is hardly to be wondered that this absurd construction has collapsed at the very first blow. And the case of the third murder could not be simpler. Djuraev had killed the main offender, but he was not satisfied with that. The drunkenness had passed, but the pain of the insult inflicted on his master continued to torment his savage heart. After all, the woman who had very nearly become his master's wife had insulted him even more deeply than Poggio. Not only had she betrayed him, she had behaved like a contemptible loose woman. In the Islamic world, as we know, such women are stoned to death. And that was what Djuraev did. He took a stone and he killed Telianova. And as for the fact that he also killed the entirely innocent maid, what did one more Christian soul mean to a savage like him?"

Gurii Samsonovich sighed sorrowfully and gestured briefly with one hand.

"And now the final thing. Do not forget that, at the arrest, it was Djuraev who offered resistance to the authorities. Naturally—he was the only one who had good reason to do so."

Lomeiko concluded hastily and unspectacularly, which was evidently the very latest chic fashion in the capital.

"That is all I have to say, gentlemen. As you see, I have tormented you less than the prosecutor did. Because I have arguments, and he has only sentiments. Decide—it is your right and your duty. But the matter is absolutely clear."

THERE WAS NO ovation because the reaction to the speech was mixed: Bubentsov's supporters were openly triumphant and his opponents were quite clearly nonplussed.

The prosecutor immediately raised his hand and the debate between the two sides began.

"And so your defendant is an innocent lamb who did not even suspect what a wolf he was warming under his coat?" Berdichevsky vehemently declaimed the excellent phrase that had only just come to mind.

Many people laughed, because Vladimir Lvovich did not resemble a lamb in the least. Encouraged, Matvei Bentsionovich continued: "Does the counsel for the defense not feel that the business of the heads was altogether too convenient for the synodical inspector? No sooner had Bubentsov arrived here in Zavolzhie to eradicate the practice of paganism than all of a sudden headless bodies were discovered, exactly as in the famous four-hundred-years-old chronicle!"

Lomeiko inquired ironically: "Perhaps my client wrote the chronicle himself?"

Again there was laughter, and rather louder than the previous time. When it came to the art of bandying words, Matvei Bentsionovich was clearly no match for the fencer from the capital.

"It does not matter so much who actually carried out the killing," said Berdichevsky, making a cardinal concession, because he had no way to refute the defense's arguments. "It is possible that Bubentsov did not dirty his own hands. But if the blood was spilled by Djuraev, he was acting with Bubentsov's knowledge!"

"Do you have proof?" asked the advocate, screwing up his eyes, "or are you simply vaporing, as you did so recently?"

"An ignorant, benighted Caucasian could not have worked out such a cunning plot by himself," Berdichevsky began anxiously. "And he was hardly likely to have understood the subtleties of photographic art. He not only tore up the photographs, but also smashed the plates. Where did he come by such knowledge of the photographic process? And, let me remind you, the murderer removed precisely the picture and the plate that could have given away the spot where the bodies were buried. How will you explain that?"

Gurii Samsonovich smiled condescendingly.

"Why, very simply, my dear colleague. As he was wrecking the exhibition, Djuraev noticed that one of the pictures showed a place that he remembered only too well. On looking more closely, he saw the mattock that he had forgotten. It was not hard to imagine what danger this picture posed for the murderer. There is the answer to your riddle. And in addition, Mr. Prosecutor, I should like to protest in the most vigorous terms against the revolting contempt for other nationalities implied by your words. 'An ignorant, benighted Caucasian.' You make it sound as if he were not entirely human. And yet he was very human indeed, only with different traditions and beliefs, and with his own ideas of honor, far stricter than ours. It is a great pity that the police killed Djuraev. I would have gladly argued in his defense. We always measure everyone with our own yardstick, but Russians are not the only people in this world."

The defender's reward for these just words was passionate applause from the progressive section of the public, with the journalists applauding most loudly of all. Berdichevsky blushed painfully, because he subscribed to the very same views.

"And what of the attempt to escape? Why did Bubentsov need to flee, if he was innocent?" asked Matvei Bentsionovich, suddenly recollecting this point.

Lomeiko paused, as if he was embarrassed by such a simpleminded question.

"I beg your pardon, but what else was there left for him to do when the Circassian opened fire? Your valiant plodders would have riddled all three of them with bullets. And Bubentsov could not possibly believe that there would be a fair trial. And we can see that he was right."

Berdichevsky looked at the defendant and saw Vladimir Lvovich's lips tremble in a triumphant smile.

"How long can this go on?" the deputy chief procurator said rather loudly. "It seems that everything could hardly be any clearer."

Matvei Bentsionovich cast a glance filled with anguish at His Grace Mitrofanii, who suddenly gave him a certain sign.

"Mr. Chairman," Berdichevsky immediately declared. "I would like to ask you to hear a witness for the prosecution."

When it emerged that the bishop of the province himself was going to testify, the defender leapt to his feet and shouted: "I protest! The bishop had nothing to do with the investigation; I have studied the materials of the case very closely. And so His Grace's speaking can be nothing other than an attempt to exploit the authority of such a respected individual to influence the jury."

Mitrofanii smiled, amused at the thought that the court might not allow him to speak. The chairman of the court, his swollen-veined physiognomy flushed bright scarlet, replied sharply to the luminary from the capital.

"Not so! Although the bishop did not formally take part in the investigation, it is well known to everyone that he guided the activities of the investigators. In addition, His Grace's perspicacity in such matters is well known, and not only in our province"—the judge pronounced the last word with especial emphasis, in rancorous revenge on the barrister for his earlier jibes—"but also beyond its boundaries."

"As you wish," said Gurii Samsonovich, bowing his head meekly, but before he sat down, he added: "I implore you, Your Grace, not to abuse your word as a pastor! It carries great weight, but the responsibility that comes with it is also great."

THE ENTRANCE OF this witness created a genuine sensation, and in his zeal one of the illustrators even slid down from his chair onto the floor and gradually crept closer in order to capture the bishop's solemn and majestic posture as he pronounced the words of the oath.

Mitrofanii did not address the jury directly, but immediately turned to face the counsel for the defense, as if acknowledging that he was the key figure in this bitter legal battle.

"You spoke of responsibility," His Grace began clearly and loudly. "And you spoke the absolute truth. Everyone who speaks before a human court of law bears a great responsibility. But we bear an incomparably greater responsibility before another court to come. However, you appear to have forgotten about that."

Gurii Samsonovich lowered his head meekly, as if not daring to contradict such a venerable opponent while yet remaining true to his own opinion.

"You are, after all, a talented man with a subtle mind," Mitrofanii continued reproachfully. "Why do you indulge in these verbal acrobatics? The merchant and his son, the three poor Zyts, the artist, the two young women, and this Caucasian as well—see how many souls have perished. And all of them, as ill luck would have it, are connected with Bubentsov. You will not attempt to deny that, surely? Here in Zavolzhie everything had been calm and peaceful. Then this man appeared and it was as if he had cast a curse on our blessed district. There came murders, mutual suspicion, hatred, baseness, informing, mistrust in families, fear. I shall now say something that many freethinkers and atheists will regard as superstition and backwardness, but it is the pure truth. Prowling around us and among us are those who bear in their souls the spirit of evil. There are many of these people, and they look exactly the same as everyone else. Therefore we do not fear them, but we open our hearts and our embraces to them." At this point His Grace scanned with an expressive glance the gallery where the ladies of

Zavolzhsk were sitting. "And we only come to recognize these bearers of evil when for some reason, for certain requirements of their own, they decide to wound us or destroy us. And then we wail and lament, but it is nearly too late to save ourselves, because these evil powers have teeth of steel, claws of iron, and their hearts are hewn from stone."

The bishop resembled an Old Testament prophet now, and Mitrofanii's voice thundered as if he were leading his cavalry squadron into the attack on the English hussars in the Valley of Death at Balaclava.

"Do you know what a disaster befell our province? Evil came to us. And we who live here have all felt it—some sooner and some later. Your defendant is not only an evil man, he is a servant of evil. His entire life, his entire behavior, testify to that. And a dangerous servant, because he is intelligent, cunning, resourceful, bold, and handsome. Yes, yes, handsome. The Evil One has endowed him with a mellifluous tongue, an entrancing voice, and the power to subdue the weak with many other gifts."

At this point Bubentsov did something foolish: He pretended to menace the bishop from behind with horns, and he stuck out his tongue. Someone snorted in laughter, but on the majority of those present the antic left an extremely unpleasant impression.

"Let us look at those things he has done that even you will not dispute," the bishop continued, still addressing the advocate alone. "You said it was not he who killed the Vonifatievs, father and son, but his underling. Let us assume—merely assume—that to be the case. Out of one terrible crime, Bubentsov created another, even worse: He made a false allegation against an entire people, raised up a storm of hatred and intolerance, organized a shameful and repulsive hunt against those of a different faith. And how did he behave with Naina Telianova? He debauched that young woman, destroyed her life, and mocked her sinful but sincere feelings. And he did not even debauch her out of love, or even out of passion, but out of a momentary whim or, even worse, out of cupidity. Deliberately or otherwise, Bubentsov pushed Naina Telianova into committing the most repulsive acts and into direct complicity with a monstrous murder. And afterward he destroyed her. Yes, yes, in any case it was he who destroyed both Naina Georgievna and her maid, and the artist."

This was already more than Lomeiko could stand, since he could see the effect that the bishop's speech was having on the members of the jury.

"But by your leave!" the advocate exclaimed, rising to his feet. "You say this in a figurative sense, but the law does not acknowledge figures of speech! Mr. Chairman, this is in total breach of procedure and the regulations! I protest!"

"I can also speak non-figuratively," Mitrofanii said in a much quieter voice. "What were those arguments that you used in an attempt to refute the accusation? That the frail Bubentsov would not have had the strength to force the heavy tripod from the photographic apparatus through Poggio's chest? I believe that you used the phrase 'satanic strength.' A most apt expression. For I also think of satanic strength when I see how much evil energy and devilish stamina Mr. Bubentsov has displayed in the course of his tumultuous activities in our province. Yes, he is slender and gaunt, but it is a well-known fact that people with his physique possess special resources of nervous energy. In a frenzy or a fury they are capable of demonstrating miraculous strength, as medical science confirms. There is no need to seek too far." The bishop looked as if a fortunate example had just at that moment occurred to him. "Last year during the trial of a certain Miss Baranova, you yourself described it quite remarkably. Your defendant, a seventeen-year-old seamstress, choked her tormentor with her bare hands and in her passion she also dragged his two-hundred-fifty-pound carcass to a pond. I read your speech, which won Baranova a light sentence, in the newspapers. Do you remember your own explanation of nervous frenzy?"

This was a crushing blow, and all the more so because it took Gurii Samsonovich entirely by surprise. Who could have expected a provincial bishop to be so well informed?

But the bishop was already proceeding further.

"Since you have studied the materials of the case, you are aware that someone attempted to kill the nun Pelagia Lisitsyna after she exposed Naina Telianova's mischief with the white bulldogs. The material evidence includes a sack and a rope, the weapons used in the attempted murder. Bubentsov was present when Telianova was exposed, but

Murad Djuraev was not. If Djuraev is the only criminal, then how did he know that Sister Pelagia was dangerous?"

The advocate cast an inquiring glance at Vladimir Lvovich, who merely shrugged.

"And in addition . . ." Mitrofanii paused, making it clear that he was coming to the most important point of all. "Tell me, Mr. Defender, with whom was Telianova in love—Murad Djuraev or Bubentsov?"

The public did not immediately appreciate the significance of the question, but the sharp-witted Gurii Samsonovich turned pale and tugged on his beard.

"Dead men, Mr. Advocate, can also testify. The Lord has given them that power. Engrossed in your game of words, you lost sight of the main thing: that Naina Telianova would have committed such insane acts—concealing the whereabouts of the remains, killing the dogs—only for someone whom she loved with all her heart. But not for the ignorant Circassian whom you so diligently urge upon us as the likely murderer. What have you to say to that? Who is it that cannot see the wood for the trees here?"

Half a minute passed, a minute. The luminary of legal thought was silent. The hall held its breath, sensing that the outcome of the entire trial was being decided at that very moment.

Then for the first time in his entire speech, Mitrofanii turned to the accused and asked sharply: "And what have you to say to that, Mr. Criminal?"

Vladimir Lvovich flushed and was on the point of opening his mouth to speak, but that very instant something happened that very probably even the perspicacious bishop could not have foreseen.

"A-A-A-A-GH!" THERE WAS a sickening howl, or rather a whine, and Tikhon Ieremeevich Spasyonny, who had hitherto been sitting absolutely quiet, so that everybody had almost forgotten about him, ran out of the fenced-off enclosure for the accused into the center of the hall.

He collapsed onto his knees and bowed three times down to the floor: to the court, the jurors, and the hall, all the while choking on his own convulsive sobs. The guards took hold of him under the arms and tried to lift him up, but the accused resolutely refused to stand, and he had to be dragged bodily back to the bench.

"Greatly, most greatly sinful!" the crazed secretary cried. "Woe is me, I am cursed!"

The judge rang his bell menacingly and Spasyonny bowed penitently once again.

"Your Grace," he sobbed. "Allow me to make a candid confession."

Then he turned to his companion on the bench and, folding his hands prayerfully, appealed to him.

"Confess, Vladimir Lvovich! Forgive me, feebleminded as I am, but I have no more strength! Many are the sins that we bear, oh, many! The bishop spoke truly about evildoers, and even such are you and I. In the name of Christ our Lord, I implore you, repent."

The policemen were obliged to take hold of Bubentsov by the shoulders and the two of them were scarcely able to restrain the inspector, who was white with fury, which most convincingly confirmed what the bishop had said about the strength of nervous frenzy.

Mitrofanii proceeded majestically back to his place. They did not applaud him—they did not dare—but the respectful silence that accompanied His Grace on his way was more triumphant than any ovation.

"Do you wish to give testimony?" the chairman asked.

"Yes! I do!" Spasyonny wiped his tear-stained face with his sleeve. "Candid testimony. I wish to unburden my soul!"

He stood up and began speaking in a trembling voice.

"Verily, evil is ubiquitous, and I am its most loathsome servant! Vladimir Lvovich, Mr. Bubentsov, is guilty of all these terrible murders; he killed those people, but I, sinner that I am, am also guilty, for I kept silent, concealed and facilitated—out of weakness and out of fear for my own life!"

Vladimir Lvovich jerked so hard that his guards were sent flying, but another two came dashing to their aid, and the four of them managed to sit the wrathful accused back in his place. Vladimir Lvovich could not move, but he shouted: "What's wrong with you, Undershirt, have you gone mad?"

"There, you see," said Tikhon Ieremeevich, trembling all over. "Even now I shudder and shake at the very sound of his voice. Verily he is Satan. Alluring and full of temptation. He has been granted great power over men. And I, worm that I am, could not resist his temptation, when I realized how broad was the span of his wing. He came to this peaceful town to reduce it to dust, ashes, and groans—and all in the name of his own aggrandizement. It was his plan to elevate himself to the very peak of earthly power, and for that he would have halted at nothing. He told me: 'Cling tight, Undershirt, to my coattails and do not be timid, do not unclench your fingers. I shall soar aloft and raise you up with me.' But he also said: 'Beware, Undershirt, that you do not go against me, for I will crush you like a worm.' And he would have crushed me, for he is that kind of man. He deceived me, intimidated me, and flattered me, and I became his devoted dog. Most basely and most vilely have I acted, sinner that I am. The only thing in which I have not defiled myself is murder, but that only because my nerves are weak."

Spasyonny broke down, sobbing and unable to carry on speaking, so that the bailiff was obliged to give him some water. Calming somewhat, the penitent continued.

"He joked about it. About the saying that other ambitious men 'walk on people's heads,' but he was literally scrambling over heads to high places. There is much that I could tell you, about how he confused, tormented, and frightened those unfortunate Zyts . . . And I was no better, I wanted to earn his approval. What happened with the Vonifatievs was this . . . Vladimir Lvovich has horrendous debts, from the old days. Here in Zavolzhsk he strode about like a lion, but in Peter he darts about like a hare, hiding from his creditors. It is a hindrance to his career, and Konstantin Petrovich has reproached him for it— told him it is not seemly for a synodical official. And then, when we were staying with the general's widow at Drozdovka, the talk turned to the merchant who had arrived. Vladimir Lvovich whispered in my ear: Ask Sytnikov how much he expects to pay for the forest."

"Why are you lying?" Bubentsov shouted furiously from his seat, and the judge warned him: One more word and he would be removed from the hall.

"What point is there in lying now?" asked Spasyonny, glancing around fearfully at his former protector. "Now is the time to tell the truth. And so, when he learned that this Vonifatiev was going to get thirty thousand, or perhaps even forty, his eyes lit up. I sat there, thinking nothing of it. When Sytnikov grew angry with Vladimir Lvovich and got up to leave, he said to me: Overtake him and ask him not to be angry with me, and ask him at the same time whether he will bring his guest here; it would be interesting to take a look at such a savage. I thought he had some business in mind—he was planning at the time to discredit the Old Believers. It was only later that he was inspired to switch his attention to the pagans. Very well, I came back and reported to him: No, he says he won't bring him. The merchant is traveling on once the deal is done, despite it being so late. Very well, said Vladimir Lvovich, and he seemed to lose interest. That is all that happened. But that night I knocked at his door—I had an idea, a base little idea, I won't say what it was, because I'm ashamed of it and it has nothing to do with the case. I knocked and knocked, but he didn't answer. At first I was surprised, because he is a light sleeper, but afterward I decided that he must be spending the night with the young mistress of Drozdovka."

Tikhon Ieremeevich wiped his forehead with his massive, clawlike hand and took another sip of water.

"And when I went into his room in the morning, I noticed that his cloak was wet—it had started to rain just before dawn. But even then I didn't think that it was important. Several days went by and they found the headless bodies, and Vladimir Lvovich immediately began talking about Zyt sacrifices. He turned out to know so much about their beliefs and customs—I was simply amazed. Well, and I was glad, of course. What a wonderful turn things had taken, just as if we had ordered it."

The speaker paused and raised one hand.

"No, I will not distort the truth now. I want everything to be as open as at confession. I felt the worm of suspicion gnawing at me from the very beginning. Things were working out far too smoothly, I thought. As if the devil himself had dealt our hand. The idea that Vladimir Lvovich himself had planted the headless bodies never entered my head, of course. It is only now, when everything has come together and I remember about Sytnikov, and about the empty room, and about the wet cloak . . . and the artist, too; it's clear now how he arranged everything. He plied Murad with drink himself; no one else could have done it. To make sure I did not get under his feet, so that I would wander around the taverns all night, trailing after Murad like a little dog. I think that even then Vladimir Lvovich was intending to blame the murders on Murad if anything went wrong. Otherwise, why did he need the tripod?" Tikhon Ieremeevich pointed at the material evidence. "It could have been done more simply somehow. And Vladimir Lvovich has great strength; he only looks puny, but he is sinewy, and when he gets into a fury—God help you if you get in his way. And then toward the end he stopped trying to conceal things from me altogether. After the investigative experiment, when the young woman Telianova began threatening him openly, he turned as dark as thunder. He walked around his room, thinking, and then suddenly said: 'I'm going out for a while before bed. And if anyone calls or asks for me, tell them that I'm already asleep.' He didn't get back until early in the morning. Soaking wet, covered in mud—"

Tikhon Ieremeevich's testimony was suddenly interrupted in the most outrageous and indecorous fashion.

Sensing that the guards had relaxed their vigilance, Vladimir Lvovich vaulted easily, even gracefully, over the barrier and flew at his unfaithful henchman, dealing him a swingeing blow to the ear, then knocked him to the floor and clutched his throat tight in his small but tenacious hands.

The guards dashed to Spasyonny's rescue and a most unedifying scene ensued, so that the session had to be declared suspended.

WHEN THE TRIAL reconvened, the accused were seated separately, with Bubentsov sitting between two guards and wearing chains on his wrists. The inspector's appearance was not in the least synodical: He had a substantial bruise on his forehead, his collar was ripped, his eyes were gleaming feverishly—in short, he looked a genuine Satan.

Tikhon Ieremeevich had fared even worse. His ear was swollen, bulging out from the side of his head, his nose resembled a beetroot

(Bubentsov had even managed to seize hold of it with his teeth), and the worst thing of all was that the victim of the assault could not speak anymore, for Vladimir Lvovich's iron fingers had crushed his throat. That is, Tikhon Ieremeevich had made an attempt to speak, but his hoarse gasps had proved entirely incomprehensible, and the chairman had decided not to prolong his sufferings, especially since the case was turning out to be quite clear.

As he was preparing to issue his instructions to the members of the jury, the judge asked, more for the sake of form than anything else, whether anyone present was in possession of any other information that could be of assistance to the prosecution or the defense.

At that very moment a court officer handed him a small scrap of paper. The judge read it, raised his eyebrows in astonishment, and with a shrug of his shoulders declared: "Another witness has come forward. It is Sister Pelagia Lisitsyna. By law I am obliged to allow her to speak. Do you wish to speak in support of the prosecution?"

He peered around the hall over the top of his spectacles, trying to spot someone rising from their seat.

There was a buzz in the hall, because the witness had risen to her feet behind the judge, from the chairs for especially distinguished guests.

The little figure in black was greeted with a murmur of discontent. Everyone was thoroughly tired from sitting for so long through such powerful emotions, and what more could there possibly be to add now? In any case, the accused would not receive anything more than hard labor for life, and he would not be let off with anything less. Even the bishop shook his monk's headdress in disapproval, evidently considering that his spiritual daughter had succumbed to the temptation of idle vanity.

PELAGIA LISITSYNA'S SPEECH may not have been long, but it was of extreme importance to the outcome of the trial, and therefore we shall adduce it verbatim and in full, for this purpose temporarily abandoning our narrative and entrusting it to the impartial minutes of the trial. The stenographer at the trial was Leonid Krestovozdvizhensky, the son of our dean and a very capable young man, for whom many foretold outstanding achievements in the field of literature. However, he drew up the minutes in a most conscientious fashion, without any embellishments—apart from including several comments in his enthusiasm, and so making this official document somewhat reminiscent of a play. But let it remain so. As for ourselves, we shall merely add that during her address Sister Pelagia spoke in a very quiet voice, so that many people in the back rows could not hear everything.

And so we shall start from the point at which the witness, having pronounced the words of the oath, begins her own testimony.

**Lisitsyna:** Gentlemen judges and of the jury, Bubentsov did not commit the murders of which he is accused.

*Noise and shouts in the hall. Obvious agitation among the jurors.*

**Chairman:** An interesting statement. But then who did?

**Lisitsyna:** Bubentsov, of course, is a villain. His Grace the bishop described all that quite correctly. But he is not a murderer. The Vonifatievs and Arkadii Sergeevich and Naina Georgievna and her maid were all killed by that man there. He also tried to kill me twice, but God spared my life.

*She points at the accused Spasyonny. He tries to shout something, but cannot because of his wounded throat. Loud noise in the hall.*

**Chairman:** [*ringing his bell*] What grounds have you for making such a statement?

**Lisitsyna:** May I first explain why Bubentsov is not the murderer? This business with the heads—it always bothered me that although Naina Georgievna gave Bubentsov hints and even threatened him, he showed no signs of concern and only enflamed her further with his disdain. Why would he wish to play with fire like that? He only had to say a single word to her and she would have become as meek as a lamb. I could not understand it. On the other hand, in such a terrible business, the princess would not have protected anyone apart from Bubentsov, and it was clear from her entire manner that she knew something special about him. And today, when His Grace drew our attention to the fact in demonstrating the groundlessness of the suspicions cast on Murad Djuraev, I suddenly recalled the words that Naina Georgievna spoke on that last evening, as Bubentsov was preparing to leave after the investigative experiment. 'The same cloak. The same cap. How it gleamed in the moonlight.' Nobody present at the time understood those words, and they were all accustomed to the princess's predilection for expressing herself mysteriously. But now it is as if a veil has been lifted from my eyes. When Naina Georgievna said that, Bubentsov was already walking toward the door, and she saw him from the back. Do you understand?

**Chairman:** I do not understand a thing. But continue.

**Lisitsyna:** But you must see! I see very clearly now how it all happened. On the night when the Vonifatievs were killed, she was strolling through the garden. Perhaps she was hoping that Bubentsov would come out, but by that time he had already cooled toward her, since he was now counting on insinuating himself into the company of Tatishcheva's heirs without Naina Georgievna's assistance. Or perhaps she simply could not sleep, overcome by an understandable agitation. Then suddenly she sees Bubentsov there among the trees, or rather she sees his silhouette: the cloak, the familiar cap. She probably saw him from a distance, otherwise she would certainly have called out to him. Bubentsov was behaving in such a mysterious way that the young woman decided not to betray her own presence and follow him. I do not know if by this time the murderer had already thrown the bodies into the River, but Telianova undoubtedly saw him bury the heads. Being an impressionable girl with a tendency to fantasize, she no doubt took this incredible scene for some kind of secret ritual. Or she simply froze to the spot in horror—which is only natural in such circumstances. It was in precisely this condition—of numb horror—that I discovered her when I arrived in Drozdovka three days later. Naina Georgievna zealously preserved the secret of the burial place, for which she even had to kill the white bulldogs that were so dear to her own grandmother's heart, but the princess's feelings for Bubentsov were in a state of total confusion. However, when Vladimir Lvovich appeared once again and announced the beginning of an investigation directed against the bloodthirsty pagan believers, Naina Georgievna imagined that now she understood her beloved's plan: It was monstrously daring and breathtakingly inhuman. That was the occasion when she spoke about the Demon. No doubt this satanic toying with people's fates seemed to her an art far more intoxicating than the theater or painting. She is not the first to have fallen victim to this temptation.

**Chairman:** This is all very plausible. But why have you decided that the culprit must be Spasyonny?

**Lisitsyna:** He himself told us that he asked Sytnikov about the visiting merchant. And we only have Spasyonny's word that he took up the conversation at Vladimir Lvovich's request. At the same time, although Bubentsov is mired up to his eyes in debt, thirty-five thousand is not the kind of money that would save him. People in town say that Bubentsov has debts of hundreds of thousands. Would he really have soiled his hands for the sake of a sum that is so insignificant by his standards? Spasyonny is quite a different case. For him thirty-five thousand is an entire fortune. And apart from his own enrichment, he had another goal: to assist his patron in his career and to rise alongside him. And so he did not sever the heads simply in order to cover his tracks, but with a farsighted plan in mind, and one that worked excellently. Perhaps Spasyonny even prompted Bubentsov's idea of making use of the headless bodies for the Zyt case. [*Agitation in the hall.*] Tikhon Ieremeevich is a man of exceptional prudence. In committing each of his crimes, he took precautions. When he set out to kill the Vonifatievs, he took his superior's cloak and cap—as a precaution. Just in case someone might see him. And someone did! And on the night of Poggio's murder, it was probably Spasyonny who plied Murad Djuraev with drink. It was no problem for him to absent himself for an hour while the Circassian was drinking in one of the taverns.

**Chairman:** To say "It was no problem" is not proof.

**Lisitsyna:** You are right, Your Honor. But if you will permit me . . . [*She walks over to the table of material evidence and picks up the photographic tripod, then carries it across to the accused Bubentsov.*] Vladimir Lvovich, will you hold out your hands please. [*The accused Bubentsov sits without moving, looking at Lisitsyna. Then he extends his shackled hands over the barrier.*] Try to grasp the tripod in your fingers. You see, gentlemen? He has small hands. He simply could not have had a strong enough grip on this weighty tripod to strike a blow of such great force. From which it is perfectly obvious that he did not kill Arkadii Sergeevich Poggio.

*Loud noise in the hall. Cries of: "Ah, but that's right!" "Well done, little nun!" and the like. The chairman rings his bell.*

**Lisitsyna:** Permit me one more demonstration. [*She takes the tripod over to the accused Spasyonny.*] And now, Tikhon Ieremeevich, why don't you try?

*Spasyonny hastily conceals his hands, which were previously lying on the barrier, behind his back. Many people in the hall leap to their feet. The chairman rings his bell.*

**Lisitsyna:** The stand is so large that an ordinary man can hardly get his fingers around it, but Mr. Spasyonny has exceptionally large hands. For him the task presented no difficulty. . . . And I have one more request to make of the court. Would it be possible to conduct a physical examination of Mr. Spasyonny? Specifically to examine his right hip and thigh. You see, when the sack was thrown over my head in the park at Drozdovka, I stuck my knitting needles into my attacker's leg twice. Rather deeply. There ought to be four puncture marks left.

**Spasyonny:** [*jumping to his feet and hissing from his place*] You witch! You witch!

# CHAPTER 12

# The Black Monk

AFTER SISTER PELAGIA'S performance the court remained in session for a while longer, but the outcome of the case was already clear, and the public's attention was already wandering. Tikhon Ieremeevich was taken away and examined, and—true enough—there on his right leg four pink spots were discovered. No debate ensued between the sides, because so many sudden twists and turns had reduced the prosecutor to a state of stupefaction, while the counsel for the defense appeared perfectly satisfied. His client's affairs were shaping up quite nicely, and the famous advocate did not regard Spasyonny's fate as his responsibility.

Strangely enough, Tikhon Ieremeevich did not start weeping and moaning. When asked if he admitted his guilt for the murders, he only shook his head. He sat with an expressionless face and his eyes half-closed, and did not even seem to be listening to the judge's directions to the jury, or the jury's reply, or even to the pronouncement of sentence. His crumpled little face had become smooth and even acquired a certain air of significance previously quite alien to his features. Bubentsov, by contrast, behaved in an extremely nervous manner: He kept fidgeting in his seat, sometimes glancing at his secretary, sometimes twisting his neck around to look at Sister Pelagia, and at such moments he had a perplexed and even slightly stupid air. The nun, by the way, remained seated until the very end of the trial, without once raising her eyes, so that she probably never noticed Vladimir Lvovich's indecorous behavior.

The sentence was no surprise to anyone. Tikhon Ieremeevich

Spasyonny, who had still not confessed or returned the stolen money, was given hard labor for life. Vladimir Lvovich was released from arrest there and then in the courthouse, and an hour later he had left our provincial capital, disgraced in the eyes of the majority, but also secretly lamented by certain ladies.

And after that, everything in Zavolzhsk gradually became calmer and settled back down. As if a stone had fallen into a pond and at first the water had been roiled, and the waves had radiated out in circles, but soon they slowed and died away, and the surface became smooth and flat and the peaceful backwater was still again, although for a time bubbles continued to rise and pop at the surface.

Ludmila Platonovna von Haggenau went to confession with the bishop again following a long absence. She emerged with a face that was red and tear-stained, but her eyes were clear. Later Mitrofanii also had a lengthy conversation with the governor, whom he reassured completely, giving Anton Antonovich to understand that there was nothing for him to feel alarmed about. His Grace did not reveal the secrets of the confessional and he expressed himself largely in hints, but even so he imposed a strict penance upon himself afterward.

Matvei Bentsionovich petitioned the bishop on behalf of the chief of police, Lagrange, but was rebuffed. He could have regarded his debt of gratitude as fully discharged at that, but Berdichevsky went back to the bishop again—without the slightest hope, purely in order to make sure that his own conscience was clear. However, Mitrofanii unexpectedly took a sympathetic attitude to his intercession and said: "Lagrange does not have to be tried. And there is no need to dismiss him from his post. I do not regard him as a totally hopeless case. After all, he could quite easily have arranged things so that Murad killed you and no one would have been any the wiser. Tell Felix Stanislavovich that I will have a word with the governor." The chief of police remained in office, and now he also goes to confession with His Grace.

BUT EVEN BEFORE all these events—in fact, on the very day of the trial itself—a certain event took place that is worthy of special mention.

When the members of the jury withdrew to deliberate and everyone in the hall began talking at once, sharing their impressions of the trial and their expectations concerning the imminent verdict, the bishop, feeling it unbecoming to his rank to linger among the idly chattering crowd, withdrew at the chairman's invitation to the room reserved for honored guests. With his finger he beckoned for Sister Pelagia to follow him. He walked down the corridor with a gloomy air, looking down at his feet and tapping his bishop's crook angrily on the floor.

When they were alone, the nun kissed His Grace's ring with a guilty expression and began speaking incoherently.

"You are right, father, Bubentsov is an evildoer and the devil incarnate. Now he will go free and, although his synodical career is over, in his lifetime he will still work a great deal of all manner of evil. He has great strength. He will lick his wounds and rise again and once again begin sowing hatred and grief. But falsehood cannot be eradicated by means of falsehood! I only truly realized at the very last moment how things happened, or I would certainly have asked your blessing before speaking out. Or rather, I would have asked you to testify. But there was no time at all for explanations; the judge was already preparing to adjourn the trial. That is why I butted in with my arguments. And it turned out that I exposed you to the public eye in an unfavorable light. Can you forgive me?"

She looked at the bishop fearfully, almost despairingly. Mitrofanii sighed heavily and patted his spiritual daughter on the head.

"As for your exposing me as an arrogant fool, that is no more than I deserved. A lesson to me not to be so swollen-headed. And not to steal others' laurels. I know that I have that sinful weakness, and I have been punished for it. But that is only half the problem. You have made me feel ashamed, Pelagia, greatly ashamed. And afraid. How neatly everything works out when one views the world through colored glass. And one chooses the color to suit one's own preferences. Then your personal enemy appears as not merely someone who wishes you ill, but a criminal, the enemy of all mankind. Or else suddenly, no matter how many his transgressions, as a shining angel. Let the politicians look at the world through pieces of colored glass, but a pastor must not. The glass must be clear; it is even better if there is no glass at all." The bishop shook his head ruefully. "And you are also right when you say that evil cannot be eradicated with evil. In the place of one evil you simply establish another, even stronger. But Bubentsov's evil is special. It does not attack the laws so much as people's very souls. It is the church's duty to be watchful for evil and to denounce it."

The sister roused herself and started speaking quickly.

"But it seems to me, father, that God's church has a quite different purpose. We should not be watchful for evil, or denounce it, either. Because that produces fear. We should not deal with evil, but with good. With meekness and love. Nothing good will ever come of fear."

"And is that how you would limn the fear of God?" the bishop asked menacingly. "Think well, Pelagia."

"Yes, about that, too. God should not be feared, He should be loved. And the church should not be feared, but loved. In general it is a sin for the church to mingle with earthly power."

"How is it a sin?" asked Mitrofanii, more in surprise than anger. "How is Zavolzhsk any the worse because Anton Antonovich listens to me?"

Unfortunately the conversation was never concluded, because an agitated Berdichevsky put his face in at the door and declared: "Your Grace, it is all over! The jurors came back out almost immediately. Spasyonny is guilty—by unanimous decision. Bubentsov is innocent—also by unanimous decision. The reporters did not even bother to wait for the sentence. They are all here, jostling in the corridor. Waiting for you."

"Me?" the bishop asked with a trembling voice. "Well, then, let me drain the bitter cup. I deserve it." He rose resolutely to his feet and pulled Pelagia up by the hand. "You go first. This is your hour. Only try not to be too proud. Remember that you are a bride of Christ."

The moment she stepped out into the corridor, Pelagia was blinded by magnesium flashes, and after taking only two short steps she halted in confusion. She had only caught a brief glimpse of a large number of excited male faces, most of them beardless and with curled mustaches.

Strong shoulders shoved the nun aside. Frock coats and jackets surrounded the figure of the bishop, stooping in penitence.

An unattractive-looking man with high cheekbones—Tsarenko himself, the famous feature writer from St. Petersburg—said in a respectful voice: "Your Grace, your majestic wisdom has produced a most profound impression. You delivered an outstanding speech, denouncing evil in the person of Inspector Bubentsov, who may not be guilty before the court of man, but is guilty a hundred times over before the court of God. You left the petty murderer, an ordinary criminal, to be exposed by your assistant, which she did competently, undoubtedly following your instructions."

"No, no, she did it herself!" Mitrofanii exclaimed in fright. "Pelagia did it all!"

This truly touching expression of modesty was greeted with understanding smiles, and many of the reporters immediately took down the bishop's words in their notebooks, seeing in them an admirable humility and rejection of vanity.

"Of course," said Tsarenko, also smiling shrewdly. "You had nothing at all to do with it. And the credit for all the previous cases solved with your involvement also belongs to your Sister Polixena."

"Pelagia," the bishop corrected him, looking around in confusion for his assistant.

Pelagia was standing by the open window, with her back turned to the journalists. Offended? Insulted?

Let us hasten to reassure the reader. The sister was not offended in the least. She was simply standing and looking out of the window because, outside, an event that we have mentioned previously was about to take place—in fact it had already begun happening.

The square onto which the windows of the district court looked out was already almost completely empty by this hour of the early evening. Two mongrels were yelping lazily at each other beside a streetlamp and a boy in a cloth jacket and blacked boots was hopping over a puddle on one leg. But from the far end of the square, where it runs into Malaya Kupecheskaya Street, there came the resounding clop of hooves over cobblestones, the rumbling of wheels, and the jingling of harness. These combined noises approached at a brisk pace, and soon it was possible to make out a lathered pair of piebald grays pulling along a sprung carriage. Standing on the box, waving a whip, was a dusty monk in a black cassock that fluttered behind him in the wind, and his head was uncovered, so that his long locks were tousled and tangled. Then it became clear that the forehead of this terrible coach-man was covered in blood and his eyes were bulging out of his head. The small number of people in the street who saw this sight all froze on the spot.

Approaching the court building, the monk pulled back on the reins, halting the dashing horses, jumped to the ground, and shouted to Pelagia.

But then, we shall not relate here exactly what the messenger shouted, because that will be the beginning of an entirely different story, one even stranger than the story of the white bulldog.

Pelagia turned back quickly toward the bishop. Mitrofanii had not seen the strange monk or heard his shout, but he immediately sensed that something was wrong. He pushed the correspondent aside gently but firmly and . . .

TO BE CONTINUED IN

*Sister Pelagia and the Black Monk*

*The following article and interview were published in the Italian newspaper* Il Messaggero *on May 30, 2003, the day of Boris Akunin's appearance at the Massenzio Literature Festival in Rome, where he was promoting the Italian edition of* Sister Pelagia and the White Bulldog.

## Akunin: "My Russia Is at a Crossroads"

FRANCESCO FANTASIA

A veritable phenomenon has emerged from the round belly of the nesting doll set of Russian literature: He is a writer who goes by the pen name of Boris Akunin but whose given name is the unpronounceable Grigory Chkhartishvili. Born in 1956, a Georgian transplant in Moscow, Akunin would have settled for his dual career as an editor and literary translator. But when he realized that Russian literature needed an equivalent of [Andrea] Camilleri, that there was a niche for a "literary project that would unite first-rate storytelling with popular narrative," he took up his pen and began writing mystery novels full of verve and with extremely intelligent plots. All the novels are set in nineteenth-century Russia, and up to now they have all had as their protagonist the eccentric Fandorin, a detective working for the czar who, depending on the circumstance, can become a spy or simply a snoop.

Surrounded by an aura of fame that has for some time traveled beyond the borders of Russia, Akunin arrives in Rome bearing a copy of his latest thriller, *Sister Pelagia and the White Bulldog*, hot off the press. It's a novel that, surprisingly, sets aside Fandorin in favor of a brand-new protagonist—a heroine who wears a veil, as a matter of fact. Pelagia is a young redheaded nun who reluctantly turns investigator in a string of murders that take place in a country villa, in the fashion of Chekhov's *The Cherry Orchard*, which is set in the same time period.

As he did in the novels featuring Erast Fandorin, Akunin is still peppering black humor throughout this new mystery. He wins over the reader with his prose, which is refined and entertaining at the same time. Akunin takes the genre of the thriller apart and puts it back together as he pleases. On page after page, the author's subtle play of references is evocative of authors such as Leskov, Chesterton, Bulgakov, and Umberto Eco. Akunin seems to feel an overwhelming passion for negative characters. Even when the good characters prove to be right, the doubt still remains: Were the other guys, the bad guys, really wrong? "Deep down," says Akunin, "this is precisely the question I want the reader to ask, because the human soul is laden with unresolved mysteries. The good is the norm, whereas evil is an anomaly, but an interesting anomaly because of its variety. This is why I am attracted to negative characters: They are the most complex and multifaceted. It's not by chance that I chose a pseudonym—Akunin—that means 'wrongdoer' in Japanese."

**Francesco Fantasia:** Excuse me, Mr. Akunin, but after all of the success reaped by Detective Fandorin, why did you decide to switch gears and create the character of Sister Pelagia?

**Boris Akunin:** Fandorin was tired, and I knew he would become tired, which is why I had prepared myself to launch a new character, one who would be completely different from Fandorin. Sister Pelagia is a tribute to Chesterton: a nun blessed with superior intelligence whose only weapons are knitting needles. But you might ask, why a nun, precisely? I admit that love and sex scenes are not my strong point. With a female detective who wears a nun's habit, I am off the hook.

**FF:** Fandorin and Sister Pelagia carry out their investigations in a nineteenth-century Russia whose resemblance to contemporary Russia is striking: a rising middle class, disparities among social classes, greedy upstarts, and politicians with a questionable past. . . .

**BA:** The problems that Russia faced at the end of the nineteenth century are essentially the same problems we have in Russia today. I don't want to go on at great length about the political and economic aspects of these problems. That's not really the point. Right now there is an ongoing debate in my country about which values deserve the highest priority: whether individual values need to be emphasized, or whether we should return to social and collective interests. Last century, Russia chose an answer to this question that led to the tragedies of the twentieth century. Now we find ourselves at a similar crossroads, but we don't know yet which road will be taken this time.

**FF:** Your novels are replete with references to contemporary Russian politics. To what extent is it appropriate to refer to your mysteries as "political"?

**BA:** My thrillers are written for entertainment, but each of them can be considered in some measure a political novel, because politics is everywhere in Russia. If you don't deal with politics, politics will deal with you.

**FF:** One of your mysteries, *The Death of Achilles*, is set against the background of Russia's cruel colonization of Chechnya in the nineteenth century. What would Detective Fandorin say today about Putin's policy regarding the republic of Chechnya?

**BA:** I don't believe that Fandorin would have taken part in Putin's military campaign against Chechnya. Yes, Fandorin is a detective in the czar's police force, but he is above all a man of solid moral principles. The war against Chechnya is taking place in an atmosphere of immorality.

**FF:** Some critics in your country have accused you of conservatism. How do you respond to this?

**BA:** People can think and write whatever they please. In any case, if nineteenth-century Russia is dear to me, it is for its literary, not its political, history.

**FF:** During perestroika, under Gorbachev, a whole new generation of Russian writers landed in the West. But now, internationally known Russian writers can be counted on one hand. How do you explain this?

**BA:** It's simple: Russia is out of fashion. In the time of perestroika, all eyes were on the USSR. And even in the field of literature, everything that came out of Moscow was well received. But now Russia is like an old-fashioned, outdated suit. It doesn't interest people, especially on the literary front.

BORIS AKUNIN is the pen name of Grigory Chkhartishvili, who was born in the USSR in 1956. A philologist, critic, essayist, and translator of Japanese, Akunin published his first detective stories in 1998 and has already become one of the most widely read authors in Russia. In addition to the Sister Pelagia series, he is also the author of eleven Fandorin novels, including *The Winter Queen, The Turkish Gambit, Murder on the Leviathan*, and *The Death of Achilles*, all available from Random House Trade Paperbacks. He lives in Moscow.

ABOUT THE TRANSLATOR

ANDREW BROMFIELD was born in Hull in Yorkshire, England, and is the acclaimed translator of the stories and novels of Victor Pelevin. He also translated into English Boris Akunin's first four Erast Fandorin mysteries, *The Winter Queen, The Turkish Gambit, Murder on the Leviathan*, and *The Death of Achilles*.

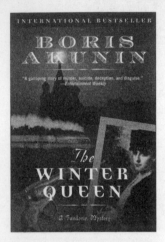
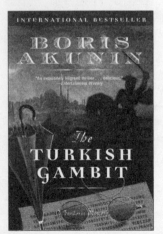

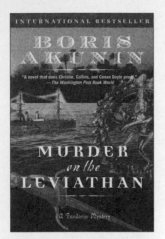

## Murder on the Leviathan

In 1878, aboard a luxury liner headed for Calcutta, Erast Fandorin joins forces with Parisian police commissioner "Papa" Gauche to determine which of ten suspicious passengers now trapped on the ship is guilty of a rising number of despicable murders.

"With a cast of eccentrics [and] a plot bristling with surprises . . . this is a novel that does Christie, Collins, and Conan Doyle proud."
—*The Washington Post Book World*

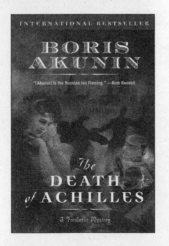

## The Death of Achilles

In 1882, Erast Fandorin returns to Moscow to find his old war-hero friend General Michel Sobolev ("Achilles" to the crowd) dead of an apparent heart attack. But Fandorin suspects unnatural causes and follows his suspicions to the boudoir of Wanda, a beautiful singer in whose bed the general secretly breathed his last.

"Stunning fiction . . . *The Death of Achilles* is a book that thrills in the manner of the detective fiction of the genre's greatest writers."
—*The Washington Times*